Elizabeth Hayes grew up in Sussex. She works as a police intelligence analyst and lives in Kent with her husband and son. *Into the Darkest Corner* is her first novel.

INTO THE DARKEST CORNER

Catherine has been enjoying the single life long enough to know a great catch when she sees one. Gorgeous, charismatic, spontaneous — Lee seems almost too good to be true. And her friends clearly agree, as each in turn falls under his spell. But Lee's erratic and sometime controlling behaviour makes Catherine feel increasingly isolated. Driven into the darkest corner of her world, and trusting no one, she plans a meticulous escape. Four years later, and struggling to overcome her demons, Catherine dares to believe she might be safe from harm. Until one phone call changes everything.

ELIZABETH HAYNES

INTO THE DARKEST CORNER

Complete and Unabridged

CHARNWOOD
Leicester

First published in Great Britain in 2011 by
Myriad Editions
Brighton

First Charnwood Edition
published 2013
by arrangement with
Myriad Editions
Brighton

The moral right of the author has been asserted

*A catalogue record for this book is available
from the British Library.*

ISBN 978–1–4448–1659–4

Published by
F. A. Thorpe (Publishing)
Anstey, Leicestershire

Set by Words & Graphics Ltd.
Anstey, Leicestershire
Printed and bound in Great Britain by
T. J. International Ltd., Padstow, Cornwall

This book is printed on acid-free paper

For Wendy George and Jackie Moscicki
— strong and inspirational women

Lancaster Crown Court

R-v-BRIGHTMAN

Wednesday 11 May 2005

Morning Session
Before:
THE HONOURABLE MR JUSTICE NOLAN

MR MACLEAN	Would you please state your full name?
MR BRIGHTMAN	Lee Anthony Brightman.
MR MACLEAN	Thank you. Now, Mr Brightman, you had a relationship with Miss Bailey, is that correct?
MR BRIGHTMAN	Yes.
MR MACLEAN	For how long?
MR BRIGHTMAN	I met her at the end of October in 2003. We were seeing each other until the middle of June last year.
MR MACLEAN	And how did you meet?
MR BRIGHTMAN	At work. I was working on an operation and I happened to meet her through the course of that.

1

MR MACLEAN	And you formed a relationship?
MR BRIGHTMAN	Yes.
MR MACLEAN	You said that the relationship ended in June. Was that a mutual decision?
MR BRIGHTMAN	Things had been going wrong for a while. Catherine was very jealous of the time I spent away from her working. She was convinced I was having an affair.
MR MACLEAN	And were you?
MR BRIGHTMAN	No. My job takes me away from home for days at a time, and the nature of it means that I can't tell anyone, not even my girlfriend, where I am or when I'll be home.
MR MACLEAN	Did your time away from Miss Bailey cause arguments between you?
MR BRIGHTMAN	Yes. She would check my mobile for messages from other women, demand to know where I'd been, who I'd been seeing. When I got back from a job, all I wanted to do was forget about work and relax a bit. It started to feel like I never had the chance to do that.

MR MACLEAN	So you ended the relationship?
MR BRIGHTMAN	No. We had rows sometimes, but I loved her. I knew she had some emotional problems. When she went for me, I always told myself that it wasn't her fault.
MR MACLEAN	What do you mean by 'emotional problems'?
MR BRIGHTMAN	Well, she told me she had suffered from anxiety in the past. The more time I spent with her, the more I saw that coming out. She would go out drinking with her friends, or drink at home, and when I got home she would start an argument and lash out at me.
MR MACLEAN	Just with regard to the emotional problems, I would like to ask you about that further. Did you, over the course of your relationship, see any evidence that Miss Bailey would harm herself at times of emotional stress?
MR BRIGHTMAN	No. Her friends had told me that she had cut herself in the past.
MR LEWIS	Objection, Your Honour.

3

The witness was not asked about the opinions of Miss Bailey's friends.

MR JUSTICE NOLAN	Mr Brightman, please keep to the questions you are asked. Thank you.
MR MACLEAN	Mr Brightman, you mentioned that Miss Bailey would 'lash out' at you. Can you explain what you mean by 'lash out'?
MR BRIGHTMAN	She would shout, push me, slap me, kick me. That kind of thing.
MR MACLEAN	She was violent towards you?
MR BRIGHTMAN	Yes. Well, yes. She was.
MR MACLEAN	On how many occasions, would you say?
MR BRIGHTMAN	I don't know. I didn't keep count.
MR MACLEAN	And what did you generally do, on these occasions when she 'lashed out' at you?
MR BRIGHTMAN	I would walk away from it. I deal with that enough at work; I don't need it when I get home.
MR MACLEAN	And were you ever violent towards her?
MR BRIGHTMAN	Only the last time. She had locked me in the house and hidden the key somewhere. She went mad at me. I'd

4

been working on a particularly difficult job and something inside me snapped. I hit her back. It was the first time I'd ever hit a woman.

MR MACLEAN The last time — what date are you talking about, exactly?

MR BRIGHTMAN It was in June. The 13th, I think.

MR MACLEAN Would you take us through that day?

MR BRIGHTMAN I stayed the night before at Catherine's house. I was on duty that weekend so I left for work before Catherine woke up. When I came back to her house that evening she was at home and she had been drinking. She accused me of spending the day with another woman — the same thing I heard over and over again. I took it for a while, but after a couple of hours I had had enough. I went to walk away but she had double-locked the front door. She was screaming and swearing at me, over and over again, slapping me with her hands, scratching my face. I pushed

	her backwards, just enough to get her away. Then she just threw herself at me again and I hit her.
MR MACLEAN	How did you hit her, Mr Brightman? Was it a punch, a slap?
MR BRIGHTMAN	I hit her with a closed fist.
MR MACLEAN	I see. And what happened then?
MR BRIGHTMAN	She didn't stop; she just yelled louder and came at me again. So I hit her again. I guess it was probably harder. She fell over backwards and I went to see if she was alright, to help her up. I think I must have trodden on her hand. She screamed and yelled at me and threw something. It was the key to the front door.
MR MACLEAN	What did you do next?
MR BRIGHTMAN	I took the key, unlocked the front door and left.
MR MACLEAN	What time was that?
MR BRIGHTMAN	It must have been about a quarter past seven.
MR MACLEAN	And when you left her, what condition was she in?
MR BRIGHTMAN	She was still shouting and screaming.
MR MACLEAN	Was she injured, bleeding?

MR BRIGHTMAN	I think she may have been bleeding.
MR MACLEAN	Could you elaborate, Mr Brightman?
MR BRIGHTMAN	She had some blood on her face. I don't know where it came from. It wasn't a lot of blood.
MR MACLEAN	And did you have any injuries yourself?
MR BRIGHTMAN	I just had some scratches.
MR MACLEAN	Did you consider that she might have needed medical attention?
MR BRIGHTMAN	No.
MR MACLEAN	Even though she was apparently bleeding, and crying out?
MR BRIGHTMAN	I don't recall that she was crying out. As I left the house she was shouting and swearing at me. If she needed medical attention I believe she could have got it herself, without my help.
MR MACLEAN	I see. So after you left the house at a quarter past seven, did you see Miss Bailey again?
MR BRIGHTMAN	No. I didn't see her again.
MR MACLEAN	Did you contact her by telephone?
MR BRIGHTMAN	No.
MR MACLEAN	Mr Brightman, I want you

	to think very carefully before answering my next question. How do you feel now with regard to the incidents of that day?
MR BRIGHTMAN	I have deep regret for everything that happened. I loved Catherine. I had asked her to marry me. I had no idea she was so emotionally disturbed and I wish to God I hadn't retaliated. I wish I had just tried harder to calm her down.
MR MACLEAN	Thank you. No further questions, Your Honour.

— CROSS-EXAMINATION —

MR LEWIS	Mr Brightman, would you have described your relationship with Miss Bailey as a serious one?
MR BRIGHTMAN	I thought it was, yes.
MR LEWIS	Do you understand that it is part of your terms and conditions of employment that you will inform your employers of changes in your personal circumstances, including providing the details of your relationships?
MR BRIGHTMAN	Yes.

MR LEWIS	And yet you chose not to inform anyone you work with about your relationship with Miss Bailey, is that not the case?
MR BRIGHTMAN	I had planned to do so when Catherine agreed to marry me. My vetting review was due at the end of September; I would have mentioned it then in any case.
MR LEWIS	Now, I would like to draw your attention to Exhibit WL/1 — this is on page fourteen of the exhibit packs — which is the statement by PC William Lay. PC Lay arrested you on Tuesday 15th June 2004 at your home address. In his statement he asserts that when he asked you about Miss Bailey, you at first stated, and I quote: 'I don't know who you are talking about.' Is that correct?
MR BRIGHTMAN	I don't remember exactly what I said.
MR LEWIS	This is the woman you have subsequently stated that you were in love with, that you intended to marry. Is that correct?
MR BRIGHTMAN	PC Lay and PC Newman

9

	turned up at my house at six in the morning. I'd been working for the past three nights and I had only just gone to bed. I was disorientated.
MR LEWIS	Did you also state when questioned at Lancaster Police Station later that same day — and I'm quoting again from your statement: 'She was just someone I was investigating. When I left her she was fine. She had emotional issues, mental health issues.'?
MR BRIGHTMAN	*(inaudible)*
MR JUSTICE NOLAN	Mr Brightman, could you speak up?
MR BRIGHTMAN	Yes.
MR LEWIS	And were you conducting an investigation into Miss Bailey?
MR BRIGHTMAN	No.
MR LEWIS	I have no further questions.
MR JUSTICE NOLAN	Thank you. In that case, ladies and gentlemen, we will adjourn for lunch.

Thursday 21 June 2001

As far as days to die were concerned, the longest day of the year was as good a day as any.

Naomi Bennett lay with her eyes open at the bottom of a ditch while the blood that had kept her alive for all of her twenty-four years pulsed away into the grit and rubble beneath her.

As she drifted in and out of awareness, she contemplated the irony of it all: how she was going to die now — having survived so much, and thinking that freedom was so close — at the hands of the only man who had ever really loved her and shown her kindness. He stood at the edge of the ditch above her, his face in shadow as the sun shone through the bright green leaves and cast dappled light over him, his hair halo-bright. Waiting.

The blood filled her lungs and she coughed, blowing scarlet bubbles that foamed over her chin.

He stood motionless, one hand on the shovel, watching the blood flow out of her and marvelling at its glorious colour, a liquid jewel, and at how even at the moment of death she was still the most beautiful woman he'd ever seen.

Once the flow slowed to a mere trickle he turned away, casting a glance across the derelict no-man's-land between the back of the industrial estate and the beginnings of farmland. Nobody came here, not even dog-walkers; the ground was rough and scarred with manufacturing rubbish accumulated over decades, weeds growing through empty cable reels, brown fluid leaking out of rusted oil drums, and at the edge, beneath a long row of lime trees, a six-foot ditch that brought dirty water when it rained, draining a mile away into the river.

Several minutes passed.

She was dead.

The wind had started to pick up and he looked up through the canopy of leaves to the clouds chasing each other across the sky.

He scrambled carefully down the rough slope into the bottom of the ditch, using the shovel for support, and then without hesitation drove it into her skull, bouncing roughly off the first time, then with a dull crack breaking the bone and splintering it into her flesh. Again and again, gasping with the effort, smashing her face away, breaking teeth, bone and flesh into one ghastly mixture.

After that, she wasn't his Naomi any more.

He used the knife again to slice away at each of her fingers in turn, her palms, until nothing identifiable was left.

Finally, he used the bloody shovel to cover her over with the rubble, sand and rubbish that had collected in the ditch. It wasn't a very good job. The blood was everywhere.

But as he finished — wiping away the tears that he'd been shedding from the moment she'd said his name in surprise, just as he'd sliced her throat — the first spots of rain fell from the darkening sky.

Wednesday 31 October 2007

Erin had been standing in the doorway for almost a minute; I could see her reflection in the darkened window. I carried on scrolling through the spreadsheet on the screen, wondering how it could be that it was dark when I left for work this morning and now it was dark again already.

'Cathy?'

I turned my head. 'Sorry,' I said, 'I was miles away. What?'

She leaned against the door, one hand on a hip, her long russet hair wound back into a bun. 'I said, are you nearly finished?'

'Not quite. Why?'

'Don't forget it's Emily's leaving do tonight. You are coming, aren't you?'

I turned back to the screen. 'I'm not sure, to be honest — I need to get this finished. You go on ahead. I'll try and get there later if I can.'

'Alright,' she said at last. She made a show of stomping off, although she didn't make much noise in those pumps.

Not tonight, I thought. Especially not tonight. It was all I could manage to agree to go to the sodding Christmas party, let alone a night out to celebrate someone's departure, someone I scarcely know. They'd been planning the Christmas do since August; as far as I'm concerned the end of November is too bloody

13

early for a Christmas night out, but it's the date they all chose. They're all partying from then on, right up to Christmas. Early or not, I was going to have to go, otherwise I could see comments being made about me not being a 'team player', and God knows I need this job.

As soon as the last person left the office, I closed down the spreadsheet and turned off the computer.

Friday 31 October 2003

Friday night, Hallowe'en, and the bars in town were all full to the cauldron's brim.

In the Cheshire Arms I'd drunk cider and vodka and somehow lost Claire and Louise and Sylvia, and gained a new friend called Kelly. Kelly had been to the same school as me, although I didn't remember her. That was no matter to either of us; Kelly was dressed as a witch without a broomstick, all stripy orange tights and black nylon wig, me like the bride of Satan, a fitted red satin dress and cherry-red silk shoes that had cost more than the dress. I'd already been groped a few times.

By one, most people were heading for the night bus, or the taxi rank, or staggering away from the town centre into the freezing night. Kelly and I headed for the River bar, since it was the only place likely still to let us in.

'You are *so* going to pull wearing that dress, Catherine,' Kelly said, her teeth chattering.

'I fucking hope so, it cost me enough.'

'Do you think there will be anything decent in there?' she said, peering hopefully at the bedraggled queue.

'I doubt it. Anyway, I thought you said that you were off men?'

'I said I've given up on relationships. Doesn't mean I'm off sex.'

It was bitterly cold and starting to drizzle, the wind whipping the smells of a Friday night around me, blowing up my skirt. I pulled my jacket tighter around me and crossed my arms over it.

We headed for the VIP entrance. I remember wondering if this was a good idea, whether it might not be better to call it a night, when I realised Kelly had been let in already and I went to follow her. I was blocked by a wall of charcoal-grey suit.

I looked up to see a pair of incredible blue eyes, short blond hair. Not someone you'd want to have an argument with.

'Hold up,' said the voice, and I looked up at the doorman. He wasn't massive like the other two, but still taller than me. He had a very appealing smile.

'Hello,' I said. 'Am I allowed to go in with my friend?'

He paused for a moment and looked at me just a fraction longer than was seemly. 'Yes,' he said at last. 'Of course. Just . . . '

I waited for him to continue. 'Just what?'

He glanced across to where the other door staff were chatting up some teenagers who were busy trying their hardest to get in.

'Just couldn't believe my luck for a moment, that's all.'

I laughed at his cheek. 'Not been a good night, then?'

'I have a thing for red dresses,' he said.

'I don't think this one would fit you.'

He laughed and held the velvet rope to one side to let me in. I felt him watching me as I handed my jacket in to the cloakroom; chanced a glance back to the door and saw him again, just watching me. I gave him a smile and went up the steps to the bar.

All I could think of that night was dancing until I was numb, smiling and laughing at people with my new best friend, dancing in that red dress until I caught the eye of someone, anyone, and best of all finding some dark corner of the club and being fucked against a wall.

Thursday 1 November 2007

It took me a long, long time to get out of the flat this morning. It wasn't the cold, although the heating in the flat seems to take an age to have any effect. Nor was it the dark. I'm up every day before five; it's been dark at that time since September.

Getting up isn't my problem, getting out of the house is. Once I'm showered and dressed, have had something to eat, I start the process of checking that the flat is secure before I go to work. It's like a reverse of the process I go through in the evening, but worse somehow, because I know that time is against me. I can spend all night checking if I want to, but I know I have to get to work, so in the mornings I can only do it so many times. I have to leave the curtains in the lounge and in the dining room, by the balcony, open to exactly the right width every day or I can't come back in the flat again. There are sixteen panes in each of the patio doors; the curtains have to be open so that I can see just eight panes of each door if I look up to the flat from the path at the back of the house. If I can see a sliver of the dining room through the other panes, or if the curtains aren't hanging straight, then I'll have to go back up to the flat and start again.

I've got quite good at getting this right, but it still takes a long time. The more thorough I am, the less likely I'll find myself on the path behind the house cursing my carelessness and checking my watch.

The door is particularly bad. At least in the last place, that poky basement in Kilburn, I had my own front door. Here I have to check and re-check the flat door properly six or twelve times, and then the communal front door as well.

The flat in Kilburn did have a front door but nothing at all at the back, no back door, no windows. It was like living in a cave. I didn't have an escape route, which meant that I never felt really safe in there. Here, things are much better: I have French doors which lead onto a small balcony. Just below that is the roof of the shed which is shared with the other flats, although I don't know if anyone else uses it. I can get out of the French doors, jump down to the shed roof, and from there down onto the grass. Through the garden and out the gate into the alleyway at the back. I can do it in less than half a minute.

Sometimes I have to go back and check the flat door again. If one of the other tenants has left the front door on the latch again I definitely have to check the flat door. Anyone could have been in.

This morning, for example, was one of the worst.

Not only was the front door on the latch, it was actually slightly ajar. As I reached for it, a man in a suit pushed it open towards me which made me jump. Behind him, another man, younger, tall, wearing jeans and a hooded top. Dark hair cropped close to his head, unshaven, tired green eyes. He gave me a smile, and mouthed 'sorry', which helped.

Suits still freak me out. I tried not to look at the suit at all, but I heard it say as it went up the stairs, ' . . . this one's only just become available, you'll have to move fast if you want it.'

A lettings agent, then.

The Chinese students who'd been on the top floor must have finally decided to move on. They weren't students any more, they graduated in the summer — the party they'd had had gone on all night, while I lay in my bed underneath listening to the sound of feet marching up and down the stairs. The front door had been on the latch all night. I'd barricaded myself in by pushing the dining table against the flat door, but the noise had kept me awake and anxious.

I watched the second man following the suit up the stairs.

To my horror the man in jeans turned halfway up the first flight and gave me another smile, a rueful one this time, raising his eyes as if he was already sick of the letting agent's voice. I felt myself blushing furiously. It's been a long time since I made eye contact with a stranger.

I listened to the footsteps heading up to the top floor, meaning they'd gone past my front door. I checked my watch — a quarter past eight already! I couldn't just go and leave them inside the house.

I shut the front door firmly and unclipped the latch, checking that it had shot home by rattling the door a few times. With my fingertips I traced around the edge of the doorframe, feeling that the door was flush with the frame. I turned the doorknob six times, to make sure it was properly closed. One, two, three, four, five, six. Then the doorframe again. Then the doorknob, six times. One, two, three, four, five, six. Then the latch. Once, and again. Then the doorframe. Lastly the knob, six times. I felt the relief that comes when I manage to do this properly.

Then I marched back up to the flat, fuming that these two idiots were going to make me late.

I sat on the edge of my bed for a while with my eyes lifted to the ceiling, as if I could see them through the plaster and the rafters. All the time I was fighting the urge to start checking the window locks again.

I concentrated on my breathing, my eyes closed, trying to calm my racing heart. They won't be long, I told myself. He's only looking. They won't be long. Everything is fine. The flat is safe. I'm safe. I did it properly before. The front door is shut. Everything is fine.

Every so often a small sound made me jump, even though it seemed to come from a long way away. A cupboard door banging? Maybe. What if they'd opened a window up there? I could hear a vague murmur, far too far away to make out words. I wondered what price they were asking for it — it might be nicer to be higher up. But then I wouldn't have the balcony. As much as I love being out of reach, having an escape route is just as important.

I checked my watch — nearly a quarter to nine. What the fuck were they doing up there? I made the mistake of glancing at the bedroom window, and then of course I had to check it. And that started me off, so I had to start again at the door, and I was on my second round, standing on the lid of the toilet, feeling my way with my fingertips around the edge of the frosted window which doesn't even open, when I heard the door shutting upstairs and the sound of footsteps on the stairs outside.

' . . . nice safe area, at least. Never need to worry about leaving your car outside.'

'Yeah, well, I'd probably get the bus. Or I might use my bike.'

'I think there's a communal shed in the garden; I'll check when we get back to the office.'

'Cheers. I'd probably leave it in the hallway.'

Leave it in the hallway? Bloody cheek. It was untidy enough as it was. But then, maybe someone other than me would make a point of locking the front door.

I finished off the check, and then did the flat door. Not too bad. I waited for it, the anxiety, the need to go round and start again, but it was okay. I'd done it right, and only two times. The house was silent, which made things easier. Best of all, this time the front door was firmly fastened, indicating that the man in jeans had shut it properly behind him. Maybe he wouldn't be a bad tenant after all.

It was nearly nine-thirty by the time I finally got to the Tube.

Tuesday 11 November 2003

When I saw him for the second time, the memory had gone completely and I spent several moments looking at him. Tasty-looking, sensual mouth, definitely looked familiar — someone I'd snogged in a bar?

'You don't remember,' he said, disappointment clear in his voice. 'You had a red dress on. I was on the door at the River.'

'Oh, of course! Sorry,' I said, shaking my head as though that would waggle some sense into it. 'I just . . . didn't recognise you without that suit.' This gave me a reason to look him up and down appraisingly. He was dressed in shorts, trainers, and a black vest — spot on for the gym, but very different from how I'd last seen him.

'No, well, not really much good for running in, that one.'

'I guess not.'

Suddenly aware that I was still staring at his thighs, I realised I must look appalling, having just finished an hour's session in the gym — hair tied back, bits of it sticking to my flushed cheeks, sweaty top. Lovely.

'Well, it's good to see you again,' he said, running his eyes from my chest down to my toes and back up again in a fraction of a second.

I wasn't sure whether he was being cheeky or a little bit out of order. But then he finished it with a slightly lopsided grin that wasn't lewd at all, just very sexy.

'Yes, and you. I'm — going to get a shower.'

'Sure. I'll see you soon,' and with that, he turned and ran up the stairs to the gym, taking them two at a time.

As I showered, I found myself wishing I'd met him when I had been heading for the gym too, instead of just coming out. Then we could have had a proper conversation, and I wouldn't have been looking like such a train wreck. For a few moments I contemplated hanging around in the coffee shop, waiting for him to finish his workout — would that look too easy? Too desperate?

Well, what can I say? It had been a while. The last few men I liked had been one-nighters; sometimes I was verging on being too drunk to recall the details. Nothing wrong with it, of course, I was just enjoying myself while I could. Had enough of relationships for the time being, enjoying being single, all of that rubbish. Maybe it was time to start calming down a little. Maybe it was time to start thinking of the future.

As I dried myself off, the changing rooms empty, a sudden thought occurred to me — I can't have looked that bad, or he wouldn't have recognised me. The last time he'd seen me, I had been dressed in a scarlet satin dress, my hair loose over my shoulders. Today I was dressed in sweaty gym gear, with no make-up and with my hair tied back — quite different. And yet he'd recognised me the instant I looked up — I saw it in his eyes.

And he'd said, 'Hello again.'

I hadn't been back to the River since, although I'd been out several times each week. Last weekend I was visiting friends in Scotland, an exhausting weekend with very little sleep — but that hadn't stopped me going out for drinks after work. On Friday we ended up in the Roadhouse, a new bar which had opened in the Market Square. It was heaving with people thanks to their opening weekend drinks promotions, and Sam and Claire had both copped off with blokes within the first half-hour of arriving. For a while, I'd danced and drunk, drunk and danced, happy on my own, seeing people I know and chatting with them, shouting into people's ears to be heard above the noise. There were some pretty tasty men in there, but there weren't many single ones. The ones that were left were men I knew, either because I'd been out with them before, or they'd been out with one or other of my friends.

Now I was already looking forward to next weekend. Friday night I was planning to go out

23

with Claire, Louise and her sister Emma, and then after that the weekend was mine. Smiling to myself, I sauntered back to the car, thinking that maybe we could find our way to the River.

Monday 5 November 2007

By leaving work late I miss the worst of the crush on the Tube. When I first moved here I made the mistake of fighting my way through the rush hour, and every day the panic got worse. There were too many faces to scan, too many bodies pressing in from all sides. There were too many hiding places, and not enough room for me to run. So I leave work late, which makes up for me getting in late. I keep moving, up and down stairs, along the platform, until the last possible moment and the doors are just closing, before I jump on the train. That way I know for sure who I'm travelling with.

Tonight I took a while to decide which way to go home. Every day I take different routes on the Tube, getting off a stop later or a stop earlier, walking a mile or so, then onto a bus, or back onto the Tube.

Usually I walk the last mile, taking different roads. It's been two years since I moved here from Lancaster, and already I know the London Transport system as well as a native. It takes a long time and it wears me out, but it's not as though I have to rush home. And it's safer.

Once I got off the bus at Steward Gardens my walk home was punctuated by fireworks, the smell of them sour in the cold, damp air. I walked across the High Street, skirting the edge of the park. Doubled back down Lorimer Road. Through the alleyway — I hate the alleyway, but at least it's well lit — and back behind the garages. I checked over the wall — the light was on in my dining room, the curtains half-closed. I counted the sixteen panes, eight on each door, which showed up as yellow rectangles, with neat edges where the curtains fell dead straight on either side. No extra bits of light showed through. No one had touched the curtains while I'd been away from the flat. I repeated this over and over again as I carried on walking. The flat is safe, nobody has been in there.

At the end of the alleyway, a sharp turn left and I was nearly home — Talbot Street. I resisted the urge to walk to the end of the road at least once before turning back; tonight I managed to get inside at the first attempt. I looked back while turning the key, which had been held ready in my hand since I got off the bus. The front door locked behind me. I felt around the edges of the door, checking it was flush against the doorframe, careful not to miss any bump which might indicate that the door wasn't properly shut. I checked it six times, counting each time: one, two, three, four, five, six. I turned the doorknob, six times.

Right on cue, Mrs Mackenzie opened the door of the downstairs flat, Flat 1.

'Coo-ee, Cathy! How are you?'

'I'm fine, thanks,' I said, giving her my best smile. 'You?'

25

She nodded and regarded me, her head on one side for a moment as she usually does and then went back inside. I could hear her television turned up to full volume the way it always is. The evening news. She does this every evening. She's never once asked me what I'm doing.

I went back to the checking, wondering if she does it on purpose, to interrupt me, knowing I'll have to start again from scratch. I'm alright as long as I don't get stuck. Sometimes I do. So — the doorframe, the doorknob — do it properly, Cathy. Don't fuck it up or we'll be here all bloody night.

At last I finished checking the front door. Then up the stairs. Checked to the top of the staircase. Listened to the stillness in the house, the noise of a siren a few streets away, the television on in the flat downstairs. More fireworks, going off a long way away. A scream from somewhere out in the street made me catch my breath, but then soon after a man's voice, a female laughing, reproachful.

I unlocked my front door, looked behind me at the staircase again, then took one step inside, closed the door, locked it. Bolt at the bottom, chain in the middle, deadlock at the top. Listened at the door. Nothing at all from the other side. Looked through the peephole. Nobody there; just the stairs, the landing, the light overhead. I ran my fingers around the doorframe, turned the door handle six times one way, six times the other way. One, two, three, four, five, six. The bolts held the door shut. I turned the Yale lock six times. I slid each bolt six times and back again, each time turning the doorknob six times. When I'd done all that, I could start on the rest of the flat.

The first thing I did was to check all the windows, and close the curtains, going round the flat in the same order. First the front window onto the street. All the locks secure. I ran my fingers around the windowframe. Then I could close the curtains tight against the darkness outside. From the street, nobody can see me unless I stand close up against the glass. I checked the edges of the curtains in case I could see part of the window. Then I moved over to the balcony, the double doors. In the summer I look out over the garden, checking the perimeter wall, but at this time of year there was only darkness outside. I checked the deadbolts on the balcony doors, felt all the way around the edge, turned the handle six times. The lock held true, the handle rattled loosely. Then I closed the heavy lined curtains against the blackness.

The kitchen — the windows in here don't open, but I checked them anyway. The blind came down. I stood in front of the drawer for several minutes, picturing what the contents looked like. When I pulled it open, I looked at the tray — the forks on the left, the knives in the middle, the spoons on the right. I closed the drawer, then I opened it again to make sure. Knives definitely in the middle, forks on the left, spoons on the right. How did I know? Maybe I did something wrong. I opened the drawer again, to check. This time it was all right.

Then the bathroom — the window is high up

and frosted, and again this one doesn't open, but I stood on the toilet lid and checked the edges nevertheless, ensuring it was closed tightly, then I pulled down the blinds. Through to my bedroom. Big windows in here which looked out onto the back garden, but the curtains were closed already as I left them before work this morning. The room was in darkness. I plucked up my courage and opened the curtains, checking the wide sash windows. I had fitted extra locks to this window when I moved in, and I checked each one, turning and re-turning the keys six times so that I knew they were secure. Then I closed the curtains, pulling them right across on each side so that there wasn't a fragment of dark window showing. Then I turned on the light beside the bed. For a moment I sat on the edge of the bed, breathing deeply, trying to calm the rising panic. At 7.30pm there was a programme I wanted to watch. The bedside clock said that the time was 7.27pm. I wanted to go and watch television. But the panic was still there, despite reasoning with myself, despite telling myself that I'd done it all, I'd checked everything, there was nothing to worry about, the flat was secure, I was safe, I was home safe for another day.

My heart was still pounding.

With a sigh, I got up from my bed and crossed to the front door, to start it all over again.

This cannot continue. It's been more than three years. It has to stop, it *has* to stop.

This time I went through the whole process of

checking the door twelve times before I moved on to the front window.

Sunday 16 November 2003

In the end, it wasn't at the River; it was back at the gym.

Friday night had been a bit pathetic, really. Too many nights out on the trot with no time to recover. It was all catching up with me and I felt tired, irrationally miserable and not at all inclined to go hunting for sexy doormen. We had three drinks in the Pitcher and Piano, a further two in the Queen's Head, and by that time I'd had enough. Sam looked at me as though I was joking when I said I was heading for home. Saturday I spent recovering, watching movies on the sofa.

On Sunday morning I woke up at ten, feeling refreshed for the first time in weeks. Outside the sun was shining, the air crisp and still, a great day to go for a run. I'd do that, then go and shop for some healthy food, have an early night.

A few steps on the icy pavement put paid to that idea. Instead, I bundled some clean clothes into my bag and drove the five miles to the gym.

This time, I recognised him before he saw me. He was standing by the swimming pool, adjusting a pair of goggles. Not bothering to worry about whether he could see through the glass window to where I stood ogling him, I watched him slide into the water and kick off the wall into an easy, gliding front crawl. The water barely moved as he slipped through it. I watched him do two lengths, hypnotised by his rhythm, until someone almost fell over my gym bag and broke the spell.

In the changing rooms, I stowed the bag in a locker and pulled out my MP3 player, strapping it to my arm. As I headed for the gym, I caught sight of myself in one of the mirrors. My cheeks were flushed, and the look in my eyes made me stop short. My God, I thought, unable to wipe the stupid grin off my face, he really is fucking sexy.

Monday 12 November 2007

After work this evening something out of the ordinary happened.

Out-of-the-ordinary things are never good for me. Sometimes, if I'm having a good day, I can look back on them and smile, but at the time it's never good. The day the pipes burst and the plumber had to come into my flat caused the biggest panic attack I've had.

I still don't know how I survived that one.

I'm wondering about this evening, because at the moment I'm okay. I'm half-expecting a panic attack to hit me later on, just when I'm least prepared for it, but at the moment everything is okay and I feel alright.

I had just finished eating, and there was a knock at the door.

I froze, my whole body tense. I don't think I even breathed. My door buzzer hadn't sounded, so it was either someone in the house, or the door had been left on the latch again. Whatever — even if my life depended on it, my body wasn't going to let me move an inch. I felt tears sliding down my cheeks.

Another knock, slightly louder. Nobody has ever knocked on my flat door before.

I had a clear view to the door from where I was sitting on the sofa, stared at it and at the peephole. The light from the hallway, which normally shone through like a little beacon, was blocked by whoever was on the other side and all I could see was a round dot of darkness. I stared with such fierce concentration, it was almost as though I could make out the bulky shape of him through the solid wood, and I held my breath until my head pounded and my fingers started to tingle.

Then I heard footsteps retreating, going up the stairs, not down, and the sound of the door to the top floor flat opening and closing.

So, it was him. The man upstairs.

I'd seen him come and go a few times, from the living room window. Once he was coming in just as I was about to leave the flat for work. I noticed that the front door was firmly shut, which made me feel a bit better, although I still had to check it, of course. The bike still hadn't appeared in the hallway, and I hadn't seen him in the garden, so maybe he was parking his car outside after all.

He seemed to come and go at irregular hours. Mrs Mackenzie was reassuringly predictable since she didn't go out at all, at least not as far as I'd noticed. She'd appear in the doorway of Flat most evenings when I came home, say hello and go back inside. I heard the sounds of her television coming up through the floorboards. Other people might find that difficult, but not me. I liked it.

And now, upstairs, Mr Unpredictable.

I wondered what on earth he wanted. It was nearly nine — not a very good time for a social call. Maybe he needed help?

After a while, my breathing calm, back to normal, I wondered if I should go upstairs and knock on *his* door. I found myself having the conversation in my head:

Oh, hello. Did you knock? I was in the shower . . .

No, that wouldn't do it — how would I have known it was him?

Again, I heard my mantra coming unwanted into my mind: *This isn't normal. This isn't how normal people think.*

Fuck off, world — what the hell is normal anyway?

Sunday 16 November 2003

Even before I saw him, I knew where he'd be.

He was in the coffee bar, reading a copy of *The Times*, looking smart in an open-necked white shirt, freshly showered.

I hesitated, wondering whether it would be a good thing to stop and say hi, and at that moment he looked up from his newspaper. He didn't smile for a second, just met my gaze, and

I thought about what might lie behind it. It felt like the beginning; as though this was the turning point. I had had the chance to walk away, and I had stood my ground. Now came the reckoning.

When he smiled, I found myself crossing the foyer of the gym to where he sat. 'Hello,' I said, thinking how lame it sounded. 'I saw you in the pool.'

'I know,' he answered, 'I saw you too.' He folded the newspaper and laid it carefully on the table next to his coffee. 'What are you having?'

Walking away didn't seem to be an option any more. 'Tea, please.'

I sat down as he stood, fitting into the seat opposite his, my heart pounding. However long I'd spent in the changing rooms after the shower getting ready, in case he was out here, it wasn't enough.

A few minutes later he came back with a small tray with a teapot, cup and a jug of milk. 'My name's Lee,' he said, offering me his hand.

I looked up into a pair of very blue eyes. 'Catherine,' I said. His hand was warm, his grip firm, and hours later when I lay in bed I could still smell the scent of him, faint, on the palm of my hand.

The fact that I couldn't decide on anything to say almost made me laugh — normally it was difficult to shut me up. I wanted to ask if he'd enjoyed his swim, but that sounded inane; I wanted to ask if he was single, but that was too direct. I wanted to know if he'd been waiting for me. All of these questions, and, I realised, I already knew the answers. Yes, yes and yes.

'I've been wondering what your name was,' he said at last. 'I tried to have a guess, but didn't get anywhere near it.'

'So, if I don't look like a Catherine, what do I look like?'

He'd not broken eye contact with me for a moment. 'I can't remember now. Now I know you're Catherine, nothing else is good enough.'

His gaze was almost uncomfortable, and I felt myself blushing under the force of it, so I concentrated on pouring my tea and took my time stirring it, mixing a little milk, then a little more, until it was exactly the right shade.

'So,' he said, with a deep breath, 'have you not been back to the River since I last saw you, or have I just been unlucky and missed you?'

'No, I haven't been back. Just been busy doing other things.'

'I see. Family things?'

He was fishing to see if I was single. 'Friend things. I don't have any family. Both my parents died when I was at university, and I'm an only child.'

He nodded. 'That's tough. All my family live in Cornwall.'

'Is that where you're from?'

'A village near Penzance. Moved away as soon as I could. Villages are grim places sometimes — everybody knows your business.'

There was another brief pause, until I broke it. 'So, do you just work at the River?'

He grinned and downed the last of his coffee. 'Yes, just at the River, three nights a week.

34

Helping a friend out, mainly. Will you have dinner with me later?'

His question came out of the blue; the look in his eyes showed the hint of nerves that his voice hadn't given away.

I smiled at him and drank my tea.

'Yes, that would be lovely.'

When I got up to leave, the card with his phone number in my jacket pocket, I felt his eyes follow me all the way to the door. When I turned to wave, he was still looking. But he did at least manage a smile.

Saturday 17 November 2007

My weekends are a curious mixture of relaxation and stress. Some weekends are good; others, not so. Certain dates are good. I can only go food shopping on even-numbered days. If the 13th falls on a weekend, I can't do anything at all. On odd-numbered days, I can exercise, but only if it's cloudy or raining, not if it's sunny. On odd-numbered days, I can't cook food, I can only eat cold things or heat stuff up.

All of this is to keep my brain placated. All of the time, day and night, my brain generates images of things that have happened to me and things that might happen. It's like watching a horror movie over and over again, without ever becoming immune to the terror. If I can get things right, do things in the right order, check things properly, follow the correct rhythm, then the pictures go away for a while. If I can get out of the door and know for sure that everything is definitely secure in the flat, then I will get a few hours where the worst feeling I have is a vague discomfort, as though something's amiss but I can't put my finger on it. More often, though, I do the best I can with the checking and, assuming I make it out of the house at all, I then spend the rest of the day fretting about whether I did it right. Then the whole day will be filled with these images of what might be waiting for me when I get home. If I don't choose a different route home every night, then someone will follow me. You get the picture. It's not a pretty one.

Whatever this is, it snuck up on me and now it's here to stay. Every once in a while I catch myself forming a new rule. Last week I found myself counting steps again, something I've not done for years. That's certainly one I can do without. But I don't seem to be able to control myself any more. I'm getting worse, not better.

So, it was Saturday again, and an odd-numbered day, and I'd run out of bread and teabags. The teabag issue was a big one, because tea is another important rule, particularly at weekends. I know that if I don't have cups of tea at eight, ten, four and eight o'clock I will grow increasingly anxious, both from the failure to get things right, and probably from the lack of caffeine. I looked at the bin, where my 8am teabag, stupidly discarded before I saw that it was the last one, lay among potato peelings and last night's pasta sauce, and for a brief moment I considered fishing it out to reuse. But that wouldn't have worked either.

The mere fact that I had been stupid enough to run out of teabags was enough to cause a heightened state of anxiety; I'm very good at the self-blame thing. If I went out to buy teabags, I would not be able to check the house properly because it wasn't an even-numbered day today. I might be able to get teabags and bring them back to the house, but in the meantime someone could have broken in, and would be waiting for me to return.

I spent more than an hour fretting over which was the worst of the two options — which rule was the more important? In order to try to get the images out of my head, I checked the flat several times, each time getting it slightly wrong. The more times I did it, the more tired I was getting. Sometimes I get stuck like this. Eventually I physically can't check any more.

And a small, small voice of reason at the back of my head, trying to be heard above the cacophony of self-reproach, was screaming *this is not normal.*

By a quarter to ten, I was scrunched into a corner, a small tight knot on the verge of self-destruction, when I heard it — the sound of the front door being closed — properly — and footsteps on the stairs.

Before I had a chance to think, I saw a way of escape. If I couldn't buy teabags, maybe I could borrow them . . .

The footsteps passed my door and carried on upstairs to the top flat. I waited for a moment, rubbing my cheeks to get rid of the tears, dragging my fingers through my hair. There was no time to check the flat. The front door wasn't on the latch; I'd heard him shut it, I'd definitely heard him shut it. I would have to just *go*.

Taking my door key, and locking the flat just once, checking it just once, I went up the stairs, pausing outside his front door. I'd never been up here before. There was a window on the landing, but no other light. I looked down the stairs. I could just about see my own door. I knocked, listening to the silence and then the footsteps on the other side.

When he opened the door, I jumped a little. Everything sounded so loud.

He had a nice smile. 'Hi,' he said. 'You okay?'

'Yes. I wondered if you have any teabags. That I could borrow. I mean, have. I've run out.'

He gave me a curious look. I was trying so hard to look normal but I must have been giving off desperation out of every pore.

'Sure,' he said. 'Come on in.'

He held the door open and retreated into the flat, leaving me standing on the doorstep watching his back. In normal circumstances I would rather have died than follow a stranger into an enclosed space, but these weren't normal circumstances, and if I was to get teabags by ten o'clock I would have to do it.

At the end of the long hallway was the kitchen, which I worked out was directly over my bedroom. No wonder those Chinese students had kept me awake with their party, I thought. Three shopping bags were on the kitchen table and he was rooting around in them.

'I just bought tea — ran out myself yesterday. I'm Stuart, by the way. Stuart Richardson. Just moved in.'

He offered me his hand, and I shook it, with the brightest smile I could conjure up. 'Pleased to meet you. I'm Cathy Bailey. From downstairs.'

'Hello, Cathy,' he said. 'I saw you on the day the agent showed me around.'

'Yes.' *Just give me the teabags,* I was thinking. *Please give me the fucking teabags. And stop looking at me like that.*

'Look,' he said then, after a moment's hesitation, 'I could do with a brew. Why don't you put the kettle on while I put this stuff away? Would you mind? Or are you busy?'

Put on the spot, I couldn't very well admit that I had nothing better to do than worry about where my next teabag was coming from, and besides, my watch now showed three minutes until ten o'clock, which meant I wasn't going to get the tea in time unless I made it now.

So I did it. I found mismatched mugs on the worktop next to the sink, choosing two and rinsing them out under the tap. Milk was in the fridge. I put fresh water in the kettle and boiled it, and made the tea, stirring and adding milk drop by drop until it was exactly the right colour, while Stuart put his shopping away and chatted away about the weather and how good it had been to find such a great flat just a few streets from the Northern Line.

I got to drink my first scalding sip of tea just as the second hand hit the twelve. I felt myself relax, the relief immediate, even though I was drinking it in a stranger's flat, with a man I'd only just met, and I hadn't even left my own flat secure.

I placed his mug on a coaster on the kitchen table, turning the handle exactly ninety degrees from the edge of the table, which wasn't terribly easy because it was a round table. It took me a few attempts before it looked right. He looked at me and raised an eyebrow, and this time I managed a smile.

'Sorry,' I said. 'I'm just a bit — um. I don't know. I needed a nice cup of tea, I guess.'

He shrugged and gave me a smile. 'Don't worry. It's a treat to get someone else to make it.'

We sat at the kitchen table in a companionable silence for a moment, sipping tea. Then: 'I knocked on your door the other evening. I think you must have been out.'

'Really?' I said. 'What night was that?'

He considered. 'Monday, I guess. Must have been seven-thirty, eightish.'

More like nine, I thought. I tried to look vague. 'I didn't hear it. Maybe I was in the shower or something. I hope it wasn't urgent.'

'Not really — just thought I should say hello and introduce myself. I wanted to apologise if I disturb you when I come in at night. I work late sometimes, never know when I'll get back.'

'That must be tough,' I said.

He nodded. 'You get used to it after a while. But I always think it must be really loud, those stairs.'

'No,' I lied, 'once I'm asleep I don't hear anything.'

He regarded me for a moment as though he knew full well this was completely untrue, but accepted it nonetheless. 'If I ever do disturb you, I'm sorry anyway.'

I started to say something, and stopped myself.

'Go on,' he said.

'It's the door,' I said.

'The door?'

'The front door. I worry about it being left on the latch. Sometimes people come and go, and leave the door open.'

'Don't worry,' he said, 'I always make sure I close it.'

'Especially at night,' I said, with emphasis.

'Yes, especially at night. I promise you I will make sure it's locked every night.' It had the sound of a solemn vow, and he said it without a smile.

I felt myself — almost — starting to exhale. 'Thank you,' I said. I'd finished my tea and stood up, aware again of my surroundings and keen to get back to the flat.

'Here,' Stuart said. He took a roll of small food bags from a drawer and used the bag as a glove to pull out a handful of teabags from the box, turning the bag inside out and twisting it at the top.

'Thank you,' I said again, taking the bag. 'I'll get some in tomorrow.' I paused for a moment, and then surprised myself by saying, 'If you ever run out of anything . . . you know. Give me a knock.'

He grinned. 'Will do.'

He let me walk several paces ahead of him to the door, not crowding me, and I let myself out of his flat. 'See you soon,' he said, as I headed down the stairs.

I hope so, said a small voice inside me.

And the most curious thing happened. I got back into my flat, sat down in front of the television and watched an hour and a half of a film before I realised I hadn't even checked the flat.

That little oversight cost me the rest of the afternoon and several hours into the evening.

Sunday 16 November 2003

By eleven-thirty, I was in love. Well, maybe in lust. And maybe my perception was slightly clouded by ridiculously expensive red wine and a glass of brandy.

Lee had met me in the town centre at eight, and when he arrived he looked even less like a doorman, despite the fact that he was wearing a suit again. This one was beautifully cut, the jacket straining just slightly across the biceps, a dark shirt underneath. His short blond hair was still slightly damp. He kissed my cheek and offered me his arm.

As we waited for our meal, he talked about fate. He took my hand and ran his thumb over the back of it, lightly, explaining how he nearly never got to meet me; how the weekend before Hallowe'en was supposed to have been his last time working at the River; how he'd only agreed to work the extra shifts to help out the owner, who was a good friend.

'I might never have met you,' he said.

'Well, you did,' I said, 'and here we are.' I raised my wine glass to him and sipped a toast to the future, to what lay ahead.

Much later, we left the restaurant and walked into the icy air. A brisk wind was blowing by the time we got to the taxi rank in Penny Street. Lee took off his suit jacket and slipped it over my shoulders. It smelled warm and faintly of him, that cologne he wore. I slotted my arms into the sleeves and felt the silk lining against my bare skin, the warmth of him, and how small and safe I felt inside the space of it. Despite it, my teeth chattered.

'Come here, you're shivering,' he said, and pulled me to him, rubbing my back and arms gently. My head, heavy with wine and too many late nights, nestled into his shoulder. I could have stayed like that, leaning against him, forever.

'You feel nice.'

'That's good,' he said. There was a pause, and then he added, 'I'd like to point out that you look incredibly sexy wearing a little black dress and my jacket.'

I raised my head, and his kiss was subtle, like the rest of him; the merest brush of his lips across mine. His hand cupped my cheek, and held it, my hair between his fingers. I tried to read his expression but it was dark, his face in shadow.

Just then a taxi pulled up and he opened the door for me.

43

'Queen's Road, please,' I said.

He shut the door behind me, and I wound down the window. 'Aren't you coming?'

He shook his head with a smile. 'You need to get some sleep — work tomorrow. I'll see you soon.'

Before I had a chance to reply, the taxi sped me away.

I didn't know whether I was just completely in love with him, or ever so slightly disappointed. It was only when I got home that I realised I was still wearing his jacket.

Wednesday 21 November 2007

After Saturday, it felt as if I saw Stuart all the time. When I left for work on Monday morning, he was leaving for work too. He looked badly in need of a shave and several more hours' sleep.

'Morning, Cathy,' he said, when he saw me.

'Hi,' I said. 'You off to work?'

'Yeah,' he said. 'Feels like I only just got in, but apparently I've been asleep since then.'

I watched him as he gave me a half-hearted little wave, then closed the door behind me, pulling it to and checking it by giving it a rattle. I stood outside the door for a moment, giving him a chance to disappear up the street and round the corner, before I checked it myself. It was closed. It was definitely closed. I checked it again.

On Tuesday I heard him coming up the stairs at just gone eleven. Even his footsteps sounded exhausted. I wondered what job he did that was so pressured.

This morning, he opened the front door just as I was checking the door of my flat. I heard him coming up the stairs behind me but carried on checking until the last minute; I was late as it was.

'Good morning,' he said brightly, 'how are you today?'

He looked much better.

'I'm fine. How are you? Aren't you going the wrong way?'

He smiled. 'Me? No. It's my day off today. I've just been to the deli to get some croissants.' He held up the carrier bag in case I needed proof of where he'd been. 'I'm going to slob around and eat too much. Don't suppose you'd like one?'

I must have looked aghast for a minute, because he smiled and said, 'I guess you're on your way to work, though . . . '

'Yes,' I said, perhaps a little too eagerly. 'Another time — maybe.'

He smiled again and gave me a cheeky wink. 'I might hold you to that.' He looked past me. 'Your door alright?'

'My door?'

'Doesn't it shut properly?'

I still had my hand on the doorknob. 'Oh — yes. It — it just sticks a little sometimes, that's all.' I gave it a tug.

Look, just go — please — I was saying in my head, but he wasn't taking the hint. In the end I had to say goodbye and leave the flat door unchecked.

Although a small compensation was that, since Stuart had moved in, I hadn't found the door on the latch once.

Monday 17 November 2003

I spent the whole of the next day in a state of excitement, reliving the best moments of the night before, agonising over when he might phone — would he ever phone? And what would I say to him if he did?

In the end, he called that afternoon, when I was just about to leave work.

'Hi, it's me. Did you have a good day?'

'Well, you know — I was at work. I've still got your jacket.'

He laughed a little. 'Yes. Don't worry about that. Give it to me when you see me.'

'And when might I expect that to be?'

'As soon as possible,' he said, his voice suddenly quite serious. 'I've not been able to stop thinking about you all day.'

I thought for a moment. 'At the weekend?'

A pause on the other end of the line. 'I can't at the weekend, I'm working. And besides, I can't wait that long. How about tonight?'

Saturday 24 November 2007

Christmas party last night.

I feel as though something has shifted in my life. For the worse, of course — just as I was

46

starting to feel safer here, too. This morning I feel unsteady on my feet, and it's nothing to do with any alcohol I did or didn't drink last night. Truth be told, I've not drunk alcohol for more than a year — I don't think I could handle it these days.

No: this morning the ground feels different under me, as though it might collapse at any moment. I've been checking the flat more or less constantly since I got up at four, and each time I had to hold on to the walls as I worked my way through the routine. I'm still not happy with it. I think I shall have to go and check it again in a moment.

Last night, I summoned up all my courage and went out. I started preparing for it early. In the old days, getting ready for a night out would have meant a shower, at least half an hour choosing a dress and shoes, doing my make-up and hair while drinking glasses of cold white wine, receiving and replying to texts from my friends. *What u wearing tonight? No wear the blue one. See you later.*

These days, preparing to go out means checking everything. Checking again. Then once more because I only started it at one minute past the hour. Then again because it took two minutes' less time than it should have done. From the minute I got in from work last night until it was time to go, I was checking.

It was ten to eight by the time I made it out of the front door, which was a huge relief.

Already I'd missed the visit to the pub, but I'd be able to catch up with them — maybe they'd be walking to the restaurant by now. Mentally rehearsing my excuses for being late, I quickened my pace up towards the High Street when I saw Stuart coming towards me. Despite the dark, and the fact that I was wrapped up in a long black coat with a scarf wrapped around my neck, he saw me too.

'Hello, Cathy. You off for a night out?' He had a dark brown jacket on, some sort of university scarf under that. His breath came in clouds.

I didn't want to speak to him. I wanted to nod and give a vague smile, but he was blocking the pavement ahead of me. 'Yes,' I said. 'Work Christmas party.'

'Ah,' he said, nodding. 'I've got one of those next week. Might see you out later; I'm meeting some friends.'

'That would be nice,' I found myself saying, as though some sort of autopilot had taken over.

He gave me a warm smile. 'See you later, then,' he said, and let me pass.

I felt him watching me as I walked away. I couldn't decide whether this was a good thing or not. Before, it had been a bad thing to be watched like that. I'd felt eyes on me all the time in the last few years, it was a feeling I could never seem to shake. But this time it felt different. It felt safe.

I wasn't as late as I'd thought, because the office crowd were still busy having drinks, in a bar called Dixey's. The place was busy even though it was still early, and the girls from work were already half-pissed, loud and excited and wearing next to nothing. I must have looked like their chaperone, their maiden aunt, wearing my smartest black trousers and grey silk shirt. It was well cut, but hardly revealing. And not very festive.

Caroline, the finance manager, seemed to feel the need to keep me company for most of the evening. Maybe she felt a bit out of it, too. She was the only married one, older than me by a few years with three children. Her hair was greying, like mine, but she'd done the decent thing and dyed it one of those chocolate-brown colours, with some reddish highlights. All I could bring myself to do was cut mine short, in a monthly ordeal at the hairdresser, the only one I could find who didn't talk to me while she cut my hair.

At least Caroline didn't ask me too many questions. She was happy enough telling me stuff, which I was only partly taking in. There was more to Caroline than that, however. I didn't believe she was one for inane chatter. I think she knew that I was struggling in this environment, and if she asked me how I was, or if I was alright, I might just fall apart.

So, when we got to the Thai Palace I sat at the end of the long table, and Caroline sat opposite me. She probably thought that I just wanted to sit away from the noise, but in reality being trapped in the middle of a long table in a densely occupied restaurant was a frightening place to be. At the end, nearest to the door, one eye on the fire exit marked at the back, I could see everyone who came in through the door, before they saw me. I could hide.

In the meantime, the girls were talking more loudly than I thought necessary and laughing at things that, surely, weren't funny and never had been. They were all slender gangly arms and huge earrings and razor-straight shiny hair. I'd never been like that — had I?

Robin was certainly enjoying himself, sandwiched between Lucy and Diane, directly across the table from Alison's impressive cleavage. He had one of those laughs that grated on me, and tonight he was louder than ever. I thought he was an odious man, with a shiny face and gelled hair, damp hands and a red, full mouth. He had that swagger of arrogance that only ever comes from low self-esteem. Nevertheless he wasn't afraid to wave his money around, and he could be very attentive. The girls all loved him.

He'd tried it on with me, once, not long after I'd started. Cornered me in the photocopy room and asked me if I'd like to meet him for a drink after work. Despite the panic I managed to smile, and say, 'No, thanks.' I didn't want to appear too chilly, but I obviously had, because the next thing I heard was the rumour that I was gay. That one made me smile. I guess the short hair and lack of make-up might have given support to that idea. Well, it suited me fine — at least that might put some of the lairy sales reps off.

Before the main course, but after yet another round of drinks, the Secret Santa sack came out and, needless to say, Robin was more than happy to be the centre of attention and play Santa.

He had a body that suggested he used to work

out once upon a time but now preferred to restrict his exercise to a stroll around the golf course once or twice a week. I guess if you could ignore his voice and his laugh it might be possible to think of him as good-looking. Caroline had told me in a low voice that he was seeing Amanda, one of the reps, and that his marriage was in trouble. This didn't come as a surprise.

Seeing Amanda didn't seem to be putting him off flirting, I noticed, and he was having a good old go at both the girls on either side of him — one of whom was young enough to be his daughter. She was looking at him shyly and I wondered whether she was going to find herself in some hotel room with him later on.

My Secret Santa present lay unopened on my placemat. It was beautifully wrapped, which was a good sign. For a moment I wondered whether someone had bought me something rude, which would be quite funny, but the wrapping didn't really do that justice. I would just have to open it.

All around the table, whoops and shouts and laughter mingled with the noise of paper being torn. Someone had given Caroline a bottle of red wine — not very original, but she looked pleased enough.

The second the wrapping had been pulled aside, I wished with my whole heart I'd not opened it at all.

It was a pair of handcuffs, lined with a pink fluffy material, and a red satin camisole top.

My heart was pounding, for the wrong

reasons. I looked around the table and, at the far end, Erin was looking back at me anxiously — it must have been her. I smiled as best I could, mouthed, 'Thank you,' and folded the items carefully back into the wrapping paper, tucking it under my chair.

I don't know which of those two things set it off. The red satin top was beautiful, well made, and it would have fitted me perfectly. Maybe it wasn't that — maybe it was the — other things.

'You okay?' Caroline asked. Her face was pink and she was starting to slur her words a little. 'You're white as a sheet.'

I nodded, not trusting myself to speak.

A few moments later I slipped away to the ladies', the Secret Santa package half-heartedly stuffed into the top of my bag. Pushing through the double doors, I noticed my hand was shaking. Fortunately there was nobody in there. I went into the cubicle first, rested my hands lightly on the back of the door, trying to breathe, trying to calm down. My heart was beating so fast there seemed to be nothing but thudding.

I pulled the package out of my bag. The wrapping paper meant at least I didn't have to touch it, and the contents hadn't touched the inside of my bag, just the paper. Still shaking, I lifted the whole lid off the sanitary bin and, wrinkling my nose at the sudden stink, shoved the package inside.

The relief was small, but instant. I retrieved my handbag and flushed the loo, just as the door opened and three young girls came in, laughing and talking loudly about some guy called

Graham and what a shit he was. I washed my hands while they busied themselves in the cubicles, shouting at each other and laughing. Washed them again. Washed them a third time. When all three toilets flushed simultaneously and the doors unlocked, I dried my hands on a paper towel and left them to it.

The rest of the meal was alright. Once the food arrived and I had something to do, I think I calmed down a little. Everyone was happy and busy talking, which meant I could watch the other diners and look out of the window.

The High Street was busy, with groups of people passing in front of the window heading to one of the pubs or restaurants, most of them happy and laughing. After a while I realised I was scanning the faces looking for Stuart. That was no good. I turned back to the table and tried my hardest to get involved in the conversation.

When the meal was over, I had been intending to sneak off and get back home as soon as I could, but that didn't quite happen.

'Come for a drink,' Caroline said, 'go on — just for one. We're going to the Lloyd George. Don't leave me on my own with all the kiddos.' She'd got her arm through mine, and was steering me away from Talbot Street and home. I let her steer me. I don't know why. Part of me just felt like fighting the urges tonight. I wanted to remember what it felt like to be free.

The Lloyd George was warm and, unlike the other pubs, not completely full. This place had once been a theatre, and the high ceilings and balcony running around the top gave the place a bright, open feel. I got myself an orange juice and stood with Caroline near the bar while she rattled on about her trip to Florida and how cheap the petrol had been. I saw Stuart before he saw me, but only just before — he caught me looking at him and before I had a chance to look away he'd smiled, said something to the bloke he was with, and come over.

'Hello, Cathy,' he said, shouting above the loud clamour of conversation, 'are you having a good night?'

'Yes,' I replied, 'you?'

He grimaced. 'Better now you're here. I was dying of boredom talking to Ralphie.' He pointed his beer bottle in the direction of his previous companion, a geeky-looking guy wearing glasses and a scarf of an indiscriminate brown, who was now pretending to be involved in a conversation to his right.

'Someone you work with?' I asked.

He laughed. 'My baby brother.' He took a swig from the bottle. 'How's the Christmas do?'

'Not bad. Long time since I went out for a meal.' Stupid thing to say, I thought. The trouble was, this frightened person wasn't me. I was used to making conversation with people. I was vivacious, friendly, talkative. Keeping my mouth shut was always a struggle. I wondered if I would ever get used to it.

Robin's hooting laughter rose above the general throng, and Stuart cast him a glance. 'Is he with you?'

I nodded, raising my eyes. 'He's an arse,' I said.

There was a moment's pause where we both wondered what on earth to say next.

'So,' he said at last, tilting his head in the direction of Talbot Street, 'you lived here long?'

'A year or so.'

He nodded. 'I like that house. Feels like home already.'

I found myself smiling at him. His green eyes were regarding me, a boyish sparkle to them — it had been a long time since I'd met anyone with that sort of enthusiasm. 'Good.'

Above the racket I heard someone shout 'Stu!' and we both turned to see Ralphie at the door, beckoning him on. He returned a salute.

'I'd better go,' he said.

'Right.'

'Might see you later?' he asked.

A few years ago the answer to this question would have been an automatic yes. I'd be out all night, moving from one drinking hole to another, meeting friends, leaving some of them behind in one place and meeting up with them again in another, moving from pub to club to bar without a care in the world. Seeing someone later could mean just that, or it could mean snogging in some doorway, staggering home and fucking them all night, before waking up the next day with a blinding headache and an urgent need to throw up.

'I don't know,' I said. 'I'll probably be heading home in a minute.'

'Want me to wait? I'll walk you home.'

I tried to see from his eyes whether he meant that, whether he was prepared to walk me home to see me safely to the front door, or if he meant he wanted to walk me home and then see what happened.

'Thanks,' I said, 'but I'll be fine. It's not exactly far. You go and have a good time. I'll see you soon.'

He hesitated for a moment, then gave me a smile, leaned over me slightly to put his empty bottle down on the bar, and followed Ralph out into the night.

'That your boyfriend?' said Caroline, turning back from the bar.

I shook my head.

'Shame,' she said, 'he's nice. And obviously fancies the pants off you.'

'You think?' I asked, wondering if that was a good thing or not.

She nodded vigorously. 'I can always tell these things. The way he was looking at you. Who is he, then?'

'Lives in the flat upstairs,' I said. 'His name's Stuart.'

'Well,' she said, 'I'd get in there if I were you. Before someone else does.'

I watched the others as they debated where the rest of the night would take them. They were arguing over getting a cab and going straight to the West End, or whether to have one more drink in the Red Lion, because apparently Erin had a bit of a thing for one of the barmen in there. Either way, I wasn't going with them. And I definitely wasn't going anywhere near the Red Lion. That one had people on the door.

We all poured back out onto the pavement

again and started threading our way through the crowds back up towards the Red Lion, and Talbot Street, where I was planning on diverting in the direction of home. I walked deliberately slowly so that I'd fall behind and not be noticed when I sneaked off.

I heard a noise behind me, a shout.

It was Robin, coming out of the Lloyd George still doing up his flies. He had apparently given up on Diane and Lucy, because for some reason he seemed to feel like starting on me. 'Cath-aay,' he said, breathing beer and whisky and Thai green chicken curry all over me. 'Did I tell you how sensational you're looking tonight?'

He slung an arm over my shoulder. He was so close to me I could feel the heat of him. I ducked from under his arm and quickened my steps to try to catch up with the others, not wanting to reply, not trusting myself with any answer.

'What's the matter, beautiful? You not talking to me tonight?'

'You're drunk,' I said quietly, staring at Caroline's back to try to make her turn around, to come and rescue me.

'Well, love,' he said, with emphasis, 'of course I'm drunk, it's the fucking Christmas party, right? Tha's the whole fucking point.'

I stopped walking and turned to face him. Somewhere inside me, the fear had been taken over by fury. 'Go and annoy someone else, Robin.'

He stopped too, and his attractive face had become a sneer. 'Frigid cow,' he said loudly. 'Bet you only get wet for your girlfriend.'

This, for some unfathomable reason, made me smile.

Whatever, it was clearly the wrong response for him. Before I knew what was happening, he'd pushed me back hard, my feet stumbling backwards, until I hit a brick wall, his whole body against me. The breath knocked out of me in one go, I couldn't take any in because of his weight, and then his face in mine, his mouth on mine, his tongue in my mouth.

Monday 17 November 2003

It was nearly midnight when Lee finally put in an appearance.

He'd said he'd be at my house at eight, or thereabouts, and then nothing — no call, no text, nothing at all until nearly midnight. At eleven, pissed off, I had nearly gone out, but decided to go to bed instead. All night I'd been fighting the urge to phone him, to say 'Where are you?' but instead I tidied up, cleaned the bathroom, emailed some friends and got steadily more and more mad.

Until the knock on the door.

Lying in bed, staring at the ceiling, I wasn't sure I'd heard it until a second knock, slightly harder. I contemplated ignoring it; that would serve him bloody right, standing me up like that! And besides, I was in my pyjamas.

I waited a few moments and no more knocks came, but I couldn't lie there any more. The anger was sitting on my stomach like a dead weight. With a sigh, I got out of bed and padded downstairs, putting on the light in the hallway. I opened the door, mentally rehearsing giving him a piece of my mind.

Blood on his face.

'Oh, my God! Oh, shit, what happened?' Barefoot, I leapt from the doorway, touching his cheek, his face, feeling him wince.

'Can I come in?' he said, with a cheeky smile.

He wasn't drunk at all, which had been my first thought. The way he was dressed was very different from the last time I'd seen him: grubby-looking jeans, a shirt that might once have been pale blue but was now decorated with spots of blood and smears of grease, a tatty brown jacket, trainers that must have been years old. But I couldn't smell alcohol on him — just sweat, dirt, the smell of the cold night outside.

My second thought, which I voiced, was, 'What the fuck happened to you?'

He didn't reply, but I didn't give him much of a chance, dragging him in and sitting him on the sofa, while I ran around getting some Dettol and cotton wool and warm water and a towel. In the semi darkness, the light from the hallway, I dabbed away at the blood around his eye, feeling the swelling beneath the skin give. Blood oozed from the cut in his eyebrow.

'Are you going to tell me?' I said quietly.

He gazed at me, stroked my cheek. 'You look so good,' he said. 'I'm sorry I'm so late.'

'Lee, please. What happened?'

He shook his head.

'I can't tell you. All I can say is that I'm sorry

I didn't make it for eight. I tried everything I could to get to a phone, but it didn't happen.'

I stopped fussing around his face and looked at him. He was telling the truth about that, at least.

'It's okay,' I said. 'You're here now.' I held a cotton pad up to his eyebrow for a moment. 'Although dinner's ruined.'

He laughed, and then winced.

'Lift up your shirt,' I ordered, and when he didn't immediately comply I started to undo his buttons, pulling his shirt open. The side of his chest was red and scratched — the bruises wouldn't show for a while. 'Jesus,' I said, 'you should be in A&E, not my front room.'

His hands went to my back and pulled me down towards him. 'I'm going nowhere.'

His kiss started gently, but only for a moment. Then it was fierce and hard, and I was kissing him back harder. His hands were threaded through my hair, pulling my face into his. After a moment I fought against him, but only so I could pull my T-shirt off over my head.

For a first time, it wasn't very special. He smelled of engine oil and tasted of day-old instant coffee; his face was rough with stubble and he was heavy against me, but still I wanted him badly. Although he seemed to have forgotten that it might be an idea to use a condom, I wasn't about to stop him now; it was fast and awkward, a tangle of legs and arms, and clothes still getting in the way. His breath was coming fast and rasping against my throat, and a few minutes later he pulled out of me and came over my belly.

In the semi-darkness I saw his blue eyes fill with tears as his breathing slowed, heard the gasp, the sob, pulled him back against me, cradling his head against mine; felt the warmth of droplets on my chest, blood or tears, I wasn't sure. 'I'm sorry,' he said. 'It's all so shit. I didn't want it to be like this. I wanted this to work, properly work. I always do this, I always end up fucking everything up.'

'Lee,' I said, 'it's alright. Really.'

When he was calm again I left him on the sofa and made a cup of tea and some toast. He ate it as though he hadn't seen food for weeks, while I sat opposite, watching him, wondering what had happened and how I could get him to talk to me about it. After that, I ran a shower and stood with him under the spray, cleaning him properly this time. He stood half-propped against the wall, eyes closed, as I sponged the dirt away from his neck, his back. His right shoulder was one big graze, as though he'd fallen out of a car onto the tarmac. His right hand was swollen, the knuckles scraped; clearly the fight he'd been in hadn't been one-sided. Under his left arm, the deep red marks went all the way down and round to his lower back. Maybe he'd broken some ribs. I reached up and washed his hair, using the shower spray to rinse it back, away from his eyes. There was more blood in his hair above his right ear, lots of it, matted into a solid lump, but no apparent wound. Whatever — it sluiced away down the plughole and was gone.

I pushed as hard as I could and felt a scream that wouldn't come, utter terror making my heart pound, trying to get my knee up to connect with his groin; and then, just as quickly, he was pulled back off me with a grunt.

For a moment all I could see was a man dragging Robin off by the scruff of his neck, then pushing him hard so that he fell to the floor. 'Fuck off,' said a voice. 'Go on, fuck off now before I smack you one.'

'Alright, mate, alright, calm down. No problem.' Robin scrambled to his feet, dusted off his trousers and marched off after the rest of them, none of whom was any the wiser.

It was Stuart.

I was still frozen to the spot, my back against some grubby graffitied wall, breathing coming in short gasps, my hands in tight fists, fingers already beginning to tingle. I could feel it coming on, fighting it as hard as I could. I really didn't need to be having a panic attack at eleven o'clock at night in the High Street.

He came back over to me, but not too close. He stood to one side so that the light from the estate agent's window fell on his face, so that I could see it was him. 'You alright? No, silly question. Okay. Deep breaths — come on, breathe with me.'

He put one hand on my upper arm, and ignored my flinch. He made me look him in the eye. 'Take one deep breath and hold it. Come on. One breath — hold it.' His voice was calm, soothing, but it wasn't helping.

'I need to get home, I — '

'Just wait a second. Get your breath back.'

'I — '

'I'm here. It's okay. That idiot won't come back. Now breathe, slowly, come on, breathe with me for a bit. Look at me. That's it.'

So I stood still and concentrated on breathing. Despite it all, despite the terror and the shock of it, I could feel my heart rate slowing. The shaking wouldn't stop, though.

His steady, unflinching eye contact was unnerving and reassuring all at the same time.

'Right, that's much better,' he said, after a few minutes. 'Are you okay to walk?'

I nodded, not trusting myself to speak, and set off. My legs were shaking, and I stumbled.

'Here,' he said, and offered me his arm.

I hesitated for a moment, feeling the terror coming back. I wanted to run, I wanted to run fast and hard and not look back. But then I took his arm, and we started to walk up towards Talbot Street and home.

A police car suddenly pulled to a stop beside us, and a tall, lanky officer got out. 'Hold up a second, please,' he said to us.

The shaking got worse.

'Alright?' said Stuart.

'CCTV saw you back there,' the officer said to me. His radio, clipped to the front of his stab vest, was bleeping and talking to itself. 'Looks like someone was giving you some trouble. Everything alright?'

I nodded, vigorously.

63

'You're looking a bit shaky,' the police officer said, eyeing me doubtfully. 'Had a lot to drink?'

I shook my head. 'Just — cold,' I said, my teeth chattering.

'You know this gentleman?' the police officer said to me.

I nodded again.

'I'm going to walk her home,' said Stuart. 'Just around the corner.'

The officer nodded, checking us both out. From the car, the other officer said, 'Rob — flash call just come in.'

'Long as you're alright,' he said, but he was already halfway inside the car, and the sirens started a second later, making me jump half out of my skin.

We carried on walking. I'd not drunk anything stronger than fruit juice, but each step felt as if the ground was swaying.

'You don't like police, huh,' Stuart said. It wasn't a question.

I didn't answer. Tears were pouring one after the other down my cheeks. I'd felt the panic at the mere sight of him, at the cuffs buttoned to the front of his stab vest, and the siren had just about finished me off.

By the time we got to the front door, he was just about holding me up. I was gripping his arm like a lifeline, too afraid to let go. 'Come upstairs, I'll make you a cup of tea,' he said.

As soon as the front door was shut behind us, I let go of him. I checked it, just once, even though he was there. I opened the latch and closed it again, pulled the door to, pulled it again

64

and heard it rattle, ran my fingers over the edge where the door met the jamb, checking that it wasn't still slightly open. I wanted to check it again but I realised he was watching me. I managed a weak smile.

'Thanks. I'll be alright now.'

I waited for him to go up the stairs so I could check the door again, but he stood his ground.

'Please. Just come and have a cup of tea. We'll leave my door open so you can leave if you want to. Okay?'

I stared at him. 'I'll be fine. Thank you.'

He didn't move.

'Please, Stuart, you can go back out and find your friends. I'm alright now, honest.'

'Just come and have a cup of tea. The door's locked, I saw you do it. You're safe.' He was holding out his hand, waiting for me to take it.

I didn't take it, but I did manage to give up on the checking. 'Alright. Thanks.'

You're safe? What an odd thing to say, I thought, following him up the stairs. I couldn't look at my flat door as we passed it, because I wouldn't have been able to resist the urge to start checking. As it was, I knew I wouldn't be able to sleep tonight.

He turned on all the lights in his flat as he went in, putting the kettle on in the kitchen. To the left of the kitchen area was a large, open-plan living room, with two bay windows on to the front. Leafy green plants on the windowsills. I wandered over to them and looked out. Despite the dark, there was a good view over to the High Street, crowds of people still walking up and down without a care in the world. From up here you could see over the rooftops of the houses across the street, down across the twinkling orange streetlights of London towards the river, in the distance the lights on top of Canary Wharf flashing on and off, and beyond it, the Dome, lit up like a landed spacecraft.

He put a mug of tea for me down on the coffee table and sat in one of the armchairs. 'How are you feeling?' he asked gently.

'I'm okay,' I lied, my teeth chattering. I sat on the sofa, which was low and deep and surprisingly comfortable, hugging my knees. I felt so tired, all of a sudden.

'Will you be alright later?' he asked.

'Sure,' I said.

He hesitated, and took a drink from his mug. 'If you start feeling like you're getting a panic attack, will you call me? Come and knock on the door?'

I spent a moment contemplating this, not answering. *I'd like to*, was what I wanted to say, because I knew full well that he was right, I would undoubtedly have a panic attack later on, and I also knew that wild horses wouldn't be able to get me out of my own flat when it happened.

I thought my hands might have stopped shaking enough to risk picking up the mug, and I took a gulp of tea. It was hot, and funnily enough he hadn't done a bad job of making it. Not quite enough milk, but good enough to make it drinkable.

'I'm sorry,' I said.

'You don't need to be sorry,' he answered. 'Don't be sorry. It wasn't your fault.'

Those words started the tears falling again, and I put the mug down and covered my face with both my hands. I half-expected him to come over, to try to hold me, and I braced myself for the shock of it, but he didn't move. After a few moments I opened my eyes and found a box of tissues were on the table in front of me. I gave a short laugh and took one, wiping my face.

'You have OCD,' I heard him say.

I found my voice again. 'Yes, thanks for pointing it out.'

'Are you getting any help?'

I shook my head. 'What's the point?' I cast him a glance and he was watching me impassively.

He gave a little shrug. 'Maybe it could give you some more free time?'

'I don't need any more free time, thanks. My calendar's hardly what you'd call packed.'

I realised I was probably starting to sound a bit hostile, so I took another drink of tea to calm myself down. 'Sorry,' I said again. 'I didn't mean to bite your head off.'

'Don't worry,' he said. 'You're right, it's absolutely none of my business. And very rude of me to point it out.'

I gave him a weak smile. 'What are you, some kind of shrink?'

He laughed, and nodded. 'Some kind. I'm a doctor at the Maudsley.'

'What sort of doctor?'

'A clinical psychologist. I work on an assessment ward as well as doing some outpatient clinics. I specialise in treating depression but I've seen plenty of people with OCD in the past.'

Oh, fuck, I thought. That was it. Now somebody else knew that I was turning into a nutcase. I would have to move house.

He finished his tea, stood up and took the mug out to the kitchen. When he came back, he had a small piece of paper which he put carefully on the table in front of me.

'What's that?' I said suspiciously.

'The last time I'll mention it, I promise. It's the name of one of my colleagues. If you change your mind about getting some advice, some help, ask the Community Mental Health Team to refer you to him. He's a top bloke. And he specialises in OCD.'

I took the piece of paper. In neat letters, the words 'Alistair Hodge'. Under that, the word 'Stuart' and a mobile number.

'That's my number,' he said. 'If you have a panic attack later, you can call me. I'll come down and sit with you.'

Yes, I thought, like *that's* going to happen.

'I can't go and see anyone. I really can't. What about work? I'd never be able to get a promotion again if they know I'm nuts.'

He smiled. 'You're not 'nuts' at all. There's no reason why your employer needs to know about it. And even if you decide not to go and see anyone, there are a lot of things you can do on your own which might help. I could recommend you some books. You could try some relaxation therapies, that kind of thing. None of that would ever go on your records.'

I turned the piece of paper over and over in my fingers. 'I'll think about it.'

From outside, a sound of a police siren filtered up to the top floor. 'I should go home,' I said.

I stood and made my way to the front door. It was still open, giving me easy access to the hallway beyond. 'Thanks,' I said, turning towards him. For a moment I wanted to give him a hug. I wanted to feel what it was like to have his arms around me, whether it would feel safe, or not. But I could still feel the pressure of Robin's body against me, and it held me back.

'Can I ask you something?' I said.

'Sure.'

'Couldn't *you* do it? Couldn't you treat me?'

He gave me a smile. I was outside the flat, he was inside it, keeping that space between us. 'Conflict of interest,' he said.

I must have looked confused.

'If we're going to be friends,' he said, 'I'm too involved. It would be unprofessional.'

Before I had a chance to react to this, he'd given me a smile, said goodnight, and closed the door. I went all the way downstairs to the front door, and started the checking.

Monday 17 November 2003

In the early hours of the morning, just before it got light, just as I was about to fall asleep, he

69

pulled himself closer to me, gritting his teeth against the pain.

'Catherine,' he whispered, close to my ear.

'Mm?'

A pause. I opened my eyes, making out the shape of him, close to me. 'I lied to you,' he said.

I tried to sit up, but he held me down. 'Just listen. I lied to you about what I do. I'm not just working on the door at the River; there's other stuff I do as well.'

'What other stuff?' I murmured.

'I can't tell you, not yet. I'm sorry, and I promise I will never lie to you about anything ever again.'

'Why can't you tell me?'

'Lots of reasons.'

'Will you ever be able to tell me?'

'Probably. Just not yet.'

'Is it something bad?'

'Sometimes.'

There was a pause. I felt his hand stroking my hair, stroking it back from my face, incredibly gently.

'If you ask me about anything else, I'll answer it,' he said.

'Are you married?' I said.

'No.'

'With someone?'

'No.'

I thought about this for a moment. 'Am I going to regret falling for you?'

He gave a small laugh and kissed my cheek, very softly. 'Probably. Anything else?'

'Are you a good man or a bad man?'

'That depends on whether you're a good woman or a bad woman.'

I considered this response and decided it was a clever one.

'Are you going to turn up on my doorstep with injuries on a regular basis?'

'I hope not.'

'What happened to the other bloke?'

'What other bloke?'

'The one you were fighting with.'

A pause.

'He's in hospital.'

'Oh.'

'But he'll be okay.'

'Am I going to be able to introduce you to my friends?'

'Not yet. Soon, I guess. If you want to.'

His hand ran from my cheek, down the side of my neck and over my naked skin, touching me softly, tenderly. 'Any more questions?'

'Do you think you could make love to me again?'

His mouth against mine. 'I think I could give it a try.'

Saturday 24 November 2007

The panic attack hit me just before four this morning. I'd been trying to sleep, but of course I hadn't been able to. I was lying on the bed, thinking about it all and trying not to think about it at the same time. I'd put myself in danger by going out. The flat felt violated just as

I did, even though it had happened outside in the street. I could sense his presence everywhere. There was only one thing that could possibly help me feel better, so I got up and started checking.

The first set of checks didn't alleviate the panic, and I realised it was because I was still contaminated by him, so I stripped all my clothes off and put them into a black bin liner. I tipped the contents of my handbag out onto the kitchen worktop and stuffed the handbag into the bin liner too. I put the bin bag outside on the landing.

I went into the shower and scrubbed myself from head to foot, trying to get the feeling of Robin off me. My skin was red by the time I'd finished. I brushed my teeth until my gums bled, gargled with mouthwash, dressed in a pair of clean jogging pants and a sweatshirt.

After that, I checked the flat again. It was no good. Half an hour later, when I was still standing on the toilet seat, checking the stupid bathroom window which didn't even open anyway, I realised I still felt dirty. It was the tears, flowing down my cheeks, contaminating my hot skin.

I stripped off again. Clothes that had been clean out of the airing cupboard, shoved into the laundry bin.

Back into the shower. For a full thirty minutes I stood there, letting the water flow over my skin, aware that it stung from the last time I scrubbed it, trying to make myself believe that this meant I was clean.

There's nothing left, I told myself. He's gone, there's no trace of him left. He is *not here.*

Still not clean, I retrieved my nailbrush and the antibacterial soap and started scrubbing again. This time, by the time I was done, the water was running pink down the drain. It brought back memories of something, vague, painful, like an old wound.

I sat on the edge of the bath, wrapped in another clean towel, almost too tired to start again, but knowing I had to.

When at last I'd finished the whole thing, again, still wrapped in the towel, I put on a clean top and a pair of leggings from the airing cupboard. This was a bad one. I was stuck. The urge to start again, do it properly, just once more, to be certain, to be absolutely sure that the flat was safe, was very strong.

I was cold, shivery, and the feel of the clothes on my skin was scratchy, irritating, not soothing.

I did the only thing I could do: went back to the flat door and started again.

By half-past seven I was so tired I physically couldn't do any more. I held off the panic a while longer by making myself a hot drink. I sat shivering on the couch, cradling my mug of tea, knowing what was coming but trying to keep it at bay. There was nothing at all worth watching on the television at this unearthly time of the night, but I found myself watching a repeat of some quiz show with dry eyes, my skin all over my body tight and sore. The sound of the voices was curiously soothing. Maybe this would do the trick.

When the shivering subsided, the tiredness overtook me and I drifted off for a while. The next thing I knew, the sound of sirens jerked me back awake.

The quiz had finished and one of those interminable real-life police shows had taken its place. Sirens everywhere. It's only the television, I told myself, but it was too late. Somehow I managed to find the remote and turn it off.

I curled into the corner of the sofa, trying not to breathe too loudly, listening out for any noises in the flat. The shaking was worse now, my skin like gooseflesh from my scalp to my feet.

Had I been dreaming about him, or had he really been here? All I could see was him: his whole weight on top of me, pinning me down. I imagined those handcuffs, which had already broken the skin on my wrists, cutting into my swollen flesh. The smell of him; stale alcohol, breathing it into my open mouth.

This isn't real. He's not real . . .

When I opened my eyes, I thought I saw Robin's face; he was in here somewhere, hiding. Waiting for me to fall asleep again.

It was bright daylight when the trembling and the tears finally began to ease off. I felt shattered, completely exhausted, too afraid to go back to sleep. I forced myself to stand up and stretch. The urge to go and start checking the flat was strong, but I was too tired, too stiff. I could barely move.

I limped to the kitchen, shivering with cold

74

now rather than the effects of the panic attack. I put the central heating on and switched on the kettle.

The garden under my kitchen window was bare and grey; the grass was the only splash of colour. The trees all naked now, brown decaying leaves littered in piles in the corners of the garden wall. The wind blew the top branches; if I could hear them from here, it would have been a rattling sigh. The kettle roared away in the stillness, my eyes back to feeling dry and sore as if they'd never be able to cry again. It looked cold outside. I yawned.

I took my tea into the bedroom, opening the curtains fully so that I could see the tops of the trees moving in the wind when I lay down on my bed.

I watched the branches swaying, dancing, the grey clouds behind them scudding along at a merry pace. The tops of the branches waving at me, lying wretched and scrubbed to pieces on top of the duvet.

All I have to do is stay alive.

Tuesday 18 November 2003

The next morning he was dressed and gone before the alarm clock woke me at seven.

The shower was usually the only thing that really woke me up, and I moved from the blissful dreamy warmth of having had a seriously good seeing-to into a kind of queasy discomfort, as though I'd been a bit on the drunk side of tipsy and had somehow misbehaved. I hadn't, of course, I hadn't drunk anything at all last night — I could remember every delicious detail of the sex that had taken up much of the dark hours. But even so, in the cleansing warmth of the shower, the familiar scent of my shampoo and soap somehow grounding me back into normal life, I couldn't escape from the earlier part of the evening. What the fuck was that all about?

I took myself off to work and ploughed through a few jobs that had been hanging over my head for a while, trying to clear my head of the tiredness that comes from not much sleep and lots of sex. Just when I'd managed to forget about him, my phone buzzed on my desk with a text.

Sorry about last night. Was not v good impression. Forgive me?

I left the phone on the desk for a while and pondered my reply. If I closed my eyes for a second I could see his face on the pillow next to me, the light from the bedside lamp, his blond hair shining at the edges, those blue eyes dark and regarding me with something I couldn't fathom. And the dark red bruise around his eye, swelling under his eyebrow, the cut skin. And the fact that despite it all he was smiling.

It's fine.

I looked at my reply for minutes, thinking about what else I wanted to say. 'It's fine, don't worry about it, feel free to turn up in whatever state takes your fancy'? 'It's fine, thanks for coming'? 'It's fine, at least the sex part was, not sure about the rest of it'?

In the end I hit the back button, deleted my reply, and left his text unanswered. As my English teacher used to tell me, if you can't think of the right thing to say, say nothing at all.

Monday 26 November 2007

I went back to work on Monday the way I always did, one foot in front of the other, so tired I almost couldn't remember which routes I'd taken last week. The bus stop I wanted was a mile away and I was already late. I tried to hurry but my feet were sluggish. I'd not seen or heard Stuart since Saturday night. For all I knew he was still inside his flat and hadn't been out at all on Sunday. Sometimes I heard noises from upstairs, a soft footfall, a cupboard door, the noise of bathwater draining away. But more often there was no noise at all.

Caroline came to find me at eleven.

'You coming down for a coffee?' she asked chirpily.

I wondered how much sleep *she'd* had this weekend. 'Maybe later, I just want to finish this.'

'Christ, you look like death. I didn't think you'd drunk that much.'

She made me laugh in spite of myself. 'Cheers for that.'

'Are you alright, Cathy? One minute you were

there on Saturday and then you'd gone. Robin said something about you wanting to have an early night.'

'Yes — I just didn't feel — I mean . . . I don't know. I'm not really the going out type.'

She smiled. 'They are a bit loud, aren't they? The girls, I mean. You've no excuse though. You're younger than me. How old are you? Thirty-five? No excuse.'

Twenty-eight, I wanted to say, but hell, it didn't matter how old I was. I might as well be sixty.

'Well, come down and find me later, won't you? I want to hear more about that sexy young man who lives upstairs.' And with a wink, she was gone.

I'd been dreading bumping into Robin. Fortunately he worked out of another office most of the time. With luck it might be months before he turned up again.

I looked out of the window and thought about the man who lives upstairs.

Friday 28 November 2003

When I got to the Paradise Café, Sylvia was already waiting for me at the corner table, a pot of tea and a double espresso on the table in front of her. The window where she sat was steamed up and the whole place was warm and damp and fragrant like a freshly showered Sunday morning.

'Am I late?'

'I didn't order you a muffin,' she said, kissing

me on both cheeks with enthusiasm, 'I thought you'd like to choose one yourself. They've got apple and cinnamon ones.'

'Then I'll get us a couple of those, shall I?' I said.

The Paradise was like an old friend. Years ago, Sylvia and I, and the three other girls I'd shared a house with at university, used to meet up here once a month, chatting about our lives, wasting an afternoon over coffee and food. Karen and Lesley had both moved away; Karen to Canada, where she'd taken a teaching post at the St George campus of Toronto University, and Lesley to Dublin, where her family lived. Last year Sylvia had had a big falling out with Sasha, and she didn't come along any more. Sometimes I had an email from her, but she'd got a new boyfriend who had become a fiancée, and they'd moved into a new house, and gradually Sasha's life had diverted away from the life we had shared.

So now it was just me and Sylvia. She was working as a journalist on Lancaster's regional newspaper, but was desperate to get out of the boring provinces and move to London. She would suit London, I always thought. Already she was too vivacious and bold for Lancaster, her blonde hair and jewel-bright outfits setting her in bold relief against the sandstone and the concrete.

'You look like you've got some news,' I said. Sylvia was fidgeting in her seat, and it wasn't like her to be first to arrive.

'Not yet,' Sylvia said wickedly. 'Firstly, what's

79

this I hear about a new man? A little magpie told me you were out having dinner with a man in a suit.'

The magpie would have been Maggie, who had been Sylvia's flatmate when we'd first graduated. She'd got her nickname because she only ever wore black, very occasionally with something white, and had a penchant for bling.

I found the smile that had barely left my lips had returned.

'Well?'

'Shit, Sylvia, I can't keep anything from you, can I?'

Sylvia gave a little squeak of delight. 'I knew it! What's his name, where did you meet him and what's he like in bed?'

'God, you're dreadful.'

'You know you want to tell me.'

I took several sips of tea whilst Sylvia hopped from one bum cheek to the other.

'His name's Lee, I met him at the River, and it's none of your damn business.'

'And is he absolutely stunning?'

I fished out my mobile phone from my bag and scrolled through the menus until I got to the photo I'd taken of him, the only photo I had. Fresh out of the shower, dressed only in a white towel, hair damp, the bruises on his face and on his side fading. The look on his face lecherous.

'Oh, my God. Catherine. He's a bit of alright, isn't he? Why the fuck didn't I see him first?'

Makes a change, I thought, allowing myself to feel a tiny bit smug.

A small frown furrowed between Sylvia's

neatly styled eyebrows. 'What's with all the bruises? Is he some sort of cage fighter? Stunt man?'

'You tell me. He's being all secretive.'

That got Sylvia's interest piqued. 'Really? Secretive how?'

'I don't know what he does. He turned up at my house one night looking like he'd been in some fight and then jumped out of the car on the way home. He wouldn't tell me what had happened.'

'Was he pissed?'

'No.'

'Oh, my God, he's a gangster.'

I laughed. 'I don't think so.'

'A drug dealer?'

I shook my head.

'Well, why won't he tell you what he's been up to, then?'

'I've no idea. But I trust him.'

'You trust someone who gets into fights and then won't tell you what happened?'

'He's been honest with me about everything else.'

'Has he? How do you know?'

Sylvia was entirely right. I knew that if he did have a job, the hours were irregular and he was often away for days at a time. I hadn't met any of his friends, his family — having them all the way down in Cornwall was convenient, to say the least. I hadn't even been to his flat.

'If you met him, you'd know. He says everything with his eyes.'

She hooted with laughter and kicked me

81

under the table. 'Get a grip on yourself!' She swirled the last of the coffee around in her cup and looked at me from under her eyelashes. 'Well, it's about time I did meet him anyway. Why don't you bring him along to my farewell party?'

'What farewell party?'

The excitement of holding her news in bubbled over at last and Sylvia's eyes sparkled with delight.

'I've got myself a job at the *Daily Mail*. I'm starting in January.'

'Shut up! No way!'

'Yes way. I am getting out of this town. Finally.'

Genuinely thrilled, I gave her a hug whilst Sylvia squealed and jumped up and down. The other occupants of the Paradise Café, an elderly couple and a few students, watched us warily, whilst Irene behind the counter gave us an indulgent smile.

That was it, then, I thought. I'd be left here in Lancaster whilst my oldest friends went off pursuing their lives around the world. If it weren't for Lee, I'd be looking to escape myself.

'So what's all this about a party?'

Monday 26 November 2007

When I got home there was post for me on the table downstairs in the hallway. In addition to the usual bills, there was a large brown envelope with just the word 'Cathy' on the front in black marker.

'Coo-ee, Cathy! You alright?'

'Yes, thanks, Mrs Mackenzie. How are you?'

'I'm fine, dear.' She gave me that hard stare again, while I looked at the envelope on the table without picking it up, and then she went back into her flat and shut the door.

I left it where it was and checked the door again, twice over, start to finish. I could have got away with once, but the second time enabled me to pick up the envelope with the other stuff and take it upstairs.

I dropped it on the coffee table while I did the checks, but I found I rushed through the first two times because I wanted to see what was in the envelope. I had to force myself to slow down the third time, do it properly, concentrate. When I'd finished I paused. Was that good enough? Should I do it again for good measure, just to be sure? Maybe I'd missed something.

I started again.

It was nearly nine when I sat on the sofa and opened the envelope. A pile of papers, some of them clipped together with a paperclip, and a handwritten note at the front.

Cathy —
Thought these might be useful. Let me know if you need anything. Or if you want to ask any questions.

Stuart

I looked at the note for ages, the way he'd written my name, the way he'd signed his name. I wondered if he'd had to think about what to write. It looked utterly carefree, easy, as though he'd picked up the pile of papers somewhere, casually, and then just scribbled off two lines without even thinking about it.

I went through the pile, and quickly I noticed that there was nothing careless about it at all. The first thing was a sheet about the Centre for Anxiety Disorders and Trauma at the Maudsley Hospital in Denmark Hill, and the specialist outpatient clinic for OCD. Then there were articles that he'd printed off various websites, with bits underlined. There was a study about OCD and new therapy options for treating patients presenting with severe symptoms, written by Dr Alistair Hodge, C.Psychol., AFBPsS, B.Sc. (Hons)., M.Sc., Clin. Psych, Dip., C.B.T., PsychD., DCHyp., SMBCSHA, UKCP and BABCP Registered — and half a dozen other people with equally impressive qualifications. There was a page of alternative therapists that he'd printed off from somewhere, with two handwritten ones added to the bottom, a yoga class meeting at the local primary school on a Wednesday evening, and a Core Relaxation Therapist, whatever that was, with a phone number. The page below that was a list of OCD support groups, with one highlighted and handwritten in the margin 'meets in Camden 7.30pm third Tues of month, phone Ellen for details' and a number. Under that, three chapters from a book called Unstuck: Techniques for Freeing Yourself from OCD, with various bits underlined. Then there were three different questionnaires which seemed to be about determining whether you actually have OCD or not.

Finally, unexpectedly, the last page was another handwritten note.

Cathy —
Thanks for looking at all this. You've made a start.
  Ring me, okay?

Stuart

Then his phone number again, just in case I'd lost the last one he'd given me, which of course I hadn't. I knew exactly where the bit of paper was, just in case I needed it, which I never would since I knew his number off by heart already.

Not that I was going to use it.

Friday 28 November 2003

Lee was working at the River.

I went to see him, wearing that red satin dress. His face when he saw me was incredible. I gave him a smile and a wink as I passed him going into the club. Through the night, dancing with people I knew, chatting at the bar with some people I hadn't seen for a few months, then later on when Claire and Louise turned up, I kept seeing his face in the crowd, at the edge of the dance floor, watching me.

By midnight, several drinks down me, I was more bold. Dancing, on my own, I saw him again in the doorway, ostensibly watching the crowd, in practice watching me. I crossed the dance floor to him; his eyes never left mine. He took me by the hand and pulled me towards the corridor connecting the main club with the bar at the front, his steps rapid, making me stumble, all the while shouting, 'Lee! Lee? What the . . . ?'

He pushed open a doorway marked 'Staff Only' and the music suddenly dulled as the fire door slammed behind us, my heels skittering down the concrete corridor, another door to the side — an office. The only light came from the CCTV screens, showing the dance floor, the door, the stairs, the area outside the toilets. He pushed a pile of paperwork off the desk, papers scattering everywhere, lifting me between his two hands as though I weighed nothing, his mouth on mine, hungry. I tugged at my skirt, pulling it up and out of his way. With one hand he pulled my knickers aside, ripping them, discarding them into the room, and then fucking me, hard.

A few minutes later, not a word spoken, he adjusted his suit and, without looking back at me, left the room. Sitting on the desk, legs still splayed and trembling with the force of him, I watched the CCTV screens until he reappeared at the main door of the club, looking for all the world as though he'd just been checking the dance floor for trouble.

Until he looked up at the camera, right into my eyes, and stared.

Looking round the office at the paperwork all over the floor, my underwear torn, discarded in the corner, I found myself thinking: this is so crazy — what the fuck am I doing? What am I doing?

Monday 3 December 2007

I've been dragging my feet from one day to another for a week. The flashbacks are bad, which correspondingly means my checking is bad. I know this is because of what happened with Robin. It will take a while to get it out of my system, then at some point it will start to ease off, then I can just get back to checking normally and making myself half an hour late instead of three hours late.

I'm not sure if coming home and reading about OCD is really helping, to be honest. The medical terms remind me of the hospital and I try not to think about all that. I don't remember that much about it, anyway. It's as if all that happened to someone else. It's as if I fell asleep when it all got too difficult, and then I woke up some time about eighteen months ago, gradually, with a kind of dull awareness that I was still alive, and that all I had to do was carry on, put one foot in front of the other, move forwards and not backwards. Of course I should stop bloody reading about all this and start actually doing something constructive.

I've heard Stuart coming home, late at night. I think sometimes I lie there waiting to hear his feet on the stairs outside. I know he tries to be quiet when he comes up the stairs but to be honest I'd hear him in any case. I feel safer when

I've heard him go past because I know for sure the door will be locked downstairs. After he's been past I can go to sleep. Sometimes it's been nearly midnight, though. He must be shattered.

Today I found myself walking past the library on my way home. The lights were all on, and the doors slid open automatically as I walked past, like an invitation. I avoid places like this, public places, but something made me go inside. It was nearly empty. Students at desks, a couple of people on the internet terminals, two members of staff stamping books and chatting in loud whispers.

I browsed my way around until I got to the psychology section, looking along the titles for anything that might relate to obsessions and compulsions. I recognised the title of a book that Stuart had recommended, ran my finger along the spine.

It was quiet in here. I pulled out a volume about anxiety and flicked to the chapter headings. Not very cheerful. I heard a sound behind me, and looked over my shoulder. From where I stood between the shelves I could see nobody, not a single human being.

I put the book back in its place and walked back to the end of the aisle. There were still two people working at long tables, books spread out, notepads, highlighter pens. Only one person working at the main counter now, a woman with short hair and impossibly long earrings. She was accepting a pile of books that a man had just passed over the counter to her.

I caught a flash of blond hair, a bulky physique, navy blue sweatshirt, a confident, purposeful stride. It was him.

I felt light-headed, ducked back behind the shelves, my heart pounding. The lightness didn't go away, and then it was blackness, and the room started to swim. I didn't even feel the floor.

It must only have been a few moments later when I opened my eyes and saw the library woman and some other people standing over me. I tried to get up quickly, my head spinning, disorientated.

'Stay there, you're okay. Just take a moment.' It was one of the students, a fair-haired man who looked far too young to have a beard of that magnitude.

'Would you like me to call you an ambulance?' said the library woman. 'I'm afraid there aren't any First Aiders on duty this time of night, so I don't know . . . '

'I'm fine, really. Sorry. I just felt faint.' I tried to get up again. This time the young man helped me. They'd put a chair behind me. I sat down gratefully.

'Put your head down, that's it.'

I looked around for the blond man as best I could before the student put his hand on the back of my neck and shoved my head downwards. There was no sign of him.

'Have you had anything to eat?' said the student.

'Are you a doctor?' the librarian asked.

'I'm a lifeguard, I've done First Aid,' he said. 'She just fainted, that's all. Give her a minute, she'll be fine . . . I've got some chocolate in my bag,' he said to me. 'Would you like that?'

The librarian started to say something I suspected would be connected with rules about eating in the library.

'Thanks.' I raised my head. 'I'll be alright. I feel better now.'

She caught sight of the queue forming at the desk and hurried off, leaving me with the student. He had a mess of strawberry-blond hair, heading somewhere towards an afro, and a beard that looked capable of holding enough food to sustain a family of four. 'My name's Joe,' he said cheerfully, offering his hand. He was crouched next to my chair, which was oddly positioned in the middle of the psychology section.

'Cathy,' I said, shaking his hand. 'Thanks, Joe. Sorry for the — for causing a scene. Interrupting your studies.'

'S'okay. I was just about falling asleep over there.'

I stood up. He stood next to me as if half-expecting me to keel over again. 'You're feeling okay?'

'Yes,' I said, 'thanks. I'm fine.' I gave him my brightest smile.

'You look a bit better than you did. You went down with a hell of a bang.'

I looked at him and nodded. 'Well, I'd better go.'

'Sure, see you around then. Take care.'

'You too. Bye. Thanks again.'

I scurried out of the library, giving the woman

behind the desk a half-smile as I passed.

In the fresh air I felt better. I knew it hadn't been him, the man I'd seen. He was the wrong shape, his hair the wrong colour. It was dyed blond, not natural the way his had been.

I see him everywhere, all the time. I know it can't be him, he's hundreds of miles away and safely in prison. But still he haunts me, a regular apparition, reminding me that I'll never get away from him. How can I get away, when he's still inside my head?

On my way back home, to start the checking, I fished out my mobile and sent a text to Stuart.

Hello, thanks for all the OCD stuff. Hope you're not working too hard. C

A few moments passed, I was just about to turn the corner into Talbot Street, and the reply came.

No problem, hope it's useful. Do you fancy a brew? S

I looked up at the front of the house, all the way up to the top floor. All his windows were lit up. The floor below, just the lights from the dining room in my flat shining dimly through to the front. His windows looked much more welcoming than mine. I sent a reply:

I'm just on my way home. Give me half an hour? C

Friday night, and all my friends out in town, getting drunk and flirting and shouting and dancing . . . Waving at strangers and bent double laughing, knees squeezed together in delicious hysterical agony, at the lad who's tried to jump over a bin in the Market Square and landed flat on his face . . . Walking from one bar to the other holding each other up, trying to pretend we're less drunk than we actually are, although we're more drunk than we were in the last place because of the cold, the fresh air . . . Having serious discussions in toilet cubicles, holding your friend who's crying because she thinks he doesn't like her any more and anyway he's such a twat, he doesn't deserve you . . . Repairing make-up again, crowded round the neon-lit mirror, the floor skiddy with water from the sinks, at least one of them always full and blocked with tissue . . . At the end of the evening holding back someone's hair, probably Claire, she's such a lightweight, at least she made it into the loos this time, while later some poor girl nobody recognises sits barefoot on the steps outside, legs splayed at odd angles, mascara-streaks down her sorrowful cheeks, her shoes on their sides next to her, her bag hanging round her neck . . . Walking home together arm in arm because there's no money left for a cab, too late, too early, if it wasn't winter it would be light by now, not feeling the cold because we're so full of vodka and friendship and love for each other and anyone else who'll stand still long enough . . .

I wasn't out tonight, though, I was at home with Lee. He turned up at my house at seven, with three carrier bags and a tagine. He shut me out of my kitchen and I sat watching television, hugging my knees and drinking the frosty-cold white wine he brought with him, listening to him singing along to the radio, lots of banging of cupboard doors and rattling of pans.

He'd told me he wasn't working again until Tuesday. I thought of the long weekend stretching ahead of us like a beautiful promise, all the places we could go together, falling asleep with him, waking up with him still there, and shivered with delight.

Every so often the kitchen door opened and he emerged with something else for the table — cutlery, bread, some small pots of something unidentified with spoons sticking out of them.

'Anything I can do?'

'Sit there and look beautiful.'

I thought about the girls. They'd gone to the opening night of the Red Divine, a nightclub in a converted chapel. It had finally managed to open despite complaints from former worshippers, who failed to see that if they'd not stopped attending services the chapel would still be a thriving Christian oasis in the seething heathen mass of the town centre, instead of a state-of-the-art club with three bars, leather seating and a VIP area. They'd wanted to call it Angels and Demons but that part at least had been vetoed by the licensing department at the council. There was one bonus, though: the local newspaper said that all the people who'd put in a complaint had received VIP tickets to the opening night.

I was dying to see the inside of it. Next weekend?

The kitchen door opened again, a rush of warm air and the sound of voices on the radio against sizzling, the smell of something spicy and meaty and delicious.

He didn't even look flushed, just cool and completely in control, humming to himself as he put out some serving spoons and arranged the placemats in preparation for something hot in the middle of the table.

'Sure I can't help?'

He came over to me and bent to kiss me. I snaked my arm around his neck to pull him closer, but he untangled himself. 'Don't distract me, I'm nearly done.'

I went back to the television with a smile on my face. My mouth was watering.

Monday 3 December 2007

I knew I only had thirty minutes to do all the checking, so that meant I couldn't rush it, I had to do it properly first time. No mistakes. Everything six times, get the pattern right.

It was all right.

I made it up the stairs half an hour after I'd sent him the text. I'd not even managed to take my coat off.

When he opened the door and saw me, he frowned. 'Are you okay?'

'Yes,' I said, following him in. His hallway was bright.

'You look really pale.'

'Oh. I fainted in the library.'

We were in the kitchen. He'd taken my coat and hung it on a hook on the back of the door, over his brown jacket. He looked smarter today, I guess he hadn't had time to get changed out of his work clothes: dark grey smart trousers and a blue shirt, sleeves rolled up to his elbows. 'You fainted? How come?' He pulled out one of the kitchen chairs for me to sit on.

I shrugged. 'I don't know. Maybe I didn't eat enough today, or I'm just tired, or something.'

'You're staying for supper, then,' he said.

'No — I mean — I wasn't hinting or anything — '

'You're staying for supper.'

He was stirring soup on the hob that smelled home-made. While he did that he made tea, even though I really wanted to make it myself, just to be sure it was right. He was busy stirring mugs and adding milk and chatting away about how mad his week had been. And something about how he'd found a really good shop four streets away that sold spices that he'd not seen anywhere else.

I got my mug of tea and, like last time, it wasn't too bad at all. Certainly drinkable.

He got some bread rolls out of a paper bag and put them in the oven to warm through. I watched the way he moved in his kitchen, feeling drowsy. It hadn't escaped my attention that he hadn't mentioned OCD once.

'Thanks again for all that stuff you left for me. It was really interesting.'

He stopped what he was doing and looked at me. For a moment it seemed as if he'd had a weight lifted off him.

'That's good to hear. Have you thought any more about getting some help?'

'I've thought about it. It's hard, though, you know?'

He put a tub of sunflower spread on the table, side plates, knives, spoons. 'I know.'

'I don't do these things for fun, for no reason. Checking, I mean. It helps me to feel safe. If I didn't check, how would I know I was safe?'

'It would be better, though, wouldn't it, if you could just check once and be sure you're safe?'

'Of course.'

'You know yourself that there's no logical reason why you need to check things more than once. You complete these safety behaviours because of the way you feel, not because something has physically changed to make things unsafe.'

'I somehow doubt therapy is going to fix that.'

'It's got to be worth a try, though? Hasn't it?'

He brought over two steaming bowls of soup and put them on the table. Then the bread rolls, quickly, from the oven, juggling them from one hand to the other.

He sat opposite me and looked me in the eye.

'Thank you, for this. It's very kind.'

'It's just chicken soup. But you're welcome.'

He was still holding that eye contact with me, expectantly, as though he was waiting for me to

96

say something or do something that would move things forward somehow. I wondered if he did this at work, stared at his patients until they said something to break the silence. I didn't want to say anything, though. I just wanted to look, to have a reason to look, to keep looking.

In the end it was him that gave up first. He looked down and started on his soup, his cheeks flushed. I chalked it up as a small victory to me. I could outstare anyone, any time, anywhere. A little trick I learned in the hospital.

The soup was good, incredible in fact. I felt warm from the inside, and the more I ate, the more I was aware of how hungry I had been. 'When's the last time you ate?' he asked, when I used the last of my bread to collect the final bit of soup from the bottom of the bowl.

'I can't remember. I doubt it was that long ago.'

'Do you want me to make some more?'

'No, really, it's fine. Thank you.'

'Do you want me to come with you?'

The sudden change of subject put me off guard. 'Come with me? Where to?'

'To see your GP. Not in with you of course, but I'll come with you to the surgery. Would that help? Bit of moral support?'

'No, thanks,' I said, not looking at him.

'It's not a problem. I should be able to get some time off.'

'I don't even have a GP, Stuart. I've never bothered registering with one since I moved down here.'

I stood, the chair scraping noisily on the tiled floor.

'Thanks for the soup. I've got to go. You know how it is, I've got important things I need to be getting on with.' I pulled my coat off the hook and made off down the corridor back towards the front door, feeling a little bit like the walls were getting narrower the further down I went.

'Wait a sec. Cathy, wait.'

I thought he was going to go on about it some more, doctors, therapy, talking about it, getting better, all of that shite, but instead he just gave me a carrier bag with something heavy inside it. 'What is it?'

'More soup. Two portions, frozen. Just keep eating, okay?'

'Thanks.'

I practically ran down the stairs and back into my flat. I stood for a moment on the other side of the door, breathing fast. The bag in my hand was heavy. I took it through to the kitchen and put the two solid blocks of soup into the freezer. There wasn't much in the fridge, I noticed. He was right, I should really start paying more attention to eating. After all, I didn't want to faint again — it might happen at work.

I checked the flat, but my heart wasn't in it. I kept thinking about Stuart. I'd been very rude, walking out on him like that. It wasn't something I could really help. I can't take pressure.

I don't trust doctors any more, not after what happened in the hospital. If I start giving in to them, if I start looking for help, it might just happen all over again, just when I've started to make progress, just when I've got a job and a flat and a life, of a sort. Stuart sees me as I am now: someone who spends so much time fiddling with the front door that she forgets to eat, someone who faints in the library, someone who can't take any sort of confrontation or advice.

He didn't see me as I was then. He doesn't know how far I've come with this already.

Sunday 7 December 2003

On Sunday morning we went for a walk on the beach at Morecambe. It was bitterly cold, the wind blowing up the sand into our faces, stinging and making my eyes water. My hair blew around in crazy shapes.

I faced into the wind and forced it back behind my head, twisting it round and tying it in a knot. It wouldn't hold for long, but it would do for now.

He took hold of my hand again, 'Beautiful.' He had to shout above the noise of the wind. We walked down to where the waves were crashing against the sand, our feet leaving wet trails. I picked up a shell, translucent and glistening with saltwater. My hair was working its way loose again. The clouds overhead were racing across the sky, getting darker, threatening rain. I unwound my thin cotton scarf from around my neck and disentangled it from my coat, the wind whipping it away as I tried to stretch it out. I wound it round my hair, trying to tie it, all the while the wind fighting me for it, laughing at my efforts.

'Lee,' I shouted. He was throwing pebbles into the surf.

He heard me and came back to where I stood, but didn't wait for me to speak. He cupped my face in his hands and kissed me, his mouth warm and salty-tasting. I gave up on my hair and it flew around us, just at the same moment as my scarf, which I'd even forgotten I was holding, took flight and soared into the air like a skinny bird.

Lee let go of me and chased after it while I stood laughing, the sound snatched from my lips before I could even hear it. The scarf fell and rose and twisted in different directions, the fronds at either end flapping crazily.

It landed in the wet and foamy sand, as I knew it would, and he brought it back to me, draped over one finger, cold and forlorn and dripping.

We gave up on the wind and walked hand in hand back towards the town. The smells of the seaside were too tempting and we went into a chip shop, the quiet when the door shut behind us almost deafening. We bought a portion of chips to share and sat with flushed cheeks at the Formica table by the window, watching through the condensation as people walked along the front at odd angles, coats and trousers whipped by the wind.

'I wish every day could be like today,' I said.

Lee was watching me thoughtfully the way he often did. 'You should give up work,' he said.

'What?'

He shrugged. 'Give up work. Then, whenever

I've got a day off, we can spend it together doing things like this.'

I laughed. 'What am I supposed to live on?'

'I've got plenty. We could get a place together.'

I thought he was joking at first, but he wasn't. 'I love my job,' I said.

That made him laugh. 'You're always complaining about it,' he said.

'Still, I wouldn't give it up. Thanks, though. It's tempting.'

Outside, a police car crawled past. It came to a stop outside the shop next door, but nobody got out. 'Wonder what they're doing,' I said.

He caught my eye then, bright blue eyes.

'What?' I said, smiling.

'I need to tell you something.' He took another chip and munched on it, his eyes still on me.

'Go on,' I said, thinking it didn't sound good.

'It's just between you and me. Alright?'

'Yes, of course.'

I didn't know what I thought it was. I just knew it was going to be something else that was going to change everything. The moment had that feel about it, that before-and-after feel, as though this was going to be the end of one time and the beginning of another.

My hair hung around my face and shoulders, sticky with the salt wind, full of bits of sand, blown into a thick brittle cloud like dark brown candyfloss. He reached out and tried to put his hand through it, but couldn't. It made him laugh. He looked out to the street again, at the police car parked outside and at the rain that had started lashing the window. Then he looked back

101

to me and took my hand in his.

'It's just that I love you,' he said. 'That's all.'

My heart soared, of course it did, and from then on every time I looked at him and remembered him saying it my heart jumped and everything in me wanted to smile and yell about it.

But there was something else. I couldn't shake the feeling that he'd been about to tell me something else, something completely different, something bad; and at the last moment he'd changed his mind.

Wednesday 5 December 2007

I was getting ready for bed and I made the mistake of checking, just once more. It was almost like a guilty pleasure, something I was going to permit myself to do, to help me feel totally safe before I went to sleep. But doing it on an empty stomach, having had little sleep for the past few nights, wasn't a good idea. I got stuck again. Each time I checked, I did it wrong somehow, lost count, didn't do things in exactly the right order, didn't have my hand on the door for long enough, it just didn't feel right.

Hour after hour, I started again and again and again . . . I had a shower at about one in the morning to try to wake myself up a bit, shivering when I got out. I got some joggers and a T-shirt on and started again at the flat door.

Still no good. I ended up sitting by the door, my head on my knees, sobbing and shaking, making such a racket that I didn't hear him coming up the stairs. He knocked on the door and made me jump out of my skin.

'Cathy? It's me. Are you okay?'

I couldn't reply, I just gasped and sobbed. He was just on the other side of the door.

'What's happened?' he said, louder this time. 'Cathy? Can you let me in?'

After a moment I just said, 'I'm okay, go away. Please — just go away.'

I waited for the sound of footsteps going upstairs, but they didn't come. And a few moments later, the sound of him sitting down on the landing outside my door. I cried harder, although not so much with fear as fury, fury at him taking control of my panic, blocking the door, interrupting whatever I could have conceivably done to protect myself. Ironically enough, though, I wasn't trapped any more. It's the same when Mrs Mackenzie interrupts the checking downstairs.

I crawled away from the door and sat on the carpet looking at it, thinking of him sitting outside. What on earth must he think of me?

I cleared my throat and spoke as clearly and firmly as I could. 'I'm alright now.'

I heard shuffling as he got to his feet. 'Are you?'

'Yes. Thank you.'

He coughed. 'Do you want anything? Shall I make you a cup of tea, or something like that?'

'No. I'm alright.' It felt like madness, talking to my door.

'Okay.'

There was a pause, as though he was uncertain whether to believe me, then finally the sound of footsteps on the stairs up to the top floor.

Monday 8 December 2003

I had contemplated taking Monday off, or even phoning in sick and spending the day in bed with Lee.

If he'd stayed in bed it would have been too tempting to get back under the covers, but he got up when I went to have a shower, and by the time I came downstairs in my work clothes he had made me tea, and a sandwich to take to work with me.

'You didn't have to do that,' I said.

He wrapped his arms around me and kissed me. 'You should think about what I said,' he whispered at last. 'If you weren't working we could go back to bed.'

'You're such a tease.'

It was wet and windy and still almost dark outside, and the temptation to go back inside and spend another day with him was almost unbearable. I'd left a door key on the dining room table so that he could lock up if he wanted to go out. It seemed like a completely natural thing to do; I already knew I wasn't going to ask for it back tonight. We'd spent two whole days in each other's company, two blissful days and three nights of complete happiness. Not a moment of discomfort or awkwardness or bickering. Not a moment had gone by when I hadn't been glad he was there.

I'd been at work all of ten minutes when my phone rang: it was Sylvia. She had a few more weeks at her old job before moving to London.

'Hiya,' I said. 'How was the Red Divine?'

'Divine, darling,' she said. 'No, seriously, it's ace. You missed a good night.'

'What's it like, then?'

'Oh, it's just lovely. Lots of red leather sofas and chrome and glass — and the toilets! My God, you'd have loved it, they had flowers in there and proper hand towels and bottles of moisturiser. And that barman, you remember the one who used to work in the Pitcher and Piano, the one you fancied — what was his name? Jeff? Julian?'

'Jamie.'

'Well, he was in there behind the bar, too. The bar staff are all wearing red horns. And right over the bar is the old stained glass window with lights behind, so you're drinking your demon sauces underneath the gaze of the saints. Fantastic.'

'Wow. You going again next weekend?'

'Maybe. Probably. Anyway, darling, I wasn't calling to tell you about *that*,' she said, before pausing for effect.

'What, something more exciting than the opening night of the Red Divine?'

'*Much* more exciting. I'm having a dinner party, just for close friends. At Maggie's house, not mine, of course, I've started packing up, it's hideous, I can't believe I'm surviving, but anyway — so can you come?'

'When?' I asked, not sure if she'd actually said.

'Next Thursday night. Can you come? Sevenish?'

'Sure I can come, wouldn't miss it for the world. Do you want me to bring anything? Dessert? Salad?'

'New boyfriend,' she said coyly.

'Oh, I think he's going to be working,' I said.

'Oh.'

'I'll ask him, anyway, maybe he could get out of it.'

'Sean's going to be there. And Lennon. And Charlie. And I was going to bring Stevie, just for a giggle.'

In other words, come with a bloke or be the only Betty No Mates.

'I'll ask him, okay? If not, I'll see you at the Spread Eagle for the party. There's no way I'm missing that one.'

'Okay, darling, let me know by Wednesday night so I know how much stuff to buy? And in the meantime, be good. And if you can't be good, be bad.'

'I will. See you then.'

'Ciao, baby.'

Was it too early to ask Lee to a dinner with all my friends? He was going to be scrutinised at Sylvia's party anyway; surely it would be just bringing that forward? And parties at Maggie's house were always good. She was a fantastic cook, too, and the thought of missing out on one of Maggie's dinners just because my partner was too busy at work to accompany me was a truly dreadful thought.

I ploughed on with work, getting ready for a meeting at ten. Lots of meeting notes to prepare, still thinking about the last dinner party at Maggie's, a girls-only one, eating crème brûlée and drinking too much brandy.

After the meeting, I had a missed call from Lee's mobile, so I rang him back.

'Hi, gorgeous,' he said.

'Hi,' I said. 'What are you up to?'

'I've just done the washing-up. And now I'm going to go out and get some shopping so I can make you something nice for dinner. Is there anything you need?'

'I don't think so. Lee, are you working next Thursday night?'

'Why?'

'We've been invited to a dinner party at Maggie's.'

There was a pause. 'Do you want me to go?'

Of course, I thought, otherwise I wouldn't have asked. 'Yes,' I said.

'I was supposed to go somewhere, but I should be able to put it off. I'll make a few phone calls and let you know. How does that sound?'

'Brilliant.'

'Alright, then. What time will you be home?'

'I'm not sure. Half-sixish?'

'I'll have dinner ready.'

'That sounds wonderful. Thank you.'

'I'll see you later.'

Back to work, Monday morning. Getting out of the house wasn't too bad — I think it's because the sun was shining. I'd managed to sleep better over the weekend, more than a few hours at a time. I made sure I ate three times a day, had some proper dinners, and it seemed to do the trick.

Even though the Monday morning checking went well, I was still late, hurrying along the pavement, my breath in clouds in the frosty air. I heard someone behind me and turned with a start. It was Stuart. He looked so wonderful, so happy, so out of breath. 'Hiya,' he said. 'You walking to the Tube?'

'Yes,' I said. My step felt lighter already as he walked along beside me. 'Listen, Stuart, I know I keep saying this every time I see you, but I'm sorry.'

'Sorry?' he said. 'Why?'

'You get enough of that sort of shit at work, I expect. You don't need it when you're off duty. And the other day, when you made me soup and I ran out on you. I'm sorry for that too. It was really rude.'

He didn't say anything for a moment, his chin buried in the collar of his jacket. I chanced a look at him. 'No, I've been thinking about that. I was pressuring you. I shouldn't have done that.'

'But you were right. I need to do it. I've been thinking about it over the weekend. I'm going to go and find a GP to register with.' The words were out before I even really thought about them

108

— where the hell did that come from? It was him, it was the fact that he was here and for some crazy reason I wanted to see him smile.

He stopped in his tracks. 'Really?'

'Yes, sure.'

The look on his face made me laugh.

He carried on walking. We crossed the main road together, the noise of the traffic roaring. 'Listen,' he said, 'sign on at the Willow Road Medical Centre. They're the best round here, lots of really good clinics, they're great, really friendly. Sanj — Dr Malhotra — when you've registered, make an appointment to see him, okay? He's a good bloke. He's nice, too.'

'Alright. I will. Thanks.'

We went through the barriers at the Tube and parted company: he was going south, I was going north. I watched him walk away down the tiled corridor, a bag slung over one shoulder.

Monday 8 December 2003

In the end I was home at a quarter to seven, held up dealing with some grievance procedure against a member of staff at the London office which had somehow become my responsibility.

The table was all set, wine on the table, Lee in the kitchen, everything spotlessly clean. I had no idea how he did that — cook a meal without accumulating dirty dishes as he went along. He kissed me on the cheek. As well as cooking dinner, he was fresh out of the shower, his cheek damp and shaved and fragrant.

'Sorry I'm late,' I said.

'No problem,' he said. 'It's ready. Go and sit.'

This time it was spicy chicken with salad, fresh herbs, warm bread, cold sancerre.

'I rang a few people,' he said, chewing. 'It should be okay for Thursday. Might be cutting it a bit fine, probably best if I meet you there.'

'Oh. Okay.'

There was a pause while he drank. 'You sure about this?'

'About what?'

'Me meeting your friends.'

'Of course. Why wouldn't I be?'

He shrugged, regarding me steadily. 'It's a big thing for me. Meeting people. Just so you know.'

'You don't strike me as the sort of person who has trouble in social situations.'

'You still don't know me very well, then.'

There was a long pause. 'I'd like to know what job you do,' I said.

He stopped eating and looked at me for a long time. 'You know most of it,' he said. 'I work in the security industry.'

'That could mean anything,' I said. 'I'm worried.'

'You don't need to worry,' he said, his voice gentle. 'Look, I just have to be careful, that's all. It's just better for you if you don't know about it.'

'Don't you trust me?'

His eyes clouded. 'I could ask you the same thing.'

I gave up, then. 'Look, we don't have to go. To

110

Maggie's, I mean. Honestly. If you'd rather not — '

'It's fine,' he said. 'We'll go.'

'Lee, it's just dinner. It's not a test.'

He chewed, then put his knife and fork down. 'Dessert?'

Dessert turned out to be hothouse strawberries and muscat, which we ate and drank in bed. He didn't say anything else about dinner at Maggie's, or his job, and I didn't either. I lost myself in the taste of him, in the sensation of his warm hands on my bare skin, knowing that tomorrow morning he'd be gone and I'd be back to being on my own again.

Tuesday 11 December 2007

I did it. I finally did it. Tonight I got off the Tube at a different stop, a two-mile walk home, but one that took me down Willow Road. I was half-hoping that the surgery wouldn't still be open at this time of the evening, but it was.

Willow Road led off one of the main routes, but it was surprisingly quiet, mews-like; the surgery had a small car park and several buildings grouped around it, including a dental surgery and a pharmacy. Everything was brightly lit up and the car park was full. Inside, everything was new and clean. Despite its being busy, the waiting area half-full, it all seemed calm and quiet and peaceful. In the corner was a small Christmas tree, twinkling lights and multicoloured tinsel draped randomly around it.

'Can I help you?' the receptionist said as I got close to the desk. She actually smiled at me. I hadn't been expecting that. She was young, petite, with a shiny bob of red hair.

'I was wondering if I could register as a patient,' I said.

'Of course,' she answered. 'Hold on a moment, I'll just get you the forms.'

I looked around at the waiting room. There was a corner set aside for children, with a bookshelf, and a big crate full of wooden toys. Three toddlers were steadily and purposefully removing everything from the box. An old man in a huge coat was asleep in the corner, his head resting back against the wall, mouth open to reveal a single tooth.

'Is he alright?' I said, when she came back.

'George? Oh, yeah, he's fine. I'll wake him up in a bit. He comes in here for a kip sometimes when it's cold outside. Don't worry, he's not been waiting hours for an appointment or anything.'

She handed me a big brown envelope. 'It's not all forms. There's a load of leaflets in there about all the clinics we run. Do you need to make an appointment now?'

'Oh. Should I?'

'Not if you're okay. Often people only get around to registering when they've got something that they need to see the doctor for.'

I thought about it and wondered whether I would actually make it back here for an appointment unless I booked it now. 'I think I do

— need an appointment, I mean. Is it possible to see Dr Malhotra?'

'Let's see. Would you prefer to come after work?'

'Yes, if that's possible.'

'Thursday at a quarter to seven? Would that do?'

'Yes, that would be fine. Thank you.'

'What name is it?'

'Cathy Bailey. Cathy with a C.'

She wrote out a card for me. 'If you can bring the forms back before your appointment that would be great. If not, you can bring them with you on Thursday.'

'Thanks,' I said. 'But I could fill them in now, couldn't I?'

I sat in the waiting room with a pen and the envelope on my knee as a makeshift support and filled it in. It was hard going. I didn't want to think about my medical history, never mind write about it. But at least here, in this place, I could do it without falling apart. I sat next to George while he snored, and wrote about depression and anxiety and panic attacks.

I finished the forms and handed them back to the receptionist, made my way out into the dark street and headed back up to the noise and traffic. I fished in my pocket for my phone and sent a text.

S, I did it. Got appt for Thurs. C

A few minutes later, as I jumped on a bus that just happened to be going in the right direction, I heard the beep of a reply.

That's great news. Fancy a brew? ;) S x

For some stupid, crazy, bizarre reason, the text wink and the 'x' meant that I only had to check the front door once when I got in. Just once. I couldn't remember how long since it had been just once. I stood there when I'd finished, waiting for Mrs Mackenzie to come out, wondering how it was that I'd done it right first time. How was such a thing possible? I reached out to touch the door, faltering, when I heard the door to Flat 1 behind me.

'Cathy? Is that you?'

'Yes, Mrs Mackenzie. How are you?'

'Fine, dear, you alright too? Cold out there, is it?'

'Yes, you'd better get back inside, you're letting all your heat out.'

She went back in — to *EastEnders*, by the sounds of it — and the door shut again. I looked at the front door, at the locks, and I turned and went upstairs to start the checks.

Stuart took a while to open the door when I finally got up the stairs, and there he was, left arm in one of those slings made out of fetching pink sponge.

'What happened?' I asked, shutting the door behind me.

'Ah, I got kicked in the shoulder. It popped out. Bloody painful.'

He stood in the kitchen while I made the tea and he watched me. 'I'm glad you're here,' he said. 'How are you doing?'

'Me? I'm fine. Really. Don't you want to sit down?'

'Nah. I've been sitting down all day, it's driving me mad.'

'So who kicked you in the shoulder, some sort of ninja?'

He laughed. 'No, it was a patient. It was my fault — he got a bit distressed while I was asking some questions in an assessment. I got booted before I could get to the panic button. It's happened before. I got a kick in the nuts once — now that *was* painful.'

'I kind of assumed you just sat with people and listened to them talking about their childhood.'

'I do that too, in clinics. But I spend a lot of the time on the short-stay crisis ward. In between all that I'm doing research, paperwork. Hence the long hours.'

I put a mug of tea on the counter next to him and made a start on the small mountain of washing-up that had accumulated in the sink.

'I was just getting round to that,' he said.

'You were going to do it one-handed?'

He watched me and sipped his tea. 'Amazing the things you can do one-handed if you put your mind to it,' he said. 'So you're going to see Sanj?'

'Yes. They're nice in there, aren't they? There was an old guy in the waiting room, fast asleep. They were just letting him sleep. I thought that was good.'

'Not George, was it?'

'Yes.'

'I could come with you on Thursday, if you like,' he said.

I looked at him, just a quick look up from his socked feet up to the jeans and dark green sweater that matched his eyes, to his poor tired face.

'No, thanks.'

After the washing-up I microwaved some beef chilli he'd made and frozen last week, and we sat on the sofa and ate. He told me about the two years he'd spent travelling in between his degree and his doctorate. He went into his bedroom and fished out a memory stick which he said held several hundred pictures, if I ever fancied a look at them. He said he'd always meant to get them put into albums but had never got around to it. Talking about travelling got him onto the topic of this crazy comedy show that he'd seen in Australia, and from there the DVD filmed at the Sydney Opera House came out, and as I laughed with him I realised that I was starting to relax. I was warm and tired and I was actually starting to relax.

Wednesday 17 December 2003

When Lee was working, he was away for days at a time. Some days he phoned me constantly, texting me in between, asking how I was, wishing he was with me, asking what I was doing. Some days he clearly couldn't use the phone at all and I was all alone.

Wednesday evening, heading home from work in the dark. I hadn't heard from him since Saturday. I stopped at the supermarket and got myself some shopping for dinner. I was going to make a chicken casserole, keep some for tomorrow.

Sunday and Monday I'd spent most of the day checking my phone just in case he'd called. Tuesday I only checked it a few times. Today I'd hardly checked at all. I wondered if he was alright. As I browsed through the fruit and vegetables I found myself thinking back to how long he'd been away. What was the longest time he'd been away from me, since we met? A few days, a week, but usually no more than a day or two would go past without some contact. I'd sent him a text on Monday evening but I'd not had a reply. I tried to ring and the phone was switched off. This in itself wasn't unusual; when he was working he often turned the phone off, or found himself somewhere where he couldn't charge it up.

It felt strange, being without him. Despite how stifled I felt sometimes when he was with me, he made me feel safe at the same time. Now I was back to being alone, I felt exposed, insecure, vulnerable. In the supermarket I couldn't help feeling that there was someone watching me.

By the time I'd got home, dumped all the shopping in the kitchen and turned some of the lights on, I felt better. There was a missed call on the home phone; the number was withheld. I wondered if it was Lee trying to call, but he would have called my mobile first. I made dinner and sang to myself, looking forward to a soak in the bath with a book. When it was all ready I grabbed cutlery from the drawer in the kitchen and sat on the sofa to eat.

If anything happened to Lee while he was at work, would I ever find out? Would I ever get to hear about it? He'd made it clear that none of the people he worked with knew anything about me. It was 'better that way — safer'. What if he was hurt? What if he got into another fight, a bad one, and he ended up stabbed, or shot? Would I even know?

I washed up the dishes in the sink and dried them, still thinking about him, where he might be, what he might be doing. I put the knife and fork away in the drawer and something looked odd. The knives and forks had been swapped over in the drawer. I'd shoved the clean ones back in, and they were in the wrong place — one fork nestled in with the knives, one knife in with the forks.

They hadn't been like that this morning. Or had they? I forced myself to remember making the toast. Where had I got the knife from? It must have been in the right place then or else I'd have been trying to spread my toast with a fork.

I grabbed handfuls of cutlery and swapped them back over.

I couldn't understand what had happened. I went upstairs to run the bath and as soon as I turned on the bathroom light I saw it — the laundry basket had been moved from the left side of the sink to the right side. It looked odd straight away.

I moved it back.

Someone had been in here.

I went from room to room, looking for changes, looking for things that were different. It took me an hour to go through everything and when I'd finished I still wasn't convinced that I'd done it properly. Was I going mad? Surely I couldn't forget something like moving furniture around, or changing my cutlery drawer? And why would I even do something like that? The laundry basket didn't even fit properly on the right side of the sink — there wasn't enough room between it and the bath, it stuck out.

The question in my mind was not so much who had been in here — there were no signs that anyone had broken in, therefore whoever it was had a key, which meant it had to have been Lee. The question was more — why? Why would he come in here and just start moving things around?

I kept looking, in case somewhere there was a note explaining it, that maybe had fluttered down out of sight when he'd shut the front door behind him. There was no note.

Wednesday 12 December 2007

I woke up and for a moment I had no idea where I was. I seemed to be buried under a pile of coats, as though I'd been to some crazy party and had ended up in a drunken heap on the bed upstairs.

The shock of it made me cry out, a strangled

119

yell. I struggled to my feet, tangling myself in the coats and a blanket, falling onto my knees on the carpet with a crash and getting to my feet just as a figure came running into my peripheral vision. That made me scream, properly scream.

'Cathy?'

It was Stuart. With the merest of glances I took in that he was only wearing a pair of shorts and he was holding onto his bad arm.

I was in Stuart's living room, I'd been curled up on the sofa. I was still wearing my work clothes, my skirt and blouse both hideously crumpled by the look of it, my shoes on their sides on the floor. On the floor was a tangle of a fleece blanket, and on top of that was my black wool coat, and Stuart's brown jacket, and some sort of heavy all-weather type jacket of the sort you might wear to go up a mountain.

My heart was thudding, my breathing fast. 'What — what am I doing here?'

'It's okay,' he said. 'You fell asleep. I didn't want to wake you up.'

The clock on the wall in the kitchen area said it was half-past six — just about starting to get light outside.

I couldn't remember falling asleep. Just sitting here on the sofa with Stuart, watching a DVD of some comedian he'd seen when he was in Australia, laughing and then crying because I was laughing so hard.

My breathing was slowing down, my heart finally catching up. 'I'd better go,' I said.

'Sorry,' he said. 'I didn't mean to give you a fright.'

I looked him up and down, standing there in his kitchen in his boxer shorts — I should be grateful he didn't sleep naked.

I collected my shoes and struggled into them, my balance still impaired. I grabbed my coat from the tangle of blankets and piled the rest of it in a big heap back onto the sofa.

'I'm sorry for . . . you know . . . making such a racket,' I said at last. 'Is your arm okay?'

'It bloody hurts, to be honest. I'll have some more tablets in a minute.'

'I'd better go,' I said again.

'Alright.'

He let me out and I cast a glance back at him, thinking what a stupid fucking idea it had been of his not to wake me up last night, and at the same time thinking about him running out of his bedroom when he heard me scream.

Thursday 18 December 2003

'Catherine, darling!' Sylvia threw open the door to Maggie's, since of course she was the hostess even if she didn't actually live here any more, and pulled me into a tight squeeze.

At the same time looking pointedly over my shoulder.

'He's been held up,' I said, by way of explanation. 'Sorry. Hopefully he'll be here soon.'

'Held up?' she echoed. 'Is he off stealing the crown jewels or something?'

I laughed. 'Probably.'

I went into the living room and said hello to everyone. Claire and Lennon were on the sofa, Lennon looking vaguely uncomfortable about the fact that Claire was lying across his lap, her legs on the arm of the sofa; he sat there rigid while she laughed raucously about something Louise had said.

'Catherine! About time,' Louise said, getting up in one lithe, unfolding movement from the floor where she'd been sitting. She kissed my cheek. 'Claire's pissed already.'

'Claire, you're such a lightweight.'

'I know, I know,' she said, tears still on her cheeks from laughing so hard. 'Seriously, Lou, don't do that to me, I nearly had a Tena moment.'

Still sitting stiffly under Claire's posterior, Lennon's eyes widened.

'Where is he, then?' Charlie said. Charlie was Lou's temporary cuddle, a bit too cerebral for her, we all thought, all long hair and consciousness and roll-ups.

'He's been held up,' I repeated. 'He said not to wait.'

'Would we have waited?' Charlie said, 'I doubt it, to be honest.'

You're such a cock, I thought, but I said nothing.

Max, Maggie's husband, was in the kitchen arguing with her in a not very subtle way about how much coriander had been added to whatever it was simmering away on the Aga hotplate.

I gave them both a kiss hello and they happily

carried on bickering as though I wasn't there.

Stevie appeared from the bathroom. 'Where's the new guy, then?' he asked, kissing me on both cheeks.

'Oh, God, you guys, honestly. You're not going to grill him when he gets here, are you?'

'Depends how tasty he is,' Sylvia said, handing me a glass of wine the size of a fruit bowl. In deference to Maggie's taste for monochrome, she was wearing a zebra-print skirt; below that, fuchsia fishnet stockings that only someone with Sylvia's legs could possibly get away with. The black and white theme began and ended with the skirt, though, because her top was various shades of purple and pink. She looked, as always, stunning.

Stevie was one of Sylvia's several fuckbuddies — my particular favourite, and I was pleased he was here. He was married, but he happily shagged anyone who caught his attention, as did his wife, Elaine. Sylvia got a good seeing-to once every couple of months, and in between seeings-to they sometimes had fun out in town with their clothes on, too. Elaine had been out with us on the odd occasion. She was a good laugh. Sylvia once told me she'd woken up after a particularly heavy night in town in the middle of Stevie and Elaine's kingsize bed, cuddling up to both of them.

The doorbell went and everyone looked at me expectantly. I gave them all a look which said please behave, but when I opened the front door it was Sam and Sean.

'Oh, is he not here?' Sam said, when she made

her way into the living room.

'For fuck's sake,' I said, 'seriously, will you lot all just calm down about it?'

I regretted it the moment I'd said it. Why was I being so uptight? These were my best friends, at least the girls were, people I'd spent practically my whole life with. We'd all been pissing about with relationships for years, far too long; if any of them had turned up at Maggie's with anyone remotely serious I probably would have been just as curious as they all were.

'Sylvia,' Sam said, 'is that thing made out of a real zebra?'

'Of course not, darling, I got it in Harrogate.'

'But it's furry.'

Maggie did her best to delay dinner, but after half an hour Max started grumbling so we all sat down, everybody talking at once, passing bread and wine and spoons and bowls of vegetables. I sat in a miserable silence next to the one empty seat, scooping food onto my plate and wishing I were somewhere else.

Wednesday 12 December 2007

I saw Stuart in the High Street, struggling with some carrier bags weighing him down on one side, his jacket sleeve on the other side empty. He had his back to me, heading in the direction of Talbot Street, making slow progress.

I should have immediately caught up with him, offered to give him a hand with the bags, and enjoyed his company on the last few

124

hundred yards back to the house.

Of course, I did none of these things. I skulked around in the doorway of the hairdresser's for a few minutes, then pretended to study the window of the bookshop, keeping my head down until he'd turned the corner and was out of sight.

It wasn't just the embarrassment about screaming my head off just because I'd woken up on his sofa. The more I'd thought about it since, the worse it got. He was a doctor, a mental health practitioner at that. He was everyone and everything I'd spent the last three years trying to avoid. He smelled of hospitals, he emanated authority like a scent: people telling you what to do, diagnosing you, feeding you drugs, making decisions for you, steering your life down a path they could control.

I chanced a glance up to the right, around the various bodies wrapped in warm coats and cars and buses, to see if he was still there.

'Thought it was you. How are you?'

I spun round to find him at my left shoulder, another bag added to those weighing him down.

'I'm okay, thanks. Gosh, those look heavy.'

'They are, a bit.'

He must have turned around when I wasn't looking, gone back into the pharmacy on the corner. I hesitated for a moment, knowing that I couldn't very well leave him to walk home with those bags and realising that it would mean I couldn't take my usual route home via the alleyway at the back.

'Are you walking my way?' he said with a smile.

I felt unreasonably bad-tempered, mainly at my pathetic attempt to avoid him and the fact that I'd not had the sense to go inside the shop and hide myself away properly. I contemplated saying no, I thought about making some excuse about meeting someone, but sometimes it was just easier to give in.

'Here, let me take those bags for you,' I said as we started walking.

'It's alright, really,' he said.

'Some of them, then.'

'Thanks.' He handed over two of the lightest ones and we carried on walking.

'How's the shoulder?'

'Bit better today, I think. It'll probably hurt more later. I only came out to get some milk.'

We walked along in silence for a while. I felt jumpy, as if I wanted to break into a run. He kept a respectable distance between us, so much that people walking in the opposite direction kept walking in between us. I wondered if he was having trouble keeping up with me.

'It's your appointment tomorrow, isn't it?' he asked at last.

I slowed down a little until he drew level. I didn't want to be talking about medical shit in the High Street. 'Yes, it is.'

'You feeling okay about it?'

'I guess so.'

We crossed the road and turned into Talbot Street. There were fewer people down here, and the pavement was narrower.

'Sorry I gave you a fright the other day. I should have woken you up, I think.'

'I shouldn't have fallen asleep in the first place. Don't worry, it won't happen again.'

I felt him give me a look, but I kept my eyes straight ahead.

'I know this must be hard for you,' he said.

That did it. I turned to face him, the bags swinging round abruptly and hitting my legs. 'No, Stuart, you don't know at all,' I said. 'You have no idea. You think you know everything just because you peer into people's minds every day. Well, you know nothing at all about what's going on in mine.'

It might well be true that he was used to outbursts like this, used to people challenging him, but perhaps not on the pavement outside his house. He looked startled, and for a moment he was lost for words, so I seized the chance that gave me.

'I'll see you soon,' I said, putting the bags down. He would have to carry them upstairs himself.

'Where are you going?'

'No idea,' I said, walking away. 'I just don't feel like going in yet.'

I heard the door open and slam shut behind him, and only then did I look over my shoulder. He'd gone inside. I was nearly level with the alleyway, and for a moment I thought about going straight down there and checking the house from the back, but I was too angry. I felt agitated, my nerves twanging like an elastic band that had been stretched too thin.

I didn't even hear the doorbell go, but all of a sudden I noticed Maggie had left the table and then she was back and Lee was with her.

'Hi,' he said, 'sorry I'm so late.'

There was a moment — just a moment — of shocked silence as everyone took him in, his dark grey suit, blond hair, bright blue eyes — his warm smile. And then all the girls started talking at the same time.

Sylvia jumped up from her position at the head of the table and threw her arms around his neck while everyone else stood and waited to either kiss him on the cheek or shake him by the hand. I was last, of course, but then I was kind of trapped around the other side of the table. When he got a chance to sit down, he gave me a kiss and a wink, and a whispered 'sorry'.

I felt as if I was on fire. I'd not seen him for nearly a week, during which time I'd imagined him dead in a ditch on more than one occasion. I'd felt lonely and alone. I'd felt as if I was being followed, being watched. But now, suddenly, everything was fine: my beautiful, sexy boyfriend was back and I'd almost forgotten just how lovely he was.

Everyone had relaxed, Louise was happily telling everyone about the time Claire laughed so much she wet herself in the Queen's Head and had to dry her knickers off under the hand dryer, Stevie was talking to Lee about the car he'd just bought and I was glowing. The way he looked — so beautiful and cool, serene; the way he'd smiled at them all and apologised for being late; the fact that he'd somehow found the time to buy Sylvia a bottle of Cristal and Maggie a bunch of long-stemmed white roses; but above all the way all the girls had looked at him dumbstruck, with a kind of awe — and here he was, sitting next to me, giving Stevie his undivided attention, his right hand under the table, on my thigh.

I heard my mobile buzzing in my bag and I fished around in there for it, thinking it was probably a delayed text from Lee to say he was on his way.

Bizarrely, it was from Sylv.

Are his eyes really that colour or are they lenses?

One-handed, I thumbed a reply:

Lol, they're real

I looked at her at the other end of the table, chatting away happily to Max, who at last was starting to calm down and lose some of the purple in his face that always seemed to develop at any sort of stress.

Claire was starting to look very pink around the cheeks. 'Are you going to pause for a bit, Claire?' Sam said, giving her a look. 'We don't want a repeat performance of the other night in the Cheshire, do we?'

'Don't be mean.' Claire pouted. 'Anyway, that reminds me, you haven't told them all about what happened with Jack in the Cheshire, have you?'

'Oh, God, that was funny.'

'Tell them,' Claire insisted, and then, not pausing for breath, 'Jack was in the Cheshire and he'd got to the point where he was completely off his face, and he knew he was going to chuck up everywhere — '

'As you do,' said Lennon.

' — And he went running into the gents,' continued Sam, since Claire was having trouble controlling herself, 'and he was in such a hurry he just rammed open one of the toilet doors . . . and some poor bloke was sitting in there having a crap and got the fright of his life when Jack slammed the door open on him. But the problem was Jack couldn't hold it in any longer — '

' — Or maybe he was just too pissed to realise the toilet wasn't actually empty,' added Claire, tears running down her cheeks.

'So he ended up vomming into this poor bloke's lap . . . '

'Oh, God, that's not even the funniest bit . . . '

'And as soon as he could pause for breath he managed to think, hang on, I've just puked all over a stranger, if I were him I'd be a bit pissed off, and he started to consider that maybe attack was the best form of defence, so he punched him in the face and ran back out of the toilet.'

Everyone was laughing now, except Charlie.

'Oh, God,' said Claire, 'I'm going for a wee. Back in a minute.'

'So you mean,' said Charlie seriously, 'he

130

puked all over some stranger's legs and then punched him in the face? For no reason?'

'Summat like that, yeah,' said Sam, wiping her eyes.

'Would someone pass me the gravy?' Charlie said.

'Charlie, you're such a spoon,' Louise said.

'I'm sure I recognise your face, Lee,' Stevie was saying. 'Have we met through work or something?'

'I don't think so. I've been working on the door at the River,' Lee said. 'Maybe it was there.'

'Could've been. Have you been to see the new competition yet? It's pretty impressive in there. The Red Divine, I mean — we went there on Friday.'

'No. I'm not much of a clubber, to be honest — too many nights spent seeing the aftermath of it all.'

'Good on you,' Max boomed from the opposite side of the table. 'That's what I keep trying to tell this lot: they're better off growing up and spending their money on sensible things, or better still investing it somewhere.'

'Oh, shut up, you old grouch,' Maggie said playfully. 'Just ignore grandad, girls. He's forgotten how to have fun.'

'I have perfectly excellent fun, thank you very much.'

' . . . With the crossword and Radio Three, of course you do.'

We ate and we talked, and every so often Lee's hand would drop under the table and find my thigh, and just rest there, warm and heavy, not

131

requiring a response.

When I'd finished eating I took hold of his hand under the table and gave it a squeeze. He looked at me questioningly. His eyes really were so beautiful, so open. Everyone else was busy talking and not paying any attention to us.

I whispered in his ear, 'Were you in the house today?'

He looked mystified. 'I was working. Why?'

'Someone changed the knives and forks over.'

He gave me a look that said, *why on earth would anyone do that?* But at the same time he had a twinkle in his eye.

'Did you do it for a laugh?'

'I just wanted you to know I was looking out for you.'

I felt my cheeks flush. I don't know why I suddenly felt so uncomfortable, but I did.

'You could have left me a note,' I said.

'Too obvious,' he said, with a wink and a smile.

I drank the last of my wine and thought about it for a moment, laughing at something Sylvia had said.

Lee's thumb was stroking the back of my hand, gently, making me shiver.

'Lee,' I said, quietly.

'Hm?'

'Don't do it again. Please.'

'Do what?'

'Don't move my stuff around. Please. Okay?'

His face clouded a little, but he nodded. A few moments later he let go of my hand when Maggie collected our plates. He didn't take hold of it again after that.

The surgery was busier than it had been a few nights ago, more people waiting, more noise. I sat in the corner, knees clamped together, trying to remember why I was doing this to myself. Directly across from me, a man kept coughing without putting his hand over his mouth. A baby wearing a grubby sleepsuit was throwing blocks from the toybox at his brother, while their mother ignored them both and talked to the woman next to her about fibroids, and *The X Factor*. More than once I thought about getting up and walking out. After all, I wasn't exactly ill — there were many people in here clearly in a far worse state than me. Surely I was wasting their time?

'Cathy Bailey?' The voice came from a side corridor and I looked up to see a man peering around the corner.

I leapt up as if I'd been stung.

I hurried down the corridor with Dr Malhotra, into a room that had that unfortunate smell of disinfectant, alcohol-based hand sanitiser.

'You're a friend of Stuart's?' was the first thing he asked.

'Yes,' I said, wondering how he knew that.

'He's a good bloke.'

Sanjeev Malhotra was slight, smartly dressed in dark trousers, pink shirt and tie, a neatly trimmed black beard and funky-looking glasses. 'What can I do for you?' he said.

I told him about the checking, and the panic attacks. I told him about them getting worse. He asked me if I ever thought about hurting myself. I told him I didn't. He asked me if something had happened to trigger these attacks and I told him about Robin. Then of course I had to tell him about everything else, as well. I kept that part brief. I told him I was trying hard to put all that behind me.

He clicked on the computer a few times. Just as Stuart said, he told me he'd refer me to the Community Mental Health Team for an assessment. He said it would probably be a few weeks before I'd get seen.

That seemed to be it.

'I hear Stuart's out of action at the moment,' he said, at the end.

'He dislocated his shoulder.'

'Shame. Still, at least it means we've got a chance of winning on Sunday.'

I caught the bus back to Talbot Street. I felt strange, as though I'd dreamed the whole thing, and a little queasy. Already all I could think about was getting home so I could start the checking. I had a feeling it was going to be difficult to get it right.

Monday 22 December 2003

The last Monday before Christmas, late-night shopping, the final push towards the great two-day festive shut-down.

It was six-thirty and the town centre was still heaving. I got changed at work, dressed up for a night out with the girls, and went into the town to look for a present for Lee before meeting them in the Cheshire. He'd been working this week, not at the River but at this other, unnamed job that took him away from me for days at a time and spat him back out the other end, exhausted, and occasionally bad-tempered.

In Marks & Spencer I browsed through the men's shirts, looking for something I could see him wearing, something that would bring out the blue in his eyes.

I was completely away with the moment, dreaming about Christmas, humming along to 'Santa Baby' which was playing just about audibly, when a figure appeared in front of me and stopped.

I looked up and it was Lee, looking triumphant.

I squealed as he grabbed me into a bear hug, then treated me to a long, long kiss. He tasted minty.

'I thought you were working,' I said, when we were sitting at a table in the coffee shop a few minutes later.

'I am working,' he said, 'just having a bit of a break, that's all.'

The coffee shop was quiet, just us, a young couple sitting near the door, an elderly couple with a pot of tea and two fish suppers over by the big picture windows which looked out over the Christmas lights in the High Street. Behind the counter, the staff were wiping surfaces and wrapping things in clingfilm.

'I missed you last night,' he said. 'I couldn't stop thinking about you. And your wet cunt.'

I felt my skin flush and looked around. Nobody was near enough to hear, but even so, he'd not dropped his voice.

'Are you wet now?' he asked, not taking his eyes off mine.

I couldn't help myself. 'I'm getting there.'

He sat back in his chair and glanced down into his lap. I was starting to feel a bit queasy. Leaning forward, across the table, I followed his glance and saw what I'd expected to see.

'Lee, seriously. Not here.'

For a moment I thought he was going to object, push me into putting my hand under the table, but instead he sighed and sat straight again. 'Where are you off to, then, dressed up like that?'

'I'm meeting Louise and Claire in the Cheshire.'

He continued looking at me and in the end I laughed. 'What? What is it?'

'Find anything you want? In the shops?'

'That's for me to know.'

'Been in enough of them. Burton, Principles, Next, and now here.'

'Have you been following me?'

He shrugged, but suddenly his cheeky smile was back. I wasn't sure if he was winding me up. 'Let's just say I'm one of many men who've been letching over you in that skirt this evening.'

'Well, at least you're the lucky one who gets to play with what's inside,' I said.

He drank the last of his coffee and stood. 'I've got to get back to work,' he said, dropping his

136

head and kissing my mouth hard. 'Don't be late home.'

The elderly couple by the main window got to their feet, scraping chairs and sorting out bags and bags of shopping, just as a woman in the coffee shop uniform came over and offered to take their tray.

I sat for a second, cradling my coffee cup, wondering whether I really wanted to go to the Cheshire after all, when suddenly he reappeared, standing like a brick wall between me and the rest of the coffee shop.

'Take off your knickers,' he said.

I looked up at him. 'You're joking.'

'I'm not joking. Take them off. No one will see.'

Making as little movement as possible, I hoiked up my skirt and wriggled my knickers down to my knees, pushed them down to my ankles and stepped out of them as quickly as I could, balling them up into my fist.

'Let's have them,' he said, holding out his hand.

'What for?' But I handed them over anyway.

He slipped his hand into his jacket pocket, then kissed me again, gently this time. 'Good girl.'

I sat very still, knees pressed together, staring straight ahead until I was sure he'd gone, then I slid to the edge of the seat and stood. I felt light-headed, afraid, and aroused, all at the same time.

I'd had enough of shopping. I reached for the nearest blue shirt, took it to the counter and paid.

All the way up the High Street towards the

Cheshire, dodging my way through the shoppers, squeezing round behind queues of people waiting for buses, feeling the chill of the night air under my skirt — a nice feeling, in different circumstances — all the time thinking that he was probably still watching me, I wondered if this was a test. Was I supposed to spot him? I tried not to look obvious, glancing through the faces, looking in shops, in alleyways, but I must have been. Despite how odd it felt, how wrong, to be out here in December in a short skirt and no underwear, I was still feeling undeniably frisky at his unexpected appearance and was half-wishing I'd taken hold of him under the table when I'd had the chance.

Thursday 13 December 2007

I'd been home an hour and a half, and the checking was going badly wrong. Every time I thought I had done it, the uncertainty was there, the fear. There was no point doing it if I didn't do it properly. By that time my hands were shaking and I could hardly see through the tears, and I hadn't even made it beyond the flat door.

I heard the footsteps this time, I heard his flat door upstairs open and close, and I stood still, holding my breath, trying not to make a sound.

He knocked gently, but it still made me jump. 'Cathy? It's me. Are you okay?'

I couldn't reply, I just gasped and sobbed.

I thought I heard a sigh.

'You're not okay,' he said. 'What happened?'

I took a deep, shuddering breath. 'Nothing, I'm alright.'

'Can you open the door?'

'No. Leave me alone.'

'I just want to help, Cathy,' he said.

'You can't help me. Go away.'

I cried harder, angry now as well as afraid, furious at him for being there, for not letting me fall apart.

He wasn't going to go away.

At last I tried to stand, pulling myself up on the door handle. Through the peephole, I could see him, his face distorted. There was nobody else in the hallway.

My hands were shaking. I pulled back the bolt at the top, the key took longer. The mortise lock took longer still. By the time I got everything open and the door was unlocked my knees gave way and I dropped to a crumpled heap on the floor.

He pushed open the door from the other side and came in, bringing with him the chilly air, the smell of winter. He closed the door behind him and sat down next to me. He didn't come too close, just sat there with me.

I couldn't look at him at first.

'Try and take a breath and hold it,' he said quietly.

I tried. There was just a lot of gasping. 'I'm so — I'm . . . I'm so tired. I couldn't . . . I couldn't do it . . . couldn't check.'

'I know,' he said. 'Try and think about your breathing, nothing else. Just your breathing, for now.'

I tried. My fingers were tingling. The skin on my face, tingling.

'Can you hold my hand?' He held it out across the gap between us, steady.

I reached out, touched it, withdrew, touched it again, and he took hold of me. His hand was cold, icy. 'Sorry, cold hands. Now try again with your breathing. Can you look at me?'

I tried that too. The breathing was still all over the place. If I couldn't get the breathing calmed down I was going to keel over.

'Just think about your breathing. Breathe with me. In — hold it. Keep holding. That's better. And out. Good, come on, do it again . . . '

It seemed to take forever, but in the end it got better. I started to get some feeling back in my hands. The breathing slowed, I got it back under control. I gripped his hand as though I was drowning.

'Well done,' he said, quietly, 'you did it.'

I shook my head, still not quite ready to speak. The tears kept coming. I looked up at him and his eyes, kind eyes, looking at me completely without judgement. I shifted a little, towards him, and he moved and stretched his legs out, sitting with his back against my front door, and I moved closer and then he had his good arm around me and I had my face into his chest, where it was warm and smelled of him. He put his hand on my head, stroking my hair.

'It's okay, Cathy,' he said, and I felt his voice rumble in his chest. 'It's okay. You're safe. You're alright.'

I felt so tired I could have almost slept there,

on the floor next to him, just as long as he kept hold of me and didn't let go. I opened my eyes and I could just see blue cotton, his shirt, and the way it moved as he breathed. I thought I should move. Everything was starting to ache, and the fear had been replaced with a gradual, crippling embarrassment.

At last I lifted my head and he eased away from me, gently. 'Come on,' he said, 'let's get you somewhere more comfortable.'

He stood and helped me to my feet, then led me to the sofa. I sat down and folded myself into a ball. I wanted him to sit down next to me. If he had done that I would have snuggled up to him again.

'Can I make you a cup of tea?' he said.

I nodded, shivering. 'Thanks.'

I listened to the noise of him filling the kettle, the clinking of mugs. Opening cupboards looking for the tea. Opening the fridge. The kettle roaring into life. It felt strange, having him here. I'd never had another person set foot inside the flat since I'd lived here, apart from that plumber the day the stupid pipes burst.

By the time I heard him putting the mugs down on the coffee table in front of me I'd been dozing a little.

'Will you be alright now?' he asked.

I sat up, putting my fingers around the mug. My hands weren't shaking any more, but my voice was hoarse, my throat raw. 'Yes,' I said. 'I'll be fine. Thank you. Thanks for the tea.'

He watched me while I drank. He looked bone-tired too.

'Have you eaten?'

'Yes,' I lied. 'How's your shoulder?'

He smiled. 'Painful.'

'I'm sorry about all this. How did you know?'

'I heard you crying.'

'You should have left me to it.'

Stuart shook his head. 'Couldn't do it.' He drank some of his tea. 'Are they getting worse, the panic attacks? More frequent?'

'I think so.'

He nodded. 'Was that a bad one?'

I shrugged. 'I've had worse.'

He was watching me steadily, appraisingly, like a fucking doctor. That was exactly the way they used to look at me in the hospital, as though they were waiting for me to do something, say something, demonstrate some symptom or other so they could finally agree what was wrong.

'I'm sorry, I thought you'd be okay. Sanj — he's alright really. He can be a bit casual sometimes. What did he say?'

'It was okay. He was alright. He's going to refer me for an assessment, or something. What did he mean when he said with you out of action they've got a chance of winning on Sunday?'

He laughed. 'Cheeky bugger. I'm in the NHS Trust's rugby team. Sanj seems to think I'm some kind of handicap.'

I finished my tea at the same time he did.

'Anyway, you did it,' he said, looking at me. 'You took that first step.'

'Yes,' I said. I'd caught the eye contact and now I couldn't look away.

'Will you tell me about it?' he said it so quietly I almost didn't hear.

'About what?'

'About what started it all?'

I didn't answer.

After a while he said, 'Do you want me to stay here while you sleep?'

I shook my head. 'Really, I'll be alright now. Thanks.'

He left, a bit after that. I felt more awake and I wanted him to hold me again, if I'm honest, I wanted him to hold me tightly and stay with me, but it wasn't fair to ask him to do that. So he left, and I locked the door behind him, and went to bed.

Now I need to think about carrying on with all this. Facing the rest of my life. One day at a time, one foot in front of the other. I can't do this for much longer. I can't keep doing this.

Wednesday 24 December 2003

Until Christmas, everything was fine.

Well, not entirely fine. Going out with someone who was away working for days at a time wasn't fine at all, really, but when he was around, everything was good. When he was going to be working on a job for several days, he warned me first. And when he reappeared, I was always so ridiculously relieved to see him back in one piece that any reproach I had just melted away.

When he was around, he practically lived with

me in my house. When I was at work, he would tidy up, fix things that needed mending, cook dinner for when I got home.

When he was away, I missed him more than I thought it possible. Every night I wondered if he was safe, and whether I would ever get to find out if anything bad happened to him. Although he usually turned up shattered, starving hungry and in need of a shower, he didn't appear again at my front door with any injuries. Whatever happened that first time, I wanted to believe that he was more careful now, because of me.

Not for the first time in my life, I was alone on Christmas Eve. Lee was working somewhere — it was his turn, he said. He'd tried to get out of it so that he could spend time with me. He said he was going to try to leave early, but by ten o'clock on Christmas Eve there was no sign of him.

Fuck it, I thought.

Getting ready to go out didn't take that long. My favourite dress, heels, a quick bit of make-up, hair up, bits of it falling down just moments later, and I was ready.

By ten-thirty I was in the Cheshire, and Sam and Claire were in there too. I was several shots behind them and had some serious catching up to do. Claire had already found a likely candidate for a festive night in; he looked rather young, though, and a wee bit too pissed to be able to put up much of a performance.

'Don't fancy hers much,' I yelled into Sam's ear, above the noise of Wizzard singing 'I Wish It Could Be Christmas Every Day' for the millionth time since October.

'Yeah, but you should see his mate,' Sam shouted back, pointing with the top of her beer bottle over to the corner, where someone dark and much more appealing was watching them both with an expression that was hard to determine.

'Friendly, is he?'

'Not so far.'

The friend came over and introduced himself, and actually he turned out to be rather nice. His name was Simon, and he was in the army, he said into my ear. Off to Afghanistan in two weeks' time. I listened, and watched Sam's eyes which showed total adulation, and slight mortification that this dark-eyed sex god seemed to be paying rather too much attention to me.

'Simon,' I shouted into his ear, 'this is Sam. I'm just leaving. Happy Christmas!' I gave him a quick kiss on the cheek, for luck maybe, gave Sam a wink, and went off to find where I'd left my coat.

The Cheshire was out, then. And I wasn't nearly pissed enough yet, I thought, as I clattered up Bridge Street to see if the Hole In The Wall was too packed. Grateful that I'd actually worn my coat over my dress, because it was starting to rain. Not cold enough to snow, but it felt freezing none the less, and for a moment I wondered if I'd have been better off staying at home after all.

'No, mate, I'm not fucking doing it. No way. You can fuck off!'

The sound of an argument from an alleyway,

145

and something made me look over. There were three men having a bit of a set-to, one of them drunker than the rest. Half in shadow. Probably a drug deal, I thought absently, head down, keep walking, you don't want to know.

There was a queue outside the Hole in the Wall, but not a big one. I huddled into the doorway of the supermarket, next door, along with a couple of other people I knew vaguely.

Just in time to see two of the three men who'd been arguing in the doorway walking up Bridge Street past us.

One of them was Lee.

He didn't look over, just kept walking, laughing at something the other man was saying, hands in the pockets of his jeans.

Just then, a pile of drunken blokes spilled out onto the pavement and moved off in search of a festive kebab. The noise from the bar crashed out with them, some Christmas music, just for a change, along with a gust of warmth and a smell of beer and sweat.

'You coming in, or what?' said the doorman, holding the door open for me.

Fuck it, I thought. And I gave the doorman a Christmas kiss on the cheek and sidled into the warmth and the chaos.

Friday 21 December 2007

When I got home from work tonight, there was a note waiting for me.

Seeing it made me smile. It was waiting for me

outside the flat, on the landing, just outside my front door. I guess Stuart thought I might have some objection to it being pushed under the door into the flat itself, and had left it outside, knowing that nobody was going to be coming past my door apart from him.

I picked it up before I started checking the door, put it into my coat pocket, and finally got to read it an hour and a half later, when I sat down in my living room at last.

C, hope you are well. Been thinking about you. Fancy going for a drink or something on Saturday? S x

God, yes, I do, was my first thought. This in itself made me laugh. Me, go out for a drink? With a man who knew I'd got mental health issues, who'd seen me having a panic attack? I must be getting better.

I'd been practising deep breathing, as suggested by some of the material Stuart had printed off for me. I had tried this before, last year, when it was getting worse and worse, but back then the panic attacks and the terrible thoughts were sneaking up on me, and I was already panicking before I could start trying to calm myself. Then I would start panicking because I wasn't breathing properly, wasn't doing it right, and it would just make it worse somehow.

Now that I was more aware of the things that triggered it, it might just work. So every evening after work I built a new rule into my daily regime. After checking the flat, I would sit on the floor of my living room, close my eyes and breathe. Slowly, in and out. I made myself start by doing it for three minutes. I set the kitchen timer. At first it was a struggle to keep my eyes closed for that long; every sound disturbed me. The first few times I did it, I found the old perfectionism, the desire to control my life, meant that I would admonish myself for getting it wrong if I opened my eyes before the timer went off, if I turned my head to the window at the sound of a noise in the street below.

This is how it all starts. I do something that seems like a good idea. Locking the flat is a good idea, after all, right? Then for some reason I've not done it properly one day, and that's no good at all, because if you're going to do something that's for your own benefit, you've got to do it properly or there's no point. Then I start fretting about it and picturing all the bad things that might happen if I get it all wrong, if I cock it up the way I've cocked up so many other things in my waste of a life.

So, the first time I tried my deep breathing exercises, it was all a bit crap and I ended up doing it twice, failing both times, and then going to check the flat again three times to make up for my failure.

That was all a bit shitty, and I found myself wondering whether seeing a doctor and being in touch with the medical profession again had been the best way forward. I was doing alright, wasn't I? I was still alive, wasn't I?

I tried again, later, before bedtime, and the

second time wasn't so bad. In fact, while I was doing the deep breathing I found myself remembering Stuart, his hand holding mine, talking me through my breathing just as he had sitting on my cold floor, his voice soothing, calm, his eyes anxious. Before I knew it the timer was going off, and I'd managed three minutes without opening my eyes.

That night I slept better than I had in a long time.

I placed Stuart's note on the floor in front of me, crossed my legs, spent a moment listening out for sounds in the flat and outside, and then shut my eyes and started. In. Out. In. Out. Picturing Stuart with me was the only way it was going to work, I decided. What the hell, if it worked it had to be a good thing, right? So I took him away from the cold, draughty floor and went upstairs instead, into his living room, the wide, deep sofas, relaxed back into their softness. It was sunny and warm, the sun streaming through the windows onto his face, and he'd got one hand on my upper arm, and was saying the things he'd said to me before, and a few other things too.

'I'm here. It's alright, you're safe. Now breathe — in. And out. And again, in . . . and out. That's it, you're doing fine. In. And out.'

Five minutes later I opened one eye and looked across to the kitchen clock.

I'd forgotten to set the bloody timer.

By the time I made it home, it was nearly two in the morning. I had company most of the way back: three drunken lads and two of their girlfriends happened to be staggering in my direction, and I walked with them, chatting to one of the girls, Chrissie, who turned out to be a cousin of Sam's.

The last little walk along Queen's Road wasn't too bad, really. The wind had dropped a little and although it was frosty, I'd had enough vodka to keep the worst of the chill off. And my wool coat was warm and toasty. I might make a nice cup of tea when I get in, I was thinking, and then a nice long lie-in in the morning . . .

A figure was sitting on my doorstep, and stood up when I approached.

Lee.

'Where have you been?' he asked.

I fished my keys out from the bottom of my handbag. 'Out, in town,' I said. 'Didn't feel like staying in. Have you been here long?'

'Ten minutes.' He gave me a kiss on the cheek. 'Are we going in? Fucking freezing my nuts off out here.'

'Why didn't you use your key?'

'You told me not to, remember?'

'What?'

'You said I wasn't to come in and mess up your stuff.'

'I didn't mean it like that. Of course you can come in.'

Inside the doorway, he pulled me round and

pinned me against the wall, pulling my coat open, his mouth invading mine. His kiss was forceful, and dry, and tasted of him — not alcohol. Not drunk, then. Just hard.

'I couldn't stop thinking about you today,' he whispered into my neck, his hands sliding over my dress, over the satin. 'This dress makes me want you so much.'

I undid his trousers, tugging the belt free, pushing them over his backside. Right here in the hallway, I thought to myself. Good a place as any.

'Just tell me,' he said, groaning, into my hair, 'tell me you've not fucked anyone else in that dress.'

'No,' I said, 'only you. It's yours. I'm yours.'

Saturday 22 December 2007

The weather's been great today. I'm taking it as a sign. And, of course, it's an even-numbered day, which means going out for a drink is a fabulous idea.

He was waiting for me when I knocked. I'd suggested calling for him when I was ready; that way he wouldn't have to wait another half-hour while I checked everything. I was all done with my checking, and it had gone well.

'How's your shoulder?' I asked.

'Better,' he said. He was doing without the sling. 'The tablets do the trick at least.'

The High Street was still heaving with shoppers, taking advantage of the last few shopping days before Christmas, but Stuart steered me into a side road, then down a narrow alleyway. There was a pub at the end of the passage, comfortingly called the Rest Assured, with a chalkboard outside advertising 'good food', and he opened the door for me.

It was just opening, and we were the first customers. The bar was small, with two deep sofas beside an open fire that was just chewing its way through some balled-up newspaper, prior to tucking into the logs that had been neatly stacked on top. Fairy lights were strung around the bar, and a real fir tree in the corner was tastefully decorated with silver and white. Thankfully, in here at least, no carols.

He got me a glass of wine and I sank down into one sofa, near the fire. I put out my hands to warm them, but it wasn't throwing out much heat yet.

'You look tired,' I said, when he sat down opposite me. 'Did you get much sleep?'

'Not much, to be honest. But I'm used to all that. When I come in late from work I usually find it quite hard to sleep.'

I took a sip of the wine, feeling it going to my head almost straight away. What was it about him that made me feel safe enough to think about having a drink?

'I've been practising the deep breathing thing,' I said. 'There was a whole chapter on it in that pile of stuff you gave me.'

Stuart leaned forward and put his Guinness on the table between us. 'Really? That sounds promising. You just need to keep practising until it becomes second nature, so you can do it when you need to, without thinking too hard.'

I nodded. 'I've never been much good at relaxing, but it's going okay so far.'

He raised his glass. 'Here's to a new start, then.'

There was a pause. I was starting to feel sleepy.

'Have you had any more trouble with that idiot sales manager?' he asked.

I shook my head. 'Fortunately I've not seen him. No idea what I'm going to say to him when our paths do cross, but I'll worry about that when it happens.' I thought about this for a moment. 'I never really thanked you for — well, you know. For getting him off me. And for being honest with me about things. If it hadn't happened, I'd probably still be in a crumpled heap somewhere. I feel like I'm making progress with it, at last.'

He smiled. 'Don't mention it. Anyway, *I* should be thanking *you*.'

'Me? Why?'

He sighed, and regarded me for a moment as if wondering whether to say what he was thinking. 'I wasn't in the best frame of mind when I moved in. I didn't want to move from my last house, in fact, but I had to. But the house — I don't know — it feels like home. And I think that's got a lot to do with you.'

'With me? But why?'

He shrugged, and I realised he was looking a bit uncomfortable. 'I have no idea. I just — look forward to seeing you.' He laughed, clearly a bit embarrassed, and I suddenly became aware that he liked me. I mean, he really liked me, and he was trying to tell me about it without freaking me out.

I wanted to say, *but you hardly know me* — but it wasn't true. He knew a lot more about me than anyone I work with, and I don't have any friends any more.

In a small voice, which seemed to come from somewhere else, I heard myself saying, 'You make me feel safe.'

The atmosphere changed a bit after that. I don't know if I'd just had too much to drink — almost a whole glass, for heaven's sake — or if it was the fact that the pub had suddenly got busy, the bar crowded with people. Stuart looked at me for a long time, and I held his gaze.

Someone came over to collect our glasses, and that broke the spell. 'Another drink?' he asked, and although I started to get up to go and get the drinks, he waved me back down.

The sofa was comfortable, I could quite easily have gone to sleep.

'Anyone sitting here?' a voice asked, a young woman and an older lady behind her — mother and daughter out for a shopping expedition, judging by the bags.

'Yes, but you can sit there — there's room here,' I said, patting the sofa next to me, wondering how long I could hold out before all this exposure to the general public was going to catch up with me.

I grabbed Stuart's jacket off the sofa opposite and draped it over the back of the sofa next to me. I had to fight the urge to sniff it, and that made me giggle. Oh, God, I was drunk already. I could only have one more drink. One more.

Stuart came back after what seemed like an age, shot barely a glance at the two women who were now chattering away about someone called Frank and how he'd made a terrible mistake in leaving Juliette, and sat down next to me. It wasn't a big sofa.

It was a test, really. If I could do this, if I could have him sitting this close to me, in public, if I could hold a conversation — of sorts — with this man I still hardly knew, and yet already instinctively liked and trusted, then maybe something could happen. At some point in the future.

'You okay?' he asked me.

Okay about what? I wanted to say, but he meant the fact that I was sitting so close to him that his thigh was touching mine. Other than Robin launching himself at me, and Stuart looking after me through the panic attack, it was the first time I'd had any physical contact from a man since *him*.

'I'm fine,' I said, wondering just how flushed my cheeks were. 'I was just wondering — how come I feel so . . . I don't know. I'm just not scared with you. I'm scared with everyone. Anyone. And yet I'm not scared when you're here. I don't know anything about you.'

He downed half of his pint in one go, placed it decisively on the table in front of him.

'I'm glad you're not scared with me. You don't need to be.' He took my hand and held it. I

155

looked down at my fingers inside his, wondering how my own were still cold when the rest of me was so warm, abstractly thinking that his hands were big and strong, his nails short. I looked for the panic, but it wasn't there. My heart was beating quite fast, but not with fear.

'As for knowing things about me . . . well, I need to tell you things. I've wanted to tell you for a while, but I just haven't had a chance. So here goes.'

I was about to say something about me not letting him ever get a word in edgeways whenever he saw me, but fortunately I managed to keep my mouth shut.

'Before I moved here, I was living in Hampstead with my girlfriend, Hannah. Well, she was my fiancée, I suppose, not my girlfriend. I thought we were happy, but apparently we weren't.'

He stopped abruptly, looking at my hand curled around his. I gave it a little squeeze. 'What happened?'

'She was seeing someone else. Someone she worked with. She got pregnant and had a termination. I only found out about that after it had happened. That was — difficult.'

'That's awful,' I said, and I felt it, the hurt, emanating from him like a scent.

His thumb stroked the top of my hand gently, making me shiver.

'So I guess you're not quite ready for another relationship just yet, then?' I said, baldly, trying to soften it a little with a smile. Nothing like coming out with it, I told myself.

Lord knows what I'd be like if I had a few more drinks.

Fortunately, he smiled back. 'Not really, no.' He finished off his pint, and then looked at our hands again and said, 'But something tells me you're not quite ready for one, either.'

I shook my head. I thought and thought about it, and eventually all I could manage to say was, 'I don't know if I ever will be.'

'Was it bad?' he asked.

I nodded. I'd only ever really talked about it when the police interviewed me, and even then I'd only really answered their direct questions, I didn't volunteer any details about what happened. They tried to get me to talk about that in hospital. I learned about which bits I could tell them, things I could say that would keep them happy, reassure them that I was recovering, in the hope that they'd let me out and leave me the hell alone. When they did let me out, they were supposed to sort me out with counselling, but it never happened. I wouldn't have gone, in any case. All I wanted to do was run, run fast and never look back.

I didn't think for one minute I was going to talk about it now, but it started to come out of my mouth as though someone else was saying it, and I was just sitting back and listening. 'I was attacked.'

He didn't speak for a moment. Then, 'Did they find the person that did it?'

I nodded. 'He's in prison. He got three years for it.'

'Three years? That's not long.'

I shrugged. 'It's just time, isn't it? Three years, thirty years. They might never have found him at all. At least it gave me long enough to escape.'

Thursday 25 December 2003

Christmas Day, I woke up to bright sunshine. Lee wasn't in bed next to me. From downstairs I heard noises of pots and pans banging along with my headache. I looked across to the alarm clock — half-past nine.

I tried to feel excited, and happy, and Christmassy, but for the time being my head needed nursing.

I fell asleep again and when I next opened my eyes Lee was there with a tray full of breakfast. 'Wake up, beautiful,' he said.

I sat up and tried to ignore the way my head felt. 'Wow,' I said. Toast, juice, and, because I clearly hadn't had enough to drink in the last twenty-four hours, champagne.

Lee pulled off his jeans and T-shirt and climbed back into bed next to me, pinching a piece of toast and munching on it. 'Happy Christmas,' he said.

I kissed him. Then I kissed him again, until I nearly kicked the tray over, and after that I sat up and drank some juice.

'I was out of order last night,' he said.

I looked at him in surprise. 'Out of order? Why?'

He looked at me steadily. 'I was mad jealous that you'd gone out wearing that dress. I'm sorry, it was wrong.'

There was a long pause, broken only by him munching.

'Why do you have a thing for red dresses?' I said.

He shrugged. 'I don't really have a thing for *all* red dresses. Just yours. And you in it.'

'I saw you in town last night,' I said. 'You were having an argument with someone in an alleyway.'

He didn't say anything, just put the tray down by the side of the bed.

'It looked like a drugs deal. Or something. Is that what you do? Deal?'

'There's no point in you asking me these questions, Catherine. You know I'm not going to answer.'

'Your job scares me,' I said.

'That's why I don't talk to you about it,' he said.

'If you got hurt — like, seriously hurt — would I even find out about it? Would someone call me?'

'I'm not going to get hurt.'

'But what if you do?'

'I'm not going to get hurt,' he said again. He took the empty glass out of my hand and put it on the table next to the bed, then pulled me down onto the bed and kissed me.

'Lee, I've got such a cracking head.'

'I've got something that will make that better,' he said.

It didn't make it better, of course, but it was worth a try.

I let go of his hand and had a drink, letting the coldness of the wine sink into me. I felt a bit queasy, and wondered if it was the wine, or the subject matter.

'I think I'm a bit pissed,' I said with a smile.

He looked at me appraisingly.

'Well, you are a bit pink . . . '

'Shall we go home?' I said. Suddenly I didn't really want to be out any more. Two drinks, honestly, I was useless. In years gone by I would have drunk all night and still been fine the next day.

When we got outside the cold air hit me hard and I felt my legs wobble.

He put his arm around me. 'Steady. You okay?'

It was a little, internal flinch, and I don't think he felt it. I wanted this — I wanted him, so much, and yet it was as if my body wasn't going to allow me near him.

'I was thinking about what you said before, about socialising. About how getting treatment for OCD might give me more time to socialise.'

'Yes?'

'Yes. Now I'm thinking that your kind of socialising is far less threatening than the kind I'm used to.'

'My kind? Is that some sort of back-handed compliment?'

I laughed. 'Maybe. I wasn't always like this,' I said, my teeth chattering a little, as we threaded our way through the throngs of people back towards Talbot Street.

'No?' he said, laughing. 'What, you were sober once?'

I gave him a little shove, then got his arm back around me for support as quickly as I could. 'No. I mean, I used to be a real party animal. Out every night. Drinking a lot. I was never in. Stupid, really.'

'Why stupid?'

'Well, I put myself at risk all the time. I used to get drunk, and then end up in strangers' houses, or I'd invite people back to mine. Sometimes I'd wake up somewhere with no memory at all of where I was or what I'd done. When I look back on that now, I can't believe I'm still here.'

'I'm glad you're still here.'

'Bet you wish you'd met me back then, huh?' I said jokingly.

He gave me a squeeze. 'I'm just glad I met you at all.'

Oh, God, I thought, please stop being so bloody nice to me, I can't take it, I don't deserve it.

'Look,' I said, 'I got sectioned. Twice. I thought you should know.'

'After you were attacked?'

'First time was immediately after. They let me out of the hospital after I'd recovered from the physical injuries. I don't think they really thought about what was going on in my head. I wasn't really looking after myself, anyway. So I ended up making a scene in some all-night pharmacy and the men in white coats came. Or whoever they were.'

'Probably paramedics, maybe with some help

from the police,' he said helpfully.

'After that it was about a year until the case went to court. Then I had a bit of a relapse; that was the second time.'

'Did you get proper help — therapy?'

I shrugged. 'Whatever. I'm here now, at least. I've come a long way, you know. A long way.'

He nodded. 'I can see that.'

'I just wanted you to know,' I said, 'in case.'

'In case what?'

'In case it makes a difference.'

We were back outside the house. He opened the door for me and stood aside to let me in. In the hallway, he stood back and said to me, calmly, 'Check it once. Just once.'

I gave him a look which said *I'll check the door however many times I fucking want to, thanks all the same*, but I checked it once. And once felt enough, because he was there.

He went up the stairs first, and outside the door of my flat he paused, waiting on the other side of the door so he wasn't blocking my way. 'Thanks for coming out,' he said.

I stood still for a moment looking at him, feeling the gulf between us like a void and wanting to cross it.

I don't know who moved first, whether it was him or me, but suddenly he'd got me, my arms were around him, inside his jacket, holding him as tight as I could. One of his big hands was cradling my head, and the oddest thought came into my head about how strange it felt, and I realised my hair was short now and not long. It was like a realisation that I wasn't that person

162

any more. Suddenly I wanted to grow my hair long again, just so I could feel what it would be like to have his fingers through it, holding my head.

He let out a breath, like a sigh, and I lifted my head and kissed him. At first he didn't kiss me back — he froze, just for a moment. Then the hand that had been cradling my head came round to my cheek, his fingers cool against my burning skin, and then he was kissing me too. He tasted faintly like Guinness. I felt my knees start to give, and his hold around my waist tightened a little. He felt so strong, despite his injured shoulder.

I should be panicking. I should be fucking terrified, I thought. But I wasn't. I didn't want him to let me go.

He pulled away from me to look at me, one of his hands supporting me at my back, the other at my cheek. Perhaps he's trying to see just how pissed I am, I thought, curiously. But it wasn't that. There was anxiety in those green eyes. He was checking I was okay.

Clearly I was fine, because he kissed me again, then, and I think it was a bit more forceful than he meant it to be — the day's worth of stubble grazing my mouth.

Gradually he began to release me, and my hand slipped reluctantly from the skin of his lower back, which it had found by somehow getting up inside his shirt. He took a step backwards so he could look at me.

I thought, *don't you dare apologise for what just happened. Don't you fucking dare say sorry.*

'Will you come inside?' I asked, casting a glance at the door of the flat. I wanted to take his clothes off, and I wanted him to screw me. Right then, right at that moment, I think I might even have paid him to do it.

There was a long pause, which grew more terrible with every moment. Then he shook his head. He looked as though he was debating with himself over what to do next, and some sort of internal battle was suddenly won, because he took a step forward and kissed me again, quickly, on my hot cheek this time, and whispered, 'I'll see you tomorrow,' before turning and taking the stairs up to his flat two at a time. I heard the key in the lock, the door opening, and closing, and then it was silent and I was all alone outside my flat as though I'd just got in from work.

Except I was swaying a little as though there was a strong wind, and I was desperate for a wee.

Thursday 25 December 2003

My mobile rang while we were still tangled up in each other. I found it easy to tune out the sound, concentrating on Lee's body and the rhythm of it. He grimaced and I felt him tense, distracted. 'Fucking phone,' he muttered, running a hand across his forehead.

'Don't worry,' I said. 'Leave it. Don't stop.'

It changed the mood. He pushed me off roughly, took a handful of my hair and turned me onto my front. I yelped with the sudden pain but he took no notice, forcing himself into me from behind. I struggled against him but he pulled my head back and carried on, harder.

It only took a minute longer. I heard the noise he made when he came, then he pulled out of me and got off the bed immediately, went into the bathroom and slammed the door behind him with such force that the window rattled.

My scalp was tingling from where he'd pulled my hair as I lay still, listening to my heart pounding in my chest. What the hell was that all about? I heard the shower starting.

When the phone rang again I answered it.

'Darling! Happy Christmas.' It was Sylvia.

'Hello, love, how are you?'

'Not drunk enough. You?'

'It's only half-past twelve,' I said, checking the clock. 'You've started already?'

'Course. Don't tell me you're still in bed.'

'Might be.'

'Well,' she said huffily, 'I probably would be too if I had Lee to keep me company.'

'You're welcome to him,' I said, 'he's got a right cob on this morning.'

'Hm,' she said. 'Want me to come over and kick him into shape?'

'No, you're alright,' I said, laughing at the thought of it. 'What are you up to?'

'You know, stuff . . . Mother wants me to help her cook lunch, I want to go out in my new clothes. Same old.'

I finished the call a few minutes later and got dressed, scruffy jeans and a sweater, warm socks. Downstairs the kitchen was a mess, toast crumbs and used teabags in the sink. I was halfway

165

through the washing-up, singing along to Christmas carols on the radio, when Lee came downstairs. He was wearing jeans, nothing else. His upper body was taut, his skin damp. He grabbed me, arms around my waist, and made me jump.

'You alright?' I said.

He buried his face in my neck. 'Yeah,' he said. 'Apart from that fucking phone. Who was it?'

'Sylvia.'

'Might've known.'

'You hurt me, you know.' I turned in the circle of his arms to face him.

'Hurt you how?'

'You pulled my hair and it really hurt.'

He gave an odd smile and rubbed the top of my head. 'Sorry 'bout that. Don't you like it rough?'

I considered. 'I'm not sure,' I said. 'Not rough like that.'

He let me go, took a step back. 'All women like it rough,' he said. 'Those that say they don't are just lying.'

'Lee!'

But he just laughed, and went into the living room. Maybe he was joking after all, I thought, maybe he didn't mean it. I ran my fingers through my hair from the roots to the ends. Long strands of it came away. I looked at the hair and shook it off my hand into the kitchen bin.

Sunday again, and it's cloudy, so technically it should be a good day. I might go for a run later.

Just at the moment, though, everything feels completely and utterly shit.

After he'd left me standing outside my flat and gone upstairs, I felt just as though I'd made a total fool of myself. It was a kind of a dull awareness, still feeling a bit warm and fuzzy due to having two glasses of wine (two glasses! My God), but now — in the cold light of a dull and windy December morning, all I can think of is how I told him happily that I'd been sectioned, not once but twice, and how he froze when I kissed him, how he extricated himself from my clutching fingers and then ran as fast as his legs would carry him up the stairs.

What on earth did I think I was doing? He must have sensed the desperation coming out of me. No wonder I'm a complete nutcase. No wonder I can't get out of the flat without checking everything forty times. Now I'm not just a nutcase, I'm a *desperate* nutcase who needs a shag so badly she practically has to pounce on the only male who's shown any interest in the last year. And as if it couldn't get any worse, this man was a psychologist — if anyone knew what madness looked like, he did.

When I got through my door, I caught sight of myself in the mirror. My face was wet with tears, which I must have been shedding without realising, whilst he'd been kissing me. Under the tears, my cheeks were fiery red. I didn't look as if

I'd just been kissed to within an inch of a heartbeat, I looked as if I'd been dumped.

Which, in a way, I had.

On a more positive note, however, all this provided such a great distraction from my normal woes that I managed to get away with only checking the flat once last night. Once.

I didn't sleep, though. I lay awake for hours, going over everything he'd said, and everything I'd said, trying to analyse the bits where I thought he'd been trying to tell me he fancied me, and all I could come up with sounded lame, could be interpreted differently: that he wasn't ready for a relationship (which he'd actually *said*) and nor was I (which *he'd* said as well) and that he'd had a shit time with his fiancée. The subtext of it all seemed to be that he needed my company and enjoyed being with me because, clearly, if neither of us wanted a relationship, then he was perfectly safe spending time with me, without me pouncing on him. All of which he'd said, right before I fucking pounced on him.

Shit.

At about three in the morning, I got out of bed, turned the heating on and sat shivering in my dressing gown for ten minutes with a cup of tea. When the warmth started to seep through, I decided to have a go at the deep breathing thing. Why not, after all? I had fuck all else to do.

This time I tried hard to do it without thinking about Stuart. Thinking about him now might make things worse, not better. Of course, the harder I tried *not* to think about him, the more impossible it became. I looked up to the ceiling, listened to the roaring silence inside my own ears, wondering if he was having trouble sleeping too. If he was, it was because he was lying there wondering what on earth he was going to say to me the next time he saw me. *'Um, hello, yes, I know I kissed you back, but really I'd rather shave my own eyebrows off than kiss you again. Would you mind not pouncing on me again? Thanks awfully.'*

I even tried giving myself a severe talking-to. *I am not going to let this hold me back. I am recovering from my OCD. I am going to get better, every day. I am recovering because I can do it. All he did was point it out; he's not making me better, I'm making myself better.*

After that, I had another go at the deep breathing, and this time I managed it. Just for three minutes, and it was a relief when the timer went off. I did feel calmer after that, crawled back into bed, and, as it started to get light outside, finally managed to sleep.

This morning I woke up and for a moment I could only remember the feeling of being kissed, how delicious he tasted, how strong and warm and safe he felt, and then I remembered the context of it all and I felt sick. After my eight o'clock cup of tea, I decided to be brave and go for a run. I got kitted out in tracksuit and trainers, eyeing the clouds through the window, daring it to rain. That would just about finish me off, I thought, and would be no more than I deserved; half an hour running through rain, or better yet sleet, would just about serve me right.

I checked the flat three times, which wasn't

bad, but not good either for a weekend. I used a big safety-pin to clip my door key inside the pocket of my tracksuit, checked it was secure, then at last I could set off.

It was windier than I'd realised, and my route to the park meant I was running into the wind most of the way. By the time I made it to the park gates I couldn't feel my face any more. Inside the park, I managed a sprint all the way up the hill, breathing until my chest hurt and then catching my breath at the top, gazing out across the view, all the way down towards the river, Canary Wharf and the Dome. The clouds were scudding across the sky, getting darker and stormier by the minute.

I headed off back down the hill, completing a circuit of the park, getting back to the gates just as the clouds broke and big droplets of icy rain began to fall. I thought about sheltering under the awning of the café, which was closed, but I don't like hanging around in the park any longer than I need to, particularly in this sort of half-light when you can't see who might be approaching. So I ran on.

And, of course, by the time I got back to Talbot Street the rain was easing off to a light drizzle. I was soaked, my hair spiked up in all directions by the rain and my own sweat, my cheeks stinging from the cold.

Just as I got to the house, the front door opened and Stuart came out. He was so busy checking that the door was properly closed behind him that he didn't see me at first, and for

170

a moment I contemplated diving behind next door's gate.

Too late.

'Hi!' he said, and his voice was so bright and friendly that I was taken aback by it.

'Hello,' I said, breathing hard, wishing I could have run just a little bit faster and made it home before he'd come out.

'I'm just going to go and buy some things for breakfast. Do you want some?'

'Um — I need to get changed,' I said, lamely.

'That's okay,' he said, eyeing my soaking wet tracksuit. 'You go and get some dry clothes on. When you're done, come up to the flat. Bacon and eggs alright?'

'Lovely,' I said.

He gave me a grin and went to pass me.

'Stuart,' I said.

He turned back to me, keys in his hand.

'I just wanted to say — er — thanks. For last night. For — you know. Not coming in. For turning me down. I'm sorry, I think the wine went to my head a bit.'

He looked confused. 'I didn't turn you down.'

'What?' I said. 'Didn't you?'

He took a step towards me, and put one hand on my upper arm, the way he'd done that night to calm me down. 'No, I didn't. I just didn't take advantage of you.'

'Isn't that the same thing?'

'No, it's not the same thing at all. I wouldn't have turned you down.'

He gave me a smile whilst my heart pounded, and not from the running. Then he said, 'See you in a minute,' and set off towards the High Street. I stood and held my breath and watched him until he turned the corner.

Thursday 25 December 2003

We ate dinner in a silence that I thought was uncomfortable. Lee had cooked it — slices of turkey, roast potatoes, gravy, even a jar of cranberry sauce. He was wearing a paper hat pulled from a cracker and watching me steadily while he drank.

I felt angry without really knowing why. I'd looked forward to this, to Christmas Day, thinking about how lovely it would be to have someone to share it with, and yet now I was half-wishing he wasn't here at all. I wondered if there was anything I could say that would get him to leave, without it provoking an argument.

Was it what he'd said, about women liking it rough? I tested the thought, but it didn't provoke the spark of anger. He might even be right. I hadn't particularly enjoyed it, that was true, but under other circumstances I might feel differently about that.

No, it wasn't that. It was the feeling that Lee was *taking over*.

I'd gone upstairs to get dressed and came down to find he'd shut me out of the kitchen. He'd told me that we would open our presents to each other after dinner and not before. I just had to sit on the sofa with my glass of champagne and be patient, he'd said. I ended up feeling like a guest in my own home.

My solution to this discomfort was going to be to get as drunk as I possibly could, and I was making good progress towards that aim.

'It's delicious,' I said at last, more to break the crushing silence than anything else.

Lee nodded. 'Glad you liked it.' He topped up my glass.

'Can I open my presents now, please?' I said as soon as he finished eating.

I was so unsteady on my feet that he had to take my hand to help me up from the table. I collapsed into a giggling heap on the floor by the tree and he sat next to me.

'I'm going to have to help you, aren't I?' he said, handing me a small, rectangular present, beautifully wrapped.

'No,' I said, gripping it a little more forcefully than I needed to. 'I can manage, thank you very much.'

It took ages, in between more glasses of wine, opening them — a couple of CDs by people I'd never heard of, a bracelet that sparkled on my wrist, a new leather purse and a silver fountain pen with my name engraved on the side — and Lee lit some candles in the fireplace and drank his wine more slowly than I did, and opened his presents too. He had fewer, mainly because I had presents from the girls to open as well. I watched him as he opened them — clothes, mainly, some aftershave, and a new phone. He looked pleased with them, really pleased . . . or maybe it was the wine, my judgment clouded by it.

Then I opened a box and found lingerie

buried within sheets of tissue paper, and of course I had to try it on immediately, stripping off clumsily, pulling at my jeans with wine-numbed fingers until he helped me, and of course I never got the new underwear on because we ended up making love again on the floor under my pathetic excuse for a Christmas tree, three feet high, a half-hearted display of white lights and a few glass baubles.

While he was pushing into me and I was gasping for air, my shoulders grazing the carpet, I felt out of myself, nauseous, and it reminded me of fucking people I didn't really know at the end of all those nights out.

I wondered with a moment of sudden startling clarity if this was right. I wondered if he was the right person for me to be with. Wasn't this just the end result of too many nights coming home drunk with a man I'd just met? Fucking someone downstairs on the carpet, my fingers and lips numb with too much alcohol? Faking it in the end because I was too goddamn tired to carry on much longer, waiting for him to hurry up and come because I wanted to be on my own, wanted to sleep. Wanted to be sick.

Lee must have sensed my discomfort because he slowed, pulled my cheek round to his face. I opened my eyes. He was directly above me, his expression unreadable. His hair was damp with sweat, the sheen of it on his forehead, the light from the candles throwing shadows across his cheek.

'Catherine,' he said, a whisper.

'Hm?' I thought he was going to ask me if I

174

was feeling alright, and I was preparing my best encouraging smile to get him to finish fucking me quickly so I could go and get a drink of water and go and lie down somewhere quiet and feel the room spinning in peace.

'Will you marry me, Catherine?'

The words shocked me as much as anything he could possibly have said.

'What?'

'Will you marry me?'

Afterwards, hours later, lying in bed with another thumping headache, I realised that the perfect answer would have been to kiss him, take control and make him carry on with what he was doing, delaying tactics to give me time to think. But my brain was full of wine and instead I hesitated a moment too long.

He moved off me and sat up, his back to the sofa.

I pushed myself upright unsteadily. 'Can I think about it?' I asked.

Lee was looking at me and to my horror there were tears on his cheeks. He was crying — this tough guy who had a job that involved pushing people around in alleyways, this man who grabbed fistfuls of my hair and told me that women like it rough — he was actually crying.

'Oh, Lee. Don't cry.' I sat astride his lap, wiping his cheeks with my finger, tilting his face so I could kiss him. 'It's okay. I just wasn't expecting it, that's all.'

But I underestimated the force of his shame. A few moments later, he got dressed and kissed me goodbye. 'I've got to work tomorrow,' he said, his voice gentle. 'I'll see you soon.'

'But you've been drinking, Lee, don't drive home.'

'I'll walk to town and get a cab,' he said.

It was what I'd wanted, after all — a few minutes ago I'd been wishing for him to get up and go home, leave me in peace, and now he'd gone. *Be careful what you wish for, Catherine,* I told myself.

Be careful.

Sunday 23 December 2007

By the time I'd showered and spent ten minutes agonising over what the most appropriate thing would be to wear for breakfast with someone I kissed last night, the smell of frying bacon was drifting all the way down the stairs and under the door of my flat.

I managed to lock the flat door, check it once, and head upstairs. The urge to go back and check it again was strong, but I was relying on the fact that I would be spending a while in Stuart's company to keep my brain occupied with nice things.

He'd left his front door open, but I knocked on it anyway. 'Hello?'

'In here,' I heard him shout, and I followed the sound to the back of the flat and the kitchen. It was really bright, the sunlight streaming in through those big bay windows into the lounge. He'd decorated the living room, a Christmas tree in the corner and lights around the windows. It looked warm and inviting and festive. On the coffee table, piled up, a selection of Sunday newspapers. On the small kitchen table, a pot of tea, a neat rack with steaming toast in it, a jar of Valencia orange marmalade.

'You're just in time,' he said.

He put two platefuls on the table and I sat opposite him and poured the tea, stirring the milk into my mug a bit at a time until it was exactly the right colour.

I felt so wildly and inexplicably happy that I couldn't keep the smile off my face. Having someone here, so close by, whom I could share a day like this with, was enough. It was almost hard to chew my breakfast because I was smiling so much. Then I chanced a glance up at him and he was looking at me intently.

'You look happy,' he said, curiously.

'I am happy,' I said, smiling, between a mouthful of bacon and toast, covered with a smear of runny egg yolk.

He was blushing, I had no idea why. It reminded me of last night.

Changing the subject in a ham-fisted way, I said, 'You are a damn fine cook. Even when you're handicapped with a bad shoulder.'

'I was thinking about that this morning,' he said.

'What?'

'Hm. What are you doing for Christmas?'

I gave a rather hollow laugh. 'Absolutely nothing, same as last year. Staying indoors and watching crappy Christmas TV.'

'I've got Al coming over for Christmas lunch.

He's got nobody to have Christmas with. Would you come too? We could all do Christmas together. What do you think?'

'Don't you have any family, anyone else you're supposed to have Christmas with?'

He shook his head, chewing. 'Not really. I could go to my sister's, but she lives in Aberdeen. Ralphie's gone back to travelling the world with his backpack. And besides, I'm supposed to be working tomorrow and Boxing Day. I was lucky to get Christmas Day off, really.'

I drank the last of my tea and wondered if it would be impolite to help myself to another cup.

'This is the same Al you told me about, right? The world's leading expert on OCD? And you want me to spend Christmas Day with him?'

'Er, yes. And me. So will you come?'

'It's really kind of you. Can I have a think about it?'

'Sure.'

When we'd finished eating, we sat in the sunny living room with the dregs of the teapot. I sat on the ivory-coloured rug and spread the *Sunday Times* out over the floor around me, absorbing myself in other parts of the world, other people's traumas, other worlds, other lives.

He sat on the sofa with the *Telegraph*, occasionally reading something out to me, laughing at something he'd read.

When my leg started to get pins and needles, I folded the paper up neatly and came to sit next to him on the sofa with the magazine. There was an article in it about

178

OCD. Normally I'd avoid reading something like this, because it was too damn close to home, but now it was fascinating. It was about famous people from history who'd suffered from OCD, and how it had so often been misinterpreted as eccentricity.

I showed it to Stuart, and he moved closer to me and read the article over my shoulder. I could feel his breath on my skin.

I felt myself tense, wondering if he was going to kiss me again and at the same time wondering if I would be able to cope with it without the comforting presence of alcohol in my bloodstream. Abruptly he got up, and went to the kitchen to put the kettle on for a fresh pot of tea, and at that moment the sun went behind a cloud and the room darkened.

'I should really be getting back,' I said.

I thought he hadn't heard me. A few minutes later he came back with the teapot, placing it carefully on the coffee table amidst all the supplements and adverts for mobility aids.

'Well, you can if you want to. But I was kind of hoping you'd stay for a bit.'

'Really?'

'You say that a lot,' he said, dropping down onto the sofa next to me. 'Like you don't believe me.'

'You're looking at me like a psychologist,' I said, frowning.

'I am a psychologist.'

'Well, I thought you were off sick.'

'Why are you getting cross?'

'Because you're starting to analyse me.'

He hid a smile behind his hand.

'And because that means you know how my mind works, and I haven't got a clue what *you're* thinking from one minute to the next, and it's doing my head in.'

He busied himself pouring me another cup of tea, no doubt completely aware that having a cup of tea — which was distractingly exactly the right colour — would prevent me from getting up and walking out.

'I kissed you last night,' I blurted out, crossly. I had no idea what it was I wanted to say.

'Yes,' he said.

'I felt my life change.'

He looked at me with those green eyes, waiting. 'Yes.'

'Change always scares me shitless.'

'Right.'

'*Yes? Right?* Is that it?'

He shrugged, refusing to take the bait at my heated tone of voice. 'I'm agreeing with you. Of course change is scary. But you get through it, and you'll get through this change as well. Won't you?'

I ran out of words, feeling the room swimming around me. This wasn't going well. How did I get from being blissfully, crazily happy just a few minutes ago, to this? I must have some huge internal self-destruct button.

'I don't know what you want from me,' I said miserably.

He did that eye contact thing again, the thing I was so afraid of, in case he could see how I felt, but what suddenly struck me was the way his eyes looked, the way he was looking at me. 'Cathy,' he said, 'it was just a kiss.'

My cheeks were burning. 'You think it didn't mean anything?'

'That's not what I said.'

'Why are you so comfortable with awkward conversations?'

He laughed. 'Maybe because I have more difficult conversations than I have simple ones.'

I had the feeling that whatever I said, he would have some smart answer, so I bit my lip. Eye contact: that was the other thing he was so good at. He won the battle this time, though. I was afraid if I looked into his eyes too long I might start to cry, so instead I drank the rest of my tea, putting the mug decisively down on the table.

'Really, I'd better go,' I said. 'Thanks for breakfast, it was very good.'

He walked with me as far as the door. 'You're welcome any time,' he said.

Stuart was right, of course he was. It was just a kiss, it was just a conversation, it was just breakfast. As I checked the door and the windows and the kitchen drawers and everything else, I considered everything he'd said and wondered what bit of it I was having such a problem understanding.

Wednesday 7 January 2004

'Hello, beautiful.'

'Shit! Lee, you just about gave me a heart attack.'

I was already in his arms by the time I'd finished the sentence, in the chilly car park at work. I'd come out late, not anticipating anything more exciting than a rush hour crawl home, and here he was, waiting by my car. The car park was badly lit, semi-dark.

He kissed me, slow and warm.

'What are you doing here?' I asked.

'I finished early,' he said. 'Thought I'd surprise you. Let's go out somewhere.'

'Can I go home and get changed?'

'You look perfect just as you are.'

'No, seriously, I've been at work all day, I'd rather get changed . . . '

'Get in.' He was holding open the door of a car parked directly behind mine.

'I like the car,' I said, sliding into the front seat. 'What's happened to yours?'

'I came straight from work,' he said. 'It's a job car.'

'Right. And that job would be?'

There was no reply to that one, of course. He was dressed smartly, dark suit with a dark grey shirt underneath, and he was freshly shaved. I wondered if he'd actually come straight from work or if he'd been to the gym. The car appeared to have nothing in it to distinguish it from any other, no CDs, no discarded car park tickets, no office parking permit attached to the windscreen.

We were heading out of town. 'Where are we going?'

'Somewhere a bit different.'

He put his hand on my thigh as he drove, not

taking his eyes off the road. The sudden contact gave me a thrill, despite how tired I was. His hand pushed my skirt up until he could feel the bare skin on my leg. I thought for a moment he was going to go further, but he stopped there, his hand resting on my thigh. I put my own hand over it.

'We're early,' he said after a while. 'I think we should stop for a bit. What do you think?'

He wasn't talking about stopping to admire the scenery, of course, although he did at least manage to wait until he found a reasonably attractive place. It was a car park at the top of the hill, the country park shut for the night, and fortunately they hadn't bothered to lock the gate. We drove down a dark track through the woods until the trees opened up in a clearing, and the lights of the town spread out in the valley below us.

Lee undid his seatbelt and glanced around in the semi-darkness outside. There was another car parked in the corner, and no sign of anyone in it, although it was too dark to see clearly.

It was awkward in the car even with the seats pushed right back, so we ended up outside, leaning back against the car door, my skirt pushed up around my waist, knickers pulled off and discarded somewhere. His face in my chest, my hands in his hair, I was shivering from the cold or the thrill of it all, my heels sinking into the soft ground.

'I shouldn't be doing this,' he said at last. No more than a sigh, against my throat.

'Why not?'

He raised his head. It was so dark I could hardly see him, just feel his solid bulk against me, make out the lightness of his hair with the breeze stirring it. 'I can't stop thinking about you,' he said. 'All I've been thinking about, all day, is how many minutes will it be until I'm with you again.'

'That's good, isn't it?' I whispered, kissing his cheek, his earlobe.

He shook his head. 'Not when I'm supposed to be concentrating on something at work. It's like cheating. I don't do it.'

'You mean cheating as in fucking someone else?'

He laughed. 'I don't fuck anyone else. Only you. I don't think about work when I'm with you, and I shouldn't be thinking about you when I'm at work.' He stood back from me then and adjusted his suit. From the pocket of his jacket he pulled out a ball of dark fabric. 'Yours, I believe?'

I opened the car door to get back into the warm. 'Hang on. These aren't the ones I had on earlier.'

'Of course not,' he said. 'I brought you some clean ones. Thought you might need them.'

'What happened to the other ones?'

He shrugged. 'I guess they're in the car park somewhere.'

'Have you got a torch? I can't just leave my knickers in the car park.'

'No, I haven't got a torch.' He'd started the engine. 'Let's go. I'm hungry.'

Half an hour later, we were in a beautiful old

184

pub by the river, waiting for a table, a big glass of red wine and a log fire warming me up. I was taking my time choosing something from the menu and Lee was sitting opposite me watching me with an amused smile on his lips.

I sensed it first. It was a sudden tension in him. Out of the corner of my eye I saw him stiffen.

I looked up and Lee was watching someone, or something, over my shoulder. Instinctively I turned to look. It was the restaurant behind me, tables full of people having dinner.

'Shit,' he said, under his breath.

'Lee? What is it?'

'Don't look round.' The tone of his voice was cold. Then, a moment later, he stood. 'Wait here, okay? I'll be back in a minute.'

I looked round then to see him heading towards the toilets in the restaurant. I felt queasy. Who had he seen? Another woman? Despite his instruction, I swivelled in my seat to face the dining room, waiting for him to emerge. The door leading to the toilets swung open but it wasn't Lee — two men, the first wearing a suit, a small rucksack slung over one shoulder, the second, older, more casually dressed with a black leather jacket and jeans. They were laughing about something. I expected them to go and sit in the dining room but instead they headed straight for me. I shrank back into the armchair and went back to the menu as they passed me. They went to the door of the pub and shook hands. The man in jeans disappeared through the door and into the car park.

When Lee came back a few moments later he was talking on a mobile phone. He sat down opposite me again. 'Yes. Okay. I'll see you outside,' he said, then snapped the phone shut and slipped it into his jacket pocket.

'Lee, what's going on?'

'I'm sorry,' he said. 'We're going to have to go and wait in the car for a bit.'

'What?'

'I need to meet someone. We can't wait in here.'

'You're joking!'

He leaned across to me and pressed the car keys into my palm. 'Shut the fuck up and go to the car. I'll be out in a minute.'

I stomped as best I could out to the car and slammed the door shut behind me, although there was nobody there to appreciate the force of my fury. Alone in the car, I opened the glove box, hoping to find something that would explain, but it was empty. Completely empty.

A few moments later I saw the side door of the pub open and watched Lee's figure walking towards the car. He opened the door and brought with him a gust of frosty night air.

I looked at him expectantly.

'That pub's a bit shit,' he said cheerfully. 'We should go somewhere else.'

'What?'

He pressed his fingers into his temple and closed his eyes as though I was giving him a headache.

'Okay,' he said, 'this is what's going to happen. In a few minutes some more cars will turn up.

186

I'll meet up with the guys who are in them and explain what's just happened, and then if we're lucky you and I can drive off and find another pub somewhere to have some dinner.'

'And if we're unlucky?'

'Then I'll have to help them out. And you'll have to stay in the car and keep your head down — and don't say a word.'

'Are you ever going to tell me what the fuck's going on?'

'When this is all over. I promise.'

He leaned over to kiss me in the darkness. At first I turned my cheek towards him, but he pulled me round, finding my mouth, his other hand slipping inside my jacket, pulling at my blouse.

The car reversed into the space next to us. I could see three figures inside, although it was too dark to see properly. 'Right,' Lee said quietly. 'You stay here, okay? Do not get out of the car. Understand?'

I nodded. He got out and climbed into the back of the other car. The interior light didn't go on when the door opened. I watched the figures in the car although I couldn't see them clearly. They looked as though they were discussing something but I couldn't hear a sound. After a few minutes all four doors opened and they got out. Lee gave me a smile and a wink. I wasn't feeling in the mood to return it. They all walked to the side door of the pub and went in, looking just as though they were mates heading off for a pint or two.

It was cold in the car. I considered turning the

engine on just to get a bit of warmth, or maybe the radio. For a brief moment, I even considered driving home and leaving him here with his mates. It wasn't so much that our romantic meal out had been so rudely interrupted, it was the way he'd been barking orders at me. I started mentally rehearsing the earful I was planning to give him, when this — whatever the fuck it was — was over.

The side door to the pub burst open and all hell broke loose.

I sat forward in my seat to get a better view, and then shrank back again when the man I'd seen earlier ran out of the door towards the car, rucksack on his shoulder, closely followed by a second man wearing a hooded top, and then Lee. Lee was shouting something and then hurling himself at the man with the bag, both of them crashing down onto the gravel just as the door opened again and two other men ran out.

I don't think I had a clue about what was going on, looking back. It was only when I saw Lee fishing around in his pocket and pulling out something that might have been a cable tie, strapping the man's wrists behind his back, and the man in the hooded top being brought back from the road, two of Lee's mates either side of him, holding him up, that it finally dawned on me that it was some kind of *arrest*.

Lee was arresting that man with the bag.

This was the day that went horribly wrong. The day my fragile world crashed down around my ears.

I finished work at four. I had been working on a recruitment campaign for a new warehouse that was being built to house our stock, on the industrial estate adjacent to the head office of the pharmaceutical company where I worked. The warehouse was due to open in April, and already we'd recruited most of the management. Now we were left with the supervisors and operatives, most of whom could probably be recruited from the local area. The newspaper adverts would run for the first six weeks of the new year. If we didn't have enough quality candidates after that, we would look to agencies.

I caught the Tube as far as Kingston Street, only about half a mile away from home. I took a circuitous route, through the alleyway so I could check the curtains at the back, then one length of Talbot Street before I could get to the front door. I'd made a conscious effort to take the same route home on the Tube two days running, and I was limiting my checking as far as I could. It was taking me about an hour in the mornings — certainly a lot better than it had been.

A few steps from the front door I heard a shout behind me and I turned, startled. It was Stuart, running up Talbot Street.

'You've finished early,' I said.

'Yes, thankfully. How are you?'

'Good, thank you.'

There was a pause. I wondered how I was going to get away with checking the door with him there.

'So — are you coming up for a drink?'

'What, now?'

'Yes, now.'

'I was going to — er — '

'Come up now, come on.'

In the hallway he let me check the door once whilst he stood there impatiently.

'There's a note for you here,' he said, pointing at the hall table.

I gritted my teeth at the interruption. If he kept talking to me we'd be here all night. 'Just let me do this, then I'll look.'

Of course, when I'd just about finished the check, the door to Flat 1 opened and Mrs Mackenzie emerged, resplendent in a floral pinny and slippers. 'Is that you, Cathy?'

'And me,' Stuart said.

'Oh, lovely! Both of you together.' She gave me a hard stare, the one I usually got when she caught me in the middle of checking the door. We all stood there for a moment looking at each other.

'Well, I can't stand here gassing all day,' Mrs Mackenzie said at last, 'I'd never get anything done.'

She went back inside, and Stuart and I looked at each other. 'Does she do that to you as well?' he whispered.

I nodded. 'Just don't mention Christmas to

her, she doesn't like it.'

'I know. I made that mistake last week. Here's that message.'

It was a 'While You Were Out' note, pre-printed, and it had my name on it. Other than the standard boxes which allow you to tick options, the only information on the form was a name — Sam Hollands — a mobile phone number and a landline number, and the message:

PLS PHONE ASAP

He handed it to me before I realised it, and of course by that point, with all the interruptions, the door was unchecked and I would have to start the whole damn thing again.

'The door is locked, Cathy,' he said gently, seeing my expression. 'We can't stand here all night. Let's go and have a drink.'

'I can't just leave it.'

'Yes, you can. Come on.'

'Why are you in such a huge hurry all of a sudden?'

'I'm not in a hurry,' he said.

He was so serene, so impossibly calm, I found myself getting wound up. 'Why don't you just go, and let me get on with it, then?'

'I'm not going to accommodate the OCD.'

I burst out laughing. 'You what?'

'Cathy, you don't need me to reassure you. You are going to get your condition under control. If I keep getting involved with your checking rituals, even by waiting for you to do

191

them, you're not going to be as motivated to work at it.'

'Oh for fuck's sake. You're such a fucking psychologist.'

'Yes, I am, as you keep pointing out. But I have actually finished work and I'd really like to go upstairs with you, right now, and have a drink. So come on.'

He made me go upstairs in front of him, the bit of paper clutched in my hand. I didn't look back at the door. On the first floor I stopped and looked at the door of my flat. The need to go in and start checking it was very strong.

'Come on, Cathy, don't stop,' Stuart said. He was halfway up the next flight of stairs already.

'I need to go and phone this person, this — ' I checked the message ' — Sam Hollands.'

'Do it from my flat,' he said.

When I still didn't move, he came back down the stairs to me. 'Your flat is still secure from when you left it this morning,' he said. 'Isn't it?'

Before I had time to consider this, he took hold of my hand. 'Come upstairs,' he said.

After that, I could move.

Stuart's flat was warmer than mine, and bright with all the lights on. He put the oven on and started busying himself in the kitchen. 'Are we having a cup of tea, or a bottle of wine?' he asked.

'Wine, I think,' I said. 'Shall I open it?'

He handed me a bottle from the fridge, and I found the glasses in the cupboard. 'You'd better ring that Sam Hollands,' he said, 'before you forget.'

192

I took the message with me into Stuart's living room and sat on the sofa, looking at it with trepidation. At this time of night, it didn't seem worth checking the landline number, it was probably an office. So I rang the mobile. It rang for an age. Eventually it was answered — a woman's voice.

'DS Sam Hollands speaking.'

DS? 'Hello. This is — Cathy Bailey. You left me a note.'

'Hold on a moment, please.' There were muffled sounds, voices in the background, as though DS Hollands was holding the phone against her jacket or something.

I felt my heart rate speeding up, my mouth dry. I felt sick. What the fuck did the police want? It couldn't possibly be anything good, could it?

'Yes, sorry about that, Miss Bailey. Cathy, was it? Thanks for ringing me back.'

More muffled sounds.

'Right. I work at the Domestic Abuse office at Camden Police Station. I called by with regard to Lee Brightman.'

'Yes?' My voice had almost gone.

'It's a courtesy call, really. I just wanted to let you know that Lee Brightman is going to be released from custody on Friday the 28th.'

'Already?' I heard my own voice as though it was coming from a long, long way away.

'I'm afraid so. He's given a release address in Lancaster, so I don't think you need to worry about bumping into him on the street, or anything like that. One of my counterparts in

Lancaster gave us a call with his details so that we can inform you.'

'Does — does he know where I am?'

'Not unless you've told him. And *we* certainly won't. I'm sure he won't travel far, Cathy, there's no need to worry. If you're concerned, just give us a call. You can ring this number, or the other number I left, any time, if you're worried about anything. Alright?'

'Thank you,' I managed to say, and disconnected.

I sat and waited for it. I felt it coming towards me like a wave, the panic. I think I was still waiting when I heard the noise, the wail, high-pitched and terrible, and wondered for a second where it was coming from until I ran out of breath and realised it was me. I shrank back into the sofa, trying to make myself as small as possible. Trying to disappear.

Moments like this are the ones I recognise as dangerous. The fear that permeates my life suddenly escalates to a new peak and my existence becomes a pointless effort, a challenge too far.

It was all a bit blurred for a moment. I saw Stuart sitting down next to me, but the whole room was shaking as though there was some sort of earthquake going on. I felt him put his arms around me, heard him saying something — *breathe*? But I couldn't tell the details — I pushed him away seconds before I started retching, and he grabbed the wastepaper bin and held it up just as I vomited.

And then just the sound of my own breathing,

or not even that — just little pants for breath in time with the shuddering, the shaking that was completely beyond my control. And my fingers were tingling, but it was too late, and the ground was coming up to meet me.

Wednesday 7 January 2004

Lee barely spoke to me all the way home.

He'd stopped and bought a bag of chips from the takeaway in Prospect Street. They were sitting unopened on my dining table, the smell of them making my mouth water, despite the fact that I'd entirely lost my appetite. We were on my sofa, in the dark. He'd sat down and pulled me onto his lap. I was rigid and frowning like a petulant child. I couldn't even remember what exactly it was I was so angry about any more.

'We need to talk about this,' he said gently. He had his arms around me, his face into my neck.

'We should have talked about it a long time ago.'

'You're right. I'm sorry. And I'm sorry for all that crap tonight.'

'Who was he? The man with the bag?'

'He's one of our targets. I've been following him for weeks. I had no idea he was using that pub as a meeting venue, obviously, otherwise I'd never have taken you there.'

'So you're a police officer?'

He nodded.

'Why couldn't you just have told me that before?'

There was a pause. Despite myself I was starting to soften. He was playing with my hand, threading his fingers through mine, bringing my hand up to his mouth so he could kiss the tips of my fingers. 'I wasn't expecting this to happen,' he said. 'I don't do this. I don't fall for women. I don't spend long enough with anyone to have to tell them anything. It's not an easy job to talk about, you know. I'm working undercover a lot of the time. It's easier to do that sort of thing on your own.'

'It looks dangerous,' I said.

'It probably looked worse than it was. I'm used to it.'

'That's what you were doing that first night, the night you came here covered in blood? I thought you'd been in a fight.'

'Yes. That one wasn't quite so straightforward. But that sort of thing doesn't happen often. Most of the time I'm just sitting in a car waiting for something to happen, or having briefings in some stuffy room with no windows, or catching up on three hundred emails.' He moved then, reaching behind his back. 'I'm sitting on some kind of brick here — what is this thing?'

It was my organiser. I'd thrown it on the sofa with my bag when we'd come in.

I disentangled myself and got up. 'I'll get the chips,' I said. 'Do you want anything with them? Or a drink?'

'No,' I heard him say.

I put the kettle on. If there was something I needed right now it was a cup of tea.

'Mind if I have a look?' he called.

I brought the mugs of tea through a few minutes later and he'd turned the lights on. My organiser was open in his lap and he was turning the pages.

'What are you doing?'

'I was curious. Who are all these people?'

The back of my organiser was full of business cards in a clear wallet. 'Just people I've met at conferences, things like that,' I said. 'You shouldn't be looking in there.'

'Why not?' he asked, but he closed it and handed it back to me.

'I'm a personnel manager, Lee. There's stuff in there about members of staff. Disciplinary meetings, things like that.'

He grinned.

'Okay. Are those chips still hot? I'm starving.'

Monday 24 December 2007

I came round slowly, my face against the carpet, the smell of vomit in my nose.

Almost immediately I started to panic again. Stuart tried to get me to breathe slowly. He held me, stroked my face, talked to me calmly, but at first it didn't work. I couldn't even hear him. I threw up again. Fortunately I was breathing enough not to pass out again, but in a way oblivion would have been kinder.

Eventually I heard him say, 'Come back to me. Breathe with me, Cathy, come on. I don't want to have to call for help. Breathe with me. You can do this, come on.'

It took a long time before I was calm enough to listen to him properly and understand what he was saying. He got me some clean clothes, some tracksuit bottoms and a T-shirt, because he didn't want to leave me in the flat alone, and I wasn't about to go downstairs. I was so weak I could barely stand, so he helped me to the bathroom and left me to get myself undressed and into the bath he'd run for me. He waited just outside the door, half open, and talked to me while I sat there, shaking, trying not to look at myself, trying not to look at the scars and what they meant.

It felt as if *he* was back in my head again. Or, not yet: but waiting. The images of him, the ones I'd fought to control, were still there. They had lost some of their sting. But now . . .

I used Stuart's shower gel, my hand shaking so much that it spilled across my wrist and into the bathwater, but I got enough of it to soap my hands and try to get rid of the smell of sick from my hair and my body. The smell of the shower gel, curiously familiar, made me feel a bit better. I splashed water on my face and rinsed my mouth out with soapy bathwater.

'I was thinking about that first time I saw you,' he was saying, his voice so close as if he was sitting right next to me, but coming through the open door. He was sitting on the floor, outside in the hallway. I could see his legs stretched out in front of him. 'That estate agent just barged in through the door; you must have been in the middle of checking. You gave me such a filthy look.'

'I don't remember — did I?' My teeth were chattering. My throat was sore. Had I been screaming? I felt as if I had.

'You did.'

'The door was open — they'd left it on the latch.'

He laughed. 'You poor old thing, how did you ever manage with them leaving the door open? Jesus.' The tone of his voice changed, then. 'You were looking at me with this sort of horror that someone had crossed the threshold when you were in the middle of checking the door. I thought you were the most beautiful ball of fury I'd ever seen.'

I pulled at the plug with numb fingers. Listening to the sound of the water pouring away. I'd listened to that noise from my bed, in the flat below, the swish and gurgle, wondering what he was doing having a bath at three in the morning.

'I'm not beautiful,' I said, quietly, looking at the scars on my left arm, the deeper ones at the tops of my legs. The worst ones were still red, the skin still tight and itchy.

'I'm afraid that's my call. Are you done?'

I managed to get up and put a towel around me. It was still a little bit damp from when he'd showered this morning. I felt completely tired, drained of all energy, and sat on the bath, waiting for my skin to dry on its own. I didn't want to touch myself.

'Will you be okay if I go and put the kettle on?' he said, the sound of his voice making me jump. 'And pass your clothes through, I'll put them in the wash.'

'All right,' I said, in a gravelly whisper. I was about to lose my voice completely. It reminded me of when it had happened, the next day when the police were trying to interview me, and I couldn't speak. I'd been screaming for three days. They had to wait days before my voice came back enough for me to be able to talk to them properly. By that time, of course, he'd done a lot of talking too.

I dressed in the T-shirt and the trousers he'd left for me. They felt peculiar, so baggy that I had to hold the waistband up as they kept slipping off. I felt half-naked, especially as my arms were still on display. The scars were bad. I didn't want him to see them. On the back of the bathroom door was a towelling robe, navy blue. When I put it on, it went round me almost twice, and reached almost to the floor. That would do.

I met him in the kitchen. The washing machine was swirling round with my clothes inside it. There was a faint smell of some sort of disinfectant. He put a cup of tea on the kitchen table and I sat there, my bare feet feeling the strangeness of the tiled floor. I'd never taken my socks off inside his flat before, let alone my whole set of clothes.

'Do you want to talk?' he said.

'I don't think I can,' I whispered.

'Can you tell me what they said on the phone?'

I considered this, testing the words out inside my head before I let them out. 'She said he's being released on the 28th.'

'The man who attacked you?'

'Yes.'

He nodded. 'Okay. Well done,' he said, as though I was a star pupil who'd just completed a complicated maths equation.

'She said he was going to an address in Lancaster. She thinks he won't come down here.'

'Does he know where you live?'

'I don't think so. I moved. I moved three times. There's only one person other than the police who knew me then — Wendy.'

'Do you think Wendy might be in any danger?'

I thought about this for a moment, then shook my head. 'I don't think he knows we became friends. I never spoke to her until the day she found me. After that he was arrested. She did testify at the trial, though.'

I drank some of my tea. It hurt the back of my throat, but it felt magical. I felt myself calming down almost straight away.

'You're going to be okay,' he said, gently. 'You're safe now. He's never going to hurt you again.'

I tried to smile. I wanted to believe him, I wanted to trust him. No, I *did* trust him, after all, I was sitting in his kitchen wearing his clothes and a robe. 'You can't promise that.'

He considered this, and replied, 'No, I can't promise you that. But you're not on your own with this any more. And you can choose to turn away from this evil man, and keep on getting better and stronger every day until you're not afraid any more, or you can let him carry on hurting you. It's a choice you can make.'

I was smiling, despite myself.

'Are you going to stay here tonight?' he asked.

I thought of the options. I wanted to go home and start checking the flat, but at the same time I was afraid. I was afraid of going home. I was afraid of being anywhere without Stuart.

'Yes,' I said.

'I'll sleep on the sofa.'

'No, I don't mind. You need your comfy bed,' I said, indicating his shoulder.

'You freaked out last time you slept on my sofa.'

'I think I'm less likely to freak out on your sofa than I am if I woke up and I was in your bed.'

'As long as you're sure. Are you hungry?'

I wasn't, but the casserole he had put in the oven hours ago was still simmering away, so we ate it from bowls on our laps, with chunks of bread to dip in the gravy. It was hot and spicy and it stung my throat. But it tasted good. He'd brought the bottle of wine that I'd never got around to opening, and we drank that.

'Probably not a good idea really,' Stuart said, finishing his first glass of wine.

'What isn't?'

'The alcohol. You've had a rough evening, and I need to be wide awake to cook Christmas lunch tomorrow.'

'It's nice, though.'

He turned to me and smiled. I thought he looked bone-tired, his eyes shadowed. 'At work today I just kept thinking that tonight I was going to come home and get drunk.'

'Why?'

'Last Christmas was a bit crap, to be honest. I'm trying to get over it. Of course, getting pissed isn't the answer, but I thought it might help.'

'What happened last Christmas?'

He poured himself some more wine and topped up my glass, although I'd only had a few sips. 'It was when it all started to go wrong with Hannah.'

'Your fiancée?'

He nodded. 'I did Christmas dinner. There were four of us — me and Hannah, and her brother Simon and his girlfriend Rosie. Simon was my best mate at uni, that's how I'd met Hannah. We'd just about finished eating and Han got a call on her mobile. She wasn't supposed to be on-call, but she told me it was an emergency and she was going in anyway. Simon had a real go at her, told her off, she told him to piss off and got her coat and she was gone. Simon was just so mad, I couldn't work it out, I kept telling him to leave it. It got really awkward, they left a bit after that and I was on my own until she came home again, three o'clock in the morning. I fell asleep on the sofa waiting up for her.'

He turned to look at me, frowned at the memory. 'Shit Christmas, it was, really. Turns out she'd promised him she was going to spend Christmas Day with him, the man she was seeing. Simon knew all about it. He was on the verge of telling me, apparently; that's why Rosie made him leave. She didn't want to spoil my Christmas.'

'When did you find out?'

'Not till July.' He leaned back on the sofa, finished the glass of wine. 'I don't want to talk about that,' he said decisively.

He washed up the bowls while I watched the late news, then he fetched his duvet from the bedroom and wrapped it round me. It was huge.

'I've got a sleeping bag in the wardrobe,' he said. 'You have this.'

'Thank you,' I said. I caught his eye for a moment and I felt my heart quicken. If he'd tried to kiss me again I don't know what I would have done. But he just smiled and went back to the bedroom. I listened to him pottering around the flat, turning off lights in the kitchen and turning on the light in the hallway, and I lay back on his sofa under the warm soft pile of duvet that smelled of washing powder and, faintly, of his aftershave. I never thought for one moment that I was going to be able to sleep. I lay there and thought about not sleeping, right up until the moment that I slept.

Saturday 17 January 2004

Sylvia's party was at the Spread Eagle, a favourite pub that had been the scene of many great nights out over the years. Sylvia had had an on-off relationship with the manager, more off than on, but they'd managed to stay friends in between arguments.

We got a cab to the Spread Eagle, and Lee was in a foul mood.

'Look, we don't have to stay long if you don't like it. Seriously. Just an hour or two, okay?'

'Yeah, whatever.'

If it hadn't been for the fact that he looked so good, I might just have told him to fuck off. I couldn't decide if he looked best suited up, shaved and smelling divine, or if I preferred him in jeans and in need of a wash. He was halfway between the two extremes tonight, jeans and a navy blue shirt that made his eyes look brighter and bluer than ever, and — at least — clean. And as we headed for the door, bracing ourselves against the racket that was emanating from within, he took my hand and gave it a squeeze.

It was all because of that stupid dress.

When he emerged from the shower, towelled dry and boldly naked, strolling into my bedroom with that swagger of confidence that only a man with his sort of physique could pull off, I was wriggling into my black velvet dress.

'Is that what you're wearing?'

He slipped his hands around my waist, pressing the length of his body against me.

'Clearly,' I said, amused.

'Why not the red one?'

'Because we're only going to the Spread Eagle. It's a pub. And not a very posh one, either. I can't wear a red satin dress, I'd look seriously overdone.'

He looked into the open wardrobe, then, and took the red satin dress from its hanger, a bright shiny jewel amongst all the blacks and purples. I thought for a moment he was going to throw it across to me, but instead he sat on the bed, undoing the buttons at the back of it, one by one.

'Lee?'

It was as if he'd forgotten I was there. He stood up beside me and buried his face into my neck, running his tongue along my skin, breathing into my ear and making all the hairs on my whole body stand up on end. 'Wear the red one,' he said softly.

'Lee, I can't. Really. What's wrong with this one?'

'Nothing's wrong with it. It's beautiful. You're beautiful. But you look good in red.'

'I look alright in black, too,' I said, contemplating our reflection in the mirrored wardrobe door. 'Don't I?'

He ran a hand up the top of my leg, round to the front, making me melt. Then the other hand pulling up my dress — and before I realised it, he'd pulled me over to the bed and pulled my dress back up over my head. I fell backwards onto the duvet, laughing, as he blew raspberries on my bare tummy and wrestled me out of the sleeves.

I let him undress me. I let him devote all his attention to my body for another half-hour, then, when he'd dressed and gone downstairs, I put the black dress on again and was ready just as the cab arrived outside. He didn't speak to me all the way to the pub.

When I opened my eyes on Christmas morning, the sun was shining in through the window, onto my face, making me think it was summer. I could hear Stuart in the kitchen, rattling pans, and I suddenly remembered it was Christmas, and that Alistair was going to turn up in a few hours' time.

He noticed me sitting up. 'Hello,' he said. 'Happy Christmas.' He'd got his jeans on, and a frayed grey T-shirt. 'I'll put the kettle on.'

'I'd better get up,' I said, still snuggled in the duvet up to my neck.

He came and sat on the sofa next to me, wincing a bit when his shoulder twisted. 'I was thinking,' he said, his eyes on me, 'I can ring Alistair and cancel if you like.'

'What? Cancel Christmas?'

'If you're feeling like you'd rather be on your own, you know. After yesterday. I'm sure he'd be okay.'

I smiled at him. 'That's kind, but I'll be fine. Really.'

I pulled the duvet up a bit, suddenly conscious of how little I was still wearing. Memories of being sick and having a panic attack last night were coming back to me. 'Better get dressed, then,' he said cheerfully. 'Do you want me to go downstairs and find you some clothes, or are the ones you had on yesterday okay? They're all clean.'

I thought about going downstairs to my flat, and being on my own while I scouted out something to wear. If it hadn't been for the sunshine, I think I would have needed him to come with me. I looked at the window, the sunlight streaming through. Nothing bad could happen on a day like this.

'I'll be alright, I think. I'll just go and get dressed and then I'll come back up.'

'Bring some stuff back with you,' he said, getting up.

'Stuff?'

'You know, toothbrush and stuff. I mean, if you wanted to stay tonight.'

I wasn't going to stay tonight. In fact, he'd be lucky if I ever managed to leave the flat again. I was going to be spending at least the next two hours checking, I thought, carrying my work clothes, neatly folded, and my shoes balanced on top, down the chilly stairs.

The flat was okay. Cold, because normally I'd be at work by now and the central heating goes off at six. The curtains were fine, the way I'd left them; everything in the flat was as it should be. I worked my way round, checking, thinking how peculiar it was doing this wearing nothing but Stuart's T-shirt and tracksuit bottoms, loose around the middle.

Once I'd managed to check three times, I had a shower to warm me up a bit and washed my hair back into some sort of reasonable shape. I looked through my wardrobe, wondering if I actually possessed anything any more that didn't make me look as if I was in my fifties, or trying to hide in a pile of shapeless fabric.

In the end I found a black fitted top that I usually wore under my suit at work, a black skirt that was short enough to be quite daring. And some black tights. I looked like a trainee ninja. Finally, at the back of the drawers, a pale pink cashmere cardigan. At least that would cover up the scars on my arms. Instead of buttoning it, I tied it at the waist.

I looked sadly at all my sensible shoes, all perfectly suitable for wearing under trousers, all just right if I ever felt the need to break into a sprint, but not exactly alluring.

Hell, I didn't need shoes anyway, I was only going upstairs.

I rubbed my hair dry with the towel and found some make-up, just a little, I didn't want to scare him, after all. After all that, I had a look in the mirror. I looked very strange, and very thin. Not like me at all. If he does come looking for me, I thought, he'll be lucky to recognise me.

I didn't want to think about that. I found a bag and stuffed a few essentials into it, toothbrush, joggers and a T-shirt, clean underwear. Just enough so I didn't need to come back downstairs later, if I didn't want to.

I put the bag right by the door so it would be handy, and started checking.

Saturday 17 January 2004

The Spread Eagle was full of people, most of them friends of Sylvia's from the *Lancaster Guardian*. The noise levels were immense and there was even a DJ, although the music was actually being drowned out by the shouts and laughter. Judging by the noise and the state of those present, they'd been drinking for most of the day.

Sylvia, who was holding court at the bar, looked even more beautiful and exotic than usual in a magenta skirt and an emerald-green silk blouse that matched her eyes, open to a low enough button to reveal a good portion of cleavage and a glimpse of cherry-coloured bra. When she saw me, she gave a shriek, peeled herself away from the men in suits either side of her, and tottered over to give me a cuddle. She smelled of expensive perfume, gin and pork scratchings.

'Oh, my GOD! Can you believe this? I'm actually fucking going to the *DAILY MAIL*!'

There was a bit of mutual jumping up and down, and then I remembered Lee, and stepped aside.

Sylvia stepped forward with her best coy smile, gave Lee her hand and made a delicate little curtsey. 'Hello again, Lee.'

To his credit, Lee gave her one of his smiles and kissed her on the cheek. This clearly wasn't enough for Sylvia, who put her arms around his neck and honoured him with a cuddle. He looked at me over Sylvia's shoulder and gave me a wink.

After that, he seemed to relax. I flitted about the pub, talking to various people I knew, drinking far more than I should have, accepting drinks from people I knew vaguely and some I'd never seen before in my life. From time to time I caught sight of Lee, and each time he seemed fine, talking to Carl Stevenson mainly, who'd been Sylvia's editor when she first joined the paper. Later on, I saw him in a group with Sylvia, who was partly talking to him and partly to the rest of the crowd. He saw me looking and gave me a smile and another wink.

So much for an hour, I thought to myself, watching with amusement as Lee stood at the bar, chatting away animatedly to Len Jones, the chief crime correspondent. He was the one who had pursued Sylvia relentlessly, back in the summer, despite the existence of Mrs Annabel Jones who had more than once threatened to castrate him with a pair of nail scissors.

I sidled up to Lee at the bar and snuggled under his arm.

In response he gave me a beery kiss just above my ear.

'Ah, you never said this lovely young vixen was yours!' said Len, raising a sloppy pint in my direction.

'Hello, Len,' I said.

'Cath, my little sexpot. How are you? And why haven't you been to talk to me?'

'I came over just to talk to you now, in fact,' I said. 'Nothing at all to do with the fact that I was hoping Lee might buy me another drink.'

He took the cue and shouted over the bar, handing over a tenner and getting me a vodka in exchange, while Len muttered something about going for a piss.

'You having a good time, then?' I asked, loudly, in his ear.

He nodded, meeting my eyes. I was getting very good at reading him. I could tell pretty much exactly what he was thinking, and it made my legs feel weak. Without taking my eyes off his, I put my hand deliberately on the front of his jeans and felt how hard he was. I gave him an appraising squeeze, watched his eyes close and his skin flush, then let him go and swallowed some of my drink.

'You are such a fucking tease,' he growled into my ear.

'Wait till I get you home,' I said.

His look told me he wasn't prepared to wait that long.

To be honest, I was enjoying the teasing part of it all a bit too much. I went to have a dance with Sylvia, who'd taken off her Louboutins and was dancing barefoot on the grotty bit of laminate that passed for a dance floor.

I saw him watching us, and Sylvia saw it too, pulling me over and giving me a good full-on snog.

'You're such a bloody minx, Sylvia!' I shouted at her, when she finally let go.

'Give over,' she shouted back. 'No chance of a threesome before I fuck off down to London, then?'

I laughed and cast him a glance. The look on his face was priceless. 'Hmm,' I said, 'what do you think he'd say if I asked him?'

She snaked an arm round my waist and we both turned to have a good look at him. 'He's

212

fucking lovely!' she yelled.

'I know, and he's all fucking mine!'

We laughed and hugged, and jumped up and down in time to 'Lady Marmalade'.

Having Sylvia's undivided attention didn't last long, though, and she was pulled away by two young sweaty-looking men I didn't recognise. I didn't think they were from the paper at all, but Sylvia didn't seem to care.

Lee had disappeared. I stayed on the dance floor, practically held up by the bodies either side, my ears ringing with the noise, half-wishing I'd worn something a bit cooler than this velvet dress.

Eventually I decided I was too desperate for the toilet to continue, so I sauntered over to the ladies', took one glance at the queue, and went into the gents' instead.

'Not looking,' I said, turning my face away from the few blokes standing at the urinals, locking myself into a cubicle and perching with relief.

When I finished, I went on the prowl for him, weaving my way between drunken bodies with serious intent. He was back propping up the bar, chatting to Len.

'Would you excuse us a moment?' I shouted politely, and Len raised an eyebrow and nodded, before turning back to the bar to call for another pint.

I took Lee by the hand and pulled him down the corridor past the toilets, out into the beer garden. The area round the door was crowded with people getting some fresh air, but I took

213

him further, through the gate at the end of the beer garden which led to the playground. This place was absolutely heaving in the summer, but right now it was deserted, and very, very dark.

I didn't have to drag him; in fact when he realised where I was taking him he took over and started pulling me instead.

I stumbled on a lumpy bit of grass and parked the edge of my behind on a picnic table, pulling up my skirt, glad I'd decided to wear stockings and equally glad that I'd left my knickers behind in the waste-paper basket in the gents' toilets.

I could just about see his outline, silhouetted against the faint orange glow from the skyline, but I could hear him breathing. I hooked one finger over the waistband of his jeans and pulled him close, undoing the buckle of his belt, unbuttoning and unzipping whilst he ran one hand up the inside of my thigh. When he realised I wasn't wearing any knickers, I heard a low groan.

He kissed me, roughly, forcing my mouth open, and then tearing it away to whisper in my ear, his voice just a rasping breath, 'You're such a dirty bitch . . . '

'Shut up,' I said into his mouth. 'Bet you're just glad I'm wearing this dress now, aren't you?'

It took longer because he'd had a bit to drink. As much fun as I was having, with him fucking me hard in the freezing night air, part of me started worrying about someone hearing the noises we were both making. And another not inconsiderable part of me was starting to worry about getting splinters in my backside.

Then he pulled out and turned me, pushing me back onto the table with one hand and dragging up my skirt again with the other until it was around my waist, before pushing into me again from behind with a sound that came from between clenched teeth. Hitting the table knocked the wind out of me a little, and I felt the rough lichen on the wood under my fingers, bracing myself for each thrust. He was holding my hips, pushing me forward against the table, and his grip was strong and bruising.

In between thrusts I could hear other noises — was that him? It sounded too far away. And then — unmistakable — a woman's giggle. Someone else was clearly enjoying a turn in the night air, and the playground was apparently the place to be. I didn't know whether to say something, and I tensed a little; clearly this had the desired effect because at that moment he came, thrusting into me with such force that I felt a sharp dig of pain on the front of my stomach as it grazed against the rough edge of the table.

Straight away, he pulled out of me and did up his jeans, leaving me to stand awkwardly and pull my dress down. I heard Lee clear his throat just as two figures emerged from behind the slide — the bright pink skirt visible even in this light. And behind Sylvia — holding onto her hand like a lifeline — was Carl Stevenson, looking sheepish and wiping his mouth across the back of his hand.

215

'Evening,' said Sylvia with a giggle, giving me a wink and heading past us back to the pub.

Hand in hand, we went through the side gate to the car park, and back round to the front to look for a taxi. I was shivering again.

'Why don't you women ever wear a coat, for fuck's sake?' he said, wrapping his arms around me.

'I've got you to keep me warm,' I said, kissing his neck.

That part of the evening was fine. The taxi ride home was fine, particularly as he'd got his hand up my skirt and was fingering me all the way back to my house.

When we got in, however, something changed. 'I think I'll go and have a shower,' I said, kicking my shoes off into the cupboard under the stairs. He was standing in the living room, his face clouded, hands in his pockets.

'I'm going home,' he said.

I came back into the room, not sure I'd heard him properly above the ringing in my ears. 'Did you say you're going home? Why? Aren't you staying?' I went up to him and slipped my hands around his waist. He kept his hands in his pockets for a moment, and then took hold of my upper arms and pushed me gently but firmly away from him.

'What's wrong?' I asked, a sinking feeling starting to take over from the feeling of being happily drunk.

He met my eyes at last, and his were dark with a level of fury I'd not seen before. 'What's wrong? You really have no fucking clue? Jesus.'

'Lee, tell me, for fuck's sake. What have I done?'

He shook his head to clear it. 'What was all that about, then? Coming out of the gents' toilets? Accidentally left your pants behind?'

'I only went in there because the ladies' had a queue. Sylvia and I always do that when it's busy,' I said in a small voice.

'Sylvia!' he exploded. 'That's a whole other issue! What did you think you were doing, snogging her face off on the dance floor? Touching her up?'

'I thought you'd think it was erotic,' I said, feeling tears starting. This was going all horribly wrong. 'It's not like I'd do anything with her.' Obviously not the moment to suggest a threesome, then.

'Oh, don't start fucking crying,' he roared. 'Just don't dare start fucking crying.'

I bit back the tears. 'Lee! I took my knickers off in the loos because I knew I was going to come straight out and find you.'

'Yeah, how am I supposed to know that? You could have been fucking anyone in there. You dirty fucking bitch.'

That hit a nerve. 'Don't you call me names, just because you've suddenly got all uptight! I didn't hear you complaining when you were fucking me in the garden.'

'And then you'd got your little friend out there, to give us a fucking audience!'

'I had no idea she was there!'

'Do that often, do you, go out there to watch each other? Fuck!'

217

'No!' This was a bit of a lie. We had done that once or twice, for a giggle. It was a challenge to see who could get someone out to the playground first. But not tonight . . .

'Lee . . . ' I touched his arm, tenderly, trying to bring him back, trying to calm him down, but he shrugged my hand away.

'Come on, I'm sorry. It wasn't like that. Lee.' I tried again, and this time he shoved me, hard, with both hands. I fell backwards onto the sofa, the breath knocked out of me.

He took a sharp breath in, turned his back on me. 'I'd better go.'

I sat back on the sofa, suddenly stunned by the force of his fury and devastated by the prospect of losing him. 'Yes, you better had.'

I spent the first hour after he'd left having a long hot shower, then walking from room to room, thinking over everything he'd said, how my behaviour had been interpreted. I hadn't fucked anyone else, I hadn't even flirted with anyone else, and you couldn't count Sylvia who was just about my best mate in the world. He'd been out of order. But then I thought about how he hadn't known anyone there except for me, how I'd abandoned him and spent the night flitting between people, laughing and joking, swishing my hair around and batting my eyelashes. And snogging Sylvia on the dance floor. Oh, God.

The second hour I spent sitting curled into the sofa, hugging my knees and staring blankly at the television screen, taking nothing in, the effects of the alcohol now worn off to the extent that I just felt sick to my stomach.

Just as I was contemplating going to bed, even though I knew I'd never be able to sleep, there was a quiet knock at the door. And then everything was alright again, because he was there, and the light from the hallway shone over his face, the tears, the hurt, the terrible, naked hurt in his eyes. He stumbled towards me, saying, 'I'm sorry, Catherine, I'm sorry . . . '

I took him in my arms and pulled him inside, kissing him tenderly, kissing the tears from his eyes. He was freezing. He'd been walking for miles. I pulled his clothes off him and put him in the shower, and it was almost a repeat of that first night when he'd stumbled into my house with blood pouring from his eyebrow and three of his ribs broken.

'I'm so sorry,' he whispered, as I lay beside him in bed, using my body to try to get some warmth back into him.

'No, Lee, you were right — I was out of order. I'm sorry. I'll never show you up like that again.'

And when he made love to me, it was very gentle.

Hours later, lying in the darkness of my bedroom, listening to his breathing, regular, deep. The question that had been swimming around in my mind, since the moment I first saw those eyes, finally found a whisper. 'Who broke your heart, Lee? Who was it?'

His reply took so long I thought he was asleep . . . and then the word, whispered into the air like a charm, like an incantation: 'Naomi.'

The next morning I had forgotten where the bruises on my arms had come from. But I never forgot the name, nor the way he said it, with such reverence: a breath, a sigh.

Tuesday 25 December 2007

When I got back upstairs I could hear voices before I even got into the flat. They'd left the door open, something that would normally send me into a tailspin, but after all this wasn't my flat.

Stuart was standing in the kitchen. When I came up the corridor towards him, having shut the door firmly behind me, he stopped talking, mid-sentence, and looked.

I rounded the corner and there, at last, was Alistair Hodge. 'Ah, and you must be the glorious Cathy; I've been hearing all about you. How are you, my dear?'

'I'm very well, thank you. It's nice to meet you.'

I shook his hand and accepted a glass of wine from him, immediately thinking that I would have to take things very easy.

'Come and sit with me, my dear, and let's see if we can find some nice festive music to listen to.'

I cast a glance over my shoulder at Stuart as Alistair led me into the living area. He gave me a smile and a wink and went back to the meal.

Alistair was a well-built man, loosely put together, with prematurely greying hair rather

220

like mine. He had a huge belly which strained the cotton shirt he was wearing and sat over the waistband of the brown cord trousers. Despite his girth he seemed peculiarly light-footed, and was happy leaping up from the sofa to go and select some more CDs from Stuart's collection when we'd looked through the first handful.

'Stuart, dear boy, you haven't any carols.'

'See if there are any on telly,' Stuart called back.

'I must admit I haven't got any carols either,' I said.

'Oh, that's such a shame. I don't feel at all Christmassy if I haven't any carols.' He flicked through the channels until he found some choirboys warbling away, their mouths angelic circles, their eyebrows somewhere up in their hairlines.

My cheeks were starting to feel flushed. I'd only had half a glass of wine.

'How's the shoulder?' Alistair called.

'Better. On the mend.'

He leaned over me conspiratorially. 'Did he tell you what happened?'

'Just that he got kicked in the shoulder by a patient.'

'Ah, you didn't get the full story, then. I might have known. He's a bit of a hero, our Dr Richardson. He got himself between a patient who was getting aggressive, and a nurse. He wrestled the man to the floor — '

'He's exaggerating,' Stuart said, suddenly appearing with the wine bottle and topping up our glasses.

221

' — and subdued him single-handedly until help arrived.'

I looked at Stuart.

'It's not usually that bad,' he said. 'Most of the patients I see are just too miserable to move. I don't often get violent ones.'

Alistair raised his eyebrows. I looked from one of them to the other.

'Anyway, Al, that's enough about work. I don't think Cathy wants to hear all the horrible details, do you?'

'Did he tell you about his award?'

'No,' I said.

Stuart made a noise of disgust and went back to the kitchen.

'He's been awarded the Wiley Prize for the research he's done into treating depression in young people. He's the first UK-based psychologist to get it. We're *ever* so proud of him in the department. Alright, alright. I'll shut up about it now. I *knew* you wouldn't have told her, though, Stuart, that's why I had to say something.'

'Do you work together, on the same ward?' I asked.

'Oh, no, not any more. I work at the Centre for Anxiety Disorders and Trauma. I'm in a different building. Stuart does the depression and mood disorder clinics, as well as working on the crisis ward. He started off with me though. Bloody brilliant chap.'

'I can hear you,' Stuart said from the kitchen.

'I know you can, dear boy, that's why I'm saying such nice things.'

Alistair went back to looking at the glorious

interior of the chapel of King's College, Cambridge and I went to check if Stuart needed any help with the dinner.

'Anything I can do to help?'

'Nope, it's all under control.'

Eventually he put me in charge of laying the table, although it was a small table for two, never mind three. I opened another bottle of wine, since the first one seemed to be empty. Alistair had brought some crackers, so I put one on each of the placemats, then I went to sit with Alistair again.

Finally, when I was about fainting with hunger and the tempting smells had nearly got the better of me, Stuart said, 'It's ready.'

Dinner was amazing. Stuart had cooked a haunch of venison in a rich plum gravy, with vegetables and roast potatoes, roast parsnips and Yorkshire puddings. The meat was meltingly velvety-delicious. The wine we were drinking was making me feel warm, and more than a little drunk.

We pulled our crackers and laughed at the appalling jokes, we drank more wine and finally had our dessert at about six in the evening, by which time we were all completely stuffed full of food. Alistair had seconds of everything, eating and chewing while Stuart and I looked at each other and smiled as though we had some private joke.

I made Stuart sit on the sofa while Alistair and I washed up, although he didn't stay there. A few minutes later he came and sat at the kitchen table and watched us, joining in the conversation while I told Alistair all about the happy world of pharmaceuticals and how I was busy recruiting warehouse staff for the new year. It all sounded hopelessly dull compared to the scary world of mental health wards, but they still listened. Stuart carved some more of the venison and wrapped it into a tinfoil parcel for Alistair to take home.

When everything was tidied away I made a pot of tea. Outside it was dark and the rain had started, pattering noisily on the glass. It was a good night to be at home.

'That was a delicious lunch,' Alistair proclaimed, displaying his vast belly like a trophy and patting it indulgently.

'Good,' Stuart said. 'Although it's a bit past lunchtime.'

Alistair had plonked himself happily on the sofa between us. 'I won't stay long,' he said, giving me a conspiratorial wink. 'I'm sure the two of you would much rather be on your own.'

I felt my cheeks flush and heard Stuart cough.

'We're just friends,' I said quickly.

'Of course you are,' Alistair said, with a broad smile.

'What's the bus service like today?' Stuart asked casually.

'Oh, a bit sporadic, to tell you the truth,' Alistair said. 'Appalling really, I mean, people have still got to get about, Christmas or no Christmas.'

'You going to be able to get home alright?'

'Hm? Oh, yes, I expect so.'

There was a long pause.

'I should think about getting back,' I said. I had a sudden horrible feeling that Stuart was trying to get rid of Alistair for some reason. Between us we'd consumed three and a half bottles of wine and the edges of the room wouldn't stay still. What if he was planning to make some kind of move? I thought back to the night before, about sleeping on his sofa, wrapped in his duvet, wearing his clothes.

'What are you up to tomorrow, Al?' Stuart said, trying again.

'Oh, lord, I've got paperwork to catch up on. No rest for the wicked, eh?'

'Better not leave it too late, then.'

'Hm?' Alistair looked up at Stuart. 'Oh! Of course, yes, I must really be going. Gosh, is that the time?' He got to his feet surprisingly quickly.

'I'd better be going, too,' I said.

'Well, my dear, I expect we shall see each other again very soon, hm?'

'Um — yes. I suppose so.'

'I'm very much looking forward to it.'

My cheeks burning, I found his coat and Stuart found his bag, and then Stuart said he would see him next week and they would meet up for a coffee to discuss something or other, and before we knew it Alistair had been shoved out of the door, and Stuart had gone downstairs to see him off the premises. I stood in the kitchen hopping nervously from one foot to the other, trying not to fall over.

I listened to the echoing voices coming up from the hallway below:

'Lovely dinner, Stuart, really first class

— thank you so much for inviting me . . . '

'Great to have you, honestly . . . '

'And,' his voice dropped but not enough for me to be spared what came next, 'I see what you mean about Cathy — she's a real treasure, isn't she? What a corker. Much better than Hannah. You've done well there, matey. Good on you. Right, better brave the rain . . . '

Then the sound of the door, the latch slotting home, and a moment later I heard him coming up the steps two at a time.

I stood there frozen, my heart thumping.

'Are you alright?' he asked.

'I feel a bit — I don't know — a bit drunk, I guess.'

He was eyeing me doubtfully. 'You look very pale all of a sudden. Come and sit down.'

'No,' I said, resisting. 'I'm going home.'

'You're sure? Stay for a bit.'

'No.'

'Cathy? What is it? I thought . . . '

'No!'

I made for the door, my feet slipping on the laminate floor in the hallway, pulling open the door. I made it down the stairs, holding on to the banister, fumbling for the key and forcing open the door, slamming it behind me, my heart thumping.

Hours later, the flat checked, exhausted, freshly showered and sitting curled into the sofa, I sent Stuart a text:

Sorry about earlier. Thank you for dinner.
C x

I waited and waited for the reply. Nearly half an hour later, it came. Just three words, more than I deserved, but even so, my heart sank.

It's fine. Whatever.

Friday 30 January 2004

I called Sylvia in January, the week after she started her new job. The first time I called it went to answering machine. I was going to send a text, but couldn't find the right words or put them in the right order. I chose a bad day to do it; my head was splitting and I was clearly suffering a bout of hormones because I couldn't stop crying.

That evening I tried again, and this time I got through. I was half-expecting the noise of a bar in the background but it was quiet. 'Hi, Sylv, it's me.'

'Catherine, how are you?'

'I'm okay, honey. How's it all going? I'm dying to hear. Is the job fab? Is it a good time for a chat?'

'It's fine. I'm going out in an hour or so, but I was just sitting here pretending to read through some bits and pieces. It's going well. Very bloody busy, though, manic in fact. Feels like the *Lancaster Guardian*'s a long way away.'

'And the flat?'

'Well, that's a whole other story. I'm sandwiched between someone who loves the

Carpenters at top volume all bloody day, and a couple who switch between arguing loudly and fucking loudly. I found myself bloody humming along to 'We've Only Just Begun' all day today. So, I'm flat-hunting.'

'I miss you, Sylv.'

'I know, lovie, I miss you too. How's Lancaster?'

'Raining.'

'And work?'

'Tiring, busy, stressful.'

'And the girls?'

'Haven't seen them for a while.'

'What? You been poorly or summat? Not been out?'

'Well, I've been out with Lee. But not seen the girls for ages.'

There was a long pause on the other end of the line. I could hear her rooting through what sounded like a pile of shoes.

'I'm worried, Sylv. It's all going wrong.'

'What is?' she said. I could still hear noises and then a muttered expletive.

'With Lee. I'm just — sometimes I'm just a bit scared.'

At last she stopped what she was doing. 'Why are you scared? You're not scared of Lee, surely — he's lovely. Are you scared of losing him, somehow?'

I paused while I tried to find the right words. 'He's not always lovely.'

'You been having rows?'

'Sort of, I guess. I don't know — I've been tired, he's been working a lot. When I do see him

228

it always seems to be on his terms, and he doesn't like me going out without him any more.'

Sylvia sighed. 'To be fair, though, honey, he's kind of got a point. Look at the way you were — the way we all were — when he met you. You were going out every night you could with the sole intention of flirting. No wonder he's nervous about letting you out.'

I didn't say anything, so she went on, 'You're in a relationship now, hon. It's a whole different ball game.'

Her voice softened a little.

'Lee's a good man, Catherine. Don't forget some of the complete shits you've been out with. I'm sure he's just being protective of you. And not only is he totally fucking gorgeous, but he loves you, he really does. Everyone said that, after the dinner party. He's so obviously completely and totally in love with you. That's what we're all waiting for. I wish I had that. I wish I had what you had.'

'I know.' I was trying not to let her hear my tears.

'Look, honey, I've got to shoot. Give me a ring at the weekend, yeah?'

'I will. You have fun. And take care, okay?'

'I'll be good! Ciao for now. Ciao, baby,' and she was gone.

Whatever.

I'd checked the flat so many times in the past twenty-four hours that I was too tired to carry on. The relief it usually brought didn't come, but the panic didn't come back either. I was thinking about Stuart and wondering if I'd blown it. Wondering if the only friend I had here was ever going to speak to me again.

He didn't understand. How could he? He hadn't a clue.

In any case, I was doing him a favour. He'd been hurt too, he'd been betrayed by Hannah. He didn't need another screwed-up relationship with someone like me.

This morning I heard voices from somewhere inside the house. I crept to the door and listened, straining to hear. It was Stuart and Mrs Mackenzie, downstairs.

' . . . keeping warm?'

I couldn't hear exactly what she said in reply. It seemed to go on and on, as though she was not pausing between one sentence and the next. I thought about opening the door so I could hear, but then I'd have to go through all the checks again.

Then I heard her laugh, and his laugh too. 'Things have come a long way since then, haven't they?' he said.

Then Mrs Mackenzie again — odd words, here and there, phrases I recognised from our brief conversations by the door: 'mustn't keep you . . . things to do . . . '

And Stuart: 'if you ever need anything, just let me know, okay? Just shout . . . '

Then the sounds of him coming up the stairs. I pressed against the door, breathless, my eye to the peephole. Was I checking that it was definitely him? Or was I just that desperate to see him, to see if he was alright?

His shape came into view, distorted by the lens in the peephole. He was carrying a bag with a loaf of bread sticking out of the top. I wanted him to pause, to hesitate, to glance in the direction of my door, but he did none of these things. He carried on up to the second floor, taking the steps two at a time.

Monday 2 February 2004

My happiness came and went like a ghostly breath. Throughout January I went from looking forward to Lee working, to missing him, to looking forward to him going back to work again.

When I opened the door my first thought was that Lee had been in the house again, moving my things around. There was a smell, a draught from somewhere. The house felt chilly, strange. I shouted 'Hello? Lee?' although I knew he was working, he'd sent me some texts earlier. I wouldn't have put it past him to come home early to surprise me, though, so I was cautious going into the lounge in case he was hiding in there and was going to jump out at me.

It wasn't messy, the way you'd expect a

burgled house to look. It was only when I realised my laptop had gone, complete with the charging lead, that I looked across to the patio doors and saw that they were slightly open, the lock damaged outside as though someone had drilled through it.

I reached in my bag for my phone and dialled Lee's number.

'Hey,' he said. 'What's up?'

'I think someone's been in my house,' I said.

'What?'

'The back door's open. My laptop's gone.'

'Where are you now?'

'In the kitchen, why?'

'Don't touch anything, go and wait in the car, okay? I'm on my way back.'

'Should I ring the police?'

'I'll do it. I'll be there in a minute. Alright? Catherine?'

'Yes — yes. I'm okay.'

Sitting in my car outside I started shaking and crying. It wasn't the laptop. It was the thought that someone had been in there, had broken into the house and been through my things. He might even still be in there.

The patrol car arrived a few minutes before Lee did, and even though I was halfway through explaining what had happened, Lee shook the officer's hand and they both went inside, leaving me outside by the car. And half an hour later, a white van with a crime scene investigator who told me her name even though I forgot what it was seconds later. I went into the house with her and showed her the lock and the dining table where my laptop had been.

Soon after that, Lee and the uniformed police officer came down from upstairs. There was a lot of handshaking and laughing and then the officer left.

I made the crime scene woman a cup of tea while she dusted for fingerprints and swabbed a few surfaces. It all looked quite random to me.

When she left, I started crying again.

'I'm sorry,' I said, as Lee took me in his arms and held me.

'It's alright,' he said. 'You're safe. I'm here.'

'I can't stand the thought that someone's been in here,' I said.

'I've called someone about the locks,' he said. 'He'll be here in a minute. Don't worry. Do you want me to stay tonight?'

'You're supposed to be working, aren't you?'

'I can get out of it. I'll just have to keep my phone on in case something kicks off, alright?'

I nodded.

Later, hours later, the back door secured with a new lock, Lee was making love to me in my bed, gentle this time, taking it slowly. I was thinking about whoever it was, wondering if he'd been in here, in our bedroom. Wondering what else he'd touched.

He was so tender with me, so loving, that finally something he did distracted me away from the thought of the intruder, and I lost myself in the sensations of Lee's fingers and mouth.

When I finally opened my eyes he was watching my face, a smile on his lips. 'You should do that more often,' he murmured.

'Do what?'

'Let go.'

'Lee, don't go anywhere, will you?'

'I'm staying here. You can sleep if you want to.' He ran his fingers over my temple, down my cheek. 'Have you thought about what I asked you?'

I wondered if it was worth pretending not to know what he was talking about. 'I've thought about it,' I said.

'And?'

I opened my eyes and looked at him sleepily. 'Keep asking,' I said. 'One day I'll surprise you and I'll say yes.'

He smiled, and reached out and stroked my cheek, a long, soft touch that started with my face and ended on the side of my thigh. He told me he loved me, his voice barely a whisper. I loved him when he was like this, gentle, calm, happy.

Friday 28 December 2007

I was sick when I woke up this morning. I just about made it to the bathroom. I spent a few minutes beside the toilet, wondering if I'd eaten anything that had disagreed with me, or whether it was a delayed reaction to the amount of alcohol I'd drunk on Christmas Day.

It was when I was sitting there on the tiled floor, shivering, that I remembered. He was getting out today.

It was just past five, still dark outside. When I was able to get up I brushed my teeth and tried to get back into bed, but I didn't quite make it. My feet veered towards the door to the flat.

I knew it was locked, but I had to check nevertheless. As I checked it, six times, one-two-three-four-five-six, I told myself it was locked. I locked it last night. I remember locking it. I remember checking it. I remember checking it for fucking hours. Even so, it might not be locked, I might have made a mistake. What if I'd unlocked it again, without realising? What if something went wrong with the checking, and I wasn't paying attention.

Again. Start again from the beginning.

The feeling of him is strong today. I can smell him, feel him in the air. I remember how it felt, waiting for him to come back, knowing there was nothing at all I could do to get away, no point in running, no point in fighting. It was easier just to give up.

And now?

I finished the door, but it still felt wrong.

I'd have to start again. My feet were freezing, my skin goosebumps all over. I should have gone to get a jumper, some socks. It wasn't right, though. The door might as well have been standing wide open, with him on the other side of it, waiting. Waiting for me to make a mistake.

I checked again, concentrating, my breathing already starting to quicken, my heart thudding in my chest. I couldn't get beyond the image of him standing just on the other side of the door, waiting for me to stop checking, waiting for me to step away from it so he could take advantage of it.

This was bad, very bad. My phone was in the kitchen, Stuart was at work, and in any case I still hadn't seen him or spoken to him since *that* text . . . I couldn't leave the door, I couldn't even get as far as the bedroom.

Just once, I told myself sternly. Once more, and it will be fine. Once more and it will be safe to leave the door. I tried deep breathing, tried to snatch more than just gasps, tried to hold it, tried to think of Stuart's voice.

I finished one lot of checks and stopped.

I was starting to feel calmer, my breathing slowing. While I had the chance I went back to the bedroom, not looking at the curtains, crawling straight back into bed. My stomach was churning and I was shivering with the cold. My bedside clock said it was twenty past seven. Two hours, just on the door.

I got out of bed again and found some socks and my hooded fleece top, then went to the kitchen to put the heating back on.

I found my phone and rang the office. I'd not taken a day off sick since I'd started working there, but today was going to have to be the exception. There was no way I was going to be able to leave the house.

I managed to hold off the checking for half an hour, then I decided I needed to open the curtains and that started me off again. Fortunately I had to stop at eight to make the obligatory cup of tea.

I sat on the sofa with my cup of tea and picked up the book I'd been reading. It was one of the OCD books Stuart had recommended for me. One of the chapters recommended identifying all the compulsions, all the rules, and listing them in order of importance. I reached for my organiser and found a piece of paper and a pen.

It took a long time, a lot of careful thought, a lot of crossing out and starting again, but in the end my list looked like this:

COMPULSIONS
Checking the front door
Checking the windows and curtains
Checking the flat door
Checking the kitchen drawer

AVOIDANCE
Red clothes
The police
Crowded places

ORDERING
Tea times
Shopping on even days
Counting steps

The front door was to be the top one, without a doubt. It occurred to me that, since Stuart had moved in, it felt as if I'd managed to abdicate responsibility for the front door to him, somehow. I wondered if I could gradually work my way out of this pit by passing some of it onto his shoulders, and if that was somehow unfair.

I looked at the clock — half-past eight.

What time did prison releases happen? Would he be out by now? What would he look like? Would he still have money? Where would he go?

I closed my eyes and tried to think of something else.

How long would it be? How long until he found me? I tried to picture him coming out of prison, going somewhere, to a friend's house, maybe, Lord knows he probably still had plenty of them. Maybe he would find someone else, some other girl. Maybe he had been changed by his time inside. Maybe he wouldn't come looking for me at all.

Now I was just lying to myself.

He was going to come for me, it was only a question of time.

I only just made it to the bathroom in time, sick again. Nothing left in there but pain.

Tuesday 24 February 2004

The burglary changed a lot of things, for me. I never felt safe after that, even when Lee was with me. When he wasn't there, when I was out in town, or at work, or even just driving from home to work or back again, I kept feeling as though I was being watched. When I was at home, alone, it felt as though someone was in the house.

It didn't help that I kept finding more and more of my things missing. If it hadn't been for the burglary I might think I'd just mislaid them, but they were things I didn't use often and I was fairly sure where I'd left them: my passport, for one. It had been in an old satchel at the back of the wardrobe, along with a wallet containing euros, which was also missing. An old diary. I couldn't begin to think why that had been taken, but it had. My old mobile phone, which didn't even work — that had been on the bookshelf in the living room.

Each time felt almost like being burgled all over again.

Lee said it was common in burglaries like this. It was a tidy search, he said. Quite often people had no idea what had been taken. He said there had been several burglaries in my area over the past few months, and some people had been targeted more than once.

He stayed over every night he wasn't working, and sometimes turned up unexpectedly when he was, letting himself in and scaring me half to death. One night he came in filthy, wearing clothes that stank as though he'd been sleeping rough. He peeled them off in the living room, left them in a reeking pile, and went straight upstairs to shower.

When he came back down he was smelling a whole lot better, and looking much better, too. I made him dinner and afterwards he made love to me downstairs in the living room, gentle, tender, loving. He listened to me telling him pointless things about what had gone on at work, stroked my hair away from my flushed cheeks, kissed my sweaty forehead and told me I was the most beautiful thing he'd seen all week. After that he got dressed again, back into the same filthy clothes, and went back out into the night.

I had another two days without him, no sign, no word, no phone call, and then on the Tuesday I came home from work early. It felt as if someone had been in here again. I had no idea what it was that made me think that; the door was double-locked, the windows all secure and shut, but the house just felt different. I checked everything before I even took my coat off, looking for whatever it was that was out of place. Nothing, not a sign. Maybe I'd imagined it, whatever it was, this presence, the feeling that Lee had been here. Maybe it was wishful thinking.

I cooked dinner and phoned Sam afterwards for a chat. I watched something inane on television. I washed up the plate and the dishes and put everything away. I hummed along to the radio while I did it.

At a quarter to twelve I turned the television off and thought about bed. The house was suddenly achingly quiet with the noise gone. The central heating had gone off an hour ago and it was cold.

I checked the front door and the back door, turning the lights off as I went round. I pulled the curtains open a little in the front room and as I did so I thought I saw something outside: a shape, a shadow, across the road — next to the house that had been up for sale for months and months. A bulky shape, like a man, standing in the dark space between the front of the house and the garage.

I waited for it to move, for my eyes to adjust to the light and tell me what it was.

It didn't move and the more I squinted at it the more I seemed to remember that there was a bush there, a tree, something. It just looked strange in the dark.

I closed the living room door and turned on the landing light, heading wearily upstairs. I got myself undressed and put on some pyjamas, cleaned my teeth. Turned on the light by the bed and pulled back the covers.

That was it, then.

Lying under the duvet, glaringly colourful against the clean white sheet, was a picture, a photo.

I stared at it for a moment, my heart beating fast.

It was a printed digital photo, of me. I picked it up, my hand shaking so much that the image was blurred, even though I recognised it and knew exactly what it showed: me, naked, on this very bed, my legs splayed, my face flushed and strands of my hair sticking to my cheek, my eyes looking directly at the camera with a look of pure lust, pure seduction, naked desire.

He'd taken this picture on one of the first weekends we spent together; the same weekend we'd fought against the wind on the beach at Morecambe, the weekend he'd told me he loved me for the first time. We'd been messing around with the camera, taking pictures of each other. We'd had fun with them afterwards and he'd let me delete them off the memory card. Clearly not before he'd managed to make a copy.

For a moment I gazed into my own eyes, wondering about the person I'd been then, the person who'd wanted this so much. I looked so happy. I looked as if I was falling in love.

Whoever that person was, it wasn't me now. I tore the picture into tiny pieces, threw the pieces down the toilet and flushed. The little bits all floated happily to the surface again and danced around like confetti on the wind.

Wednesday 9 January 2008

Caroline was finally back at work today, after a long holiday with her kids. I saw her come in through the open door of my office. I was on the phone at the time; she waved a tanned hand in my direction.

'You're looking well,' I said, when I went to find her. 'Did you have a good time?'

'Fabulous,' she said. She was dressed from head to foot in a selection of autumn colours, from her russet hair to her tan to her evergreen skirt and a jacket the colour of a pile of bonfire leaves. 'It was hot every day, the kids had fun, I got to read four paperbacks with my feet up by the pool. And I met someone called Paolo.'

'No — really?'

'Yep, he was fabulous too.'

We went down to the canteen, even though she'd barely taken her coat off. 'I can't bear to think how many emails I've got,' she said. 'Has it been horrendous?'

'Not really. I think it's about to kick off next

week, though. The CEO's coming to talk about the new warehouse.'

Caroline groaned. 'I need chocolate.'

We sat with our teas by the window, looking out over an expanse of green landscaped lawn and some colourful shrubs.

'And how was your Christmas?' she said, pulling off a chunk of chocolate muffin.

'It was good, thanks.'

'Spent it with Stuart?'

'I had lunch with him — and his friend Alistair,' I added, before she had a chance to get excited.

'Just lunch?'

'Just lunch.'

She was giving me a long look.

'It all went a bit wrong,' I said.

'Wrong how?'

'I overheard his friend talking to him about me. It just freaked me a bit, that's all. I left in a bit of a hurry, I think he was offended. I haven't heard from him since.'

It had been two weeks. I assumed he was at home, going to work every day, but I hadn't seen him. He hadn't knocked on my door, or sent any texts. I wasn't surprised, really, after I ran out on him on Christmas Day — in fact I wouldn't have been surprised if he was looking for somewhere else to live. Who needs a crazy lady living downstairs, after all?

'I thought you were onto a winner there,' she said brightly.

'No,' I said. 'It's okay, though. I'd rather just get on with things by myself.'

Caroline patted my hand, leaving crumbs of muffin behind. 'I'm sure it's nothing,' she said. 'You know what men are like, they can be ridiculously oversensitive sometimes.'

I didn't answer for a moment, drank some tea. 'You haven't told me about Paolo yet,' I said. 'Was he young and impossibly handsome?'

'Oh, my God, I can't tell you. He was one of the waiters at the hotel. Really cheesy, but at least he was handy and I didn't have to leave the kids with my mother for more than an hour at a time. She thought I was going out with this other girl we met, Miranda. It was such a hoot.'

We went back up to the office half an hour later. I climbed the stairs, thinking about Stuart. Wishing it was home time.

Friday 27 February 2004

Friday night, nine o'clock, and Lee and I were out in town. Later, he'd promised me we could go to the Red Divine and meet up with the girls, who were all out too.

I'd never before looked forward to an evening and yet dreaded it so much in equal measure. I was finally going to get to see the inside of the Red Divine, I was going to spend a night dancing and laughing and talking to my friends, and at the same time Lee was going to be right by my side the whole time. I wanted to be with him — but just not tonight.

When we got to the club it was already gone eleven. Despite the queue which snaked almost to the corner of Bridge Street, the door supervisor caught sight of Lee and waved us through to the VIP entrance. On the way in there was a lot of handshaking and backslapping and general greeting between Lee and the five or six gorillas dressed in suits who were working on the door. I kept my mouth shut and stood dutifully to one side, freezing cold and shivering.

For some reason, there had been no argument about what I was going to wear tonight. I picked out a short black dress with thin straps and a diamanté detail around the hemline. He looked at it and said, 'You can wear that as long as you wear tights.' Fair enough, I thought, too cold to go without in any case.

I took off my jacket and checked it into the cloakroom. Lee had gone back to talk to someone else on the door, a shorter man with a beard who'd just arrived. I thought it might have been the owner; I'd seen his picture in the newspaper. Barry? Brian? Something like that.

I considered going through the mirrored doors beyond which all seemed to be noise and lights and warm air, find the girls, get a drink, start to relax without him, but I didn't think about that for long. I'd better wait.

After a while he came to get me, took me by the arm, gave me a kiss on the top of my cheek and steered me through those beautiful mirrored doors.

The club was large, several rooms with dance floors and bars tucked away in odd places, which meant that although it was huge, and full of people, it felt curiously intimate. A lot of the

245

church architecture remained, with some pews against the walls, arches leading from one area to another, and then, as Sylvia had said, a giant illuminated stained glass window overlooking one of the bars. Beyond this, the space suddenly opened into what would once have been the nave, with the DJ sited at the position of the altar. The room was filled with incredible sound and lights and people dancing; above their heads two trapeze swings trailed red silk fabric just out of reach, two dancers wearing red bodysuits and horns swinging backwards and forwards, impressively in time with the main beat. Around the top of this space balconies emerged through stone arches; people with drinks leaning over chrome railings watching the dancers below.

As we weaved between the throng of bodies, my chest thumping with the bass beat, I looked and looked for the girls. Lee didn't let go of my hand until we were at one of the quieter bars, where he bought us both a drink while I stood with my back to him, longing to go and find a space to dance, to relax.

I felt a tap on my shoulder — it was Claire, at last. I gave her a hug. 'It's great in here, isn't it?' she yelled in my ear.

'Yes, it is! Where's Louise?' I yelled back.

Claire shrugged and pointed vaguely in the direction of the main dance floor. 'Where's Lee?' she shouted.

I pointed behind me to the bar. He'd seen Claire and was making 'do you want a drink' hand signals.

She shook her head and held up a bottle with

a straw sticking out of the top of it. 'He's such a sweetie, isn't he?' she yelled in my ear.

A few moments later he came back with our drinks. I drank about half of mine quickly, handed the glass to Lee and took Claire's hand. 'You dancing?' I looked at him for permission. He wasn't smiling, but he didn't say anything either. I knew he'd be watching my every move.

Claire and I threaded our way through to the main dance floor. Dancing made me feel better. For a fraction of a moment, about two songs in, I even forgot that Lee was there. For a moment, I was back to being on my own, the way things were, when I could dance however I liked, talk to anyone, flirt, chat, drink until I could barely stand if that was what I felt like doing.

Then I took a glance up at the balconies and there he was, almost invisible in his dark suit in the shadowy alcove, just illuminated quickly by the lights and then plunged into blackness again. I would have preferred it if he'd been talking to someone, or looking generally around the room, or at least looking as if he was enjoying himself. But he was just staring — at me.

I gave him a smile which he didn't return. Maybe he wasn't looking at me at all.

I started to feel a little bit queasy.

Louise, who'd found us on the dance floor, was watching me. She took my arm and shouted something in my ear but I couldn't hear a word of it above the music.

But she didn't need to, because suddenly from behind someone had taken hold of my waist and started grinding provocatively against my back-side. I jumped half out of my skin and looked over my shoulder to see it was Darren, one of Louise's friends from work whom I'd had a brief fling with last year. He kissed me quickly somewhere above my ear and looked pleased to see me, but his smile died within moments when he saw my face.

I managed a smile and moved a little away from him and carried on dancing. Darren kept dancing near to us, which, given how packed the dance floor was now, was very close indeed. When I felt brave enough I chanced a glance up to the balcony.

He had gone.

For a moment I wondered if this was my chance. 'Lou,' I yelled, 'where's the toilet?'

'You what?' She cupped a hand behind her ear as though that would make any sort of difference.

I took her hand and started to pull her off the dance floor with me towards the edge, but I was a bit too late. From the throng of bodies pressed on me from all sides I suddenly felt a touch that was just a bit too intimate, an arm snaking round my body, one firm hand cupping my breast, pulling me backwards, warm breath on my neck, his tongue suddenly on my skin, his voice loud and still barely audible in my ear. 'Where are you off to?'

Louise's grip relaxed on my hand as the momentum of the dancers carried her back into the crowd, while I danced for a moment with my lover, still holding me from behind so I couldn't see his face. Despite the bodies all around I felt every part of his body against me, I knew it so well. I rested my head back onto his shoulder and with his free hand he swept my hair off my neck so he could kiss me, bite me. My long hair wrapped around his fist like a thick black rope, pulling my head back to expose more skin, until all I could see were the swirling lights moving across the vaulted ceiling far above, the swoosh back and forth of the twin trapezes making me feel as if I was spinning.

My knees started to give. He pulled me clear of the crowds, down a narrow corridor, into a dark corner. People walking backwards and forwards, shouting above the noise, laughing, ignoring us completely. He pressed me into the wall with his bulk, one hand cupping my cheek as he kissed me. His other hand holding both my wrists above my head, pressing me into the rough stone wall. I felt something digging into my skin and struggled against his grip. He pressed harder against my wrists. I didn't want to be kissed. I felt claustrophobic and panicky.

'Suck me off,' he said, his voice low into my throat.

'No,' I said, quietly so he couldn't hear.

He started trying to push me to my knees but I resisted. His hand was suddenly firm on my cheek, pulling me into the light from the other room.

'I don't feel well,' I shouted.

He looked at me doubtfully.

'I think I need to be sick,' I said.

He must have believed me because he led me

along the corridor to where the toilets were and let go of me, momentum stumbling me through the door.

It was surprisingly quiet in here, the music just a low pounding coming from a long way away. It was full of girls, crowded around the mirrors and the sinks, helping themselves to pump bottles of moisturiser despite the humid air.

The cubicle at the end was free and I stumbled into it, shutting the door and locking it. I sat down and cried. My legs were shaking. I folded myself down across my knees into a tight ball and sobbed and rocked myself.

Minutes passed, or maybe it was seconds. I wanted to be anywhere on the planet other than here. I pulled some toilet tissue out of the dispenser and wiped my cheeks, looking at the black mascara and eyeliner and the wet, looking at the way my hand holding it was shaking. What was wrong with me? When had this all started going so wrong?

'Catherine!' I heard Louise's voice shouting and then a knock on the cubicle door. 'You in there, honey? Let me in. Are you alright?'

I reached up and unlocked the door and she came in, saw my face and locked the door again behind her. She squatted down next to me in the toilet, took my hand in hers and held it, trying to stop the shaking. 'What is it, honey? What's the matter?'

'I just — I just don't feel well,' I said, sobbing all over again.

She wrapped me in her arms and I fell into a faceful of her hair. She smelt of perfume and hairspray and sweat. I loved her and wished she were Sylvia all at the same time.

'It's okay, it's okay,' she sang, rocking me gently. She got some more toilet tissue and wiped my face. 'You want me to get Lee? Get him to take you home?'

I shook my head so hard the cubicle spun around me. 'No,' I said, 'I'll be alright. I just need a minute.'

She pushed the hair back out of my face, trying to get me to look her in the eye. 'What's the matter, honey? You're not yourself, are you. What's up?'

'It's all going wrong,' I managed to say before the tears came back. 'I can't — I can't . . . any more.'

Another bang on the door. 'Lou? 'S me. Let me in.'

It was Claire. Louise unlocked the door and Claire came in too, just about managing to squeeze behind the door to shut it again. Three of us crammed into a cubicle meant for one. It had been a while. The thought that I was back here with my girlies made me manage a weak smile.

'See, that's better,' Claire said, 'you only needed me, didn't you, love? Louise, you're such a half-job. Come here, honey.' She elbowed Louise out of the way and enfolded me into her one hundred per cent natural and proud double-G cups until I quite literally couldn't breathe.

'Give over, she's choking, can't you tell?'

Eventually all three of us were almost having a

giggle. I'd stopped crying and I didn't even feel nauseous any more. We had a group hug, then we unlocked the door and all piled out again.

'We need some repairs,' Louise said, rooting through her tiny bag for emergency make up. They both scrutinised my wreck of a face.

'So what's up?' Claire said. 'You know you can tell us. Whatever it is, honey. We'll get through it, won't we?'

'It's — I don't know. I'm not sure. Work's been a bit shit. I'm just tired all the time. Not sleeping very well. You know . . . And Lee. I'm not sure about Lee.'

'What's these marks?'

Claire had my hands, and was looking at the red marks on my wrists in the cool light from overhead. Where he'd pressed me into the rough stonework there were some long scratches, little pinprick threads of blood.

'I don't know,' I said, 'must have scratched them somehow.'

Louise and Claire exchanged glances for a fraction of a second while I stood still and had eyeliner applied to my lower lids by Louise.

'There — just as beautiful as always,' she said after a moment, and spun me to the mirror.

For a moment I didn't recognise myself.

'Come on, Lee'll be wondering what we're doing in here,' Claire said. 'I told him I was only coming in to look for you.'

'He's waiting?' I asked.

'Yes, he's right outside. He came to find me. Said you were feeling sick.'

'Oh.' I hadn't moved.

'You're so lucky with him, Catherine,' Claire said, coming back to give me a hug. 'He's fucking gorgeous, and he obviously loves you so much. I wish I had someone like him.'

'He's . . . a bit intense. Sometimes,' I said.

The washroom was full of women again, suddenly, jostling around the sink, shouting at each other.

Louise kissed me on the cheek. 'Isn't he just what we've all always wanted? Someone who's going to look you right in the eye? Someone who is going to stand and wait outside the loos for you to come back? We're too fucking used to whatever the opposite of intense is, Catherine. We're too fucking used to blokes not giving a shit. You've got someone who doesn't just give a shit, you are completely and utterly his number one priority. The world doesn't exist for him outside you. Do you have any idea how amazing that is? To find a bloke like that?'

I had no answer for that, of course, but they didn't need one: they were already weaving through the spangles and heels and LBDs towards the door to where, as they'd said, he would be waiting.

I put on the best smile I could manage, one foot in front of the other, thinking about what might happen later and how I could minimise the damage.

Stuart and I were walking to the Tube. It was still so early it was only just getting light, the roads quiet because it was Saturday and we were both up and out of the house already.

'I thought you weren't talking to me,' I said at last, trying to keep up with him. My teeth were chattering.

'What?' he said. 'What gave you that idea?'

'I thought you were pissed off with me walking out on you on Christmas Day.'

'Oh, that. Not really. I'd probably just had too much wine. Anyway, that was ages ago.'

He'd sent me a text last night, the first one since the *whatever*.

C — any plans for tomorrow? If not I'm taking you out.
Be ready at 7am. S x

Half an hour later we were at Victoria Station looking up at the electronic board. I was wrapped in Stuart's huge jacket, the one that looked as though it was supposed to be for exploring the Arctic, because it was still below freezing and I couldn't seem to warm up. The bottom of the jacket finished just above my knees. I must have looked like a kid, but at least I'd stopped shivering. He'd put a beanie hat on me as well, and some fleece gloves.

At least it was getting light, weak winter sun outside, skimming the underside of the dark grey clouds. The station was still quiet this early on a

Saturday, just a few tourists and brave pigeons snacking on bits of pastry, and a lone cleaner driving a bleeping floor polisher. I watched him for a while. He seemed to be deliberately driving it at people who were standing looking up at the giant board, waiting for information, making them pick up all their bags and move.

'Platform fourteen,' Stuart said, 'come on.'

The train was warm. We fell into opposite seats and then almost immediately I had to unwrap myself from the huge jacket, pull off the hat. I got down to my fleece underneath and Stuart stuffed the jacket into the space overhead.

'I'm probably going to end up carrying that jacket around all day, aren't I?' I said.

'No, you wait. It'll be windy. You'll be glad you brought it.'

He was right, of course. It was cold and draughty in the station at Brighton, but as we walked down the hill towards the sea the wind got stronger and stronger. By the time we got to the seafront I was even pulling the hood up over the top of the woolly hat, and Stuart was holding my hand tightly in case I blew away. The sea was grey and furious, a white wind of spray and foam stinging our cheeks. We stood for a while clutching on to the blue-painted railings separating us from the shingle and the turmoil beyond, and felt the force of it.

Stuart said something that I couldn't hear, the words snatched out of his mouth and carried away. Then he took my hand and we went back towards the shelter of the back streets.

It was still early, but even so the shops were

busy with people looking for January bargains. I pulled Stuart into a camping shop and bought another hat, a smaller navy blue one that came with free gloves, so that Stuart could have his back. We walked around for a while, then found our way into the Laines. It was still busy here, busier in fact because of the narrower spaces between the shops, but the wind wasn't so fierce, the atmosphere was more relaxed.

But I was expecting to see Lee.

I'd already had a few moments: a man who passed us on the train, bulky blue jacket, blond hair at the top — I never saw his face, but the shape of him was enough to give me a start; as we stood facing the gale on the seafront a man and a woman walking a dog, an Alsatian, along the promenade. It couldn't possibly have been him, a woman and a dog for heaven's sake, but even so it made me feel ill.

It was getting towards ten o'clock — time for tea. We found a café, in the Laines, just off a small square where a busker played into the cold air, fingerless gloves on an acoustic guitar, a rock voice without drums or a band to support him. We had a cafetière and a pot of tea between us, a small table of dark wood with wooden seats, tucked into a snug corner. Then a man came in, passed our table and walked towards the back of the café. I shrank back into my seat, turned my head.

'What?' Stuart said. 'What is it?'

I recovered myself. 'I'm sorry. It's nothing. What were you saying?'

'That man?' he asked, lowering his voice.

I nodded. 'It's fine, honestly. Sorry.'

'What was his name?' Stuart asked.

I didn't say it for a moment. I looked away, tried to work out if I was ready for this, ready to share. He didn't stop looking at me, his gaze steady, unflinching. He wasn't going to leave it. He wasn't going to rush me, either, but he wasn't going to leave it be.

'Lee,' I said. 'His name's Lee.'

He nodded. 'Lee. You think you see him.'

'Yes.' I was looking at my hand, in my lap, the nails digging into my palm.

'It's okay,' he said. 'It's all part of it, the healing.'

'I saw him even when he was still inside. It's why I don't go out much.'

He smiled at me. 'You need to let these thoughts come,' he said. 'Don't fight them. Just let them come, accept them, don't feel guilty or bad. It's all part of it. Fighting against them will make it all harder.'

He looked over my shoulder at the man I'd seen. 'He's reading the paper,' he said. 'Why don't you take a look?'

For a moment I looked at Stuart as if he'd gone completely mad. His expression didn't change. 'I'm here,' he said. 'You're safe. Have a look, go on.'

Not quite believing that I was actually doing this, I turned and peered around the edge of the wall towards the back of the café: more dark wood tables, couples having lunch just like us, a family with two children eating ice creams of all things, and right at the back, a fair-haired man

257

with a steaming cup in front of him, reading a copy of the *Daily Express*.

My breath caught in my throat and my instinct was to turn, to hide. But I kept looking. It wasn't him. I already knew it wasn't him, but it hadn't stopped the fear, the sudden panic. Now I could see it wasn't him — he was older, his hair was more grey than blond, the skin around his eyes wrinkled, his face thinner. He wasn't as bulky as Lee, in fact without his jacket this man was slender.

He felt the force of my stare and looked up from his paper. There was a moment of eye contact and he smiled. He actually smiled at me. And then there was suddenly no resemblance to Lee at all, and he was just a stranger, a friendly man who was enjoying a coffee and smiling at me.

I smiled back.

'Better?' said Stuart, when I sat back in my chair.

'Yes,' I said.

'You can do this, you know,' he said. 'You're braver than you think you are.'

'Maybe,' I said, drinking my tea. It was warm and delicious.

I was still smiling when we went out of the café back into the Laines. The sun was shining, weakly, but it cheered everything up. We walked back down towards the pier.

The wind had dropped a little but it was still gusty on the pier. We sat in a shelter on the quiet side, watching the waves and the gulls trying to balance on the railings. Out at sea the clouds were black and immense, behind us the sun making everything bright and shiny, reflecting off the wet planks with glistening brilliance.

'Bit breezy, innit?' an old chap said to me. His hat was pulled down low over his ears, fluffy tufts of grey hair waving madly. His glasses were flecked with spray from the waves.

'Just a bit,' I agreed.

He was holding tightly to his wife's hand. Their hands were old, the skin spotted and wrinkled, his wife's wedding ring worn paper-thin and loose behind the big knuckles. She had rosy cheeks and blue eyes, a patterned headscarf keeping her hair neat and her ears warm. He chuckled and pointed as a juvenile gull, all brown spots and huge webbed feet, blew off the railings and took flight, swooping madly and fighting against the wind.

We carried on walking as far as we could go. The fairground rides were mostly closed, tarpaulins flapping and seats wet. Walking down the other side of the pier was madness — the wind whipping our jeans around our legs, the spray like horizontal rain. The ghost of the West Pier floated on the surface of the rolling sea like the bones of some long-dead sea monster.

We crossed back to the other side and walked back to the seafront, into a steaming fish and chip shop full of people in damp coats, laughing about the wind. We had a big portion of chips out of the wrapper and sat on a wall outside, eating chips with our fingers and listening to the gulls shrieking and calling around us, waiting for us to drop one. I was half-expecting one of them to actually snatch a chip from my fingers.

I was listening to Stuart telling me stories about seaside trips he'd had as a child, penny arcades at the end of the pier, sunburned legs and fishing nets on bamboo poles.

'What happened to your parents?' I asked.

'My mum died of cancer when I was fifteen,' he said. 'Dad lives near Rachel. He's alright — getting on a bit. I saw him a couple of months ago, briefly. I'm going to see them next month, I've got a few days off work.'

'Rachel's your sister?'

'Yes. Older and much wiser. What about your mum and dad?'

'They died in a car accident. I was at university.'

'That must have been tough. I'm sorry.'

I nodded.

'No brothers or sisters?'

'Just me.'

We were down to the last few chips, the rock-like bits at the bottom. Ignoring the signs about not feeding the seagulls, Stuart emptied the last few into the gutter and put the wrapping in a wheelie bin.

'I feel like booking a holiday,' he said, as we walked back up the hill towards the town centre. 'Let's go and find some brochures.'

He took me straight home, which was both good and bad. I didn't even know what it was I wanted any more.

We didn't speak all the way home in the cab, even though he was holding my hand, gently but firmly. I kept my eyes focused out of the window, looking but not seeing as the raindrops chased their way across the window, sparkling like orange jewels in the light from the streetlamps.

He took my keys and opened the front door for me, standing to one side and letting me go first. I didn't sit down, and neither did he. I caught a glimpse of his face, and to my surprise he looked so broken that I couldn't look at him again.

'I think we should cool it a bit,' I said. As soon as the words were out of my mouth I felt a flood of relief.

'What?'

'I said — '

'I heard what you said. I'm just not sure I believe it. Why?'

'I just feel — I just think I need a bit of space. I want to go out with my friends more. I want some time to myself. To think.'

I sat down then, perched on the edge of the sofa, knees pressed tightly together. I could feel the tension in the air rising like a tide.

'You get lots of time to yourself when I'm at work.'

'I know,' I said, 'and I like it. I don't like coming home and finding you've been in here while I've been out. I want you to give me my spare key back.'

'Don't you trust me?'

'I just like my own space. I like to know where everything is.'

'What the fuck's that got to do with anything?'

'You coming in here when I'm out. Leaving me messages. Leaving that picture of me under the duvet.'

'I thought you'd like that. Don't you remember what happened when I took that picture? What we were doing? I remember it. I think about it all the time.'

'I remember you telling me you'd deleted it. You obviously didn't.'

He didn't answer.

'I've been scared, Lee. Since the burglary. I don't like you coming in here when I'm not at home. It's as though my house isn't mine any more.'

There was a pause. I could see him in my peripheral vision, standing to my left by the door. He hadn't moved a muscle, he'd not taken his coat off. He was like a solid shadow, a black ghost, a nightmare.

'You want to go back to shagging anyone and everyone,' he said, his voice like ice. 'You want to go back to that.'

'No,' I said. 'I just want a bit of space, that's all. I don't want to see anyone apart from my friends. I just want to — think. To be sure that this is right.'

He took a step forward then, suddenly, and I think I must have flinched or something because when I looked up at him he'd frozen again. His face looked calm, impassive, but his eyes were raging. Without another word he took a step back again, out of the door. I heard the front door open and shut again with a soft click.

He was gone.

I sat motionless for a moment, waiting for something to happen. I don't know what I was expecting. Maybe I thought he was going to come back. Maybe he was going to come back and hit me, or throw something at me, or yell and swear.

Eventually I got up, went upstairs and got changed out of that stupid black dress with its stupid sparkly bits that I'd already decided I was never going to wear again. It was going in the first charity bag that came through the door, no matter what it had cost me to buy. Along with the red one. I wanted to be rid of them both.

It was hours later, when I was lying in bed still wide awake wondering what on earth had just happened, how it had happened, that I realised that he hadn't given me my key back.

Monday 14 January 2008

Caroline and I were on our way to Windsor for a meeting with the senior management team. She was supposed to be talking about budgets, and I was there to present the recruitment plans for the new warehouse that was opening in the new year. Caroline was driving and chattering on about work as we sped along the M4. I was exhausted, my throat sore.

Going out of the office is never a good thing for me. It upsets my routine. Already I was planning the checks for when I got home, telling myself that I would have to do it right, do it properly, so that I didn't end up doing it all sodding night again, making a racket that Stuart could hear through the floorboards.

'You look worn out, love,' she said then.

'Do I?'

'Late night, was it?'

'Not really. I think I'm getting a cold or something.'

I went back to gazing out of the window. If only I could sleep, just for a few minutes, I would feel better.

'How's things going with that lovely man upstairs?'

'Oh. Well, he's still talking to me after all, it seems. He took me out for the day.'

'That sounds promising.'

'It was nice.'

'You don't sound sure.'

'We're just friends, Caroline,' I said.

'Bollocks you are,' she replied.

I laughed, in spite of myself. 'He's not up for anything else, I'm telling you.'

'I wish you'd stop bloody pacing around each other and just get on with it,' she said.

'Look,' I said, 'nothing is going to happen. If it was going to happen, it would have done by now. I do like him, at least I think I do. But I prefer being on my own.'

'Don't you get lonely sometimes?'

'No.'

'Oh, I do. Since Ian left — it's miserable really. I try to hold it all together for the kids, but you know, when they go to their dad's at the weekends, the house is so quiet. I was thinking of joining a club, or something. What do you reckon?'

'You mean like a singles thing? A dating agency?'

Her cheeks were pink. 'Well, why not? It's not easy meeting nice blokes, is it? I was kind of hoping — maybe . . . '

'Maybe what?'

'Maybe you'd come with me?'

I stared at the side of her head while she kept her eyes on the road, her fingers gripping the steering wheel. I tried to think of something to say.

'We're here,' she said, pulling into the car park. 'Are you ready to face the lions?'

Friday 12 March 2004

For the first few days I felt curiously empty, hollow, as though I'd done something immense and it hadn't sunk in properly. At the same time I felt afraid. I double-locked the front door as soon as I came in every night. I looked for signs that he'd been in the house as soon as I came home, but nothing had been moved or changed. At least, nothing that I could put my finger on.

I thought it had all been easy — I thought that he'd seen sense, maybe he'd not been as bad as I thought, and I found myself thinking that maybe I'd made a mistake; he was great in bed, able to make every time we had sex different, exciting. I considered texting him and asking him to come back, but in the end I just put my phone in my bag, out of sight, and left it there.

I didn't see him for two weeks after that night. I had been crying at night, missing him, in a bizarre sort of way. It was my problem, I realised, I was the one who was a complete commitment-phobe — no wonder he'd found it hard to be with me. No wonder he'd left and not looked back. I sent him a couple of texts but they remained unanswered. When I rang his mobile it went straight to voicemail.

Two weeks after he'd gone, I had a phone call from Claire.

I was at work, in the middle of completing a presentation that needed to be done ready for the afternoon, and suddenly Claire was on the phone. Her voice was strange, tight. She asked me how I was.

'I'm okay, love. Are you okay?'

'I just think you've made a huge mistake, that's all.' I could hear tears, somewhere not too far away, although she was fighting to keep her composure.

'A mistake? What do you mean?'

'With Lee. He told me you'd finished with him. I couldn't believe it. Why on earth would you want to do that?'

I was about to say something, but she didn't give me time to get a word in.

'He told me he was going to take you away on

266

holiday. He said he was so looking forward to it, how you've changed his life, how you made him happy when he thought he'd never be happy again. Do you know about his last girlfriend, Catherine? Did he tell you about Naomi? Do you know she killed herself? She left a note asking him to meet her and made sure it was him that found her. He's never got over it. He told me he still has nightmares about seeing her body. And then he told me that you'd ended it with him, told him you wanted to go out and start seeing people again — how could you do that, Catherine, how could you do that to him?'

'Wait, Claire — it wasn't like that — '

'Do you have any idea,' she continued, and she was crying now, gasping in between words, struggling to get them out; I could picture her perfectly, her beautiful complexion mottled with fury, fat tears running unchecked down her cheeks, 'do you have *any* idea at all how unfair all this is? I would give anything to have a man like Lee. I would give anything at all, anything in the world, to have someone be as devoted to me as he is to you. He *loves* you, Catherine, he loves you more than anything. You have absolutely fucking everything in the world, and you're just throwing it all away, and — and — breaking his heart in the process. I can't bear it.'

'It's not like that, really,' I said at last.

She'd finally run out of things to say, just the odd sob and endless sniffing. At least she hadn't hung up.

'You don't know what it's like with him. He follows me around. He lets himself into the house when I'm not here . . . '

'You gave him a *key*, Catherine. Why would you give him a fucking key if you only wanted him to go in the house when you were already inside it?'

I didn't have an answer for that. Even I knew it didn't sound bad, put like that.

'Do you know what makes it all worse? Even after what you've done to him, even after you've broken his heart, he's still completely madly in love with you. He told me all about all the things you said to him, and straight after that he said if I saw you I was to ask you if you'd go and see him. He's back working at the River. He said he wanted to see you, to check you're alright. He said he wasn't going to come to the house because you'd asked him not to. So, you going to go?'

I told her I'd think about it.

Clearly that had been more or less what she'd been expecting, because she gave me a final shot of, 'I still can't believe what you've done, I hope you're proud of yourself,' and hung up.

I cried after that, shutting the office door and hoping to God nobody would come in. Claire had never spoken to me like that before. She was a loyal friend, someone who understood that mates always came before blokes, that whatever a bloke said to you was not usually to be relied on, especially not when a bloke was bad-mouthing a friend.

I went through the rest of the day in a haze of misery. I finished my presentation as quickly as I could and delivered it without any real thought or enthusiasm. Claire's words spun round and round in my mind. I must have been really wrong, for her to talk to me like that. I thought about what she'd said, about how unhappy he was without me, how much he loved me. I thought about his last girlfriend, this Naomi — he'd never mentioned her name again after that one whisper in the middle of the night — and about why he'd chosen to talk to Claire about her, and not me. And I thought that he must have been through such a lot of misery, and how he'd been *happy*. How I'd made him happy.

I left work as soon as the presentation was finished, telling them I had a headache, which was the truth. I went home and cried some more, thinking about Claire and how I couldn't afford to lose one of my dearest friends, one of my oldest friends. Later, when I'd been lying in bed for hours, thinking about it all, I got out of my pyjamas and into the red dress. It didn't fit me as well as it had done last time I'd worn it — it was baggy around the waist and the chest, as though some large person had stretched it when I wasn't looking. But I wore it anyway. Slapped on some make-up, and went to the River looking for him.

What I really wanted, despite everything, was a repeat performance of that time when he'd fucked me in the office at the River. I wanted him to look at me as though I was the most perfect creature he'd ever laid eyes on, I wanted him to take me by the hand and haul me down the corridor to the office, as though he couldn't

269

wait another second to get inside me.

He was laughing and joking with Terry, the door supervisor, when I walked past the queue of people and up to the VIP entrance. My chest tightened when I saw him, short blond hair cropped close to his head, still improbably tanned despite the cold and the rain; that dark suit, well-cut, defining the muscles and the shape of his taut body.

'Hi,' I said.

'Catherine. What are you doing here?' he asked. He was trying to sound cold, but already I'd seen the reaction in his eyes.

'I was hoping you might let me in so I could join my friends,' I said, giving him a smile and a barely perceptible wink.

Terry came over. 'Sorry, love, it's packed in there tonight. You'll have to queue like everyone else.'

I wasn't about to be joining the ranks of the queuing public. 'It's okay,' I said, 'I'll go somewhere else instead.' I gave Lee one last lingering look, and walked in the direction of the town centre.

In fact I found the nearest taxi and went straight home. Sure enough, at three in the morning, I heard him knocking at the door.

'Why didn't you use your key?' I said as I opened the door. I didn't get time to ask anything else, and he wasn't going to reply.

He took my upper arms and pushed me backwards into the living room, not bothering to turn the lights on, not bothering to shut the front door behind him. He was breathing hard, and

270

when I touched his face it was wet. I kissed him, licking the tears away from his cheeks. He let out a rasping sob and devoured my mouth, kissing me so hard I could taste blood. With a grunt he gave me an almighty shove which sent me sprawling onto the sofa, and before I could say anything else he'd pulled my pyjama bottoms off, undone his suit trousers so quickly and clumsily that I heard the button ping off. I just had time to think, this is going to hurt, and then he was fucking me. When he pushed into me, I cried out.

Did I say no? Not that time. Did he rape me? Not really, not that time. After all, I'd opened the door to him. Earlier in the evening I'd been to the nightclub with the intention of getting him to fuck me. Now he was fucking me, and I didn't feel I had any right to complain about it.

But it hurt. The inside of my lip was cut from where his mouth had invaded mine; the next day I was so sore I could barely walk. But he was back, at least for a few hours; when I woke up the next morning, he'd already gone.

Wednesday 23 January 2008

It's time to refocus.

I had my assessment today, and it felt as if I've turned some kind of corner with this.

The Community Mental Health Team was based in Leonie Hobbs House, in the next street to Willow Road. It was a normal-looking house from the front, not unlike ours — imposing bay windows and a front door in need of a lick of paint. There was a brass sign on the gatepost and posters in the front windows advertising everything from Smoking Cessation Clinics to a Self Help Group for Post Natal Depression.

It was raining outside, which made the whole place look grimmer than it might have otherwise. The windows looked as though they were crying.

I pushed open the door and the hallway held a reception desk and some stairs going up to the first floor. Behind the reception desk the former front room of the house was crammed with desks and women, shuffling paper from one tray to another, talking and sipping from mugs. The walls were covered with posters. If you'd come for information about something in particular you wouldn't have had a hope of finding it.

'I've got an appointment for an assessment,' I said to the woman at the reception desk.

'That'll be upstairs. That's not a local accent, is it? Where are you from?'

She must have been in her late forties, long grey hair in a big plait down her back, wisps of it in a cloud around her face. 'The north,' I said. Usually I said this to anyone in London and they accepted it without question, as though the north was a single amorphous blob which began somewhere beyond the Toddington Services.

This woman was going to be an exception.

'You're from Lancaster,' she said, fortunately not waiting for my response. 'I lived there for twenty years. Then I moved down here. Better pay, but the people aren't as nice.'

I glanced into the crowded room behind her

and the six or seven ladies sitting tight-lipped listening to every word.

I climbed the stairs. At the top a dog-eared piece of paper with the words 'CMHT turn left' helpfully written in black marker was taped to the wall. Along a short corridor to the left I found another reception area, this one freshly painted in comforting shades of beige and mushroom. There was nobody behind the desk, so I sat on one of the comfy chairs and waited. I was early for the appointment.

A woman came out of a door to the right. She was dressed in a loose top and jeans, her hair tied in two bunches either side of her head that stuck straight out. She had a lip ring and a beautiful smile full of even white teeth.

'Hi,' she said. 'Would you be Cathy Bailey, by any chance?'

'Yes,' I said.

'He'll be ready in a minute. I'm Deb, one of the CPNs,' said the woman. She was still smiling. 'Did you bring your questionnaires ?'

'Oh — yes . . . ' I rooted around in my bag.

Deb took them off me. 'Saves time when you're in there, you know.'

I waited. From down the corridor, out of sight, came the sound of a door opening and footsteps getting closer and closer until a man's head appeared around the corner. 'Cathy Bailey?'

I got to my feet and followed him. I kept thinking about Stuart. I thought about him all the way through the questions the consultant psychiatrist asked. Dr Lionel Parry, his name was. He looked like a roughly shaved badger, a grey and black beard morphing seamlessly into grey and black hair at the sides of his head and growing copiously out of his ears. When he asked me how much time it took me to check the door, how much time it took to check the windows, the drawers, everything else, I thought about lying. It feels so goddamn stupid, checking the doors. I know it doesn't make sense. But I can't stop myself doing it.

So I told the truth. Sometimes it's hours. Sometimes, I'm hours late for work and I have to stay late to make up for it. Social life? Don't make me laugh. It's a good job I don't actually want to go out in the evenings, isn't it?

After that he asked me about Lee. I told him about the flashbacks, the sudden thoughts, like flashes of memory, of things he'd done. Things I'd tried to forget about. And all the rest of it. The nightmares, the panic attacks, the lying awake at four in the morning too scared to go back to sleep again. The things I try to avoid: social events, crowded places, the police, red clothes.

He listened and wrote notes and looked at me from time to time.

I was shaking.

I wasn't crying, not yet; talking about it was just making me feel shaky.

'I've been trying deep breathing,' I said, in a rush. 'I've been trying to control the panic. It works sometimes.'

'That's good,' he said. 'Then you already know that you are in charge of this. If you can control the panic sometimes, then it's just going to take practice and a few other techniques until you can control it all the time. You've made a start, you've done really well.'

'Thanks. It was Stuart, really, not me.'

'Stuart?'

'A friend. He's a psychologist.'

'He might have pointed you in the right direction, but you made the choice that you were going to try to control your panic. Nobody could have done that except you.'

'I guess not.'

'And don't forget, if you've done that already, it means you can do more. This means that you should be able to bring your checking under control too. It won't happen straight away, it will take time, but you can do it.'

'So what happens next?'

'I'm going to refer you for some cognitive behavioural therapy. In addition to that, I think you should try some medication to help with the panic attacks. They take a while to kick in, though, so don't be concerned if you don't feel the benefit straight away. You need to give it a good few weeks.'

'I tried drugs before. I'd rather avoid them if I can.'

'I've had a look at your notes, and the drugs they gave you in the hospital were different. These ones won't make you feel drowsy or spaced out. I'd like you to try them because your assessment indicates that there may be some elements of post-traumatic stress disorder, or PTSD, as well as obsessive compulsive disorder.'

'Stuart said it would be good if I could be referred to Dr Alistair Hodge.'

'Yes, I was going to suggest that. He does a clinic here, or one at the Maudsley. You'll get a letter and then you'll need to give his secretary a ring. You should be able to get to see him quite quickly, I expect. In the meantime, I'll get Deb to give you the numbers for the Crisis Team, in case you need them. But I doubt you will.'

'How long do you think it will take? To get better?'

He shrugged. 'That's very difficult to judge. Everyone is different. But you should be able to see some positive effects within a few sessions. You have to be prepared to put in some work with it — it's like a lot of things in life: the more you put in, the more you get out.'

When I finally got back out into the street, it was dark. The rain had stopped at last. The traffic outside was at a standstill, probably some accident on the North Circular jamming everything up. The buses were relatively free as far as the bus lanes went, but they weren't going to go anywhere fast.

I felt as if I'd turned some sort of corner, as though there was absolutely no turning back. It had been this that had frightened me the most, after the hospital; after being so out of control, so completely in the hands of strangers I neither liked nor trusted, having to follow their timetable and their instructions, being told when to eat and when to sleep and when to go to the toilet.

Once I'd got out of the hospital the second time, I knew I'd die before going back there. I

276

moved from Lancaster, with a bright vapid smile and empty promises of engaging with the local mental health services as soon as I could. I moved away from the doctors and the nurses and social services and the terrifying system which made no sense to me. It had served its purpose. It had hauled me to my feet and pointed out rather bluntly that, actually, I hadn't died at all, I was still very much here and I'd better pull myself together and get on with it. Not for the first time, I thought that it would have been kinder if I *had* died, rather than going through the process of recovering. But moving away made me realise that, if anyone was going to be in control of my life, it had to be me. There was no alternative. I took control, I controlled every moment of my day, timing things to the second, counting my steps, planning my cups of tea; it gave me purpose, gave me a reason to put one foot in front of the other every single day no matter how shitty, no matter how grim, no matter how lonely.

I don't want to give that up. It makes me feel safe, if only for a while.

Tuesday 16 March 2004

My mobile phone ringing made me jump. I'd been sitting waiting for something to happen, waiting for him to come back, waiting for him to ring, hoping for it and dreading it at the same time. But the name on the display wasn't Lee; it was *Sylv Mob*.

'Sylvia?' I said, trying to sound as cheerful as I possibly could. 'How the devil are you?'

'I'm fine, honey. How are you doing?'

'I'm okay. How's London?'

'How are you really?'

I couldn't reply for a moment, holding the phone tightly, looking at a spot on the wall, trying to concentrate really, really hard on not breaking down. 'I'm okay,' I said again.

'Louise says you've gone a bit funny. She's worried about you.'

'Funny? I've not gone funny at all. What's that supposed to mean?'

Her voice was curiously calm and, for Sylvia, soothing. 'Doesn't mean anything, she's just worried about you. She said you had marks on your arms. She said you went out with them last month and then went home again after half an hour. And Claire said she had Lee crying on her shoulder the other day — you'd had a row or something.'

When I didn't answer, she said, 'Hello? Catherine?'

'I'm still here.'

'Do you want me to come home, darling? I could make it at the weekend, maybe, for a day?'

'No, no. Honestly. I'm fine. It's just — things aren't going so well with Lee.'

'What's been going on?'

'He's — he . . . Sylv, he just scares me sometimes. He pushes me around a bit. I don't like it.'

There was a long, long pause. I'd done it. I'd admitted that my perfect relationship with my

278

perfect man wasn't as perfect as they all thought it was. And now everything was going to be alright, because Sylvia knew, Sylvia would have exactly the right words to say to make it better, my best friend in the whole world. I waited for her to say something sympathetic, I waited for her to tell me to dump him, get out of the relationship, tell him to fuck off using those exact words and run, and not look back. Ever.

When she next spoke I was so shocked that, for a moment, I forgot to breathe.

'Catherine, I think maybe you should see someone.'

'What . . . ?'

'You've been through a really rough time lately, lots of stress at work, lots of pressure, haven't you?'

I didn't answer. I couldn't believe what I was hearing.

'I know Louise is worried about you. We all are. Lee's worried about you too. I think you should go and talk to someone — your doctor? Or maybe someone at work?'

'Wait,' I said, 'Lee's worried about me?'

She hesitated. 'Darling, he loves you. He thinks you're just missing me, or something, but it's more than that, I know it is. He says you've been hurting yourself. You've been hurting your arms. Please don't get upset, my darling, I don't want to upset you when I'm so far away and I can't do anything about it . . .'

I heard my voice rising into some high-pitched note of hysteria. 'Sylvia! He's fucking frightening me. He tells me what to wear. He tells me when I'm allowed to go out. No matter how you try and dress it up, that isn't a fucking normal relationship!'

She was silent, then.

'Whatever it is he told you, it's not fucking true, alright?'

'Don't get upset, Catherine, please, I — '

'Don't get upset?' I echoed. 'What the fuck do you expect me to say? Since when did you and Lee start talking to each other on the phone, anyway?'

'He spoke to Louise, she told him she was worried about you. Louise rang me last night and then Lee rang me too. We're all just worried sick about you, C. You're acting really strangely and we all just want you back to your normal self again . . . '

'I don't believe I'm hearing this. This cannot be happening.'

'Listen, darling, Lee says he's trying everything to make sure you're alright, but I still think you'd be better if you saw someone. Listen to me, Catherine. I want you to get some help with this. Do you want me to try and find you some numbers?'

I removed the phone from my ear and stared at it for a moment with a fascinated horror, and then pressed the 'end' button and threw it with all my strength at the wall. It broke into at least three pieces, the main part lying on my carpet making a faint, strange high note like an animal in pain.

I put my hand against my mouth to stop — what? A scream? There was nobody left now. Nobody at all. It was just him, and me.

The bus crawled through the evening traffic. It was dark but the city was bright: shop windows, streetlights, traffic lights, the glare everywhere reflecting off the wet rainy streets. Inside the bus was warm and damp, the windows steamy, the smell of hundreds of people and grubby upholstery.

I don't like using the phone on the bus, but I was desperate to talk to him. I kept my voice low.

'Hi, it's me.'

His voice sounded a long, long way away. 'How did it go?'

'It was fine. Well, it was difficult too. But I did it. He's going to refer me to Alistair. And he gave me some tablets.'

'What are they?'

'I don't know, the prescription's in my bag. He said they were an SS-something.'

'SSRI. Selective Serotonin Reuptake Inhibitor.'

'Whatever. He said he thought I had post-traumatic stress disorder as well as OCD.'

'That's good.'

'Is it?'

'I meant it's good that he thought that. I thought it too. But it's not my place to assess you.'

'No. How's work?'

'It was okay, I guess. It's over with, anyway.'

The man across the aisle was staring at me. He didn't look remotely like Lee, but he unsettled me nonetheless. He was young, with lank hair chopped roughly around his ears, scabs on his mouth and nose. Hollow eyes with dark circles under them, staring at me.

At the next stop a few more people got off, and I contemplated leaving the bus and walking the rest of the way. The man across the aisle stood up too and I thought he was getting off, so I stayed where I was. Instead he stood in the aisle for a moment until the bus started moving again, and then sat in the seat in front of mine.

He was giving off a smell, mildewed, like clothes that had been left damp in the washing machine for a couple of days. There were spots on the back of his neck and every few seconds he sniffed — not clearing his nose, but as though he was scenting the air.

At the next stop I got off the bus. I thought he was going to follow me, but instead he stayed on. I stood at the bus stop in the rain and watched the bus move on, saw him through the window, those eyes, still staring.

Friday 19 March 2004

I stopped at the post office in town on the way home and picked up some passport forms. I had a browse around the shops while I was there, looking at clothes, but not bothering to try anything on. I just didn't feel like going home, not yet. Lee was working today, I hadn't had a text or a phone call since last night.

When I opened the front door I had that same immediate sense that something wasn't right. It wasn't a draught, or a smell, or anything tangible. The driveway just had my car on it, and there was no sign of Lee's car or any other car for that matter. I just knew that someone had been in the house while I'd been out.

I stood there on the mat for a moment, the door still open behind me, wondering if I should go inside or if I should just get in my car and drive away again. The hallway was empty, I could see all the way down to the kitchen at the back — everything was as I had left it.

This is stupid, I told myself. Nobody's been in here, it's just your fertile imagination and that bastard burglar.

I put my keys and my bag down in the kitchen and went through to the living room, and stopped dead. Lee was sitting on the sofa, watching television with the sound muted.

I gasped with shock. 'Jesus, you scared the life out of me!'

He stood up then and came towards me. 'Where the fuck have you been?'

'In town,' I said. 'I went to the post office. Don't talk to me like that, anyway, what's it matter where I've been?'

'You went to the post office for two fucking hours?'

He was standing inches away from me. I could feel the heat of his body, like the force of his anger. His hands were hanging relaxed by his sides, his voice was even.

Nevertheless, I was afraid.

'If you're going to speak to me like that I'm

going out again,' I said, and turned my back on him.

I felt his fingers circle my upper arm and he pulled me round with such force that my feet left the floor. 'Do not walk away from me,' he said into my face, his breath hot on my cheek.

'I'm sorry,' I muttered.

He let me go and I stumbled against the doorway. The instant he moved away from me I ran, bolted for the front door, never mind that my keys were in the kitchen — I had to get out, I had to run.

I never made it. He was at the front door before me and before I had any idea what was happening his fist made contact with the side of my face, the corner of my eye.

I was on the floor, by the stairs. He was standing over me, looking down. I was so shocked I couldn't catch my breath, sobbing and touching my cheek to see if I was bleeding. Then he crouched next to me and I shrank back, thinking he was going to hit me again.

'Catherine,' he said, his voice low, shockingly calm. 'Don't make me do that again, okay? Just come home on time, or let me know where you're going. It's simple. It's for your own safety. There are some really dangerous people out there. I'm the only one who's looking out for you, you know that, don't you? So make it easy for yourself and do as you're told.'

It felt like a turning point. It was as though the denial about my relationship with Lee had come to an end, I knew what he was capable of, what he could do, and what he expected of me. It was as though a door had been slammed in the face of the old, naïve, carefree Catherine. What was left was me: the one who was afraid all the time, the one who looked behind to check who was following, the one who knew that, whatever the future held, it could not possibly be good.

Hours later, when I was finally brave enough to look in the mirror, there was scarcely a mark on my face. It had felt as though he'd broken my cheekbone. My head was aching, but on the surface of the skin there was just a barely perceptible swelling and a small red mark. As though he'd not hit me at all.

Thursday 31 January 2008

I got off the bus at Denmark Hill. Across the road, King's College Hospital, brightly lit, an ambulance with lights flashing and sirens blaring going to the side entrance and the Accident and Emergency department. I stood at the pedestrian crossing, watching the ambulance, until I realised a car had stopped to let me across. I headed for the Maudsley Hospital, a beautiful old building with huge pale porticoes against red brick, just across the road.

I stood looking at it for a moment thinking of how it must have looked the same a hundred years ago, maybe with less traffic. The last time I'd been near a hospital was when I'd been taken in through the back entrance, in the back of an ambulance, sitting crouched and squeezed tightly into a corner. I promised myself I'd never go back there, I'd never let them take me like that again. Now here I was, standing in front of a psychiatric hospital and I was going to walk in through the front entrance just like a normal person. If I could just pluck up the courage to move.

'Looking for someone?'

It was Stuart. He was wearing a shirt that looked badly in need of an iron, the sleeves folded up to his elbows, his hospital ID pass clipped to his breast pocket.

'I'd almost forgotten what you look like,' I said. It had only been a couple of days, with various shift patterns and me being at work too, but it felt like years.

'Shall we go inside?' he said, after a moment.

I looked at him and looked back at the entrance. I could see people inside, walking around.

'I'm not sure,' I said.

'We could go somewhere else, if you like,' he said gently, 'but I haven't got long.'

I took a deep breath. 'No, let's do it. Just make sure I get let out again, alright?'

We walked through the main entrance and down an endless corridor, passing doctors and visitors and medical reps and orderlies, until suddenly there was a restaurant on the left. 'I take you to all the nicest places,' he said.

'It's fine. Don't be silly.'

I sat at a free table while he got us some drinks and food. I watched him in the queue. Crowds of people always made me nervous, but being in here made things worse. It was easy to spot the medical staff since they clearly belonged there; others, probably visiting family, looking up at the blackboard menu with everything except jacket potatoes scrubbed off, debating over the few remaining sandwiches or the stale cake. Maybe some of them were patients.

Three people behind Stuart in the queue, a man with his back to me was making me feel uncomfortable. He was with some other people, laughing and talking to a girl, but there was something about him that reminded me . . . the laugh? I could hear it from here. I concentrated on Stuart, watching him, but the man was still there. He had muscles, too, big shoulders. I started to feel a bit sick.

I turned in my seat towards the wall, concentrating on the bright white walls, trying to think about other things. Counting to six. It'll be fine. It's not him.

'Cheese salad or ham?' Stuart put the tray down in front of me and I jumped.

'Cheese salad, please,' I said. He passed it over and started unwrapping his ham.

'Let's go out at the weekend,' he said. 'What do you think? We'll go out Saturday — the weather's supposed to be good, isn't it? I've got a match on Sunday, assuming the shoulder's up to it.'

The man who'd been behind Stuart in the queue walked past then. He was more like him than the man in the café in Brighton had been. I looked, though. I did it. I looked at him, forced my brain to spot the differences.

Stuart followed my gaze, watched as the

man sat a few tables away, with his friends and the girl he'd been talking to. They were still laughing.

'That's Rob,' he said. 'Plays rugby with me.'

'Oh,' I said.

I looked up and saw his eyes on me. Watching me steadily. 'You alright?'

'Yes.'

'Sure?'

'Yes.'

'You look a bit — pale.'

I tried to laugh. 'I'm always pale. Really, I'm fine.'

'How long did the checks take this morning?'

I shrugged. 'Wasn't paying attention.'

He was still looking.

'Stuart, really, I'm fine. Stop it, okay?'

'Sorry.'

After we'd finished eating we walked back up the long corridor towards the entrance. The entrance hallway was still full of people coming and going. I was counting my steps back to the door, thinking of nothing except getting out, and perversely what they would do if I suddenly started to run, and then we were outside in the cold, and I could finally breathe fresh air, traffic fumes, and hear the noises of the outside, and I was free again. I wasn't even really aware that he was still there with me until he took hold of my hand.

I looked at him in surprise.

'I know this isn't the right time, or the right place,' he said. 'But I wanted to tell you something.'

I waited for him to continue, looked down at his hand holding mine. Realised he was actually nervous.

'Remember when I kissed you? And the next day I said it was just a kiss. Do you remember that?'

'Yes.'

I was too afraid of making eye contact with him, so I looked at the road, watched the traffic heading south, three buses going in the opposite direction and so far not a single one heading for the river and home.

'It wasn't just a kiss for me. I said that because — I don't know. I don't know why I said it. It was stupid. I've been thinking about it ever since.'

That was when I saw her.

On the top deck of the number 68, heading towards West Norwood. My attention caught by a bright pink beret sitting jauntily on top of a mass of blonde curls. Heading away from me, but looking at me intently. Staring.

It was Sylvia.

I turned back to him. 'What did you say?'

Saturday 20 March 2004

Lee had Saturday free, and we went to Morecambe again. I hadn't wanted to go, but it was better than staying in the house. My face still felt tender, my cheek bruised when I pressed my fingers against it, but nobody else would ever have known. He'd managed to hit me hard enough to make my teeth rattle without actually leaving a single mark.

It was warm, the sun bright in a cloudless blue sky. It was busy and it took a long time to find a parking space. In the end we walked back towards the town along the esplanade. He held my hand as we walked. I still felt nervous around him.

'I'm sorry about the other day,' he said. It was the first time he'd mentioned it.

'About what?' I asked.

'You know.'

'I want you to say it.' Maybe it was too challenging. But I felt safer here, walking along with other people, families, kids on bikes, than I did in my own home.

'I'm sorry about the argument.'

'Lee, you hit me.'

He looked genuinely astonished. 'I did not.'

I stopped walking and faced him. 'You are kidding? You hit me across the face.'

'I thought you fell over,' he said. 'Either way, I'm sorry.'

It was probably the best I was going to get. We walked on for a bit. I was warm enough to take my sweater off. The tide was out and the sea was so far away I could hardly see it beyond the expanse of sand.

'Lee, I'm sorry too,' I said.

He pulled my hand up to his mouth so he could kiss it. 'You know I love you,' he said.

Despite everything, the look in his eyes and his hesitant half-smile almost had me fooled again.

'It's no good,' I said. 'I can't do this. You make

me afraid, Lee. I don't want to be with you any more. This isn't doing either of us any good, is it?'

I saw a cloud cross his face, not anger — not that, maybe disappointment? I thought he was going to let go of my hand, but instead he held it tighter.

'Don't,' he said quietly. 'Don't do this. You regretted it last time.'

'I did. But things have happened since then.'

'What things?'

'You hitting me, for one. And you talking to Claire about me, and Sylvia. She thinks I'm going mad, Lee. It's not fair. She's my best friend and you've turned her against me.'

'What?' He gave a short laugh. 'Is that what she told you?'

I felt tears pricking my eyes. I didn't want to cry, not here. I sat down on one of the benches. He sat next to me, taking hold of my hand again.

'Did she tell you how come I had her phone number? She gave it to me that night in the Spread Eagle. She came up to me at the bar and asked me to buy her a drink, while you were off fuck knows where. I bought her a drink and she put her hand on my arse and gave it a squeeze, then she slipped a piece of paper in my jacket pocket and told me to ring her if I got bored.'

'I don't believe you.'

'Yes,' he said quietly, 'you do believe me, because you know what she's like.'

I rubbed my cheek angrily with the back of my hand.

'Come here,' he said softly, pulling me into a

hug. 'Don't cry. It's okay.'

He held me gently with both his arms around me, my head nestled in his shoulder. His fingers ran through my hair, combing it away from my face. 'You don't need to be scared, Catherine. You shouldn't be scared. It's this crazy job. I'm no good at showing how I feel, I get stressed and angry and I forget who I'm talking to. I'm sorry if I scared you.'

I pulled back from him so I could look in his eyes. 'What if I'd called the police, Lee? What if I told them what you'd done?'

'Most likely, they might send someone round to take a statement, then it would get filed and nothing else would happen.'

'Really?'

'Either that, or there'd be a prolonged internal investigation and I'd lose my job and my pension.' He stroked a finger across my cheek, wiping away the last tear. 'I've got something for you,' he said. 'I want you to have it, no matter what.'

It was a ring, inside a black velvet box. A platinum ring with a big diamond, glittering brilliantly in the sunshine. I didn't want to touch it, but he pressed it into my hand. 'I know it's a rocky start for us,' he said, 'but it will get better, I promise. In a few months I'll look for a transfer, something a bit less stressful, something that means I can be at home more. Just please say you'll think about it. Catherine? Will you at least think about it?'

I thought about it. I thought about what I would have to do to stop him hitting me again;

about being home on time, about telling him if I went anywhere without him, about wearing what he told me to wear and doing exactly what he told me to do. 'Alright,' I said. 'I'll think about it.'

He kissed me then, in the bright sunshine, and I let him.

I'd always thought that women who stayed in abusive relationships must be foolish. After all, there had to be a moment, a realisation that things had taken a wrong turn and you were suddenly afraid to be with your partner — and surely that was the moment to leave. Walk away and don't look back, I always thought. Why would you stay? And I'd seen women on television, interviewed in magazines, saying things like, 'It isn't that simple,' and I'd always thought yes, it *is* that simple — just leave, just walk away from it.

In addition to that moment of realisation, a moment that had already passed for me, there was a new realisation that walking away wasn't a simple option after all. I'd tried it and made the mistake of inviting him back. Being still in love with him, the gentle, vulnerable part of him that was still inside somewhere, was only part of it: it was also the dreadful fear of what he might do if I did anything to provoke him.

It wasn't about walking away any more. It was about running.

It was about escape.

It was sunny and almost warm, so we got the Tube down to the river and walked along the South Bank until we were too tired to walk any more. We sat on a bench outside Tate Modern and drank hot tea out of disposable cups. It felt like the first day of spring.

'When I came to see you at the hospital on Thursday, I thought I saw someone I knew.'

'Lee?' he asked.

'No. Someone else. Sylvia.'

Stuart leaned forward on the bench, his head turned to me. 'Who's Sylvia?'

I'd been thinking about this ever since Thursday: telling him. Thinking of how I could explain it.

'She was my best friend before all this happened. She moved to London because she got this amazing new job.'

'You lost touch with her?'

I nodded. 'Well, it was more than that, really. She didn't believe me. When things started to go wrong with Lee, I tried to tell her about it. I needed her to help. I don't know why she didn't. In the end I didn't contact her again.'

He waited for me to continue, putting his cup down onto the paving stone under the seat, the steam coming off what was left of his tea, curling up in beautiful patterns.

'I've been thinking about what you said, you know.'

'What I said?'

'About . . . the kiss.'

'Ah,' he said. 'I wondered if you'd even been listening, to be honest.'

'It took me a bit by surprise, that's all. I thought you weren't interested in me.'

He gave a short laugh. 'I must be better at hiding my feelings than I thought.'

There was a pause while I tried to work out what to say next.

'Look,' he said, 'don't worry about it. I know it's a difficult time for you at the moment. I don't want this to stop us being friends.'

'It's not that,' I said. 'I need to tell you about it. I need you to understand what happened to me. You can't decide how you feel until you know.'

'What — right now?'

I nodded. 'It's better out here,' I said. 'I won't fall apart out here, with all these people walking past.'

'All right,' he said.

'It's bad.'

'Yes.'

I took a deep breath. 'It was a bad relationship. It got worse and worse. In the end he nearly killed me.'

There was a long pause. He looked at me, looked at his hands. Eventually, he said, 'Someone found you?'

'Wendy. She lived next door. I must have given her such a shock.'

'I'm sorry,' he said quietly. 'Sorry you went through that.'

'I was pregnant when he attacked me. I didn't even know it until they told me afterwards in the hospital that I'd lost the baby. I don't know if I can have children now. They said it was unlikely.'

He looked away.

'I had to tell you that,' I said.

Stuart nodded. I realised he had tears in his eyes. I put my hand across his back. 'Oh, God, please don't be upset. I didn't want you to be upset.'

He put his arms around me, pulling me into a crushing hug, and we stayed like that for several moments.

'Do you know what the worst thing was?' I said at last, into his shoulder. 'It wasn't sitting in there, in that room, waiting for him to come back and kill me. It wasn't being hit, it wasn't the pain, it wasn't even being raped. It was that afterwards nobody, not even my best friend, believed me.'

I sat back then, looked out at the river, a barge going slowly past, downstream. 'I need you to believe me, Stuart. I need that more than I've ever needed anything in my whole life.'

'Of course I believe you,' he said. 'I'll always believe you.'

Stuart wiped away the tears with his finger and moved to kiss me. I put my fingers to his lips. 'Wait,' I said. 'Think about what I've told you. I need to know you can deal with it.'

He nodded. 'Okay.'

We got up and started walking back towards Waterloo Bridge. 'Why didn't she believe you?' he asked. 'She doesn't sound like much of a best friend.'

'It's the way he was. He could charm

anyone. He was nothing but charming with all of my friends. They just thought I was being ungrateful, that he couldn't possibly be all the things I said he was. Then he started talking to them when I wasn't there, telling them things about me that weren't true. He was talking to Sylvia, my other friends were talking to her too, about things that he'd told them. Before I knew what was happening, they were all busy discussing how I'd gone completely mad.'

In front of us a little boy, running to catch his older brother, fell over onto his knees. His mum picked him up and rubbed him down before he had a chance to start crying.

'And you saw her? Sylvia?'

'She was on that bus, heading south. On the top deck.'

'Did she see you?'

'She was staring at me. It was so strange.'

'Does it worry you?'

'What? Seeing Sylvia? I don't think so. It just gave me a shock, seeing her. I never thought I'd see her again, and then suddenly there she was. I mean, I knew she was in London somewhere. But even so . . . '

We were nearly back at the Tube.

'Let's go home,' he said. He pulled me into a hug.

I couldn't think of anything I wanted more.

I left my desk at exactly noon, turning off the computer screen and grabbing my coat from behind the door. The town centre was busy, but then Fridays often were; full of shoppers, pensioners, mothers, toddlers, students, and people who really should be at work but, for some inexplicable reason, weren't. The sun was shining, and that always brought more people into the town centre. I could smell summer on the breeze, although it was still chilly. Maybe the weekend would be good.

I hate crowds. I would much rather stroll through the town centre without seeing another single living person; but today I had to meet Sam.

At the Bolero Café, Sam was waiting for me, sitting at a table by the window.

'Let's sit at the back? Can we? I'm always cold by the window.'

Sam raised her eyebrows but moved her bags, and her coat, and followed me to the back of the café.

I hadn't been in here since it changed hands. It used to be the Green Kitchen, a vegetarian-vegan place selling locally sourced organic produce, with a small café at the back. It had managed to hold out for a while, but when the students departed for the long summer break it didn't have enough custom. It had reopened as the Bolero just after Christmas, and with the Pensioner Specials (tea and a teacake for a pound) it was faring much better.

'Happy birthday,' I said at last, giving Sam a kiss on the cheek. 'How are you?'

'I'm doing fine, thanks,' Sam replied. She was looking beautiful in a red cashmere sweater, a present from the new boyfriend. Well — he wasn't that new. She'd met him on Christmas Eve in the Cheshire. But it still felt new to me. I'd only seen her once since Christmas.

'More to the point, how are you?'

'More to the point? What's that supposed to mean?' I asked. I really didn't want to start on this so soon into our meeting.

'I've not seen you for ages and ages,' she said. 'I was just wondering.'

The waitress turned up just then, which was a useful distraction. I ordered a large tea and a slice of wholemeal toast. Sam ordered a latte and a cheese ploughman's.

'How's things going with Simon?' I asked.

That took care of the next half-hour, right up to halfway through Sam's lunch. She was still full of the new man, the future, maybe getting married when he was next on home leave — it was all there.

'So what about you?' she said at last, swigging down the last of her coffee. 'How are things with Lee?'

'Oh, good,' I said. 'Fine.'

'So he hasn't proposed or anything dramatic like that, then?'

'Well — yes. Kind of.'

'Kind of?'

I cast a glance at the window, just checking.

'He's always proposing. Every blinking week.'

'What — and you're not going for it? Haven't you said yes?' Sam couldn't get her head round that one, I could tell.

'I don't see the point. We're fine as we are, we get along, you know, the odd tiff here and there like everyone else; why change it?'

'Why change it? You could be having a wedding, for heaven's sake! A dress, a honeymoon, presents! A great big piss-up with all your mates there!'

I shrugged. 'I'm not saying never, I'm just saying we've got more important things on right now. I'm really busy at work. I don't want to be worrying about organising a wedding when there's so much going on.'

'Well,' Sam said, patting my hand, 'he obviously loves you to pieces, doesn't he?'

I stirred my tea slowly, watching the patterns swirl and twist on the surface of the liquid. 'Yes,' I said.

'Why so sad, then?' she asked.

I wasn't doing a very good job, here, I thought. I was supposed to be bright and cheerful and full of the happy birthday wishes, but I wasn't managing to fool her.

'I miss Sylv,' I said, which was entirely true, despite our last dreadful conversation.

'She's only down in London, you know. Hardly a million miles away.'

'We've both been really busy.'

'I heard about the row you had.'

'Did you?'

She nodded. 'Claire told me. She thinks

you've gone all weird since you met Lee.'

'I know.'

'So what's going on?'

I shrugged, contemplating telling her my side of the story and wondering whether it would actually do me any good at all. 'I'm not sure myself.'

I didn't trust her, not fully. She was the only one still in any sort of contact, and even that was sporadic. Who was to say she hadn't been talking to Lee herself? Maybe as soon as we'd finished here, she would phone him and report back what I'd said, how I looked, what I ate. In the kitchen someone dropped a plate — the sound made me jump. When I looked back at Sam, her expression was difficult to read.

'Claire's right. You've changed.'

I shook my head, knocked back the last of the coffee. 'No. Just stressed with work. Tired out. You know how it is,' I said.

She leaned across and patted my hand again. 'I'm here if you ever need to chat. You know that, don't you?'

I managed a bright smile for her. 'Of course. But I'm fine — really. I just need a bit of a break, I think. So what was last night like? Was the Cheshire busy? Did you go clubbing?'

'Yeah. Town was packed, no idea why.'

'It's the end of term today. Last night for all the students to get wrecked before they all go home and get their washing done.'

Sam laughed. 'Wasn't only students, though — loads of people. Saw Emily and Julia — she was asking after you. Roger who used to work with Emily was out too. Remember him? He was after you, once, wasn't he?'

I gave a wry grin. ' 'Fraid so. He was a bit of a mare in the end — always phoning me up at work.'

'And Katie. She asked where you were, too.'

'I'm sorry. It sounds like it was a good night out. Shame I missed it.'

'You've not been out for ages and ages.'

'I know. Look,' I said, desperate to change the subject, 'why don't we go to Manchester next weekend? Have a look for some new shoes, do lunch?'

'I can't next weekend, I'm looking at houses,' she said. 'I'll give you a ring, though, okay? We can do that soon. It sounds like a great idea. Just don't let me spend too much money.'

I paid the bill for our lunch, although Sam tried to intervene. A birthday treat, I insisted. She was the only contact I had left with my old friends. Even if I wasn't sure about her, she was all I had left.

Outside in the cold air, she hugged me so tight it hurt, all over. She put her arms around my back and patted and rubbed, as though she was trying to force some warmth inside.

'Christ, you're getting thin,' she said.

'I know,' I said. 'Fabulous, isn't it?'

She looked at me a little sternly. 'You're sure you're alright? You promise me? Because I think something's not quite right.'

'Sam, everything's fine.'

I couldn't promise. If she asked me to promise

again, I was going to break down. I was going to totally lose it. There was only so much lying I could do, and promises were important to me, I didn't take them lightly.

'You're sure?'

'I'm sure.'

She hugged me again, just in the wrong place. I was trying hard not to wince, but it hurt. My whole body hurt.

'You know where I am if you need me, alright?' she said.

I nodded, and then she headed off back up the hill towards the college where she worked. I wondered if she'd guessed what it was. She knew something wasn't quite right, but she didn't have a name for it yet.

I had names for it, but not ones I could repeat.

I looked around the Market Square for a moment, just in case I could see him, but there was no sign. That didn't mean he wasn't there. Sometimes he was, sometimes he wasn't. I was no good at telling the difference any more. I just felt as though I was being watched the whole time, every minute of every day. Sometimes that just made it easier, safer. Less likely for me to make a mistake.

I counted my steps back up to the office: four hundred and twenty-four. That was one good thing, at least.

When I got home tonight, it wasn't quite dark. The mornings were getting lighter, too, the bulbs pushing through every spare patch of soil in the greyness of London.

I indulged my vice for circuitous routes home, enjoying the not-quite darkness, thinking about what I was going to cook for dinner.

By the time I got to Talbot Street the sky was getting dark and it was getting colder. I walked along the alleyway at the back, looking up at the back of the house, at my flat, at the balcony, and the curtains. I looked at the gate, hanging off its hinges and the thick grass behind it.

The curtains hung exactly the way I'd left them. I looked at the faintly yellow space of my window, staring intently, trying to see into the room beyond.

It all looked perfectly fine, just as I'd left it.

I walked to the end of the alleyway and turned the corner, heading back to the street. As I came out of the gloom a figure passed me, walking on the other side of the street, away from the house. Something about his shape made me stop and shrink back into the shadows.

It was Lee.

In the same way it was always Lee, every time I saw a big man, that purposeful stride, fair hair, broad shoulders. I caught my breath and forced myself to look, just as the man rounded the corner at the end of the road and crossed over into the High Street. Not long enough for me to be sure. It's not him, I told myself. It's just your mind playing tricks again. It's not him, it's never him. It's just imagination.

I walked back along Talbot Street towards the house, trying to get the feeling off my shoulders, trying to get back to the way I'd been just a few moments ago, looking forward to having something to eat, a shower, watching a film or something, listening out for Stuart's footsteps on the stairs outside, going to sleep.

I got in the house, shut the door behind me and checked it, running my fingers along the edge of the door, feeling it flush with the frame, checking the lock had shot home, checking the handle, one, two, three, four, five. Checking it again, turning it.

I finished the check and waited. Something was wrong. Something was badly wrong. I started again, all the way from the beginning, checking the door, checking the lock.

What was it? What was wrong?

It wasn't the door . . .

I stared at it for a moment, all my senses alive, listening. Then I turned my head, slowly.

I looked back to the doorway of Flat 1.

Silence.

My feet didn't want to move, but I forced them. I went to the doorway and knocked, something I'd never done before, never even contemplated doing.

'Mrs Mackenzie? Are you there?'

Silence, complete echoing silence. No *East-Enders*, no sound of the news or anything else for that matter. I looked behind me, back to the door, the table in the hallway, messy with piles of post. Nothing wrong. The door was still closed.

I knocked again, harder. Maybe she'd gone out. Maybe she'd gone somewhere, gone away on holiday or something; I was thinking that thought at the same moment as knowing for a fact that something had happened to her.

I swallowed, suddenly terrified. I put my hand on the door handle, then pulled it back again. I felt in my pocket for my mobile phone.

This was bloody silly. What was I going to say? 'Oh, hi, Stuart, please can you come home? Mrs Mackenzie's turned her telly down.'

I put my hand back on the door handle and turned it. The door opened and swung open before I had a chance to stop it, swinging back on the wall with a loud bang that echoed all the way up to the top floor.

The lights were on inside, a gust of warm air, smell of cooked food, stale.

'Hello?'

I wasn't expecting a reply. I stepped over the threshold, just a step forward. Her flat matched mine, upstairs: the living room straight ahead, kitchen at the end on the right, overlooking the garden; bathroom and then bedroom to my right. I couldn't see her from where I was standing so I took another step. The carpet under my feet was wildly patterned, threadbare.

I could see through to the living room, the television — a huge one, no wonder it was so bloody loud. But it was turned off, just a big expanse of dark grey.

I was level with the bedroom door now. I looked to my right — I could see into the bedroom, lights on, but it was empty. I looked behind me to the open door, the staircase leading up to my flat and Stuart's flat beyond it.

'Mrs Mackenzie?' My voice sounded odd to me, off-key. I wanted to hear it for reassurance but the quaver in it made me even more afraid.

I took another step inside. The room opened up here, the windows to the front to my left, the curtains drawn. Ahead of me, to the right, the kitchen area. Next to me on the right, a small dining table, a neat white lace tablecloth, an African violet in a pot in the centre of it. The curtains to the back open, just blackness beyond.

She was in the kitchen. All I could see was a slippered foot.

I ran to her. 'Mrs Mackenzie! Can you hear me? Are you alright?'

She was on her side, blood on the side of her face, but she was breathing, barely; I fumbled in my pocket for my phone, dialled 999.

'*Emergency, which service do you require?*'

'Ambulance,' I said.

I told them where to come, I told them that Mrs Mackenzie was unconscious, hardly breathing, blood on her head.

I held her hand. 'It's okay, Mrs Mackenzie. The ambulance is coming, they'll be here soon. Can you hear me? It's alright now, you're going to be alright.'

She made a sound. The skin around her mouth was crusty. I found a tea towel on the counter, ran it under the tap, squeezed it so it was damp, dabbed it around her mouth.

'It's alright, it's alright,' I said softly. 'Don't

worry, you'll be fine.'

'Cath . . . '

'Yes, it's me. Don't worry, the ambulance is coming.'

'Oh . . . ' She had tears in her eyes. 'My — head . . . '

'You must have had a fall,' I said. 'Try to stay still, they'll be here in a minute.'

Her hand was cold. I went into her bedroom, looking for something warm. On the bed, a crocheted bedspread, handmade by the look of it — I pulled it clear of the bed and took it back to the figure lying on the kitchen floor, laid it over her.

Outside I could hear a siren, a long way away, getting closer. I would need to go and get the door open but for the moment I couldn't move.

'The door . . . ' she said. Her voice was faint.

'It's alright, Mrs Mackenzie. I'll let them in. Don't worry.'

'The door — it was . . . it was . . . I saw . . . outside — '

The siren stopped, right outside.

'I'll be back in a moment, Mrs Mackenzie . . . ' I ran for the front door, my hands shaking.

Green uniforms. A tall man and a short woman.

'It's this way. She's on the floor.'

I stood back and let them do what they needed to do.

'Do you know what happened?' She only looked young, the paramedic, smaller than me, dark hair cut short.

'No, I found her like this. She must have had a fall or something. I live in the flat upstairs. She normally comes out to say hello, I can hear her telly on. I thought it was odd when she didn't come out, so I knocked on the door . . . '

I was aware that I was gabbling like a mad person.

'Alright, try to take it easy,' she said. 'She'll be fine, we'll look after her. You're shaking. Are you feeling faint or anything?'

'No, no, I'm fine. Just — be careful with her, won't you?'

By the time they got her out to the ambulance I'd started to calm down a little. I stood in the doorway watching them putting the trolley, stretcher, whatever they called it, into the back of the ambulance.

I heard the sound of someone running along the pavement and looked across to see Stuart pounding up the road towards the house. 'Cathy — oh, God, I thought — ' He was out of breath, put his hands on his knees. 'I saw the ambulance, I thought . . . '

'It's Mrs Mackenzie. When I came in I suddenly realised I couldn't hear her television. Her door was unlocked, I went in and there she was, on the kitchen floor.'

'Is she in a bad way?'

They were shutting the back doors of the ambulance. 'She had blood on her head. She must have hit it on something.'

Finally, the ambulance drove away up Talbot Street.

'Come on,' Stuart said. 'Let's go inside.'

He let me check the door while he went into Mrs Mackenzie's flat to turn off the lights. When I'd finished I stood in the doorway waiting for him.

'What are you doing?'

'Looking for a key. Don't worry, I've found it.'

He turned off the last remaining lights in the flat and joined me at the door. He locked it behind us, putting the key in his pocket.

'Has she got any family? Friends?'

'Not that I've ever seen.'

On the first floor landing we both paused. 'Come up for a drink?' he said.

'Alright.'

I made the tea in Stuart's kitchen while he went to have a shower.

I felt unsettled, sitting at his kitchen table cradling my mug. I thought of Mrs Mackenzie on the floor, trying to speak, trying to tell me something. The door . . . Something about the door.

She'd seen something outside.

I wondered if it was the same thing I'd seen: the shape, the dark figure of a man. I remembered the figure I'd seen walking away, the figure who looked like Lee. Had he called at the flat? Had she seen him at the door, been startled by it?

'Try not to worry,' Stuart said, coming into the kitchen. 'I'm sure she'll be fine. We can go and visit her tomorrow, if you like.'

He was warm and smelled of shower gel, dressed in a T-shirt and a pair of jeans. The sight of him made all thoughts of evil shapes and shadowy figures evaporate from my mind. Every time I'd imagined seeing Lee these past few weeks, it had turned out to be my imagination. Why should it be him this time?

I handed him his mug of tea. It was getting cold already. I wouldn't have been able to drink it like that.

'Thanks.' He sat down opposite me and before I had time to look away he'd caught me in those eyes.

'I'm going to Aberdeen on Thursday,' he said at last.

'To see your folks?'

Stuart nodded. 'Dad's birthday. I usually go up there this time of year.' He put his mug down carefully on the table. 'I was going to ask if you wanted to come with me.'

I felt hot all of a sudden.

'But I guess it's too short notice.'

'Yes, I think it is.' As well as being completely out of the fucking blue, I thought. Why ask me when it's too late for me to do anything about it? Assuming I had wanted to go with him, even. 'Besides, my first appointment's on Friday.'

'Oh — of course it is. I forgot.'

You didn't forget, I thought, because I didn't actually tell you. And I somehow doubt that Alistair told you when it was — why would he? It was pointless second-guessing him. I was pissed off again, for no good reason.

'I wanted you to know that I've been thinking about what you told me.'

I didn't answer, draining my mug of tea to hide my discomfort. I felt tense and itchy, like a

311

jumper that was two sizes too small.

'I think we should take it slowly,' he said. 'I want to make sure you get better first.'

'Oh, that's very good of you,' I snapped.

'Cathy — '

'How about we take it slowly like we're doing now?' I said, standing up so quickly that the chair rocked on the tiled floor. 'Or how about we take it even slower than that, and give up on it completely?'

'I don't want to do that.'

'Good for you. What about what I want?'

'What *do* you want?'

'I want . . . I just want to feel *normal*. Just for a fucking change. I want to feel like a normal person again.'

I couldn't stand to look at him any more, sitting there all relaxed and sure of himself, so I turned and made for the door.

'Cathy, wait. Please.'

I turned to face him. 'I don't know how you really feel about anything,' I said.

'When I think you're in the right frame of mind to listen, I'll tell you what I feel.'

'You can be really fucking patronising sometimes, Stuart.'

'Alright,' he said, taking a step towards me, and then another. 'You want to know how I feel.'

I nodded, stood my ground, chin up, angry enough to take it, whatever ammunition he had left, whatever he had for me, verbal or physical.

'Are you listening?'

I nodded. 'Go for it.'

And then he kissed me.

It took me completely by surprise. He kissed me, leaning me back against the wall in his draughty hallway, his hand cupping my cheek. Every time I thought it was over he came back for more. His body was warm and solid against me, the pressure of him holding me there against the wall. He was so much taller than me, taller than Lee had been, his physique more athletic. I should have been terrified. I should have reacted the same way as I had when Robin had done more or less the same thing, out on the High Street, two months ago. But instead I felt myself unfurling, stretching out, tensed limbs relaxing and chilled fingers warming up.

After several long moments Stuart took an abrupt step back and regarded me with one raised eyebrow, challenging.

'Oh,' I said.

He took another step back, towards the kitchen, giving me space.

'That's how I feel,' he said.

'Right.'

He smiled then, a broad, happy smile.

I cleared my throat. 'Well, I think we'd better talk about this some more — another time, maybe.'

'Yes,' he said.

'Maybe when you get back from your trip to Scotland.'

'Fine by me.'

'I'm going home now.'

'Okay. I'll see you next week.'

Today would have been my mother's sixty-fifth birthday. I often wondered what she would have been like if she'd lived — whether we'd be going out for a meal, or whether I'd treat her to a pampering session. Or maybe a weekend away somewhere. I wondered if we'd be good friends, whether I could call her up on a whim, wanting a chat, wanting comfort, wanting to hear a friendly voice.

I missed her.

If she'd lived, my life might have been different altogether. If they'd not both died in my final year of university, I might not have behaved the way I did. I might not have got drunk every night, slept around, done drugs, woken up in strange houses wondering where I was and what I'd done the night before. I might have got a better degree; I might be some CEO now, running a global organisation, instead of running a personnel office in a plastics manufacturing plant.

I might not have been going to the River that first night, Hallowe'en, wearing a red satin dress, with my heart wide open and ready to be broken. I might not have worn that jacket, with the receipt for the last time I'd bought a tea in the gym's café, in the pocket. I might not have left the receipt in the pocket, where he could have searched and found it, and discovered a way of finding me again. I might have got away without ever seeing him again.

I might have escaped.

And even now, maybe if my mum and dad were still alive, maybe they would have been able to counsel me away from him. They would have recognised him as dangerous. Would I have listened? Maybe not.

If Mum had lived, maybe I would have married someone by now, someone kind, stable, honest; maybe I'd have a child, maybe two, maybe three.

No point in thinking about what might have been. *Today is going to be the start of my fight back*, I decided — the way I decided every day, until he turned up at my house, let himself in, and turned it back round until it was nicely under his control.

Today was different, though.

I had an email from Jonathan Baldwin. I remembered him, although not immediately. We were on a month-long training course together, four years ago, in Manchester. He appeared outgoing, enthusiastic, we had a laugh together and I seemed to remember promising to keep in touch, although we never had. He emailed me at work out of the blue, to see how I was doing. He said he was setting up a branch of his management consultancy business in New York and asked if I'd worked with anyone I could recommend. I emailed back and said I would give it some thought and let him know. It felt a bit like a sign, for me. I wondered if New York could be the answer.

Lee was waiting for me when I got home from work.

Not on the doorstep, as he used to once upon

a time — no, inside, in the kitchen, busy making us some dinner. He used to do that, before, and I would be pleased. Today, when I opened the door and smelled the cooking smells, I just wanted to run. But running didn't get me anywhere.

He would let himself in whenever he felt like it, come and go as he pleased. I remembered when this was such a big deal for me, not so long ago. I'd wanted my own space, my front door that I could lock behind me and know for sure that nobody was going to be inside there without me. I remembered telling him that I wanted that space back. I remembered asking him for the key, and him walking away from me. I remembered him simply walking away and leaving, without so much as an argument.

When I thought back to that time, I couldn't believe that he'd let me go so easily, and that I was such a fool, such a stupid fool, as to go looking for him. I could have got away. If I'd left him alone, avoided him completely, started going out with my friends again, I could have been free.

But I didn't.

Wednesday 13 February 2008

Stuart phoned me at half-past one. I was sitting in my office with Caroline at the time, discussing the applications for the warehousing jobs. 'Hello?'

'Hey, it's me. Are you free to talk?'

'Sure.'

'I've just been to see Mrs Downstairs.'

'How's she doing?'

'Not too good. She hasn't been conscious since she came in, apparently. They've done various scans. Seems like she might have hit her head harder than first thought when she went down.'

'That's awful.'

'They were asking me if we knew who her next of kin is.'

'I haven't a clue.'

Caroline gave me a questioning look to ask if I wanted her to go. I waved her back into her seat.

'Maybe we could try the management company. They might have someone on file — I don't know.'

'I'll give them a ring this afternoon if I get a chance,' Stuart said.

'If not, I could ring them.'

'I'll let you know.'

There was a little pause. I wondered if he'd been thinking about that kiss. I'd thought about it a lot.

'What time's your flight tomorrow?'

'Early. And I'm back on Sunday night. Will you miss me?'

I laughed. 'No, of course not. I hardly see you during the week as it is, you're always at work.'

'Hm. Maybe I should start rethinking my priorities.'

'Maybe.'

Was he flirting with me? It felt like he was. I wondered what this conversation would be like if he were sitting in my office instead of Caroline.

'Can I give you a call tomorrow?'

He was definitely flirting with me.

'I'm sure you'll have more important things to do.'

'You're joking — it's only Dad and Rachel.'

'Even so, you said yourself you don't see enough of them. Make the most of your time there. And you could do with a break as well, you've been working really hard.'

'I want to find out how your appointment with Alistair goes. How are you feeling about it?'

'Alright. I'm trying not to think about it, to be honest.'

'I'll call you tomorrow evening. If you don't want to talk to me you can just turn your phone off.'

'I might do that. I'll see how I feel. Look, I need to get back to work. Have a safe trip, okay? I'll see you next week.'

'Okay.'

I rang off.

'Let me guess,' Caroline said. 'Stuart?'

'Our neighbour downstairs had a fall the other night; they took her off in an ambulance. Stuart went to see her — she's not doing too well.'

'Oh, that's rough.'

'I'll try and see her tomorrow night, she might be better by then.'

'Is he going on holiday or something?'

'He's going to Aberdeen to see his Dad and sister.'

'You were giving him a hard time,' she said.

'Was I? I wasn't. Really?'

318

She raised her eyebrows at me in response.

'He asked if I was going to miss him,' I said, trying to remember if I'd imagined that tone in his voice.

'You *are* going to miss him, of course.'

'It's only four days, Caroline, for heaven's sake. He works such long hours sometimes I don't see him from one week to the next, it won't be any different just because he's gone to Aberdeen.'

'Is he going to call you?'

'Says he is.'

'That's it, then,' she said. 'If he rings you every day between now and when he comes back from Aberdeen, you'll know.'

'I'll know what, exactly?'

'That he loves you.'

I was momentarily taken aback. I'd not thought of it in those terms before. I'd thought of Stuart as being someone I could trust, someone who understood what might be going on in my head, even someone who found me attractive and probably wanted sex. But not as someone who might be in love with me. Not as someone I could be in love with.

'What are you, some kind of soothsayer?' I said, laughing at her earnest expression.

'You mark my words,' she said. 'You'll see.'

Friday 9 April 2004

I thought he was working, but he came in drunk. He let himself in with his door key when I was sitting watching the news on television. For a fleeting moment I was happy — I was back to looking forward to seeing him again, to getting things back to where we should have been, relaxed, happy, having fun as a couple.

Instead he stumbled, half-fell through the door, and as I rose from my seat to meet him his fist hit the side of my face with a crashing blow, sending me flying backwards into the side table.

I was so shocked that I didn't move, just lay there for a moment seeing the carpet against my face and wondering what on earth had happened. Then pain all over my head, excruciating pain, as he took hold of a fistful of hair and dragged me up to my knees.

'Slag,' he said, breathing hard, 'you fucking bitch . . . you complete fucking slag.'

With his left hand he slapped me, a stinging blow across my cheek. I would have fallen backwards again but he still had hold of my hair.

'What have I done?' I yelped.

'You don't get it, do you, you fucking slag?' His voice was icy cold, and I could smell the beer on him.

He let go of my hair, then, and before I could fall back or get to my feet he brought his knee up and it connected with my nose with such force that I felt it crack. I screamed, and tried to crawl away, tried to get up, still stunned. Tears were spinning down my cheeks and splattering away with the blood that was pouring from my nose and my split lip.

'You're mine,' he said, 'you are my fucking

whore. You do exactly what I tell you. You understand?'

I whimpered, clutching on to the leg of the dining room table with slippery fingers, my eyes closed. I felt him grab my hair again, yanking me away from the table, and a voice that must have been mine, pleading with him, 'Let me go, please, please . . . '

He undid his jeans with his left hand, staggering over to the sofa, pulling me along as though I were a rag doll whilst I scrabbled to get to my feet to take the pressure away from my scalp.

With a sigh, he sat back heavily onto the sofa, his jeans now at mid-thigh, his cock hard — as though the sight of me broken and bleeding was turning him on — and told me to suck.

Sobbing, blood over my hands and in my mouth, I did as I was told. I wanted to bite his fucking knob off and spit it in his face. I wanted to use my fist and punch him so hard in the balls that he'd need to get them surgically removed from his pelvic floor.

'Look at me. Fucking bitch, I said, look at me!'

I raised my eyes to his face, and saw two things that terrified me. Firstly, the smile, the look in his eyes that told me that he had me exactly where he wanted me, and that this wasn't going to end. And secondly, the black-handled lock knife that he held just a few inches away from my face.

'Do it right,' he said, 'and I might not cut your fucking nose off.'

I did it right, I did the best I could, with blood and snot and tears streaming from my face to his crotch, and he didn't cut me — not then, anyway.

I need to escape. I need to make sure that I can get away without him even realising it, because I will only get one chance.

Thursday 14 February 2008

After work on Thursday I took the Northern Line heading south of the river. I bought some flowers at a stall at Victoria, freesias and pink roses, then caught the bus to Camberwell and King's College Hospital.

Getting off the bus at the same place where I'd seen Sylvia not too long ago felt a bit peculiar. I kept looking around in case she was there again, but of course she wasn't. Not on a bus, not on the pavement either. It felt strange, too, to be so close to Stuart's workplace and yet he was hundreds of miles away by now.

It took me an age to find the ward; I went in through the main entrance and then ended up in a building adjacent to the bus stop, opposite the Maudsley. I found Mrs Mackenzie on Byron Ward, in a side room. She was either asleep or unconscious, breathing noisily through her open mouth. She had lost weight, or maybe it was my imagination; either way she seemed tiny, childlike, lost in the big hospital bed. The cabinet next to the bed already had a bunch of flowers in a vase, daffodils, in full and vibrant bloom. Next to the vase was a card.

'Hello, Mrs Mackenzie,' I said quietly, wanting to wake her and yet not wanting to, at the same time. 'I brought you some more flowers. How are you feeling?'

What a stupid question. I sat on the visitor's chair next to the bed and reached for her hand, surprisingly warm, the back of it bruised from various needles that had been inserted under the skin.

'I'm sorry I didn't find you sooner,' I said. 'I wish I'd been there.'

I thought I felt a flicker of pressure on my hand. I gave it a squeeze.

'Did you fall, Mrs Mackenzie? Was it an accident?' My voice was quavering a little. 'I wondered if you'd had a fright, or something. If you saw someone, or something, that scared you.'

There it was again, a twitch more than anything, as though she was dreaming and her hand was moving of its own volition.

'You're safe here,' I said. 'They'll help you get better. And we're keeping an eye on things, Stuart and I. You don't need to worry about anything.'

It was hard keeping up a one-sided conversation. I glanced across at the card. It was an artist's print of some red flowers, with the message 'With Best Wishes' printed at the top. My curiosity got the better of me. Inside, it read:

Get well soon, with love from Stuart (Flat 3) and Cathy (Flat 2). X

Oh, well, I thought. Hopefully when she wakes up she'll remember who we are. I added the flowers haphazardly to the vase of daffodils rather than go on the hunt for a second vase, and topped up the water from the sink in the corner.

'I'd better go,' I said, giving her hand another squeeze. 'I'll come and see you again soon, alright?'

My phone rang as soon as I turned it back on, waiting at the bus stop on Denmark Hill.

'Hello?'

'Hi, it's me.'

'Hello, me.'

'I said I'd ring, didn't I?'

'You did. How was your journey?'

'Not bad, thanks. How are you?'

'I'm okay. I'm actually standing outside the Maudsley, waiting for a bus.'

'Are you? Have you been to see Mrs M?'

'Yes. She was asleep.'

'Did they say how she is?'

'I didn't see anyone else. I just went in and stayed for a minute. Anyway, here's my bus.'

'Oh. Can you not talk to me while you're on the bus?'

I was queueing to get on, behind an elderly couple and a group of teenagers carrying skateboards.

'I could, but I'd rather not.'

'Can I ring you later, then?'

I laughed. 'If you like.'

'What time?'

'Give me at least a couple of hours — you know I'll have things to do when I get in.'

That first time Lee hurt me, I mean the first time he actually left me with physical injuries, I had to take the next week off work. I pretended I had flu — to be honest I must have sounded rough when I phoned in on the Monday morning. It took a week for the marks on my face to be sufficiently disguisable with makeup. The only thing left was the cut to my lip, which ended up looking like a particularly horrible, scabby cold sore. My nose, fortunately, didn't turn out to be broken, or, if it was, it wasn't a bad break.

Needless to say, I didn't go to the doctor.

He stayed with me for five days. The next morning he was distant. He looked at me as though I'd been especially stupid and managed to fall over in the street. Nevertheless, he made me some soup and helped to clean me up, wiping my face with surprising tenderness.

The following day he was exceptionally gentle; he told me I was the only woman he'd ever loved. He told me I was his, only his; if any man ever looked at me he would kill them. He said it dismissively, as though it were a remark that could be made casually in conversation with little meaning, but I believed he could do it. He meant it.

For the time being, I had to play along with it. For those five days, I tried to be what he wanted me to be. I told him I was his, only his. That I had made a mistake by trying to end it. That I loved him.

When he left to go back to work on the Wednesday night, I considered my options. At first I stayed at home, in bed, watching television and pretending nothing had happened. I waited, and waited, in case he came home again. In case it was a test.

I wanted to call the police, but I knew he would check my phone. I wanted to leave the house, run, run as fast as I could to the police station, and hope they would protect me. They wouldn't, of course. He would be questioned, if I was lucky, and then there would be some sort of inquiry, during which time he would be free to come and go, free to hurt me, free to kill me. It wasn't worth the risk.

On the Thursday I called an emergency locksmith and got the locks changed on the front door and the back door.

That night was the first night I started checking properly.

By the following Monday there had still been no sign of him. I wondered if he'd gone for good; some part of me hoped he was feeling remorse for what he'd done, maybe changed his mind about me, decided to leave me in peace.

Back then I was still at least partly an optimist.

I went to work on the Monday, and got a lot of sympathy from people that I didn't really deserve. Nobody doubted that I'd had the flu — I'd lost about half a stone in weight in a week, I looked pale and gaunt and had a scab on my lip. The swelling had gone down across the bridge of my nose, and the bruising was easily concealed under several layers of foundation.

I didn't stay late; I was only at work until about four. I wasn't away for long.

When I got home on that Monday afternoon, I spent the first twenty minutes or so checking all the doors and windows. Everything was secure and I heaved a sigh of relief.

I didn't check the bedroom, of course; there didn't seem to be any point.

When I went up to bed at about ten, there, on my bed, was a little pile of shiny keys, and a note:

GOT SOME MORE KEYS CUT FOR YOUR NEW LOCKS.

SEE YOU LATER XX

I spent the next hour or so going over the house again, tears pouring down my cheeks, looking for the way he'd got in, and I never found it.

That night was my first panic attack, the first of many.

Friday 15 February 2008

I took Friday afternoon off work for my first appointment with Alistair. I was expecting to be more nervous than I was. I waited upstairs at Leonie Hobbs House, thinking of Christmas Day.

The clinic was busier, several people waiting to be seen, although hopefully not all of them waiting to see Alistair. There were several clinic rooms and there was a steady traffic of people in and out. No sign of Deb and her lip-ring today; behind the clinic reception desk on the first floor was a comfortably built lady in her fifties with battleship-grey hair and an NHS badge attached to her navy cardigan proclaiming her name to be Jean.

She hadn't spoken to me, other than to ask my name. She didn't make eye contact with anyone in the waiting room, just kept a close watch on her computer screen and on the pen attached to the desk by a long, thin chain.

'Cathy?'

I jumped to my feet and walked down the corridor to the only open door, through which Alistair must have run before I saw him.

'Come in, come in. How are you, my dear? It's good to see you again.'

With his effusive welcome I was half-expecting him to jump up and kiss my cheek, but fortunately for both of us, he didn't. He was sitting on a leather armchair next to a second chair and a sofa. He looked well, smiling at me and indicating I should sit down.

I chose the chair. 'Hello again,' I said. 'Did you make it home alright on Christmas Day?'

'Oh, yes. I managed to get a cab just up the road, I was quite surprised to find one so easily. Marvellous chap. Thank you, I did have the most wonderful time. And it was lovely to meet you after hearing so many good things from Stuart.'

I was starting to feel a bit shaky.

'Now, then,' Alistair began. 'I've been looking

at your assessment. You saw Dr Parry, am I right?'

'Yes.'

'And he prescribed an SSRI for you?'

'Yes.'

'Good, good. And you've been taking that — let's see — around three weeks?'

'About that.'

'They do take a while to kick in, sometimes. It might be a while before you see any effects.'

'They've not made me feel spaced out, anyway. That's what I was worried about.'

'Hm, no, they're not at all like the drugs you've had before, looking at your notes. Much more appropriate. Do you know, I really do feel you must have had an appalling time of it. The last time you were treated, I mean.'

I didn't answer.

'I shouldn't comment, really, but — hm. Anyway. It seems to me, my dear, that you might have two issues here, existing side by side. Your assessment indicates that you're clearly suffering from OCD, and the level of that is what we would call moderate-to-severe on the Yale-Brown Compulsive Symptoms checklist, the YBOCS list. Now Dr Parry noted, and I would tend to agree, that you also have plenty of symptoms which more resemble PTSD, that's post-traumatic stress disorder. The symptoms for this can be similar to OCD in terms of stress, but include things such as flashbacks, nightmares, an exaggerated startle response, and panic attacks.'

He flipped over the pages in his notes. 'And I

think you've been suffering from all of those . . . '

'Yes. I guess so.'

'And would you say they've been getting worse?'

'They get worse and better. I mean, I had a bit of a fright at the beginning of December. I had some bad panic attacks and nightmares for a week or two after that. And the OCD was worse, too. Then things got better for a while. Then Christmas Eve something else happened to set me off, and again, everything was a bit grim for a while. At the moment, it's not too bad.'

Alistair was nodding, patting his expanse of a belly reverently as though it contained a baby rather than merely his dinner. 'It's that pernicious worm of doubt, isn't it? You know full well that the door is locked, the tap is turned off, the switch is turned off, but still there is that doubt, and you have to go back and check again . . . '

He shuffled his papers and wrote a few lines of scribble on what looked like a dog-eared bit of scrap paper. 'The good news is that the therapy we can provide will help you with both OCD and PTSD. You'll need to be willing to work on this at home, on your own — and the more you're prepared to work on it, the better the result is likely to be. There will probably be some setbacks along the way, but with a bit of time and effort you will be able to get better. Okay?'

I nodded.

'Let's start at the beginning. Can you tell me a bit about what you were like as a child?'

I told him, slowly at first, the whole sorry story — leading up to but never seeming to reach the moment when I met Lee, the moment when my precarious life veered off towards that cliff edge. That would come later.

I had an hour and a half for the first session, next week it would be an hour, and so on once a week unless I felt I needed more. I'd agreed to try out some things at home. I was going to do something called 'exposure and response prevention'. Sensibly enough, this meant exposing myself to the perceived danger, and then waiting until the anxiety subsided, without performing any of the checks or rituals which would normally help to reduce the anxiety. Theoretically, the anxiety would reduce of its own accord. Rinse, repeat again and again and again.

I remained a little sceptical, but I promised to give it a go.

My phone rang when I was still about a mile away from home. The streets were quiet, just the after-school traffic. I was thinking about going for a run with what was left of the afternoon, although it was getting dark.

'Hello?'

'Hey, it's me. How did you get on?'

'Okay. It was fine. Is that what you do?'

'Pretty much. Not much to it really, is there?'

'I guess not, if you do it every day. I kept thinking it must be really dull, having to listen to all that.'

'Not at all. Everyone's different, don't forget. Everyone travels to that difficult point from a different direction. What are you doing now?'

'I was going to go home and check three times. Why?'

'I'll call you later, shall I? I'm just going to take Dad out to the garden centre. I just wanted to . . . let you know I was thinking of you.'

'I'll ring you, if you like. When I've finished the checks. Would that be okay?'

'That would be great. I'll keep the phone handy.'

I kept thinking of one of the things I'd talked about with Alistair. Theory A and Theory B — it was something for me to consider. Theory A: that if I somehow fail to check the flat properly, someone will break in. Not just someone. That Lee will break in, and that I will not realise he's done it. That I am actually in real danger if I fail to check thoroughly. Theory B: that actually checking the door once is enough, and that checking it over and over again does not make it any more secure, and that the reason for checking is simply that I am just extremely worried about being in danger. The two theories are in opposition to each other, and they cannot both be true. The rational theory is, of course, Theory B: that what I am doing by repeatedly checking everything does not make me any safer than checking once.

Even if I accept that Theory B is possible, how can I be sure that it is the truth? The only way, according to Alistair, is to carry out some sort of scientific experiment to see which theory holds water and which one falls apart under scrutiny.

It's all very obvious where this is going. I check less, nothing bad happens, *ergo* it's a complete waste of bloody time checking everything over and over again and I should stop doing it forthwith.

I'm not an idiot — even I know it's a waste of time. That doesn't stop me doing it.

And the thing that worries me more than anything is that actually this 'scientific testing' fails to take into account that my fears aren't based on some ridiculous invented danger at all.

They're based on the fact that Lee is out there somewhere, looking for me.

Assuming he hasn't found me already.

Monday 26 April 2004

Lee was here for a few hours on Sunday; before that he was working, or whatever it is he does when he's not here. When he let himself in on Sunday night I thought he was going to hit me again, but he seemed quite happy, pleased with himself as though he'd been clever.

'Why did you change the locks?' he asked conversationally, as we ate lunch.

I tensed. 'Don't know really,' I said, brightly. 'After the burglary, you know. Thought it might be safer.'

'Were you going to give me a new key?'

'Of course.'

He laughed, although I didn't think it was funny.

When I got to work this morning I sent an email to Jonathan Baldwin asking for more details about the sort of person he was looking for, and later this afternoon I got a reply:

Catherine,
   Good to hear back from you. Initially I'm looking for someone to help me get the NY branch established, really — ideally someone with some consultancy experience, although more importantly someone with enthusiasm and commitment who can be flexible enough to spot opportunities when they arise. I remember from years back that you seemed like the sort of person who would end up running some big organisation somewhere.
   I can sort out an L1 Transfer Visa, and I also have a short lease on an apartment in the Upper East Side (nothing too spectacular, but it has a south-facing balcony which is pretty rare). At some point in the future there may be the potential for a partnership in the company if things go well.
   The downside is that I need someone quickly — I'm getting calls from NY all the time with business opportunities that I'm having to turn down because of commitments in the UK, so the sooner I can get someone out there and setting up the office, the better.
   Any ideas?

Cheers
Jonathan

I'm wondering if I could do it. If I could deal with it all by phone and email, talk to him while I'm at work and discuss the finer points, this might be my chance to escape. I could be out there and in New York before Lee knew anything about it. If I could go to New York on a short-term contract, even three months, then that might buy me some time to decide what to do next. I might be able to get a sabbatical from work.

I just need enough time to get away from him.

Friday 15 February 2008

The High Street was still busy. Round the last corner, into Talbot Street. I was tired now, I would need to concentrate extra hard on the checking so I didn't make any mistakes.

Into the alleyway, round to the back of the house. I looked up at the windows, all of them, the balcony with the eight panes of glass showing, the bedroom, curtains shut tight. Stuart's flat had one light on in the bedroom. I'd put one of my timers up there. It would go off at eleven. Downstairs, Mrs Mackenzie's flat was in darkness. It all looked okay. I carried on to the end of the alleyway, round to the front of the house.

When I'd got in, shut the front door, it occurred to me that I was the only person in the house. I'd be the only person sleeping in the whole of this great big house tonight. No Mrs Mackenzie, no Stuart. Just me. Last night I'd ended up talking to Stuart for what amounted to hours, so it felt as if he was here; it didn't feel as if I was alone. Tonight felt different.

I checked the door, running my fingers along the edge, feeling for anything, any bumps or swells, which might indicate the door had been tampered with. Then the latch. Then the lock. Turn the handle, six times one way, six times the other way. I missed the sound of Mrs Mackenzie's television. I missed her coming out to see me.

I paused at the end of the first set of checks. This was normally the point at which she would open her door behind me.

I'm not sure if I felt something, or sensed it: a draught, maybe, a scent of food cooked a long time ago, a breath of cold air. I turned slowly and looked at the door. We'd shut it, and locked it, the night that Mrs Mackenzie had been taken off in the ambulance. Stuart had phoned the management company that looked after the lease, told them what had happened. They were going to send someone over to collect the key, but so far nobody had turned up.

I frowned, squinted. The door looked odd.

I went a bit closer.

It was slightly open, a tiny sliver of blackness showing beyond the doorframe. I felt the draught again, definite this time, a whisper of cold air coming from inside.

I pulled at the door handle and it swung open. It wasn't locked. Inside, everything was dark, dark as the grave.

I shut the door again, firmly. The latch caught and when I turned the handle this time it didn't open. Stuart's spare set of keys were in my bag. He'd put the key to Mrs Mackenzie's flat on the ring along with his other ones.

I found the keys, slotted the right one in the lock and turned it. I rattled the handle. I turned the key in the Yale lock and the mortise lock held the door fast. Right, it was definitely shut and locked. If anyone was inside they would need a key to get out.

I went back to the front door for my second set of checks. It didn't do the trick, though, because all I could think about was the door to Mrs Mackenzie's flat, which I'd turned my back on. What if I hadn't locked it properly? What if the door had swung open again while my back was turned? What if it opened again by itself when I wasn't looking?

I checked it again. It was still locked. I tried the Yale lock.

I checked the front door for a third time, to balance it all out again. Finally I felt better. I went up the stairs and let myself into my flat. The dining room light was on, as I'd left it, the rest of the flat dark and chilly. I waited for a moment just inside the door, listening to the sounds of the house, straining to hear anything unusual, out of place. Nothing.

I started checking the flat door, feeling vaguely uneasy but not sure why. I couldn't get over the thought that I was on my own. Completely on my own.

By the time I finished the checks it was nearly nine. I'd been expecting to find something wrong, but everything was exactly as it should have been. It was just as well.

Finally I sat down to phone Stuart.

'Hey, it's me.'

'At last, I was about to give up hope!' He sounded tired.

'How's your Dad doing?'

Stuart sighed and dropped his voice a little. I could hear a television faintly in the background. 'He's alright, really. He's a lot frailer than the last time I saw him. I don't think Rach really notices it, she sees him every day.'

'Did you get to the garden centre?'

'Yeah, but it's raining. Ended up looking round the greenhouses mostly. You wouldn't believe how many different plants that man can look at and not get bored. And it's bloody cold up here, too. I really miss you, Cathy.'

'Do you?' I felt my cheeks flush, realising at the same time that I was missing him, too. Even if we hardly saw each other during the week, with him being away I felt the absence of him like an ache.

'Yes. I wish you were here.'

'You'll be back Sunday night. It'll go fast.'

'It won't. Not for me, anyway. What are you going to do with your Saturday?'

'I don't know. Go to the launderette. Go for a run, maybe. I haven't been for a while.'

There was a pause. 'So it went well? Your session with Alistair?'

'It was fine. I've got homework to do — scoring everything. You know.'

'And you're feeling alright now?'

I knew what he was getting at. He was trying to gauge the likelihood of my discussing my symptoms leading to a panic attack later on. 'I feel fine about all that. I'm feeling more nervous about being here on my own. I mean, no Mrs Mackenzie downstairs, no you upstairs. Just me and the ghosts.'

'Peaceful, you mean.'

'Yes. Oh, but there is one thing. We did lock her door, didn't we? I mean, we locked it with the key?'

'We did. Why?'

'The door was open when I got home. Mrs Mackenzie's door, I mean. It was actually slightly open.'

'The management company must have been in, then. They said they were going to, didn't they?'

'Yes, but surely they were supposed to lock it up, not leave it open.'

'Maybe they just weren't as careful. Anyway, I'm betting it's well locked up now!'

'I hope so.'

'Cathy, you locked it. It's fine.'

I didn't answer.

'When I first met you, you did all this alone. You locked yourself in every night, checked the doors were secure, and you were fine. You're fine now, it's no different.'

I tried to sound cheerful. 'Yes, I know. I'm alright, really I am.'

'Will you come with me to Aberdeen next time?'

'Maybe. If you give me a bit more notice.'

'Rachel's dying to meet you.'

'Stuart, honestly. Did you tell her about the OCD?'

'No. Why, should I?'

'I just want to make sure she has a full and accurate picture.'

'The OCD isn't part of you, is it? It's just a symptom. Like snot is part of a cold.'

'Lovely. What have you been telling them, then?'

'I've told them I've met this girl with silver hair and dark eyes, who is funny and clever and charming and occasionally spectacularly stroppy. She can put away fifty cups of tea a day and outstare someone with glass eyeballs.'

'Now I see why they're dying to meet me.' I tried to fight back the yawn but it was impossible.

'Am I keeping you up?'

'I'm really tired. Sorry. I didn't sleep last night, and I walked back from that place today, the buses were all jammed in traffic.'

'You walked back from Leonie Hobbs House?'

'Give over, it's not that far. I like walking.'

I yawned again.

'Take the phone with you when you go to bed, okay?' he said.

'Why?'

'If you wake up in the night, ring me. Will you?'

'I don't want to wake you up, that's not fair.'

'I don't mind. If you're awake, I want to be awake with you.'

'Stuart. This is all really weird.'

'What do you mean, weird?'

'When you come back on Sunday, it's not

340

going to be the same, is it? It's all changed. Since the other day.'

'Since I kissed you, you mean.'

'Yes.'

'It has changed, you're right. I was bloody determined to keep my distance so you could concentrate on getting better. I don't think I can do that any more. Does that worry you?'

'I'm not sure. I don't think so.'

'My flight gets in at nine-something on Sunday night. Can I come and see you when I get back home? It'll be late.'

It was that moment, that turning point.

I hesitated before answering, knowing what it would mean if I said yes, and what it might mean if I said no.

'Cathy?'

'Yes. Come and see me. I don't care how late it is.'

Friday 21 May 2004

Lee's working all this weekend; just for a change, he's told me in advance. I don't know if this is a test, to see if I'm going to do a runner. I'm certain he doesn't know about New York, so I think he is still half-expecting me to try to get away from him some other way. He even said I should go out tonight, see my friends.

For the past few weeks he has been acting more than ever as though this relationship we have is normal. He hasn't been violent towards me; he hasn't turned up unexpectedly, he hasn't

341

even made any unreasonable demands. He's actually been kind, too — looking after me when I had a cold last week, cooking me dinner and getting some shopping in. If I hadn't seen that other side of him, I think I would be pleased at the way this relationship is turning out.

Things got better when I told him I was thinking of taking a sabbatical from work. I did it as a safety precaution; if anyone from work phoned, or if I let something slip, it would give me an explanation to fall back on. And of course he'd always wanted me to give up work, right from the start. I had thought it was because he wanted to see more of me, but of course it was all about control, even then.

I know him so much better now. When I'm at work, he phones me at odd times of the day. If I get back to my desk and find a missed call from him, I have to phone him back straight away. He always asks if I'm going to be off-site, if I've got any meetings — he knows my schedule better than I do. Once I got called into a meeting with the GM for several hours; when I rang him back I was expecting him to be angry with me, but he wasn't. Turned out later that he'd driven to where I work, found my car in the car park, opened it with his spare key (he has a duplicate set of my keys now; I haven't given them to him, but he has them anyway) and checked that the mileage on my car was right, meaning that I'd not been anywhere without letting him know. He knows exactly how many miles my car has done, and how many miles it is from home to work and vice versa. I cannot deviate from the route.

I've not tried to challenge him on any of this. I know it's wrong. I know he's got me completely controlled. The fact that I know all this is my own private rebellion. He doesn't know what's going on in my head. He doesn't know that I am going to seek an opportunity to escape, or that I know I can only attempt this once. He will kill me, I know he will, if I mess this up.

I've been in touch with Jonathan. I came right out with it and told him why he should consider me for his job in New York. I don't remember telling someone that I want to set up my own company one day, but I wouldn't be surprised if I'd said it in an inebriated state at one of those conference dinners. In any case, I don't care what the job is — although I'll work hard at it — it's the escape route I've been looking for. Fortunately it should all be dealt with by email at work, nothing at all needs to go to my home address — no need for it to be. When my replacement passport arrived a week ago, I took it with me to work and left it in my drawer.

I'm hoping that Jonathan will accept me, because I've almost been assuming that this is all going to go ahead. I don't think my sanity would hold up if it doesn't. My credit card went to paperless billing a long time ago, so if I need to book flights Lee shouldn't be any the wiser. I check my emails at work. After the burglary, I didn't bother to replace my laptop. There didn't seem to be any point.

So, for now, he can watch me all he wants; my time in Lancaster is limited.

Soon I will be free.

I heard Stuart on the stairs, dragging his backpack, bumping it against the wall. I was sitting on my sofa, my socked feet tucked under me, my nerves singing like an electric fence. When I heard him I wondered whether to leave him to go all the way up to the top floor with his bag, get home, get settled in, have a shower, make a drink, whatever else people do when they get home after a journey. I wondered whether he might have forgotten about coming to see me, even though we'd talked about it on Friday night, even though he'd mentioned it again last night, even though he'd sent me a text from Heathrow to say his plane had landed and he was on his way home.

Then I remembered his shoulder, and before I had time to think about it any more I ran over to the door, unbolted everything and unlocked it and opened it.

He'd just about made it to the landing.

He was a bit out of breath, his backpack lying at his feet like some kind of hunted beast, his hand looped through the strap as though he was going to drag it back to his lair. 'God,' he said, 'this thing is fucking heavy.'

'What's in it?'

'Shitloads of books. I don't know what I thought I was doing, bringing them back. They were in Rachel's garage.'

I stared at him for a moment. 'Do you want me to give you a hand taking it upstairs?'

He didn't reply at first. He looked as though

he'd forgotten where he was and what he was doing. He looked lost.

'Can I come in?' he said at last.

I nodded and stood to one side. He left the bag where it was, stranded on its back on the landing.

I pushed the door shut as soon as he was inside, started the process of locking and checking, counting as quickly as I possibly could without making any mistakes, all the while Stuart standing there behind me, waiting.

At last he said, 'Cathy, for fuck's sake. This is torture.'

'I'm going as fast as I can.'

'Seriously. Please. Leave it now, it's locked.'

'The more you talk, the longer it'll take, so shut up, okay?'

He waited. He must have been counting with me, because just as I finished, before I could start again, he came up behind me and slipped his arms around my waist. I didn't flinch. He rested his head against mine, his breath warm against my hair. I looked down at his forearms around my middle. I turned slowly and raised my head so that I could look at him, the expression in his eyes difficult to determine.

'You're nervous,' I said.

He smiled. 'That obvious, huh?'

'It's okay,' I said, and kissed him.

After that first kiss, it got easier. I took him into my bedroom. He started undressing me and then we got tangled up and so I took over and stripped off.

The bedroom was dark, the only light coming

345

into the room from the living room, but even so I was conscious of the scars. He must have felt the scars, in the dark, as he ran his hands over my skin. But he didn't say anything. He must have felt them with his mouth when he kissed me, with his tongue. He didn't say a word.

The strangest thing was that I felt it, I felt everything. Normally I feel nothing but itching, discomfort, tightness, soreness. The surface of my skin is dulled by the scars, lots of it is numb — nerve damage, apparently. When he touched me, I felt everything. It was like having new skin.

Tuesday 25 May 2004

Jonathan rang me on my mobile yesterday; thankfully nobody was in my office at the time. It was supposed to be an interview of sorts, but I could tell straight away that it was just a formality. I tried to picture him, but I couldn't put the voice to the face. I was nervous in any case, trying not to let it show in my voice. Slightly exaggerating my management consultancy experience — whatever, it did the trick. He said he would employ me on a three-month temporary contract, just to get things started. If I liked it and he liked my work, he would extend it. He booked my flights and emailed me the times — I will have to pick up the tickets at the airport.

I saw my boss at the end of the day and handed in my notice. With annual leave owing, I've only got just over two weeks left with the company. She wasn't happy. I made a pretence at apologising for leaving her to find a new HR manager but in reality my heart was singing.

So, today I made one of my rare trips out in public. Although I wanted to go to the post office to get some US dollars, I was reluctant to head straight there in case Lee was watching. He was supposed to be off working somewhere, but that didn't mean he wasn't busy following me. He'd done it before; he'd done it so often that I saw his face everywhere I went. Probably most of the time I was imagining it, but not always.

I strolled around Boots for a while, pretending to look at the pregnancy tests — that ought to get him going, I thought, if he's watching — and then the make-up.

My flight was booked for 4pm on Friday 11th June — my last day at work in the UK would be the Thursday, the day before. I decided to buy a suitcase and leave it at work, sneak important things out of the house, clothing, one or two items at a time, more when he wasn't there to see. I could hide the suitcase in my storeroom at work — fortunately I was the only person who ever went in there. It wasn't ideal, it wasn't a way I'd ever packed before, but it would have to do. I'd take the minimum amount of clothes and buy new stuff when I got to New York.

There was still a lot of stuff in the house, though. I couldn't just pretend I was suddenly deciding to de-clutter — it wasn't worth the risk. With my New York salary I could afford to keep up the rent on the Lancaster house, for now. Maybe in a few months' time I could come back and hand the keys back to the landlady, and clear out my stuff. All I needed was a few months, just long enough for him to forget about me and move on.

I chanced a look up, over the top of the display counter, and there he was — right over the other side of the store, by the entrance, to one side — wearing his suit, today, I noticed — maybe he'd had some kind of a meeting with the management.

I had to pretend I hadn't seen him, although I'd have loved to have given him a wave. It put paid to my plans to visit the post office, though. I would try again tomorrow — I'd tell him I needed to collect a parcel for a friend, or something.

Friday 22 February 2008

I woke up suddenly, going from deep, dark sleep to wide awake, heart thumping, in a matter of a few seconds.

I was in Stuart's bed, and it was perfectly dark. No sound except him breathing next to me. I listened with my whole body, straining to hear whatever it was that had woken me.

Silence.

I looked down at Stuart, the shape of him illuminated in the half-light from the window, his shoulder a pale curve. I was still getting used to sleeping with him, even though we'd spent every spare minute together since he'd come back from Aberdeen. Every time I woke up and he was there, it took me a few moments to calm down and remember.

I'd been dreaming about Sylvia. Stuart was there with me, and we were naked, making love in bed as though we were all alone, just as we had been doing just a few hours ago. In my dream I'd looked up and she'd been there, in the doorway, the pink beret set firmly on her blonde hair, her mouth thin, a mean smile.

There it was again, a sound. Not in the flat, though — outside. I got out of bed and crept round to the other side, to the window, pulling Stuart's shirt off the hook on the back of the door on the way past and putting it on, wrapping it over my front.

It wasn't quite dawn, still perfectly dark, the sky just beginning to turn grey. I looked out from the side of the window over the back garden, the wall a rectangle of darkness, a regular shape, the grass grey tussocks underneath. I couldn't see the shed from here, my balcony below was in the way. I leaned over the windowsill and peered down into the darkness, starting to relax, when suddenly — something moved.

At the same moment Stuart spoke from the bed and made me jump out of my skin. 'What are you doing? Come back to bed.'

'There's someone outside,' I said, an urgent whisper.

'What?' He swung his legs out of the bed and stretched for a moment before coming to stand next to me. 'Where?'

'Down there,' I whispered. 'Near the shed.'

I stood back from the window a little, not

wanting to obscure his view.

'I can't see anything.' He put his arm around my shoulders and yawned. 'You're cold, come back to bed.'

He saw my expression and looked out of the window again, then to my horror lifted the sash. It made a noise like the door to Hell creaking open. 'Look,' he said suddenly, pointing.

A shape darted across the lawn and under the gap between the gate and the lawn, a dark shape, but definitely not a human. 'A fox,' he said. 'It was a fox. Now come here.'

He pushed the sash window back down, peeled his shirt away from my shoulders and drew me back into the warm bed. My skin was cold against his but he warmed me quickly enough, with his tongue and his hands and his whole naked body against mine, until I forgot all about the shape I'd seen; forgot how it was actually nothing like a fox, but bigger and darker and bulkier; how it seemed to be on my balcony, on the floor below; and how I'd seen the reflection of the grey sky against something shiny, something long and thin and shiny, like a long knife.

Thursday 10 June 2004

It was too much to hope that Lee would be working on the day I was planning my escape. In a way, though, having him at home with me was better. If he was here watching me, I knew exactly where he was. And if I managed to leave early enough, I might even get a head start.

Last night he let himself into the house, late, when I was watching a film on the sofa. My mind was fizzing with it all, the thought of getting away from him, the fear of it all going horribly wrong. When I heard his key in the door I forced myself to smile, stay calm, not give anything away.

He was in a suit today. He hung his jacket over the back of the chair in the dining room and came to give me a kiss.

'Can I get you anything?' I asked.

'A beer would be good,' he said. He looked tired.

I got him a bottle from the fridge and brought it through.

'I was thinking,' he said, 'we should go on holiday. What do you think? Get away from it all for a bit, just you and me.'

'Sounds good.'

'Have you sent off those passport forms yet?'

I looked at him, hoping he hadn't seen me jump. 'I sent them off. Not had anything back. Takes ages, doesn't it?'

Lee raised his eyebrows and took a swig from the bottle. 'I've always fancied going to the States. Never been. Have you been?'

'No.'

'Maybe Vegas. Or New York. What do you think?'

My heart was thumping so loudly he must surely be able to hear it. 'Mm.'

'You know I love you, Catherine?'

I smiled at him, 'Of course.'

351

'I think it's important that we're honest with each other. You love me?'

'Yes.'

'We could get married. In Vegas. What do you think?'

Right at that moment, I would have agreed to anything, just to shut him up. I only needed another few hours.

'I think it sounds fabulous,' I said. And I kissed him.

Thursday 28 February 2008

I had another panic attack today.

It wasn't nearly as bad as the others I've had, and I don't think any panic attack is ever going to be as bad as the one I had on Christmas Eve when I first spoke to Sam Hollands, but, just when I was starting to think that those tablets were kicking in and I was getting better as far as the anxiety was concerned, something happened to upset the balance.

I stayed on the bus all the way to Park Grove, just around the corner from the flat. I took my regular detour through the back alleyway and spent a moment looking up at my curtains, checking each square of glass in the balcony doors to make sure the curtains were hanging properly. I looked at the gate, hanging off its hinges. There was no doubt that some animal was using this as a route: the grass was trodden into a pathway, with tufts of some greyish fur caught on the rough wood. The gate didn't look as though it had been disturbed. If someone had been on my balcony, they must have come over the wall. I looked up at it. It was well over six feet, solidly built, with no easy way over.

I was thinking about Mrs Mackenzie again, and what she'd said to me about seeing something outside. Maybe she'd meant something outside had made her jump, and that had caused her to fall.

I had a good look over the gate at the ground floor windows, at her patio doors. They all looked fine to me. The flat downstairs was in darkness, just as we'd left it.

Stuart was already home, upstairs preparing dinner. I was going to get changed from my work clothes and bring some clean clothes for tomorrow.

Checking felt like a chore tonight, especially because Stuart was upstairs and every minute I spent down here fiddling with my doors and windows was a minute wasted.

I got all the way to the bedroom before the checking went wrong. It took me a moment to notice, even.

The curtains were open.

Initially the shock was like a bucket of icy water. I felt my heart start to thump in my chest, so loud I could hear it behind the roaring of blood in my ears. I couldn't breathe for a moment, and then I was breathing fast and hard. I got as far as feeling the headswim before I kicked in with the focus — breathe deeply. Slow it down. In — hold it — and out.

I'm good at this now. And the rationalising.

Nobody has been here. You are safe. Nobody has been here — you just left the curtains open last time you were here. And breathe. Breathe deeply.

It was getting to be daylight in the mornings when I got up. I opened the curtains in Stuart's bedroom this morning, letting the light flood in. Last time I'd been in my flat was — when? Monday evening? It had been still broad daylight when I'd left the flat, when I'd gone upstairs to get the dinner on before he got in from work. What about when I'd been standing outside in the alleyway, looking up at the windows, just a few minutes ago. Had they been open then? I tried to picture it, but I couldn't say for sure — I was looking at the balcony, and then at Mrs Mackenzie's flat. I couldn't even remember looking at the bedroom window. Surely I would have noticed if I'd left them open — wouldn't I?

I'd left them open. Nobody had been in here, I'd just left them open. It was the only possible explanation.

I could just about have accepted this, that it had been light, so I wouldn't have closed the curtains, except for the fact that all the other curtains in the flat — other than the balcony curtains, which were open exactly the right amount — were closed.

Maybe I'd not even been in my bedroom on Monday evening? Had I checked the flat properly on Monday? Or had I been in such a rush that I'd missed the bedroom out altogether and left the curtains open from the previous time I'd been in here? I tried to fish out the memory of Monday, what I'd done, but it blurred into last Wednesday and the Monday before.

I kept up the breathing until I started to feel as if I could move. I got to the curtains and stood for a moment looking out at the garden, seeing if anything was different; daffodils were growing haphazardly out of the borders, the grass overgrown. There was no sign of anything being different or out of order in the garden. Nothing to worry about.

I checked the window, feeling all around it. Nothing wrong there either. I closed the curtains and got changed, telling myself all the while that I was a fool, I was stupid. My jeans were on my bed, folded exactly as I'd left them. I slipped them on, finding a clean T-shirt. From the wardrobe I got a clean blouse for tomorrow, a long skirt and the navy blue heels that went with it, folded them into a neat pile with the shoes balanced on top.

I put the clothes into a carrier bag and put it by the front door of the flat before I started going round the flat again, checking everything was secure. This time I did it properly. Left the curtains closed, all the curtains closed except for the dining room, the room I could see from the back alleyway. I left these open exactly halfway, letting the fabric fall back in the precise way that I knew I would recognise.

I was actually feeling okay as I headed up the stairs to Stuart's flat. I was feeling okay as we had dinner, telling him about how I'd nearly freaked out and lost it in my bedroom just because I'd forgotten that I'd left the curtains open this week. We laughed about it and I was

355

fine about that; I was fine all the way until we were snuggled up on the sofa in Stuart's living room, watching a comedy and laughing until the tears rolled down my cheeks.

I was fine right up until the moment I shoved my hands into my jeans pocket, searching for a tissue, and instead pulled out a button, a tiny button covered in red satin, a scrap of red satin fabric behind it, screwed up tightly as though someone had twisted and twisted it around until it had finally torn off.

And I wasn't fine at all after that.

Friday 11 June 2004

At four o'clock this afternoon, I will be free.

My eyes opened this morning and Lee was fast asleep beside me, his eyelashes fanned out across his cheek like a bird's wing. He looked beautiful, peaceful, as though he wasn't capable of hurting anybody.

It was ridiculously early, but I wasn't tired any more — my head was buzzing with nervous energy. I felt as if I was about to go on stage at the Royal Albert Hall, or pull off a mind-blowingly cunning jewel heist. I'd planned today in excruciating detail, with contingency plans in case anything went wrong. In case he was suspicious; in case something unexpected happened.

Before bed last night I'd told him I was going in to work early today; that I had a meeting this afternoon and I was going to need to go in to prepare for it. He'd not even looked concerned, not looked doubting — in fact I think he'd been barely listening. So far, so good.

A quarter to six. I got up, as quietly as I could, desperate not to wake him. I went into the bathroom to dress, my navy blue suit, shoes with just a bit of a heel, the same clothes I'd worn last week. I wanted to eat something for breakfast, but my stomach was churning so much I thought I might actually be sick.

I was going to be sick.

I made it to the downstairs bathroom just in time, watery vomit coming out of my mouth. God, I must be more nervous than I'd thought. I rinsed my mouth in cold water, my hands trembling a little.

My routine, carefully considered to be identical to a normal work day, even though Lee was still fast asleep upstairs. I pinned my hair back in a neat bun. I put on make-up, drank a glass of water, rinsed it out and put it on the drainer. After a moment's thought, I rinsed out a clean cereal bowl and spoon and put that on the drainer, too.

I collected my bag and my keys, and quietly shut the front door behind me. It was nearly half-past six.

Thursday 28 February 2008

'That's it, that's better — come on. Deep breath. Another. Slower.'

'I can't — it's bad, this — '

'It's fine. I'm here, everything's alright, Cathy.'

The little scrap of red was lying in the middle of the rug like an open wound. I couldn't look at it. In the background the television was laughing at my hysteria. I guess it must have looked quite funny to an outsider.

When I was almost calm again he took me with him to the kitchen and made me sit at the kitchen table while he made tea.

'What happened?' he said. He was always so unflappable, so bloody composed.

'It's that. It was in my pocket.'

Stuart looked across to the rug. 'What is it?'

I shook my head, side to side, until I started to feel dizzy. 'It's — just a button. It's not that. It's how did it get into my pocket? I didn't put it in there. It shouldn't be in there. It means that he's been in the flat. He got in and put it in my pocket.'

'Hey. Come on, deep breaths again. You're over this, don't let it get to you again. Here's your tea, come on, have a bit.'

I had some gulps, burned my throat, felt sick. My hands were shaking. 'You don't understand.'

He sat opposite me with his tea, and waited. Always with the unending fucking patience, it got on my nerves. It reminded me of the fucking nurses in that crazy fucked-up excuse for a hospital.

'Can we just leave it? Please? I'm fine now.'

He didn't speak.

I drank my tea. Despite myself, I was starting to calm down. I still couldn't look at it, couldn't think about it, what it meant. In the end, I managed a whisper. 'Please could you get rid of it?'

'I'll need to leave you on your own for a minute.'

'Yes. Don't go far.'

'I'll put it in the bin outside. Alright?'

He got up from the table. I put my hands over my face, blocking it out. I kept my eyes screwed shut until I heard the door to the flat shut behind him — he knew better than to leave it open these days — and his footsteps on the stairs. I wanted to scream. I wanted to scream and not stop, but I held it in, counted to ten, told myself that it was gone, it was gone forever, maybe it had never been there in the first place, maybe I'd imagined it.

He came back a few minutes later and sat back down at the kitchen table. I drank my tea and gave him a smile that I hoped was reassuring. 'See?' I said. 'Nothing to worry about. Just your crazy girlfriend flipping again for no reason.'

He just kept up that steady eye contact. 'I'd like it if you could tell me,' he said. 'I think it'll help.'

I didn't answer, wondering if I could say no, and if I did whether he would be satisfied with that or whether he would go on and on and on . . .

'This is part of my past. I want to get rid of it, forget about it,' I said.

'It's part of your past that's clearly having a significant impact on your present.'

'You think I put it in there myself?'

'I didn't say that.'

I bit my lip. My tea was only half-drunk, otherwise I would probably have got up and walked out. In any case, I wanted to go downstairs and start checking, try to work out how the hell he got in.

'Look,' he said at last, 'I'm not trying to get inside your head. I just want to know how I can help. Can you try and forget what job I do and just tell me? I'm not your therapist, Cathy. I'm just the poor bastard who's in love with you.'

I found myself smiling in spite of it all. 'I'm sorry. I've kept all this in for so long, it's hard to just let it all out, you know?'

'I know.'

I got up and went to sit on his lap, folding myself into him and tucking my head under his chin. He put his arms round me and held me.

'I had this red dress. It was what I was wearing when I met him. He got a bit obsessive about it.'

I had a momentary picture of the dress when I'd bought it, how perfectly it fitted, how I'd had to buy shoes to match. I'd loved it, at first. I'd wanted to wear it all the time.

'And this button reminds you of the ones on that dress?'

'Yes — no, it's more than that. It is from the dress, I'm sure it is — oh, I don't know!' I had been racking my memory desperately, trying to picture the dress, the exact size of the buttons, whether the backs were metal or plastic. I veered from absolute certainty that it was, back to doubt. Of course, now the button was outside in the bin I couldn't check. There was one thing that was beyond question, though. 'It's the sort of thing he'd do, Stuart. It's exactly the sort of twisted game he used to play. He put that — thing — in my pocket to let me know he's come back for me.'

Stuart's fingers were stroking the skin on my forearm, but I could feel tension in him, in the way he was holding me. I was waiting for him to say it. *It's just a button. It doesn't mean anything.*

'You could have picked it up somewhere,' he said gently.

'No,' I said. 'I don't just pick things up. Do you? Do you just go around randomly picking up other people's crap? No? I don't either.'

'Maybe it got mixed up in your washing,' he said, 'at the launderette. It's tiny. It could have been left in the washing machine by whoever used it last. It was all twisted, wasn't it? Perhaps it got caught in the machine or something. Isn't that a possibility?'

'Whose side are you on?'

I got up, suddenly suffocated by his arms around me. I crossed the room and changed my mind and came back again, pacing, trying to stop the panic and the anger and the sheer, dreadful hopelessness of it all.

'I didn't realise there were sides.'

'Shut up and stop being such an idiot!' I shouted.

He shut up. I'd crossed a line and felt bad straight away. 'I'm sorry,' I said. 'I didn't mean that.'

'You should ring the police,' he said at last.

'What for? They won't believe me,' I said miserably.

'They might.'

'You don't believe me; why should they?'

'It's not that I don't believe you. I think you're severely traumatised by what happened, you're afraid now and that's making you ignore the fact that there are potentially rational explanations for how it came to be in your pocket.'

'That's just the point, Stuart. It was *in my pocket*. It wasn't just tangled up in the washing, it was in my fucking pocket. It didn't just fall in there of its own accord, and I didn't put it there, he did. Don't you get it? He used to do things like this. He'd break into my house when I wasn't there, leave me messages, move things around. Things you wouldn't necessarily notice. It's why I started the checking.'

'He'd break into your house?'

'He was — kind of an expert in it. I never worked out how he managed to get in. He could break into just about any house without you knowing how.'

'Jesus. You mean he was a burglar?'

'No. He wasn't a burglar. He was a police officer.'

Friday 11 June 2004

I drove away from the house, not daring to look back.

The sun was bright already, the sky cloudless

362

and blue, the air chilly but not cold. It was going to be a beautiful day, a fantastic day. When I got to the end of my street, indicated right, turned the corner, I felt a scream starting to bubble up inside me, a laugh, a manic laughter of release. All the panic that had built up in me for so long.

I drove to work, let myself in through the rear doors so that I didn't have to say hello to security, and retrieved my suitcase from its hiding place. In the side pocket were my US dollars, my passport complete with three-month visa, and my travel documents. My office was bare and empty — someone else would be moving into it next week. I dragged my suitcase out to the back door, hoping that security wouldn't be looking at the CCTV cameras right at that moment, hoping that nobody would see me, ask me how I was doing and wasn't I supposed to have left already?

Part one of the plan had gone well.

Once I got to the motorway, I was singing. I drove two junctions down the motorway to Preston and negotiated my way through the gradually building rush-hour traffic to the railway station. In the next street was a second-hand car dealership. I parked on the street in front of the crowded forecourt. On the front seat next to me was the car's log book and MOT certificate. I'd signed the portion of the V5 which stated that I was selling the car, and left the remainder of it blank. Next to it I left a note:

To Whom It May Concern
  Please look after this car. I don't need it
any more.
          Thank you.

I left the keys in the ignition. Hopefully whoever found it wouldn't feel the need to report it to the police.

I pulled my suitcase from the boot and wheeled it up to the station entrance. I bought a ticket for London, paying cash, dragged my case down to the platform to wait. The London train was due in five minutes. I wanted to be gone, already, even though I knew Lee was probably still fast asleep in bed; I wanted to be away from him; I wanted to run and never look back.

The train was busy at first, each station bringing new people on and taking old people off. I wanted to relax, to read a book, to look like a normal person. I sat still and gazed out of the window at countryside and towns rushing past, each station we went through taking me further and further away from my old life and closer to freedom.

A week ago, a week to the day, he'd come in late — gone eleven o'clock. I'd thought he was out for the evening, I'd thought I'd be safe until Saturday at least, but he'd turned up and let himself in. I was watching a programme on New York and the sound of the front door opening and closing made me jump, and without thinking I turned it off.

The smell of alcohol preceded him into the

living room. It was not going to be pleasant, I knew.

'What you doing?' he demanded.

'I was just going to bed. Would you like me to make you a drink?'

'Had enough to bloody drink.'

He fell onto the sofa beside me. Still wearing the same jeans and hooded sweatshirt he'd been wearing two days before when he'd left for work. He ran a weary hand over his forehead. 'I saw you in town last night,' he said, his tone challenging.

'Did you?' I'd seen him, too, but I wasn't going to admit it. 'I was out for a drink with Sam. I told you — remember?'

'Yeah, whatever.'

'I thought you were working,' I said, wishing I could just tell him to leave me the fuck alone and stop following me.

'I was fucking working,' he said. 'I just saw you going from the Cheshire to the Druid's. Looked like you were having a right laugh. Who was that bloke?'

'What bloke?'

'Bloke with you. Had his arm round you.'

I thought, forced myself to remember. 'I don't remember him having his arm round me, but the bloke that was with us was Sam's boyfriend.'

'Come here.' His arms were held open, swaying slightly, and I gritted my teeth and snuggled up to his chest. He gave me a crushing hug, pressing my face into his sweatshirt. He smelt of pubs, tarmac, takeaway food and alcohol. His hand pushed the hair out of my face, and then he pulled my face up to his for a kiss. He was clumsy about it.

After a minute he said, 'Your time of the month?'

I thought briefly about nodding, but it wouldn't do me any good. 'No.'

'Why you being so unfriendly, then?'

'I'm not being unfriendly,' I said, trying to keep my voice bright. 'Just tired, that's all.' To prove my point, I hid a delicate yawn behind my hand.

'You're always fucking tired.'

I was at that crossroads again, the one where I could either be brave and let him have what he wanted, or try to fight it and risk getting another serious beating. When he was drunk like this, he wasn't going to let me get away with saying no, and I didn't want to risk starting my new job in New York with yellowing bruises on my face.

'I'm not *too* tired, though,' I said, with a smile. My hand in the crotch of his jeans, giving him a rub. Undoing his belt.

In the end, he beat me anyway. He fucked me and I tried hard to make sure it didn't hurt too much, trying to make it last as though I was enjoying it. I knew the way it was going when he started slapping my backside while he was fucking me, just a slap at first, but carrying on getting harder and harder until I had to cry out. That was what seemed to turn him on these days. He could fuck for hours, especially if he'd had a drink, his erection coming and going, until he found some way of hurting me — biting me, or pulling my hair until I cried out, and as soon as he heard that genuine note of pain in my voice, he'd go at it harder until he'd hurt me enough to tip him over the edge and he'd orgasm.

He pulled out of me abruptly and turned me over onto my back, his breath coming in ragged gasps, his eyes glinting with pleasure. The skin on my behind stung as it came into contact with the carpet underneath.

I wondered what he was going to do. I thought by now it wasn't possible to still be afraid of him. He'd hurt me so many times that this was now almost a regular event. He was getting ever more inventive, finding new ways to humiliate me.

'Don't hit my face,' I said quietly.

'What?'

'Anything — just not my face. They ask too many questions at work.'

He grinned, an ugly leer, and for a moment I thought he was going to do just that, hit me again and again across the face until my skin split. I felt tears start, although I hated letting him see me cry.

'That so?'

I nodded, not able to look at him any more. Then he deliberately put one hand under my chin, choosing his place, thumb on one side, fingers the other.

'No,' I said, 'please, Lee . . . '

'Fucking shut up,' he said, 'it's good like this, you're going to love it.'

While he fucked me, he took away the air from my lungs, my fingers at my throat, trying to relieve the pressure, the air burning my lungs, the roaring in my ears signalling that I was going to lose consciousness in just a matter of moments.

Then, still fucking me hard, he'd ease the pressure and I'd cough and gasp, dragging air into my lungs. The only way to stop him was to give in. I screamed, as loud and as hard as I could, tears racing down my cheeks. I'd almost seen death. I was utterly terrified and screaming was almost involuntary — so I screamed.

He didn't try to stop me, didn't put his hand over my mouth again, and just let me scream. It did the trick. A few seconds later he pulled out of me and jerked off over my face.

On the train now, the Midlands rushing by in a blur of green and sunshine, I closed my eyes against the nausea.

Afterwards, he'd picked himself up off the carpet, staggered to the downstairs toilet to wash in the sink, and then he'd gone upstairs and fallen into bed. I'd waited until I could hear him snoring, then I got myself to my hands and knees, still crying, and went to have a shower. At least the only bruises I had that time were around my throat. I wore a neck scarf to work every day this week. They all thought I'd gone and got myself a love bite, at the grand old age of twenty-four.

At nine o'clock, the train pulled in to Crewe. I heard the station announcer run through the list of stations that remained on the journey, all the way to Euston, and then, 'Due to a signalling failure at Nuneaton, this train will be delayed for half an hour.'

Half an hour? I checked my watch, although I knew what the time was. It was fine. I'd allowed an extra two hours in addition to the three-hour check-in time at Heathrow. As long as there were no further delays, there wouldn't be a problem getting there on time.

I wanted to sleep, but I was too wound-up, too fraught. When would I be able to relax? Would I relax when I was on the plane? When I got to New York? When I heard that he'd moved away from Lancaster, or when a year had passed and I hadn't heard from him?

Would I ever, ever be able to relax again?

Sunday 9 March 2008

In the end I phoned DS Hollands, in the Domestic Abuse Liaison Office at Camden Police Station, just to bring an end to the argument. When I eventually got through to her, she had completely forgotten who I was. I explained about the curtains and the button, and — stumbling over my words — how this had been typical of Lee's actions when we'd been together. Even as I said it, it sounded stupid even to me. It sounded like something someone would say just to get attention. I was half-expecting her to tell me off for wasting police time, but in fact she said very little. She said she would phone her contact in Lancashire and would get back to me if there were any concerns.

She didn't phone back.

That night Stuart didn't sleep very well. I lay next to him waiting for him to sleep, knowing that he was awake because of the things I'd told him. He deserved better than me. He deserved someone who wasn't so fucked up, someone who wasn't trailing a psychopath along with a whole host of other baggage. We lay in bed next to each other in silence, not touching. I wanted to talk some more, but there was no point.

It wasn't just a button. It wasn't even just any red button, I was certain of that now. It was a button that came from a dress that I'd worn in another life, another time, with my heart on my sleeve. A dress I'd loved and then hated. And at some point after that, fingers that had once caressed the satin with such a curious, sensual reverence had taken hold of the tiny button and twisted it round and round with force until it had torn away.

When I woke up the next morning, Stuart was already dressed and ready for work. 'We should go away this weekend,' he said.

'Away?'

'Just for a break. Somewhere out of the city. What do you think?'

In the end we spent the weekend at a hotel in the Peak District, going for long walks during the day, eating too much in the evening and then holding each other in a magnificent four-poster bed, all night. It was a wonderful weekend, and, contrary to expectations, I had no need to fiddle with the curtains.

It was the sort of weekend I would have talked over in great and extensive detail with Sylvia, in years past. Of course that won't happen now. I sometimes wonder where she is, what she's doing. It could be that she's living just up the road from me, and that I pass her house every day. I don't know where she is. I guess if I phoned up the *Daily Mail* I could probably find her, but a lot of water has passed under a lot of bridges now, and I don't know if that is something I could do. Sylvia, although she was my best friend for a long, long time, is part of my old life — the life I was convinced I couldn't go back to.

I have a new life now, and it's with Stuart.

Gradually the panic about the red button faded, and going away for the weekend gave me a chance to think about it. To me, there wasn't any rational explanation of how it came to be in my pocket, so I pretended it hadn't happened. Maybe Stuart was right — maybe I'd even picked it up myself, in some kind of reverse-psychology absent-mindedness — maybe it was some perverse new symptom of my OCD.

But when we got home I went back to checking, properly. I made a point of going into the flat every morning before work, checking and leaving everything in order, and then checking it when I got home, turning the lights on when it got dark, making it look to anyone who might have been watching from outside that I was home, even when I was upstairs with Stuart. I bought another plug socket timer, and I would turn on the television when I got home from work, leaving it to turn itself off again at eleven o'clock at night. Sometimes I managed to restrict the checking to three times, as per Alistair's instructions; sometimes it was more.

As for the feeling of being watched — that had never, ever really gone away. Now it was back properly. In every street, every shop, every time I went outside the house, I felt eyes on me. I knew it was my imagination; after all, he was miles away, wasn't he? He might well have been released at the end of December, but if he was going to come looking for me he would have done it by now.

Part of me wished he'd found some new person to be with, and another part of me hoped he hadn't, for her sake.

Friday 11 June 2004

By the time I got to Heathrow, I had less than an hour to check in. The latter part of the journey, arriving at Euston, taking the Tube to Paddington, getting the Heathrow Express, dragging my stupid suitcase from place to place, had been hard. I was getting more and more fraught.

I checked in at the American Airlines desk, and that was a defining moment. I was here, I was safe. I spent a few moments wandering around the shops in the terminal, thinking about spending money on things I didn't need. I hadn't bought any lingerie since before I'd met Lee. If I'd bought some for myself, he would have accused me of sleeping with someone else. I touched some delicate lace panties in the lingerie shop and thought about buying them. Then, looking out across the crowded terminal, I caught a glimpse of a figure that looked too much like him. I caught my breath, but the man turned and it wasn't him at all.

Lee was all the way back in Lancaster, I thought. He thought I was at work. He was five hundred miles away, and even if he found out I was gone now, I'd be safe on the plane by the time he got here. There was nothing at all he could do now.

Still, I wanted to get into the departure lounge. There was no point whatsoever in hanging around now.

Every step I took, I felt watched. Even here, miles from home, miles from Lee, I could see his face everywhere I looked. It was going to be so good to get away from all that.

I joined the queue to pass through the checkpoint into the departure lounge, casting one last glance across the terminal at the sea of faces, faces going about their business, happy holiday faces and tired business faces. Suits and shorts, sunglasses and briefcases. I was nearly there. A few more steps, another couple of hours in the departure lounge, I'd be on the plane. I'd be free.

And then, suddenly — there he was, walking past Tie Rack towards me. His eyes on me, his face impassive.

The queue was still snaking round the metal barrier — I couldn't stay here.

I just ran, panicked, ran as fast as I could, towards a security guard, a man in uniform, who was strolling along the concourse without any idea what was about to hit him. I didn't chance a look behind me. If I had, I would have seen Lee flashing his badge at the security guard whose eyes were widening as I flew towards him, my mouth open in some sort of soundless scream, some sort of 'Help me, help me' . . . and instead of putting himself between me and Lee, instead of being my protector, my saviour, he grabbed me and threw me to the floor so my face and hands and knees smacked into the granite; held my arms back while Lee pulled out his cuffs and snapped them onto my wrists. And while Lee struggled to get his breath back and gasped, 'You're nicked, you are fucking nicked,' the guard said nothing, just panted and sweated with the exertion and the excitement of being involved in something so dramatic on only his second day in the job.

I heard myself sobbing, 'Help me, please — this is all wrong, he's not arresting me, I haven't done anything . . . ' but it was no use.

The guard helped Lee haul me to my feet.

'Cheers for that, mate,' Lee said.

'No problem. You need any more help?'

'No, mate, I've got back-up outside in the van. Thanks again.'

It was all over within a minute. There wasn't any back-up in the van, of course. There wasn't even a van. There was just a car, an unmarked cop car, abandoned with its lights flashing just at the pick-up point outside the main entrance. Holding me tightly under one elbow, he frog-marched me out of the door.

I could have tried to run again. But there wasn't any point.

'Be a good girl, Catherine,' he said to me. 'Be good. You know you want to.'

He pushed me into the back of the car. I expected him to shut the door, climb in the front and drive off. But instead he got into the back with me.

I don't remember what happened after that.

Friday 14 March 2008

The next time I saw Alistair I told him that I was going through another difficult time. I told him about Lee's habit of moving things, hiding things, and about the twisted scrap of red cloth and button I'd found in my pocket. I could tell by the expression on his face that he'd never come across a story quite like this one, even if he did his best to hide it. He probably thought I did it myself. He probably wondered whether actually I've got some sort of psychosis as well as an anxiety disorder.

To his credit, he was both soothing and at the same time strict. However it happened, the button was just a button. It didn't mean anything. The world was full of red things, he said, and they didn't cause us any harm. The red button didn't actually cause me harm. It was in my pocket, I touched it, it made my anxiety levels increase, but other than that, it didn't actually hurt me, did it?

It wasn't the button that was the problem, I

wanted to shout, it's how the fuck did it get in my pocket? But there was no point going over all that with him, he couldn't help, and I was all too used to people not believing me. I needed to hear back from the police, to be reassured that Lee was safely still miles away. In any case, one thing was just starting to become clearer to me, a faint glimmer within the darkness. Whether I was picking up red objects to feed my own fears, or whether Lee was actually starting to stalk me again, what I needed from Alistair was the same. I needed to learn not to be a victim this time — of myself, or of anyone else. I needed strength, to deal with the bad things that life threw at you. I needed to take back control.

For now, Alistair said we should concentrate on the PTSD. Working on the PTSD had a number of elements. When I had flashbacks, or thoughts about Lee, I should let them come, and let them go.

I remembered being in the café in Brighton with Stuart when he'd said something similar about that man who had startled me. It was all about recognising the thoughts as being part of the disorder, rather than something that was defining me as a person.

'I'd prefer not to have the thoughts at all,' I told him, 'never mind accepting them.'

Alistair rubbed his hands together, sliding the middle fingers against each other in a regular pattern that was somehow soothing.

'The thing you need to remember, Cathy, is that these thoughts have to go somewhere. They are in your head at the moment and they have no way out. That's why they're so upsetting. You have these thoughts and when you get them, you try and bat them to the back of your mind. You try to push them away, then they will have to come back because your mind hasn't had time to process them, to deal with them. If you let them come, consider them, think about them, then you will be able to let them go. Don't be afraid of them. They are just thoughts.'

'You say that. They might be just thoughts, but they're still bloody scary. It's like living in a horror film.'

'Think of them like that, then. They are part of a horror film, and sooner or later, no matter how scary they are, they will come to an end if you just let them come, and let them go.'

His voice was calm and curiously soothing. I tried to think of Stuart in here, running a clinic, listening to people telling him about their misery, about grief, loneliness, about not understanding the world any more, about wanting it all to end.

Then I went home to try to digest it all.

As would be the case with any other addiction, on the nights when I was here alone, it would have been very easy to get away with indulging in my vice without Stuart or anyone else knowing. But checking didn't give me any actual pleasure, it never had; it was more of a relief — a temporary absence of terror. Alistair gave me a number of things to try to reduce the stress caused by not checking properly, including the deep breathing, rationalising my fears, re-naming them so that they become not real, normal fears but just a manifestation of my OCD. They're not good fears, they are part of my condition — why would I want to keep them?

Earlier this evening, just after I got home from work, I had a phone call. My first thought was that it was Stuart, but it turned out to be DS Hollands. That sudden racing heartbeat — would it ever get any better? I thought she was going to tell me that Lee was missing, Lee had told someone he was coming to get me, one of the other officers had been tricked into telling him my home address.

'I just wanted to let you know — I spoke to my colleague at Lancaster police station DA unit.'

'Yes?'

'They sent someone round to check up on Mr Brightman on the morning after you called me. Can't guarantee he hadn't been round to see you, but it's very unlikely. He was in bed having been working the night before. He's working at a nightclub in the town. The officers checked it out and he was definitely at work the night you rang. So although it's not impossible that he made a trip to London, it's pretty unlikely. Do you have any other reasons for thinking he might know where you are?'

I sighed. 'Not really. Just that I know what he's like. Isn't he supposed to have some sort of licence, if he's working as a doorman?'

'He's not a doorman; apparently he's just a glass collector. Lancaster is going to check it out, though, don't worry. Even though he's not got any conditions attached to his release, I get the impression they're keeping a close eye on him.'

Can't be close enough, I thought to myself.

'I think you can relax a bit, Cathy. If he was going to come looking for you, I think he would have done it by now. And you've got my numbers, right?'

'Yes, thanks, I have.'

'And if you think there might be someone in your flat, just dial 999 straight away. All right?'

'Yes.'

I wish I could shake off this feeling. It's not a fear that one day he might come for me, it's more certain than that. It's not *if* he finds out where I am, it's *when*. The only reason he has not put in an appearance yet, assuming of course that I did leave my own curtains open and I did somehow absent-mindedly pick up a red satin-covered button from somewhere, is that he doesn't know where I am.

But when he does, he will come for me.

Saturday 12 June 2004

The first thing I noticed was the light — bright light, into my eyes, which were closed.

My mouth was dry; I couldn't open it at first.

Had I been asleep?

For a moment I couldn't feel my arms, then I realised they were tied behind me, tightly. Everything from my shoulders to my fingertips ached, suddenly and powerfully.

Handcuffs.

I forced my eyes open, panicking now, to see that I was lying on my side, the side of my face pressed into the carpet. Grey carpet, familiar. At home, then, in the spare bedroom.

I twisted my face around as far as possible, but I couldn't see much. It took a few moments for me to remember where I'd been going, and what happened, and when I remembered it, it came like a crushing, weighty blow. I'd been going to escape. I had been . . . so . . . close . . .

There was no sign of him in here, at least, but I knew he couldn't be far away. I had no idea how long I had before he came back, so I forced myself to think.

My head hurt. I couldn't tell, at first, if it was because of lying in such an unnatural position for so long, or if he'd hit me. Every thought felt laboured and painful.

From the airport . . . back home . . . he must have driven me, in his car. I don't remember it. It must have been several hours. I don't remember any of it.

I had no idea what the time was, and I couldn't even tell if it was still daylight, because the overhead light was on. The curtains must be closed.

I tried to stretch my legs out, but they seemed to be tied up to my wrists somehow. I was completely hogtied. I could not move at all. I tried to roll over onto my back but had to stop that immediately because every movement was incredibly painful. My head was swimming and for a moment I could see nothing but stars.

What happened? I needed to think. I had to concentrate on this. It was too important.

He said he was arresting me . . . the people

380

standing watching, and some of them walking past as though nothing whatsoever was going on. He showed his warrant card to the security guards — then they were asking him if he needed any help. I must have been fighting. Dragging me away. I'd been shouting, trying to tell them that he was kidnapping me, he was going to hurt me, but of course they must have all just thought I was a raving mad woman. I would have thought the same, if I'd been in an airport, waiting for my flight to be called, off on holiday somewhere hot, somewhere exotic. Perhaps going on honeymoon, or just somewhere on a business trip. Raving mad woman, being arrested. Drugs, probably. A business trip. Maybe to New York.

I wondered what had happened to my suitcase. They must have pulled it off the plane somehow. I bet the flight was delayed.

How long would it be before I was missed? I wasn't due to start work until Tuesday — three days. Before that, the landlady of Jonathan's apartment would likely just assume I was getting a later flight. If she even noticed I wasn't there. Lee could do a lot of damage in four days.

Tears rolled from my eyes to my nose, dripping off the end and onto the carpet.

How long before he came back? I couldn't move. He couldn't just leave me here, surely? I needed to find out what he was planning to do. If he was just going to kill me, I would be dead already. Whatever it was would probably be worse.

Almost as I had that thought, I heard the

sounds — the stairs creaking, the sound I remembered from lying in bed, pretending to be asleep, waiting for him to come upstairs, wondering if he would be in a good mood and if he'd leave me in peace.

The door to the spare room was shut, and I heard a key turning, close by. I hadn't even realised the spare room door had a lock. I'd never needed it before. Just one key, then.

I felt him pulling at the back of my head, and it hurt — pulling my hair. He was untying the gag. I hadn't realised I was gagged, but I was — with some sort of cloth. And underneath it, the corners of my mouth sore, crusted with blood. I felt fresh blood start to trickle when he pulled the cloth away. I tried to speak but all that came out was a groan. I kept my eyes closed. I didn't want to look at him. I never wanted to see his face again.

'If I undo the cuffs, are you going to behave?' he asked. His voice was calm, controlled. He wasn't drunk, then. That was something.

I nodded, my cheek scraping against the carpet. It still smelled new. I felt him grab one of my wrists and unlock the cuffs, the rasping rattle as they came away. My arms contracted and I cried out with the agony of the sudden movement.

'Shut up,' he said, his voice still calm, 'or I'll knock you out again.'

I bit my lip, the tears pouring. Now the cuffs had gone, I could stretch my legs out, although that too was incredibly painful. So much for fighting back, I thought. I could barely move.

After a while, stretched out on my side, I thought I could manage to sit up. I tried to raise myself on one elbow, opened my eyes. The room swam. I could see my arm, my wrist in front of my face, swollen, the skin grazed and raw where the cuffs had chafed.

He waited there, patiently, watching me while I struggled again and again to sit up. When I managed it, and looked at him, he was sitting on the floor with his back to the door, his legs stretched out in front of him. He looked pleased with himself. I wiped the back of one hand over my mouth. It came away bloody, but not much. My head still thumped. He must have hit me somewhere to knock me out.

I was still wearing the suit — the navy blue suit I'd chosen for the journey to New York because it wouldn't crease. Well, it was creased now. The jacket was torn across one shoulder, I could feel it give as I moved. The skirt was undone at the back. Had he tried to undress me?

My ankles had rope round them, a blue nylon rope, not very thick, loose at one end. It must have been looped around the cuffs somehow. I wanted to reach down and untie them, but I had no energy at all.

'D-did you drug me?' I asked, my voice barely there. My throat was dry.

He laughed. 'Is that the only question you have for me?'

I gave a barely perceptible shrug. It had seemed like a good question a moment ago, but it suddenly wasn't relevant any more.

How did you find me? I wanted to ask. How

did you know? How did you get down to Heathrow so quickly? And above all, why . . . ? Why hadn't my plan worked? Why wasn't I on a plane, somewhere over the Atlantic? Why wasn't I in New York already?

'They'll miss me,' I said. 'When I don't turn up in New York they'll report me missing. Someone will come looking for me.'

'Who will?'

'My friend. He's going to give me a job in New York.'

'Your friend? You mean Jonathan Baldwin?'

My blood ran cold at the sound of that name on Lee's lips.

'What? What did you say?'

He reached behind and pulled something out of the back pocket of his jeans, threw it towards me. It was a business card. I picked it up with numbed fingers. On one side, in neat black letters in a corporate design of green and gold, I read:

Jonathan Baldwin BSc (Hons), MBA, CHRP, CHSC
Senior Management Consultant

I turned the card over. On the back, in my handwriting, was written:

Change Management Conference, Manchester, 5–16 June, 2000

'It was in your organiser,' he said, 'and you fucking fell for it, every bloody word of it. I

384

always knew you were naïve, Catherine, but I didn't realise you were that stupid.'

So there was no job in New York. No flat waiting for me. No escape. And nobody to notice my absence: nobody in New York, and nobody here either. It might be weeks, months even before anyone realised I was gone. By that time I would be dead. I felt a huge wave of despair, a black cloud which made it difficult to focus on anything other than the pain. This couldn't be happening, it couldn't. I'd spoken to him, he'd emailed me, it hadn't been Lee, it had been a different man, a deeper voice, a different accent. Jonathan was a real person, I remembered him. Lee couldn't have done it. He couldn't have.

'You set me up?' I sobbed. 'You set all this up?'

'In my last job, I used to do stings like this all the time. People who are committing crime are suspicious, they sometimes take ages to convince. But you fell for it straight away, didn't you? And you didn't even hesitate. You didn't even think about whether it was the right thing to do. You just jumped at the chance to fuck off and leave me behind.'

So it was true. He'd played me, he'd taken my need to escape and used it against me. There was nothing I could do. All those moments when I'd seen blue sky, when I'd seen that hint of freedom, I had still been in the cage.

My question, *the* question, had formed itself in the black fog of my brain. 'What are you going to do?'

That got him thinking. I didn't want to meet his eyes, but I could tell he was concentrating.

385

'I haven't decided yet,' he said at last.

'You can let me go,' I said.

'I don't think so,' he said straight away. 'You're mine, you know that. You tried to leave me. I gave you chances, Catherine. I gave you so many fucking chances. And you let me down.'

'You know you can't keep me here forever. They will find out. You'll lose your job.'

He gave a short laugh. 'Yeah, right. You mean if I'm planning to do anything, I'd better finish you off?'

I nodded.

'You want me to kill you?' he said, curiously.

I nodded again. All the fight in me had gone. I wanted it over with.

He got up, suddenly, stood over me. I started to feel sick. 'You see, that's what I fucking hate about you, Catherine,' he said, his voice a growl. 'You just give in too fucking easily.'

He nudged me with his knee and I toppled back onto the carpet, struggling back up to a sitting position, tears and snot running down my face into the corners of my stinging mouth.

I waited for the blow. I waited for the smack to the head, the punch, or the kick. I wanted it. I braced myself, but I longed for it too. I coveted the oblivion.

When he next spoke, it was through gritted teeth, as though he was so disgusted by me that he could hardly bring himself to speak. 'You're a piece of filth. You're a dirty, slutty whore, Catherine. I can't decide whether to kill you, fuck you or just piss on you.'

I let out a sob, as I heard the sound of his

386

jeans being unzipped, and seconds later the warm wet splashing of his piss over my hair, the remains of my smart suit, the new grey carpet. I cried, trying to keep my eyes and my mouth shut so none of it would go in. The sound of it, the smell of it. I started to retch.

When he'd finished he left the room for a minute, leaving the door wide open. I started to crawl towards it, seeing the hallway outside, the bathroom beyond, but before I got there he was back. A bucket of cold water, the sponge that I used to clean the bath out, a bar of soap. The water smelled like bleach as he dropped the bucket onto the carpet.

'Clean yourself up, you cunt,' he said.

Then he left the room, locking it behind him.

I howled. But he hadn't put the handcuffs back on.

Sunday 16 March 2008

I opened my eyes into the darkness, breathing fast, my heart pounding in my throat. For a moment I was disorientated, then Stuart moved in bed and I was there, with him, in his flat. It was just me and him. No Lee. It was another nightmare.

It's not real, I told myself. It's part of it. Let the thoughts come, let them go.

I considered waking Stuart up, but that wasn't fair. I lay still for a while in the darkness, listening.

I could hear noises.

It took me a moment to realise that they were real noises, not part of the rhythm of the house, not the noise of my blood rushing through my head.

A bang, far away. Downstairs? No, it didn't sound like it. It sounded further away. Maybe in the street. I couldn't hear the noises of the street from Stuart's flat as well as I could in my own. A car door slamming?

I looked across at Stuart's alarm clock. It was ten to three in the morning, the coldest and darkest and loneliest part of the night. I should be asleep. I should go back to my nightmare. For a moment I wondered if actually I wasn't awake at all, if I was still dreaming.

Another bang, followed by a scrape. A noise like something being dragged across a floor. Something heavy, inert.

I sat up in bed, straining to hear. For several moments, nothing. Just the noise of Stuart's breathing, deep, regular. The sound of the fridge humming in the kitchen. A car starting up outside, driving away.

Maybe that had been it — just someone going out to their car.

Stuart moved next to me and I lay back down, fitting myself into the curve of his body, pulling his arm around me, protecting me, keeping me safe. I closed my eyes and tried to think of good things, tried to fall asleep.

A few minutes later, he came and took the bucket away. I'd used it to scrub feebly at the carpet. Already I could feel the skin on my fingers burning from the bleach in the water. The patch of carpet that had been scrubbed was turning from pale grey to a dirty yellow.

After that, he didn't come back for several hours.

I spent a while sobbing, but not much. I tried getting out — I tried bashing at the door, but it held. I tried hammering at the window, but it faced out over the back and there was nobody out there to see me, or hear me. He'd left nothing at all in the room I could use as a weapon, or that I could use to try to break the window.

Before I'd left for the airport, this room had held a single bed, a wardrobe, a desk with an old computer, a chest of drawers and a small portable television, along with various other smaller bits and pieces. Now it held nothing. The only decoration was the curtain pole and the curtains hanging from them, but I had nothing at all I could use to get the curtain pole down with. I tried pulling it down, thinking I could use the pole to smash the window, but it held my body weight easily, even when I bounced up and down.

I felt thirsty, wondered what the time was, what day it was. How long had it been since I'd had something to drink? Well, I wouldn't last long at this rate. If he'd gone to work, if he was going to be away for several days, it would be dehydration that would get me first.

I tried screaming, 'Help me! Help me! Help!' over and over again, as loudly as I could, but all that seemed to do was leave me with a sore throat.

I sat for a while and tried to think of a plan. I considered using my stockings to make some sort of noose, so that I could try to put it around his neck when he came into the room, to try to choke him. That was about the best plan I could come up with. Thirst, fear and hunger were making thinking harder than it usually was.

I felt the back of my head gingerly and found a lump which hurt so much when I pressed it gently that I nearly passed out. The hair around it was matted with dried blood. He'd knocked me out, then. I wondered how long I'd been out for.

I wondered if I'd have any sort of strength left to fight him when he came back, and whether it was worth it. If I tried to attack him, he'd fight back, and then he would undoubtedly punish me for trying.

Well, I couldn't just sit here and let him do whatever he wanted. If he killed me, at least this whole shitty mess would be over and done with.

I thought about tying my stockings to the curtain pole, or pulling the curtains into strips, and hanging myself. I thought about it in such detail I even began to picture myself, and his face when he found me. It would be a victory, of sorts. Although all my friends, his work colleagues, everyone, would think I committed suicide because I was depressed. He would get away with it — nobody would ever know how he'd treated me. And he would go on to do it all over again, to someone else.

I turned a corner, then, and I decided to try to fight. I had another go at screaming.

And that was how I managed not to hear him coming in through the front door, climbing the stairs and unlocking the door to the spare room, to my prison.

Thursday 20 March 2008

When I came in from work tonight, there was a bowl and a spoon and a cup on the draining board in the kitchen.

To any sane adult, the rational explanation would be that I'd washed up my bowl after having cereal for breakfast, and had left it to dry and gone to work.

In reality, though, I'd done nothing of the kind.

It was a measure of how far I'd come already that I didn't descend into a panic attack. I didn't even go back to the front door and start the checking process all over again. I stood there and stared at the bowl, knowing what it meant. My heart was thudding in my chest and I was almost too afraid to look round, in case Lee was there standing right behind me.

He wasn't in the flat at all — I knew that, I'd already checked the whole place once. The front door downstairs had been firmly shut and latched, the way it had been every day since

Stuart moved in. The flat door had been securely locked, and I'd locked it behind me and checked. The doors to the balcony had been locked, too. The flat had been fine — *fine* — until I'd finally come to the kitchen to start making something to eat.

I waited for the anxiety to subside, determined not to give in to it. First the button — now this.

The red button with its attached scrap of cloth had been like a warning — less subtle than this new message. The first one had been like a flag, literally a red flag even though it was tiny, telling me he was back, he had found me. It was meant to be an alarm, a warning. He knew that anyone I chose to tell about it would look at me in an odd way, think about what sort of an attention-seeking person might rip a button off something, tuck it in her pocket and then have a panic attack about it. This time, though, he knew I wouldn't tell anyone at all about it. What would be the point? No rational person would believe that a person would break in — leaving no trace — just to leave some washing-up on the drying rack.

I put the bowl, the spoon and the mug into the rubbish bin and took the bag outside to the landing. After that I made a cup of tea, giving myself time to think.

I should have moved out. I should have started looking for somewhere new to live, the day after the button appeared in my jeans pocket, almost a month ago. I realised it was too late to do that now — he would be following me, he would see me going to visit new flats and he would know where I was going to live even before I'd moved in.

Even if I ran, even if I just left everything and caught a train somewhere, he would still find me. And besides, I couldn't just leave everything behind — my job, the flat, Stuart. The thoughts that had begun to form in Alistair's office crystallised into a sense of resolution. What good would running away do? It didn't work last time and it wouldn't work now either. I was going to have to stay. I was going to have to get ready to fight.

Saturday 12 June 2004

The door slammed open with such force that it made me jump and stopped me mid-scream.

I was completely unprepared for what came next — his fist coming towards my face at speed, smacking my cheekbone and propelling me backwards, the back of my head, already fragile, hitting the wall as I fell.

I couldn't move for a moment, stunned, but I didn't have time to contemplate my next move anyway. He took hold of a fistful of my hair and hauled me back to an unsteady kneel, before hitting me again, harder. This time his fist connected with my nose and I felt the blood start to pour out of it, watched through dazed eyes as it formed a splashy puddle on the grey carpet. I gagged, sobbing, retching.

'Shut the fuck up!' he yelled. 'What the fuck do you think you're doing, screaming like that?'

'Let me go,' I said, quietly, pleading.

'I don't think so, Catherine. Not now.'

This time I winced before it hit — my right eye, the bridge of my nose. My hand against my face, trying to protect it, and he pulled it away, placing it on the floor. I watched him stand on my fingers and heard a crack.

I bit back a scream, the pain going through me like a slice. 'No, please, Lee — no more. Please.'

'Take your clothes off.'

I looked up at him. My right eye felt strange, wouldn't focus.

'No, no . . . please.'

'Take your fucking clothes off, you stupid, dirty bitch. Take them off now.'

Seated, I pulled my jacket away from my shoulders. My right hand wasn't working properly, the fingers starting to swell. After a moment he lost patience and pulled my jacket away, ripping it away from my aching shoulders. My blouse he just tore off. Then he dragged me to my feet, pulling away a handful of my hair as he did so, tossing it to the carpet and wiping his hand on the back of his jeans, then pulling my skirt down.

Then he stopped. The thought of him sickened me, but even so I raised my head. I wanted to see his eyes, to see if I could find out what he intended to do to me.

I tried as hard as I could to focus on his face. The leer. Oh, my God. Oh, shit — he was enjoying it. He really was enjoying himself.

As I watched, he reached to the back pocket of his jeans and pulled out the knife, the black-handled lock knife with a curved blade, partly serrated, about five inches long.

I found my voice again, begging, pleading, my voice rising into a wail. 'No, no, no, Lee — don't, please don't . . .'

He reached forward and slid the blade under the fabric of my knickers at the side, slicing the fabric with a neat, crisp sound. I felt the coldness of the blade against my naked skin. I couldn't move. Then the other side. He reached between my legs and grabbed at the material, pulling it away.

Then he took a step back and surveyed me. 'You're ugly,' he said, a smile in his voice.

'Yes,' I said. I felt it.

'You've lost so much weight you're like a fucking skeleton.'

I gave a little shrug.

'You're so fucking skinny. I liked you before, when you had some flesh. You were so beautiful, so gorgeous I couldn't stop myself looking at you, did you know that?'

I shrugged again. My right eye was starting to close, my head was pounding. I looked down at the blood which had splashed from my broken nose down the front of my body. Blood everywhere. Who'd have thought so much could come from one nose?

He sighed heavily. 'I can't fuck you like that. You aren't even remotely attractive, you know that?'

I nodded.

He turned and left the room, but before I was even fully aware that he was gone, he was back again, something in his hand, something red. He threw it at me, and it slid across my naked skin like a kiss, so soft.

'Put it on.'

My red dress. I found the opening, slid it over my head, biting back the tears, pulling it down over myself.

I looked up at him and tried to smile. Tried to look beguiling.

Again the back of his hand this time, across my mouth. I fell to the floor and the pain was so intense, so complete, that I felt myself laugh. I was going to die here, and I couldn't stop laughing.

He was on top of me, then, forcing my legs apart, grunting with the effort, pulling the fabric of my dress up to my waist. I heard it tear, and that seemed to turn him on even more.

What made it worse was that he didn't smell of alcohol. He wasn't even drunk this time, he didn't have that excuse.

I lay there and smiled to myself, whilst he grunted and thrust at me, ramming himself into me again and again, thinking that the pain, the pain all over from the weeping grazes around my wrists, my broken fingers, my nose, my head, my right eye, the split to the corner of my mouth that let the blood seep in — I was drinking it, tasting it, almost wishing there was more — it was all just so fucking funny. So ironic! I'd nearly been on a plane to New York, and I needn't have bothered, the whole time. I could have just stayed here, locked myself in my own spare room and waited for the inevitable.

The pain of him fucking me hard, every way he could, somehow wasn't even worse than everything else. I'd been here before, after all. Whilst he was raping me he wasn't doing anything else. He wasn't killing me.

Friday 28 March 2008

'How's it been going?' Alistair said, when I got into his room.

'Not bad,' I said. I handed over the sheet of paper I'd been diligently filling out all week.

On the left, a list of my checking compulsions in order of importance, followed by a list of my avoidance compulsions, similarly ordered. We were starting with the easy ones. I'd scored each one by how much I imagined not performing each ritual would distress me, out of 100. The worst one, not checking the flat door, scored 95. The lowest, not checking the bathroom window, scored 40. The avoidance compulsions — crowded places scored 65, the police scored 50 and the colour red, of course, after the incident the other day, was the worst — 80. Below that, my ordering compulsions — not shopping on particular days, eating on certain days, neither of which seemed to be as bad as they had been in the past, and scored just 20 each. The main ordering compulsion, having cups of tea at set times — I'd given that one a 75.

I'd been set the task of challenging myself with exposures to my lowest fears, as often as possible. Next to the original scores, I'd written

397

in how much distress I'd felt after performing these exposures, once the anxiety had lessened.

Alistair was reading my list and nodding, occasionally raising his eyebrows. I felt like a pupil showing my homework to the head teacher. 'Good, very good,' he said.

'It reminds me of that bit in *Harry Potter*, you know, where they confront the thing that most scares them by magicking it into something funny.'

'Absolutely. Or, indeed, *Hamlet*.'

'*Hamlet*?'

'"For there is nothing either good or bad, but thinking makes it so." Anyway, tell me about some of the things you tried.'

I took a deep breath in. 'Well, I managed to watch some police programmes on the television. I started off with a drama, then I managed to watch one of those true life shows where they film from the back of a police car.'

'And?'

'It was okay. I wanted to turn it off, but I didn't. I kept up the deep breathing while I was doing it, and in the end it was quite interesting. I kept telling myself it wasn't real. I thought I was going to have nightmares after it, but I didn't.'

'That sounds excellent. You need to be careful about telling yourself it isn't real, though, or telling yourself anything at all, for that matter. Internal dialogue can be just another safety behaviour. Try it again but see if you can just watch it, and enjoy it. Just accept it as a television programme like any other.'

'Alright.'

'And the checking?'

'I left the bathroom alone. I skipped it out of the checking ritual when I got home.'

'And how was that?'

'Surprisingly easy.'

'You've got the distress levels here as just five — excellent.'

It was true. I'd gone straight past the bathroom. I'd had to tell myself that there was no way on earth it could be unsafe — after all, the stupid window doesn't even open — but even so, I did it. It wasn't very nice at first. When I'd finished checking everything else it still felt odd, and for a long time afterwards I was sitting staring at the bathroom door, thinking all the time about the window being fine, not open, picturing it. Eventually it subsided and I didn't feel so bad.

Seeing progress with it already was a real motivator. I wanted to go home and try some more, try some harder things.

Our hour together was nearly up when Alistair picked up my list again. 'I think you should consider that there are a few elements missing from the list,' he said.

'Such as?'

'Have a think. What's your biggest fear? The real biggie.'

I thought, not knowing what he meant at first, and then suddenly knowing and not wanting to say. I felt the anxiety responses we'd just been discussing — my heart rate speeding up, my hands starting to tremble.

'You're quite safe here. Just try and say it.'

My voice came from a long way off. 'Lee.'

'That's right. And you're going to need to tackle that fear too, otherwise tackling all the others is going to be a bit pointless. I think the sooner we deal with that one, the better. All the other fears have their source in that main one, don't they? So if we tackle how you feel about Lee, then the others should all come toppling down too. Does that make sense?'

'Yes,' I said. Of course it made sense. If I wasn't scared of Lee any more, there was no point checking the door or doing any of the other stupid pointless tasks I filled my whole day with, was there? It all sounded so bloody obvious. 'It's not a meaningless fear, though, is it? I mean, I can just about comprehend that checking the cutlery drawer six times is silly, it's a waste of time. But being afraid of Lee is about self-preservation.'

Alistair was nodding. 'Yes, but you need to consider that we're talking at cross purposes. There is Lee himself, and then there is the *thought* of Lee. Lee himself is presumably pottering about his daily life up in the north somewhere. The *thought* of Lee is disturbing your daily life. You think you see him when you're out and about. You imagine that he's going to try and break into your house. So it's the thought of him, this picture you've created in your mind of this omnipresent figure, this source of all bad things, which we need to deal with.'

I was starting to get a headache.

'So I'm not saying you need to go and find the real Lee and confront him and wait for your anxiety to subside. I think you need to tackle your perception of him, and do it in the same way that you're tackling your compulsions, with exposure and response prevention.'

'How? How can I do that?'

'By just letting the thoughts come, and letting them go. Let yourself remember. Let the anxiety come, wait for it to subside, and then, before it's gone completely, think about him again. When you're at home, imagine him coming into the room. Picture him. Think about standing in front of him, facing him. And then wait for the anxiety to subside. These are just thoughts, Cathy. Let them come, and let them go.'

He made it sound so easy.

'Will you give it a try?'

'What — now?'

'We can try now. But especially when you're at home. At first you can get Stuart to sit with you, if you like. But don't use him for reassurance. You need to be able to do this by yourself.'

'I'm not sure I can do it.'

'It's up to you, of course. But think about the implications of being unafraid of Lee. It's worth a try, isn't it? And if we try now, it might be easier to give it a go than when you're at home. At least here you won't be tempted to go and start checking the door. What do you think?'

I didn't answer.

'Have a think about how much thinking about Lee would distress you first. Let's use our scoring system. On a score of zero to one

401

hundred, how bad do you think it would be?'

'Just to think about him? Ninety.'

'Alright. Let's try — yes?'

I closed my eyes, not sure what I was doing and if it was all going to go horribly wrong. Lee wasn't hard to imagine. He was in my thoughts all the time anyway, even if I did fight against it. This time, I let it come. I pictured my flat. I was sitting on the sofa, looking back towards the door. Waiting. I pictured the door opening, and Lee standing there.

I felt the fear coming like a wave, my heart racing, tears starting in my eyes.

'That's it,' said Alistair. 'Just let it come, don't try to stop it.'

I pictured him walking towards me. Lee, as he always was, handsome, short blond hair, complexion that always seemed to be slightly tanned even in midwinter. Those eyes, bluer than the summer sky. And the size of him, too, the bulk, the muscles in his arms and across his chest. He came and stood next to the sofa and looked down at me. He even smiled.

I waited. Already I could feel the anxiety was less than when I'd started thinking. I'd expected this to end in a full-blown panic attack, but it wasn't that bad at all.

'Tell me about what you're imagining,' Alistair said.

'Lee in my flat,' I said. 'Just standing there.'

'Alright, good. Now I want you to picture him leaving again. Put him into a car and have him drive off.'

I did it. He turned, gave me a wink — where that came from I had no idea — and shut the door behind him. I went to the front windows, saw him getting into a car, a silver car, shutting the door and driving away. I pictured myself going back to the sofa and turning on the TV.

I opened my eyes.

'How was that?'

'I did it,' I said.

'And think about your anxiety. How bad is it now, thinking about him?'

'About — about seventy. Eighty maybe.'

'Good. See? You can do it. It's a good start.'

Saturday 12 June 2004

It took a long time and, in the end, I was almost sorry it was over. He pulled out, pulled himself away from me, over to the wall, sitting there, his head in his hands. I saw my own blood on his hands, his face. Then I heard him sob. I pulled myself gingerly up to a sitting position.

'What am I doing?' he said, his voice broken. 'Oh, my God. What the hell . . . ?'

I looked at him and he was actually crying.

I inched my way over to him, every bit of me sore. As he cried, I found myself sitting next to him, the wall for support, and I slipped my arm around his shoulders. He put his head against my neck, the tears from his face sliding down my skin. I put my ruined right hand, three fingers now fat as sausages and numb, cold, on the side of his cheek. 'Shh. It's okay.' My voice sounded distorted, my lip split and swollen. 'It's okay, Lee. It's alright, really.'

He cried against me for a long time, while I held him and wondered whether, actually, I was going to be all right after all.

'I'll get locked up,' he said, his breath coming in rasping sobs, 'they'll put me away for this.'

'No, they won't,' I soothed. 'I won't say. We'll be all right, honestly. Just you and me.'

'Really?' He looked up at me like a child.

I wondered if he could even see my ravaged face. Did I look suitably comforting? How could he possibly imagine that anything was ever going to be all right again?

I had to continue down this path — it was my only chance. 'You have to let me clean up a bit.'

'Of course.'

To my surprise, he got up and left the room.

I crawled across the landing to the bathroom, found my way into the shower and stood there, seeing the blood diluting as it washed away, swirling into patterns against the white enamel that were almost beautiful. I rinsed the piss out of my hair, trying not to watch as clumps of it came away in my fingers and blocked the plughole. My skin stung; my right hand was still useless. I wondered what would happen if I had broken bones in my hand and they weren't fixed.

Fortunately the towel in the bathroom was the navy blue one, not one of the white ones, so the blood that dotted it as I dried myself gingerly was not too noticeable. I was bleeding from between my legs. Probably my period, I thought, which had been overdue. I'd not thought about it, putting it down to the weight I'd lost, the stress, the fact that I wasn't eating regularly. Maybe it had been brought on by the trauma.

It was as though all this was happening to someone else. I went into the bedroom and found some sanitary towels, knickers, clothes to wear, jeans, a belt, a loose jumper. I could have run away, right then. I could have run out into the street, shouting for help.

But that was just it. I couldn't run. I had nowhere to go. I couldn't call the police, could I? He was one of them. They would look at me, and he would invent some story about me being traumatised by some incident he'd been working undercover on, how I was showing signs of mental illness and he'd been trying to help me. They'd take me to hospital, patch me up, and then I'd end up sectioned. Or worse, they'd send me home. With my left hand, I made a half-hearted attempt to clean up the blood in the spare room. It was everywhere — walls, carpet, smeared over the door. I gave up in the end, and went downstairs.

Friday 28 March 2008

On the way back from Leonie Hobbs House I walked fast, long strides, getting my heart rate up. If I was physically tired this evening at least I stood a good chance of being able to sleep. That was the theory anyway. I was finding it harder and harder to sleep in my flat, spending hours lying awake listening out for noises outside. Even sleeping with Stuart upstairs was difficult; every noise sounded as though it was coming from my flat below us.

Once I turned away from the main road into Lorimer Road, the noise of the traffic faded away.

I could hear footsteps that matched my own, perfectly. For several yards I thought they were mine. Then I realised that there was someone on the pavement behind me. I thought it was quite far away, so I chanced a look back. Just a glance.

A man was walking behind me, about thirty yards behind, matching my pace. Dark clothes, a hooded top, the hood down. I couldn't see his face because the streetlight behind him left it in shadow. Just clouds of his breath in the cold air.

I picked up my pace and waited for the sound of his steps to match mine. The sound of them was jarring.

He'd speeded up, too.

At the end of Lorimer Road, the main road again. I could see buses, still stationary in the traffic, but at least I'd be able to get on one of them if I needed to. I didn't care which one.

Before the main road, though, I realised that the noise of the steps had ceased. I looked behind. The man had gone. He must have turned into one of the houses.

At home, later, I looked and looked. I checked the door and the windows and the kitchen. I even checked the bathroom, though I'd stopped checking that weeks ago. I knew he'd been here.

I could smell him, sense his presence, as a rabbit scents a fox.

It took another hour on top of the checking I normally do before I found it. In the cutlery drawer, which I'd checked already — one single knife and one single fork, buried under all the others, carefully swapped over into the wrong section and hidden.

Saturday 12 June 2004

He was in the kitchen, stirring a cup of tea. The happy little domestic scene, after what we'd gone through half an hour before, was peculiar.

He gave me a smile. His blond hair was stained with red and brown bits at the front where he'd run his bloody hands through his hair. He gave me a kiss on the cheek and I managed a smile in return, the cut on my lip splitting open again as I did so. 'Are you okay?' he asked me.

I nodded. 'Are you?'

'Yes. I'm sorry.'

'I know.'

We went into the living room and I lowered myself onto the sofa gingerly.

'I didn't want you to go,' he said lamely. He sat in the armchair across from me, giving me some space. I felt that all the anger had gone from him. If I was going to run, now would be a good time. But I had no energy left at all.

'Well, I'm not going anywhere now, am I?' My voice sounded odd to me — not just the slurring of the words because my mouth was out of shape — I think one of my ears was funny, too. I could hear a ringing, a buzzing.

'Why did you do it?' I asked. It didn't really matter either way, now. I meant what I said. I wasn't going to run again, I'd decided.

Lee looked wasted. His skin was pale, tired, his bright blue eyes dulled. 'I wanted to see what you'd do.'

'Was that you, on the phone? Pretending to be Jonathan?'

He nodded. 'I thought you'd recognise me, but you didn't. I set up an email address. It was all pretty easy, really. I never thought you'd fall for it. You never checked to see if any of it was real, did you?'

'How did you get down to Heathrow so fast?' That was the only other thing that had bothered me.

He shook his head and sighed. 'You really are unbelievably stupid sometimes, Catherine — you know that?'

I shrugged. What the hell? He was right.

'I've got blue lights and a siren. Traffic jams and speed limits don't apply.'

Well, knowing that didn't make it any easier.

'Of course, you did give me the fucking runaround, you know.'

'Did I?'

'I didn't think you'd go by train. I thought you were going to drive all the way down to Heathrow. When I couldn't find your car on the motorway I just hammered it all the way down there. Do you realise how close you came to getting on that plane? If I'd not gone as fast as I did you would have been on that plane and away.'

I didn't want to think about it, how close I'd come to being free. It hurt too much.

'What about the CCTV in the airport? Won't they have seen you pretending to arrest me?'

'I'm not bothered about the CCTV. You know there are cameras everywhere at the airport — all the shops, all the entrances and exits, every square foot of that place is covered. But it's all owned by different companies, half the cameras aren't working at any one time, or the quality is too shit to make anything out, or the tape's overwritten every twenty-four hours because they're too tight to pay for more tapes. Often the person in charge of it is on holiday and nobody else knows how to work the system anyhow. Even if you could collect it all up, it would take someone years to review all the footage from that one day alone. And as long as you know who to call, you can deal with whatever's left. I was more worried about the ANPR, to be honest.'

'The what?'

'Automatic number plate recognition. It would prove the car went all the way down to Heathrow on a day when I was supposed to be reviewing surveillance logs in the office. Or it would have done — I switched the plates on the car.'

This wasn't getting us anywhere. I wondered how long it would be — how many days I could endure.

After the cup of tea, and a sandwich that he made me, we watched some television together in some sort of pretence at normality. At eleven o'clock, he told me to strip my clothes off. I did so without argument, although it was difficult doing it one-handed. When I was wearing just knickers, he told me to hold out my arms in front of me and I complied whilst he clipped the handcuffs back around my wrists. Instantly the cold metal sliced at the raw skin and the pain started again. He took me back upstairs to the spare bedroom, and threw a blanket in there after me.

I sat down on the floor whilst he stood in the doorway, thinking that he would leave, but after a few moments he shut the door behind him and sat with his back to the wall opposite.

'I never told you about Naomi,' he said.

Saturday 29 March 2008

I got up early on Saturday and went for a run.

I tied my hair back into a bunch, since it was at that annoying length — long enough for the wind to blow it all around my head and into my eyes, too short to do anything stylish. The bunch at the back of my head was about the size of a Brussels sprout, and all I had to tie it back with was one of those infernal red elastic bands dropped on the step outside by the postwoman. It was too early to be busy, still a bit chilly, when I started to run. I set off at a nice even pace towards the park, the pavements wet under my feet. It was cloudy now, but it might turn into a nice day later. I could go and do some shopping.

I could actually try to find some new clothes. I'd not bought anything new for a long time. And I would do some work, too. I would work on the OCD. Alistair said to keep doing it, keep challenging myself, don't let the anxiety go away completely. Get used to it. Get used to letting it go away by itself, without appeasing it by checking.

When I got back to Talbot Street I deliberately went straight in, without my usual detour through the back alley. That felt really strange, and when I'd checked the front door, and Mrs Mackenzie's door, the first thing I did in the flat was check the curtains, from the inside this time. They were fine. I checked the flat door, it was fine. I checked the rest of the flat and missed out the bathroom, fine.

I kept thinking I should go outside and check the flat from the back alley, but now I was inside it seemed a bit pointless. Nevertheless, I was anxious.

I got dressed in jeans and a jumper, and, as I was performing my checks ready to go out, I decided I was going to stop checking the cutlery drawer. I wanted to do it one last time, just to be sure, but I resisted. To make up for it, I concentrated hard on the flat door. That was probably cheating, really, replacing one safety behaviour for another, but even so it didn't make me feel a whole lot better.

By the time I was on the bus, I tried to assess my anxiety and worked out that I was probably about forty or so. That wasn't half bad. Especially considering that, realistically, I was spending most of my day in a state of tension anyway, always on the lookout for him, always waiting for something bad to happen. In fact, even after not checking the bathroom and not checking the cutlery drawer, I was probably feeling better than I usually would, going out at the weekend.

I couldn't believe this was actually working. I couldn't believe I was actually feeling better.

The bus took me towards Camden, and I got off at Camden Lock and started to wander around the shops. I'd thought about going into the city, to Oxford Street, maybe, but that really would be scary. This was a good start.

I knew what I was looking for, what I wanted to buy, and when I finally saw it in a vintage shop I knew I'd have to get it.

It was red silk, just a camisole top, not unlike the one poor Erin had got me for Christmas. It was a size ten. I stared at it for several moments, feeling my body responding to it, everything telling me to turn away, run away from it. *It's only a top*, I told myself. *It's a piece of cloth, stitched together. It's not going to hurt me, it can't hurt me.*

After a few moments I touched it. It was soft, very soft, and surprisingly warm to the touch, as though someone had just taken it off.

'Want to try it on?' I looked round to see a small girl with short black hair streaked with bits of electric blue.

'I'm just looking, thanks.'

'It's your colour,' she said. 'Go on. It can't hurt.'

I actually laughed. She was right, in so many ways. I took the hanger and went to the changing room, just an alcove at the back of the shop with a cotton curtain hanging from a rail on three rattling metal rings, my heart pounding.

Don't think. Just do it.

I pulled my jumper over my head, my back to the mirror. I took the top off its hanger and slipped it over my head, my eyes closed. I felt a bit queasy, dizzy, as though I was on some wild fairground ride. *Now you've done it*, I told myself. *Now you're going to have to open your eyes and look.*

I looked. Not in the mirror, just down at myself.

It was a different shade from the red dress. It was pinker, cherry-red, rather than the blatant scarlet of the dress. The top was peachy in texture, a beautiful thing really, a thread of gold running through the bottom edge.

I'd had enough. I took it off, replaced it on the hanger, pulled my jumper back over my head. The urge to go and wash my hands was very strong. I put the hanger back on the rack where I'd found it, and left the shop straight away, before the assistant could say anything.

Further on, there was a bench. I sat down for a few moments while people walked past, thinking about how scared I was, waiting for it to go away. I already knew what I was going to do, and the thought of it was keeping the fear there. I don't know when I suddenly got this brave. It's not something I've been good at in the past, is it?

When I felt at about level thirty, I got up again

and carried on wandering around the shops. It was busy, but not enough to make me afraid of all the people. I found a spice shop, and bought some Mexican spice blends for Stuart. Next door was a second-hand book shop, and I spent a while browsing in there, looking through novels and travel books and even, for a while, the self-help section.

After that, I sat in a café and had a pot of tea. Normally I would go to the back of any coffee shop, as far from the door as possible, out of sight, so that I could see anyone coming in before they saw me. I made myself sit in the window. Fortunately there were tables outside with people sitting at them, so I didn't feel completely exposed, but even so I wasn't exactly comfortable.

Stuart had sent me three texts already, presumably between patients. How was I doing, what was I up to, that sort of thing. I sent a reply.

S, I'm in Camden shopping. Can you believe it?

Anything you want me to get? C x

His answer came back quickly.

Does this mean we can go shopping together next weekend? S x

I laughed. He'd been trying to get me to go shopping for ages. The only way he could do it was to disguise it as a day out, the way he'd done the day we went to Brighton.

I watched the people going past, expecting to see someone who looked like Lee. In fact I was almost hoping for it, so I could test my response. Every man that passed, everyone with his physique, none of them seemed to trigger the fear.

It was time to start heading back.

I didn't think too hard, I just went back. I walked into the shop. The assistant smiled at me. 'Hi,' she said. 'I had a feeling you'd be back.'

I smiled back at her. 'Couldn't resist,' I said, taking the top and putting it down on the counter.

'What shoe size are you?' she asked, looking at me with her head appraisingly on one side.

'Six,' I said. 'Why?'

'I've just had these brought in.' She lifted a shoebox from behind the counter and lifted the lid. Inside, a pair of red suede heels, slingbacks with a peep toe at the front. Rich, cherry-red suede. They were new; they even still had the tissue paper balled into the toe. 'Try them on,' she said. 'It says they're a five but you never know.'

I pulled off my trainers and my socks and slipped my feet into the shoes. They fitted well. It felt strange standing in heels again. I looked down at my feet. How weird this all was. How strange to be wearing shoes like this and feeling alright — a little light-headed perhaps, but alright.

415

'I'll take them,' I said.

'Does a tenner sound okay? I'd not got around to pricing them.'

'Sure.'

Taking the top home, and the shoes, in a large bag, was strange too. I thought about Erin's present and how I'd had to get rid of it without so much as touching it. Now I'd gone and actually bought a top, a red silk top. The bag felt heavy and I put it on the seat next to me on the bus. I didn't look at it. I would have to be brave and take it with me when the bus got back to the High Street and I got off it. All the way home, my anxiety levels were high, probably about forty or fifty. I waited for them to subside, but they didn't go down by much.

I took a detour through the alley, but I didn't linger. I just looked. I was scared now, scared of what I'd done. I checked the front door, Mrs Mackenzie's door, all the while my shopping bags sitting on the bottom stair waiting for me. I could picture the red top, throbbing like a living thing.

It was just fabric, I thought. It couldn't hurt me.

Nevertheless I took the bag all the way up to the top floor, to Stuart's flat, and left it just inside the door.

When I got home and checked, everything was fine. Already I felt better. I left the cutlery drawer alone, left the bathroom unchecked, had a drink and a biscuit, and felt alright.

It was a start.

I didn't sleep much. I was so cold. No position was comfortable; every part of me ached. When I saw the light behind the curtains I realised I must have slept a little, but I didn't remember it.

I sobbed, quietly, for the person I'd become. I'd lost the will to fight. I wanted to give in now, I wanted it all to be over with. I was covered in shame.

And now, as if things weren't dreadful enough, all I could think about was Naomi.

★   ★   ★

'Naomi?' I'd said.

'She was a job. A source. She was married to someone we were after. I recruited her — sweet-talked her into working with us. She was going to feed us information so we could bring him down.'

He looked down at his knuckles, the bruising on them, flexed his fingers and smiled. 'She was the most beautiful woman I'd ever seen. I was supposed to be working on her, but instead I fucked her and fell in love with her. They didn't know, they thought I was just doing what I was being paid to do, but after the first time I couldn't control it. I was going to leave the job, I was going to buy her a house, miles away, somewhere she'd be safe from that shit of a husband.'

'What happened?' I whispered.

He looked at me as though he'd forgotten I

417

was there. Flexed his fingers back into a fist, looking at the skin around his knuckles turning white. 'She was screwing me over as well as screwing me. All the time she was giving me intelligence about what he was up to, he was busy telling her what to say.'

He leaned his head back against the wall with a heavy sigh, then banged it back against the brickwork. And again. 'I can't believe I was that fucking stupid. I fell for everything she said.'

'Maybe she was too afraid of her husband,' I said.

'Well, that was her mistake, wasn't it?'

I considered this for a moment. 'What happened to her?'

'There was an armed robbery, just like we'd been waiting for, except we were waiting for them on the wrong side of town. We were all sitting there parked up like idiots, while another jeweller lost a quarter of a million pounds' worth of stock and a shop assistant got her skull opened up with a baseball bat. Just when I was wondering what the fuck had gone wrong, I got a text from Naomi asking to meet me. I went to the usual place, opened her car door, and there inside was her old man. He was having a good old laugh about it. I'd served my purpose, he said. They'd both completely fucked me over.'

He brought his knees up and rested his bruised hands on them, loosely, all the tension gone.

'A week later I had a phone call from her. She was in tears, told me all this shit about him putting her under pressure, how she was scared, wanting to know if I meant what I'd said about getting her away from him. I told her to pack her bags and meet me in the usual place.'

'You helped her escape?'

He laughed. 'No. I cut her throat and left her in a ditch. Nobody reported her missing. Nobody even looked for her.'

He stood up, stretched as though he'd just told me a bedtime story, opened the door and left me behind, turning the light off and plunging the room into darkness.

Saturday 5 April 2008

I thought I saw him again today.

It was almost a relief, in the end.

Stuart had worked late, so I left him asleep and took myself off to the High Street to pick up some shopping. It started in the Co-op — the normal feeling of being watched, but stronger than usual. The shop was pretty busy, lots of people in each aisle, and everywhere I went were faces that looked familiar, people I thought I'd seen before.

When I was queueing at the checkouts behind three other people, the feeling became more acute. I looked up, and he was standing by the fruit and vegetable section, across the other side of the store, staring right at me. I had no doubt that it was him, although he looked different in some way; I couldn't work it out at first.

I told myself it was okay. In the checkout queue I practised breathing deeply, regularly,

419

making each breath the most important thing in that moment, even though I really wanted to scream and run away.

It isn't real, I told myself. This is part of the OCD. This is your fertile imagination catching up with you. He's not real. It's just some man who looks a bit like him, you know all this. He isn't here.

When I looked over again, he had gone.

I got home with my bags of shopping, checking all the time to see if I could see him anywhere — shop doorways, the front seat of passing cars, crossing the road behind me, walking away, all these were places I'd seen him before.

Nothing more. Maybe I'd imagined it — someone who looked a bit like him?

At home I checked the flat before I went upstairs to Stuart with the shopping. I started at the front door, worked my way around the whole flat, finishing up in the bedroom. Everything was normal. I was almost desperate to find something wrong, something out of place, that would prove that he had been in here, but really I hadn't been gone long enough. Not if he had been out there watching me; after all, even Lee couldn't be in two places at once.

I woke Stuart up with a cup of tea and a kiss. When he opened his eyes and yawned, he pulled back the duvet and gave me an inviting smile, so I could climb into bed next to him. I couldn't think of anything I wanted more right at that moment than to take all my clothes off and snuggle up to my warm-skinned, naked boy-friend.

I wasn't going to tell him about seeing Lee, but afterwards, when I lay with my head on his shoulder, he suddenly said, 'You're not your usual self today.'

I raised my head to look at him. 'Aren't I? What do you mean?'

He rolled onto his stomach and propped himself on his elbows so he could look at me. He took my hand and kissed the palm, then slowly stroked his fingers up my arms, across the scars, looking at them intently. 'Something happened?'

I shrugged. 'Not really. I thought I saw someone I knew in the shop, that's all.'

'You mean Lee?'

Unlike me, he had no issues with saying his name. Stuart was always very good at facing fear, naming it, dealing with it and moving on. Something I was just starting to learn.

'I thought it was. But it was only for a moment.'

He studied me with that intent green-eyed gaze he has, as though I'm the only person in the whole world. 'You see him all the time,' he said. It wasn't a question. We'd talked about this before.

'This was different.'

'Different how?'

I didn't want to do this, I didn't want to admit to it, because talking about this made it real. If I kept it to myself I could still pretend I'd imagined it. But there was no point at all in trying to end this conversation — he wouldn't let it go until he'd probed me to his complete satisfaction.

'He was wearing different clothes. His hair was shorter. Okay? Happy?' I wriggled away from him and got out of bed, pulling my clothes back on.

He watched me with that expression he has, part amusement, part curiosity. 'Remember when you asked me, months ago, why I couldn't be the one to help you?'

'Hm.'

'Well, this is why.' He caught my wrist and pulled me down onto the bed next to him, tickled me until I couldn't help laughing.

Then he stopped, and looked at me seriously. 'Move in with me,' he said.

'Give over. I practically live here as it is.'

'So move in. Save some money. Be with me all the time.'

'So you can protect me?'

'If you like.'

Sudden realisation dawned. 'You think it was him,' I said.

He'd been caught out. 'Not necessarily.'

'Not necessarily? What the fuck does that mean?'

He hesitated for a few moments before answering. 'It means I think you're a rational person. We know Lee was released from custody a few months ago. We still don't have an explanation for that button finding its way into your pocket. But besides that, I think you're aware of your condition now to the extent that you know when something is unlikely to be part of your brain's processing, and you think it might have been him, *ergo*, I think it might have been him.'

'Stop talking like a fucking psychologist,' I said, hitting him with a pillow.

'If I were to agree to that, how would it make you feel?' he said with a wry grin.

I rolled my eyes at him.

'Seriously,' he said, when I was wrapped in his arms again. 'This time it was different. So we can reach one of two conclusions — the most likely being that you saw someone who reminded you of him, but was simultaneously different enough for you to be unsure, which is unusual.'

'Who was staring at me from one side of the supermarket to the other,' I added.

'In other words, a considerable distance from where you were.'

I didn't want to think about what the second of the two conclusions might have been. I tried to distract him by kissing him, a long, slow, deep kiss that lasted for minute after minute. He was very good at kissing, without having any agenda — he could just kiss me without ever demanding more.

'Are you going to do it?' he asked, at last, quietly, his face close to mine.

'Do what?'

'Come live with me.'

'I'll think about it,' I said. I don't think he had honestly expected much more than that.

He left me alone for most of the day. From time to time I wondered if he'd gone out, and then I would hear a noise from some part of the house and realise he'd been there all along. Banging, from somewhere outside — the garage? What was he doing?

I spent some time looking out of the window, willing someone to see me. I looked over into the next-door neighbour's garden, desperate for them to come out, so that I could bang on the window. I tried banging on the glass with the handcuffs, but the noise was so terrible I was afraid he would come up the stairs. It was pointless anyway. There was nobody to hear, apart from him.

The weather had turned, and it was rainy and windy. More like October than June. I sat with my back to the wall, waiting for him to come for me. I stared at my wrists, at the scabs that had formed, thin and tight, over the scrapes the cuffs had made yesterday. If I moved too much the wounds would open again, so I sat still. The three middle fingers of my right hand wouldn't bend. The skin was purplish, mottled, but the swelling had subsided a little. I was glad I didn't have a mirror. My eye was still mostly closed, my ear still buzzing.

When it started to get dark I felt the exhaustion and thirst getting the better of me, and I lay down again, the blanket around me. I must have slept, because when I woke up he was there, standing over me, and despite itself my broken nose was detecting something.

'Get up,' he said, his voice firm but not angry. I struggled against my aching limbs to sit. On the floor, from the light of the hallway, I could see a packet of chips wrapped in paper, and a bucket of water. It didn't smell of bleach. I fought the urge to put my head into it and drink the whole thing.

He turned and locked the door behind him.

'Thank you,' I called, my voice hoarse, before I tipped the bucket and began to pour it into my dusty mouth.

The light went off, the door was locked. After a few minutes I lay on the carpet, pulling the blanket around me as best I could, and smelled the scent of piss and blood and bleach. I thought about Naomi and wondered how long I had left.

Monday 14 June 2004

When I opened my eyes, my first thought was this: *Today I'm going to die.*

I knew this because of the pain. It was at a different level, coming at me like a train from the moment I opened my eyes. I was sweating and shivering, and, although I must have been drifting in and out of consciousness for hours, I suddenly came round to reality and I knew.

Between my legs, under the thin blanket, the blood had flowed out of me during the night with such excess that I thought he must have ruptured something internally, and that I was simply going to bleed to death in my spare room.

425

He wasn't going to have to do anything else. I was simply going to die from what he'd already done.

Despite the food he'd given me, I was too weak to move, and shaking too much to be able to get a purchase on the floor and raise myself up, so I lay there, the pain everywhere, all at once, but most of all across my belly, inside of me.

I drifted in and out for a while, once even dreaming that I'd made it to New York. I was asleep in a huge bed, plate-glass windows looking out over the Statue of Liberty and Central Park, the Empire State Building and the Hoover Dam all at once. My tummy ache was because I'd eaten too much, and I had a hangover, and I just had to sleep for a while and it would go away.

So when he came in — was it hours later? It might even have been a day — I wasn't even really sure if he was there or not. Maybe I was dreaming him too. Maybe I was dreaming when he lifted my head up by my hair and dropped it back onto the carpet. I felt as if I was flying.

'Catherine.'

I heard his voice and I smiled at it. He sounded funny, like he was underwater.

'Catherine. Wake up. Open your eyes.'

He was on the floor next to me, and suddenly through the remains of my nose I could smell it — the alcohol. Or maybe I was tasting it as he breathed out, close to my face.

'Catherine, you whore. Wake up.'

Oh, God help me. I laughed then. It became a cough which hurt.

'Open your eyes.'

Only one of them opened, and then only a crack. And then all I could see was something silver and black, which swam into focus gradually and became something long, something shiny. Beautiful, almost.

In the end, I only really knew it was a knife when he cut me for the first time. I didn't make a sound. He wanted me to cry out, but I couldn't any more.

The second cut, my left upper arm, hurt a little bit, but what I felt more was warmth on my cold, cold skin.

When the next one came, and another, and another, I could hear him, sniffing, crying maybe, and I forced my eye open again, struggled to focus on him. He was going to kill me like this. Why didn't he just cut my throat? My wrists? Something to make it quicker. Not like this.

I didn't fight him off. He moved the blanket off me as he started cutting at my legs. 'Jesus,' I heard him say. I wasn't even aware that he'd stopped, but I guess at some point he must have.

I lay there and felt the wounds open, just small ones. My arms, my legs, the blood that was left inside me leaking out, the carpet under me now a long way from the pale grey.

Caroline and I have finally started the process of interviewing for the warehouse operatives at the new distribution site. The interviews, yesterday and today, were going well, until about ten o'clock when Caroline went downstairs to fetch the next candidate.

I was scanning his application form — Mike Newell, aged thirty-seven, little previous experience with warehousing, but his application form was legible, well-written and considered, which was more than most of them that we'd had to discard. No children, lived in south London, gave his interests as world history and electronics. The reason we'd invited him for interview was the sentence in response to the question 'Why do you think you would be able to fulfil this role with Lewis Pharma?' — 'Although I have limited experience in warehousing, I feel I would be able to bring enthusiasm and a willingness to learn to the role, and I would be able to offer my full commitment to the organisation' — enthusiasm, commitment, willingness — all things we could do with more of.

Caroline was talking to him as the door to the interview room opened, and I stood, preparing my welcoming smile, ready to greet the fifth person we'd interviewed that day.

My heart stood still.

It was Lee.

He gave me a warm smile and shook my hand, Caroline told him to take a seat and make himself comfortable, while I stood there with the blood drained from my face and my mouth dry.

Was I seeing things? He was here, wearing a suit, wearing a comfortable, friendly smile, and his eyes had barely met mine. He was acting completely as if he hadn't recognised me. As if his name was Mike Newell and not, actually, Lee Brightman.

I considered bolting for the door. I wondered whether I was actually going to throw up. Then I thought about his demeanour here, how he was acting completely normally, and I wondered if I'd actually flipped, gone completely mad, and this was some sort of peculiar hallucination.

'So, Mr Newell,' said Caroline briskly, 'I'll just explain a bit about the organisation and the role, and then we'll ask you a few questions to get to know you a bit better, and at the end if you have any questions for us, we'll be able to answer them then. Does that sound alright?'

'Yes, sure.' It was Lee's voice, but the accent was different — Scottish? Northern somehow, anyway.

Was it him?

While Caroline went through the practised explanation about Lewis Pharma and the current period of expansion, I watched him with a sort of fascinated horror. His hair was darker, slightly, and shorter; he was paler — well, that would figure — and he had aged a bit, wrinkles around his eyes that hadn't been there before. That would make sense, too. He was watching Caroline closely, nodding at the right moments, looking as though he was taking everything in. I'd never seen him wearing a suit like that before, either — it didn't really fit him properly. He looked as though he'd borrowed it. I couldn't imagine Lee wearing something that didn't make him look immaculate. Unless of course he was undercover, in which case he'd wear those filthy clothes that smelt as if he'd been sleeping rough.

I felt a momentary doubt that it was him.

It had been nearly three years since I'd seen him, in the dock, listening to the evidence. I hadn't been there for the sentencing, of course. Three days before the end of the trial was the second time I ended up sectioned. While he was being sent down, I was dosed up with tranquillisers and spending most of my day staring at a stain on the wall.

I tried to summon up a picture of his face back then, and it was confusing. I'd tried so hard to block him out. In my nightmares, even in those moments when I caught sight of him, out on the street, in the supermarket, he was a faceless shape now.

Was it him?

Caroline was coming to the end of her speech, and any minute now it was going to be my turn.

I realised that, without meaning to, I'd been breathing deeply and slowly, calming myself with every breath, coping, because I had to. I tried to think about my anxiety levels. At least sixty, possibly seventy. I couldn't fall apart here. I needed this job badly — they'd taken a chance on me, and I couldn't blow it. I waited for the fear to subside. It was going to take a while. I was going to have to deal with it.

'So,' I said, realising that somehow I was working on some kind of auto-pilot, 'Mr Newell.'

He looked across at me and smiled. Those eyes — they were wrong. They were too dark. It wasn't him, it couldn't be. I was imagining it, the same way I'd imagined seeing him all those other times.

'Can you tell us a bit about your last role, and why you decided to leave?'

I found myself listening to the words and not taking them in. Caroline's pen scratched across the surface of her notepad, which was good, because I wasn't going to be remembering anything about what he'd said. Something about him working overseas for the last couple of years, running a bar in Spain. Helping out a friend. Of course we'd check his references, but if it was Lee, he could fake something like that easily enough.

Internally, I was veering away from complete utter horror that I was sitting here opposite the man who'd nearly killed me, who'd beaten me and raped me. I was listening to him telling me about his career, how he'd moved from various jobs having been in the army — surely we could check that? There would be records, wouldn't there? And he was telling us his name was Mike Newell; that he'd grown up in Northumberland — not Cornwall — but spent most of his working life in Scotland. There was no mention of Lancaster. There was no mention of a criminal conviction for assault. No mention of a three-year prison sentence.

Caroline took over again and offered him the chance to ask us any questions.

'I just wondered,' he said, in that voice, that curious mixture of accents that I couldn't place, 'if there was anything you'd be looking for in your ideal candidate that I haven't been able to demonstrate for you today?'

Caroline looked across to me, trying not to let the amused smile show. 'Cathy? Could you answer that one?'

It was one of the best questions I'd ever heard anyone ask in an interview. 'Of course,' I said, trying to keep my voice steady, 'it would have been preferable if you'd had experience in warehousing, but it isn't essential. We've seen a number of very strong candidates in the last few days and we are hoping to reach a decision on the roles available by tomorrow lunchtime.'

He gave me a smile. His teeth were different from Lee's — whiter? More even? Now I looked at him again, really he was quite different. It wasn't just the eyes. The teeth, the hair — the build; he was certainly less muscular than Lee had been. Even with the badly fitting suit, I remembered the way his biceps had filled the sleeves of whatever he wore. It was all just slightly, off-puttingly different.

'Thank you very much for coming in, Mr Newell,' I said, shaking his hand. His grip was firm, warm, not sweaty — the perfect handshake for someone you'd want to employ.

Caroline took him back downstairs, leaving

me alone in the interview room, my thoughts racing. Was it him? I scanned the application form — neat handwriting, capitals — it didn't look like his handwriting, although he could have got someone to complete it for him, for heaven's sake, that didn't mean anything. He could be wearing contact lenses. He could have had his teeth fixed. He'd not been able to work out while he'd been inside. And as for the last job, two years in a bar in Spain? He'd got friends out there; anyone on the end of a phone would provide him with a reference and we'd be none the wiser. And he wasn't exactly tanned.

From outside the door, I could hear Caroline bringing the next candidate in for interview, and I prepared my welcoming smile. Behind my temples, the mother of all headaches was preparing its sting.

★ ★ ★

As soon as the interview was finished, I told Caroline I was going to get a drink and some tablets. We had a break after this one, and then three more interviews before home time.

Caroline wouldn't stop talking about Mike Newell.

'I think he's easily the best one today, don't you? Even though he's not worked in warehousing before, he's clearly intelligent and willing to learn, isn't he? And that question at the end — I'm keeping a note of that one for the next time I'm an interview candidate. You gave a brilliant answer — I had honestly no idea at all what I was going to say. And I know it's unprofessional, but my God, he's a bit easy on the eye, too, isn't he? And really charming . . . '

'I'll see you in a minute, okay?' was all I managed in response, grabbing my bag from my desk drawer and heading out towards the rear doors of the building.

I got my mobile phone out, and the scrap of paper which still contained DS Hollands' phone numbers.

The mobile was turned off, so I tried the other number. 'Public Protection, DC Lloyd speaking, can I help you?'

'Er — hi. I was hoping to speak to Sam Hollands?'

'DS Hollands is in a meeting at the moment. Can I help?'

'Yes, yes. I need someone to help.' Oh, God, how to explain all this in just a few sentences? How to tell someone how urgent this was, and yet not give them a reason to think you're a complete nutcase?

'Hello? Are you in any danger right now?'

'No, I don't think so.' I could feel the tears starting. Please, I thought, don't be kind to me, I don't think I could take it.

'What's your name?'

'Cathy. Cathy Bailey. I was assaulted by a man called Lee Brightman, four years ago. He got three years for it, and I was told he was released at Christmas. This was up north, in Lancaster.'

'Okay,' said the voice.

'DS Hollands told me he'd been released. I thought I saw him a few days ago, here in London, and I spoke to DS Hollands, she got Lancaster to check on him, and they said he was still there.'

'And you've seen him again?'

'I work as a personnel manager, and I think I've just interviewed him for a job at the company I work for.'

'You think . . . ?'

'He looked different, but not much. He was calling himself Mike Newell, but it looked so much like him — same voice, everything. I was wondering whether someone in Lancaster could check on him, like, right now? Because he's only just left here, about half an hour ago. So if it was him, he won't be in Lancaster.'

'Do you have an injunction, a restraining order, anything like that?'

'No.'

'Do you know if he has licence conditions not to contact you?'

'I don't think he does.'

'Right. But he was claiming to be someone else?'

'Yes — he's put in an application form for this job, as though he has a whole career history, but all of it could have been faked. I mean, he's claimed on this form that he's been working in Spain for the last few years.'

There was a long pause. I checked my watch — another five minutes and we'd need to start thinking about going back into the interview room.

435

'Did he threaten you at all?'

'What, in the interview? No,' I said.

'Did he give any sign that he recognised you, or that he wasn't who he was claiming to be?'

'No, he played along with it.'

'But you're certain it's him?'

I avoided the question as best I could. 'He used to do this. He used to enjoy turning up unexpectedly, scaring me. He used to watch me when I was out shopping, and if he thought I'd taken too long he would beat me when I got back home. He loves mind games, and I know he would just love turning up at my place of work and pretending to be someone he's not, just to see my reaction.'

Another long pause. I wondered if she was taking notes.

'Okay. Can I call you back on this number?'

'I'm going back into interviews until gone five, but I've got voicemail.'

'Leave it with me, I'll call you back.'

I ran back into the building, into the ladies' toilets. Washing my hands, I cast a glance at my reflection in the mirror. I looked a lot more together than I felt. My hair was growing, and I'd just had it cut in a neat bob, the ends swinging gently against my jawline. I looked pale and a little tired, the dark plum-coloured jacket giving my skin a faintly greenish tinge, but nothing a quick bit of powder wouldn't fix.

Caroline was already in the interview room. 'Ready for round three?' she said.

'Sure.'

'Are you okay?' She looked concerned, as though she'd just noticed I was starting to look flaky.

'Yeah,' I said. 'Got a pounding headache — all that concentrating.'

'Oh,' she said. 'When I brought that last one in — Newell — you looked as if you'd seen a ghost. I thought you were going to pass out.'

It was my turn to do the fetching. I gave her a smile that I hoped was bright enough to satisfy her, and went downstairs to collect the next candidate.

★　★　★

When the last interview was over, Caroline and I had a short break before meeting up to discuss the candidates and make a decision on who we were going to employ and who was going to be rejected.

I went outside to get some fresh air, my headache still pounding. The tablets I'd taken had done no good at all. I turned the phone on and left it for a moment until the beep signalled that I'd got a new message. I dialled the voicemail number.

'Yeah, this is a message for Cathy Bailey. It's Sandra Lloyd at the Camden PPU. I just wanted to let you know that I've been in touch with Lancaster and they are going to send someone out to check up on Mr Brightman. I haven't heard back from them yet but I'll let you know when I get an answer. Alright, cheers, bye for now.'

I knew it was no use — by the time they located him, enough time would have passed for him to make it back to Lancaster.

As I walked slowly around the car park, enjoying the sunshine, and wondering what time Stuart would be home from work, my phone rang. 'Hello?'

'Cathy? It's DC Lloyd here. Did you get my message?'

'Yes, thank you. Have you heard any more?'

'Lancaster just called back. They've been to check on his home address but there's nobody there. The woman I spoke to said she saw him yesterday, though, and he didn't mention that he had any plans to go to London. Were you certain that it was him that you saw?'

How could I answer that? No, I wasn't sure, but at the same time I'm not mad either. I wasn't seeing things.

'I'm not a hundred per cent certain, no.'

'I think it's very unlikely — after all, does he know you're in London? Does he know where you work?'

'I hope not.'

'Thing is, he's not under any licence conditions, which means that technically he's free to go anywhere he likes without supervision. My colleagues in Lancaster can check up on him from time to time, but they can't keep harassing him if he hasn't done anything to warrant it.'

'He nearly killed me,' I said, my voice coming from a long way away.

Sandra Lloyd had a tone of voice that suggested she was sympathetic most of the time. 'Yes, but that was a long time ago. Chances are he's moved on, in more ways than one. Now I know Lancaster will be keeping an eye on him as best they can, so try not to worry.'

'Yes,' I said, lamely, 'thank you.'

I wasn't even surprised. They hadn't believed me last time; there was no reason at all why they should believe me now.

If it wasn't him, and I was just having spectacularly real hallucinations, then I was just going to have to learn to deal with them until I was better. If it was him, then I wasn't going to be able to prove all by myself that he wasn't back up in Lancaster being a good boy.

I was going to have to wait for the moment he decided to reveal his cards, and I was going to need to be ready to play his game.

★　★　★

When I got back to the office, Caroline had her jacket on.

'Come on,' she said, 'we're getting out of here.'

'Are we?' I said. My headache was making it difficult to focus.

'We are. We need to get out of this place, come on.'

We walked out of the main entrance and around the corner to the pub just by the entrance to the business park. It was busy with office workers having a drink, but we managed to find a table at the back by the kitchen. It was dark back here.

Caroline put our drinks on the table. 'You look completely wasted,' she said.

I laughed. 'Cheers for that.'

'Seriously,' she said, 'what's wrong?'

I looked at her face, my friend, the only friend I really had here in London, apart from Stuart.

'It's a long story,' I said.

'I've got time.'

I took a deep breath in. This was so difficult. Telling this story never got any easier. I felt tears, tiredness, exhaustion, fought them all. I wasn't going to break down, not here.

'Four years ago, the man I was with attacked me and almost killed me. He was arrested and, after a long investigation and a court case, he was sentenced to three years in jail.'

'My God,' she said. 'You poor girl. You poor, poor girl.'

'I moved to London because I knew he'd be out soon enough, and that he'd come after me. That's why I'm here.'

'Was this where you were before, then? Lancaster, wasn't it?'

'Yes. I wanted to be far away when he was released. Just in case he decided to come looking for me.'

Caroline looked alarmed.

'Do you think he will?'

I gave this a bit of serious consideration. There was no way of dressing this up as anything other than the horror that it really was. 'Yes. I think he will.'

Caroline breathed out. 'So — he should be out soon, then.'

'He's already out. He was released at Christmas.'

'Oh, my God. No wonder you've been looking so pale. You must be completely terrified.'

I nodded. I felt like crying, again, but what good would it do? I just wanted to go home and be with Stuart.

'That man. Mr Newell.'

'Yes?'

'He looked like him. I thought it was him. That's why I looked so peculiar. You said I looked like I'd seen a ghost — I thought I had.'

I looked at her, warm and motherly with her dark red glossy hair, all done professionally, her neat grey suit. She had tears in her eyes. 'You poor, poor girl.'

She gave me a hug and held me longer than I thought she would. I felt the tears just behind my eyes. I would save them for being alone.

'Why didn't you tell me before?' she said, quietly. It wasn't a reproach — she wanted to help.

'I have difficulties trusting people,' I said.

★　★　★

When I finally got home, I found myself checking the door, twice. It wasn't on the latch; it was firmly shut, and the flat door looked fine, too, but it clearly wasn't. I was

441

going to have to check properly, again. It wasn't the OCD. It was self-preservation.

My mobile phone rang just as I'd finished and put the kettle on. I thought it might be Stuart, but the number that I'd programmed in earlier just said 'HOLLANDS'.

'Hello?'

'Cathy? It's Sam Hollands, Camden PPU.'

'Yes. Hello.'

'I gather you spoke to my colleague earlier today?'

'Yes, that's right. She was very helpful. Have you heard any more?'

There was a pause and a rustling of paper. 'I had a call from Lancaster. They put in another call to the address we've got for Mr Brightman about fifteen minutes ago, and he was arriving at the address just as they were knocking on the door.'

I did a quick bit of mental arithmetic — the interview had been at one-thirty, had finished just before two. It was just possible for him to have caught the train, no delays, and be back in Lancaster just as the police turned up at the door.

It was starting to feel a bit unlikely, though.

'I don't suppose they said what he was wearing?'

'No, they didn't. DC Lloyd said he turned up for an interview?'

I found myself smiling. She believed me, she really did believe me. 'Yes. I really did think it was him, but I haven't seen him for three years. He looked like he'd lost weight. But then I guess he would, wouldn't he?'

'And he didn't acknowledge you?'

'No. He just acted like anyone else coming for an interview — a bit nervous, a bit keen. But then he was always good at acting. Don't forget he was holding down a job all the time he was beating me up.'

I didn't mention what the job was. She already knew about that, after all.

'And where are you now?'

'I'm at home. I'm fine, I feel fine. Thank you. Thank you for believing me.'

'No worries. Listen — if you need help, call again, okay?'

'Yes. I will.'

'Another thing. Think of a code word, something you could say without arousing suspicion if he was there, if you were in trouble.'

'Um — what, now?'

'Yes. Something innocuous. How about 'Easter'?'

' 'Easter'?'

'Yes. If I speak to you, and you're in trouble, ask me how Easter was. Pretend I'm a friend, a work colleague. Okay?'

'Yes.'

'I'm sure you won't need it. But just to be on the safe side, I've put a marker on your home address on the system. If you call in, all calls are going to be treated as urgent. This will stay on the system for three months, and then will automatically come off if you haven't called in. If you just need a chat, or some advice, call me on the mobile.'

'Yes. Thank you, sergeant. You've been brilliant.'

'Sam, call me Sam. And save my number on your phone as 'Sam' so that you can call me if you need to.'

I hesitated. 'You think I'm in danger?'

'I just think it's always a good idea to be prepared. If he's happily going about his business in Lancashire and has no intention of paying you a visit, then we'll none of us have lost anything, will we?'

I ended the call and made my cup of tea, adding milk until it was just the right colour.

It took more than an hour of thinking, and after that I'd reached a decision.

I started up the laptop that I'd brought home, pulled up the spreadsheet of all the candidates who'd been selected for interview for the warehousing positions, and scrolled down until I found him. Mike Newell. An address in Herne Hill. A telephone number.

I hesitated for a moment, wondering if I could wait for Stuart. I wasn't planning to speak to Mr Newell. I just wanted to hear the voice. If I heard the voice again, I'd know. I would know for sure. And, of course, if he was in Lancaster, he couldn't also answer the phone in Herne Hill.

Of course, when I heard the voice, I was shocked to the core; a second later realising that, actually, I'd anticipated this all along.

'Hello?' A woman's voice, one I knew well. One word, and it told me all I needed to know.

I paused, thinking, and the pause was long enough for her to say, 'Hello? Hello, who is it?'

444

I found my voice. 'What are you doing?'

Now it was her turn to hesitate. Her 'telephone' voice — somewhere between the northwest of England and Roedean — turned chilly. 'What do you mean, what am I doing?'

I wondered if my voice conveyed the confidence I needed it to. 'When you speak to him — and I know he isn't there — you can tell him I'm not afraid of him any more.'

I put the phone down. Betrayed, again.

Wednesday 9 April 2008

These days, being awake ridiculously early felt good. I liked waking up and seeing the dawn, the sky pink and alive with promise, the birds singing their hearts out.

Stuart was asleep, in his bed, in his flat, next to me.

He looked wonderful. His face was so peaceful, the skin pale and thrown into stark shadows in the early light, those beautiful eyes closed. I wondered what he would say if I woke him up just to see his eyes open and look at me. His hand was lying across the empty space in the bed where I'd been until a few moments ago. That strong hand, the fingers supple and knowing, getting so good at turning me on.

Last night he came up to the flat, surprised that I was already there. He took my hand and led me into the bedroom before I could do anything, say anything. He removed my clothes and every time I tried to say something he stopped my mouth with a kiss — in the end, I realised how hungry I was for him.

After that, lying together in the tangle of duvet, the breeze from the open windows in the living room breathing gently over our skin and turning it into gooseflesh.

'What happened to you today?' he said, simply.

I wondered how he knew.

I didn't answer at first, wondered how to tell him in such a way that he would believe me.

'Do you remember me telling you about Sylvia?'

'The one you saw on the bus? I remember.'

I got up and wrapped myself in Stuart's shirt, discarded on the floor just outside the bedroom. It smelled of him, of his day at work, his aftershave and his sweat. In the kitchen I fetched a bottle of white wine from the fridge. Fortunately it was a screw top — I had no idea where I might find a corkscrew. Inside the bedroom I pulled the sash windows down — it was starting to get chilly.

He was sitting up in bed, his eyes tired. When he saw the bottle, he smiled. 'You were a complete abstainer until you met me,' he said.

'I know — great, isn't it?'

We took turns swigging from the bottle. It was icy cold.

He waited with infinite patience for me to find the words, despite the fact that he'd been at work for an appalling number of hours, and all he wanted to do was sleep.

'She made a statement to the police. She told

446

them that she thought I was losing it. She said that I'd become obsessed with Lee, that I'd thought he was having affairs with people. She told them that I used to go berserk if he came home late from work. She put down in her statement that I used to cut myself with razors.'

He looked at me and waited.

'I never, ever self-harmed. Even though I loathed myself after all this happened, I never did that. Before or after. It would have felt like failure. It would have been like giving up.'

'I don't get it. Why would she do something like that?' He took a long drink from the bottle and handed it to me.

I felt my cheeks warming as the alcohol spread into my bloodstream. 'He was sleeping with her, I think.'

He took the bottle out of my hands and put it carefully on the bedside table. 'You never told me about what it was like going to court,' he said.

'No. In many ways it was worse than the actual assault.'

'I guess it would be,' he said.

'I didn't last through the whole trial. I think it was the third day I didn't make it into the court; the day after that I was sectioned. But from what they told me afterwards, they had an internal investigation and decided that he was going to be charged with grievous bodily harm. And something about perverting the course of justice, because they proved that he'd lied about something the first time they interviewed him.'

'Surely he tried to kill you, though? What

447

about doing him for attempted murder?'

'Lee was a detective sergeant. He'd been working as a covert operations officer for nearly four years. Before that he'd worked in their intelligence unit providing technical support for covert jobs. Before that, he was in the military, although he never told me what or where. He had a completely spotless record. When they investigated what I'd told them, he provided a whole counter-story about how I'd stalked him, how I was making things difficult for him, how he should really have reported me before now but he felt sorry for me, all this crap.'

Stuart shook his head slowly. 'That's — but what about your injuries?'

I shrugged. 'He said most of them were self-inflicted after he'd walked out. He admitted that he'd restrained me, for my own safety and for his, and he admitted that he'd gone about things in the wrong way but said that he'd only done it because he genuinely cared about me, didn't want to see me getting into trouble for what I'd done. He said I must have broken my nose when I'd tried to head-butt him. It wasn't much of an explanation, but all it needed to do was sow the seeds of doubt in their minds.'

'And they had Sylvia backing up his story?'

'Exactly. And before they called me to give evidence, I was sectioned. They never got to hear what actually happened. They never heard my side of it.'

'Even so — didn't anyone give medical evidence?'

'The only medic who gave evidence was the

nice psychiatrist who told them that I couldn't come and give evidence because I'd been forcibly taken away for my own safety and was in a closed ward having a breakdown.'

'But physically — not mentally. You were injured, for goodness' sake . . . '

'When they first took me to the hospital I weighed six and a half stone. They estimated I'd lost four pints of blood through more than one hundred and twenty lacerations on my arms, legs and torso, and through the miscarriage that was already starting.'

He shook his head slowly. He'd not taken his eyes off me for one moment. 'How the hell could they even think that it was self-inflicted?'

I shrugged. 'Once he'd finished with the knife, he wiped it down and then put it into my hand. None of the cuts were in places that I couldn't have reached on my own. In the end, the only injuries that he admitted to were the bruises on my upper arms where he'd gripped me, and the bruises to my face which he'd said were made in self-defence when I'd come at him with the knife. Oh, and he admitted we'd been enjoying what he called 'rough sex' before he said I'd flipped and started attacking him.'

'But anyone who knows anything about self-harming could tell that the cuts weren't made by you. Nobody self-harms like that. They just don't.'

I reached across him for the bottle, and sat cross-legged on the bed, taking a drink. This was harder than I'd thought it was going to be.

'I know it sounds ridiculous. I've been over

449

this whole thing countless times in my head — how unfair it all is, how they could do this to me. But it doesn't help. When you break it down, it was his word against mine. And he was there, wearing a smart suit, in his own comfortable law enforcement environment, using their language, telling them how it all went wrong but his intentions had always been good, and how sorry he was. And I was in a secure ward having a breakdown. Who were they going to believe? It's a wonder they prosecuted him at all, really. It's a wonder they didn't send him away with a fucking medal.'

Even through the pleasant, warm haze of more than half a bottle of wine, I could tell he'd heard enough. I could see that look in his eyes, the one I'd seen in Caroline's eyes earlier. It wasn't disbelief, thankfully. It was just — horror.

I knew that this was enough for now and that I couldn't tell him the rest of it. I couldn't tell him about seeing Lee today. It was all getting just a bit too much, as though the nightmares he saw every day at work were suddenly starting to invade his life at home.

'Look,' I said, putting the bottle back on the bedside table, 'I am better, Stuart. Look at me.'

He looked.

Even in the half-light, my scars everywhere were visible, a pattern of destruction on my skin.

'I'm not bleeding now. I'm not hurting any more. It's over, alright? We can't change what happened, but we can change what happens from now on. You've taught me such a lot about that, about healing. It's only good things from now on.'

He reached out a hand and ran his fingers down my body, from my shoulder, across my breast, down my stomach. I moved closer, close enough that his mouth could follow the path that his fingers had taken.

There was nothing more to be said.

Sunday 13 April 2008

I caught the bus to Herne Hill.

It was the first really warm day of the year, and I was regretting bringing my jacket. When I'd set out this morning, the sun hadn't got above the rooftops and it had been chilly. Now I was holding it under my arm and it was getting to be a pain.

I took a long walk around to the house, although I knew where it was — I'd studied the *A to Z* before I'd left home. The streets were empty, London surprisingly peaceful, as though everybody had gone away to the seaside and left the urban sprawl just for me.

By the time I stood in front of the house, I'd managed to work myself up into a fervent indignation, which I hoped was going to be enough.

The house was a lot like ours: a big Victorian terrace, matching the others row upon row in this street, the next, the one after that. There was a basement flat with a separate entrance; a set of little winding stone steps down to a bright red front door. Then an elegant stone staircase leading up to a black front door, sadly in need of a lick of paint, and a row of five doorbells indicating the flats inside. I climbed the steps to the main door. Flat 2, the application form had said. There was no name on the doorbell, although all the others had them. Flat 1 — Leibowicz. Flat 4a — Ola Henriksen. Flat 4b — Lewis. Flat 5 — Smith & Roberts. What happened to Flat 3, I wondered?

I pressed the bell for Flat 2 and waited.

There was no reply.

I debated going home again, and sat for a moment on the top step, feeling the sunshine warm on my face. Then I turned to look at the door, stood, gave it a little push. It opened immediately, and a hallway opened up beyond, complete with the original black and white chequerboard floor tiles.

Flat 2 was at the back of the house, on the ground floor. The door to the flat was a plain hardboard one with a single Yale lock. I knocked on it sharply and waited.

I heard steps from within and someone muttering.

Then the door opened, abruptly, and there stood Sylvia, a towel wrapped around her head, another towel draped loosely around her body.

'Oh,' she said, 'it's you.'

'It's me. Can I come in?'

'What for?' She was wearing her petulant expression, one I'd seen her offer to other people — waitresses, bar staff, members of the public, officials — but never to me.

'I'd like to talk to you.'

She took her hand away from the door and walked back into the flat, leaving it wide open for me to enter.

'I'm going out soon,' she said.

'I'm not planning on staying long, don't worry,' I said.

While I waited for her to get dressed I wandered into her living room, taking in the typical Sylvia clutter — the huge art posters on the walls, overwhelming the tiny space; the sofa draped with several different brightly coloured throws; the kitchenette which had probably never been used for anything more enterprising than chilling bottles of sauvignon blanc.

There was no sign of Lee. I'd been half-expecting to see some of his clothes, shoes, a bag — something. Maybe even a photograph of him. But it was as though he'd never been in here.

Behind some huge, heavy terracotta curtains that were several inches too long for the height of the room, a pair of patio doors led out onto the garden beyond. The grass was overgrown, full of weeds, here and there the odd burst of colour from when the garden had belonged to someone who cared.

I wondered who lived in the basement flat, and felt for them, in their subterranean world. I'd been there too.

'Right,' she said, breezing back into the room and making it feel instantly crowded. 'What do you want?'

I shrugged. 'Just to see you, I guess.'

She looked confused. 'Well, here I am. You've seen me.'

She looked thinner than when I'd last seen her, and although the clothes she wore were still the typical Sylvia bright — pillarbox-red jeans, a purple jumper with an emerald leather belt, and pumps which sparkled, glittery — the vivid colours made her look dulled, her hair more ash-blonde than golden-blonde, her curls heavy and dragged back into a plain black clip. Under the make-up, she looked pale.

'I'm sorry,' I said, simply. 'I came to say that, as well. I'm sorry.'

She wasn't expecting that, either.

'I'm sorry I didn't keep in touch when you left.'

'It was hard, down here, you know? Tougher than I thought it would be. I missed you.'

'I missed you, too. I felt I suddenly had no friends left. It was as though the sun had gone behind a cloud, after you'd gone.'

'I guess I should have tried harder to keep in touch, too,' she admitted.

I thought: *by that time you were too busy fucking my ex-boyfriend anyway, weren't you?*

She smiled, softened. If I was going to have to pander to her, flatter her, I'd do it.

'Look,' she said, 'do you want something? Wine? A cup of tea?'

'A cup of tea would be great. Thanks.'

She put the kettle on in the kitchen and banged about in the cupboards for a while. 'I got this flat last year. Nice, isn't it?' she shouted above the rattle of the water in the kettle.

'Yes,' I said. 'It's very you.'

She smiled and thanked me as though I'd paid her a compliment. 'What about you? You're living down here now?'

'Yes,' I said.

'Then it was you I saw at the bus stop,' she said.

'Yes.'

'I wasn't sure. You look very different, with your hair . . . short like that.'

She tugged and pulled at the patio doors until they creaked open, the metal frame scraping painfully across a paving slab outside, the deep groove through it testament to how long it had been like that, unfixed. We sat outside with our mugs of tea, on the low wall separating the patio from the grass.

'Cost me a bloody fortune, of course. You'd be able to get a four-bedroomed mansion back home for the amount I spent on this flat.'

'I bet.' There was a grille below the patio doors, about three feet wide, no doubt some windows below, giving the basement flat a little bit of natural light. Not an escape route, though. Those bars would give me the creeps if I lived there.

'You look good,' she said.

I'd not noticed that she'd been staring at me. I smiled at her. 'I feel good. Better than I ever did, probably.'

She put a hand on my knee. 'I'm glad, Catherine, really. Perhaps we can all put that nasty business behind us. It was all such a shame.'

My indignation simmered. I needed to keep it simmering, because with not much more provocation it would become a murderous, vengeful rage which I could not control.

'Yes,' I said.

Sylvia sipped her tea. The birds were singing and the garden was quiet, peaceful. We could have been in the country somewhere, the sun warm on the top of my head.

Suddenly she gave her tinkling, melodic laugh. 'I bet it was a shock when he turned up at work, wasn't it? Calm as you please. Here I am for my interview.'

'Yes, something like that.'

'I did tell him not to do it, plenty more jobs in London, all that, but he wanted to surprise you. He said he was going to try and make peace with you, see if we could all just get back to being friends again.'

'I don't think he got a chance to speak socially, really. We had a lot of interviews to do.'

She gave me a sideways glance. 'Going to give him the job?'

'We've still got some people to see.'

She frowned. 'He's a good man, you know that, don't you? A good man.'

I wondered what planet she was on, what he'd said to her, what he'd done to her to make her believe him instead of me. Maybe she just believed what she wanted to believe.

I wanted to play the game, agree with her, *yes, he's a good man*, but that was a step too far. All I could do was pretend that she was actually talking about Stuart, and then I could nod.

'He had a really hard time of it, you know. They don't tend to like ex-police in prison.'

Good, I thought. What did she expect me to say? Poor Lee, what a horrible ordeal for him?

'Have you got someone else?' she asked, that coquettish smile back in her voice, nudging me with her elbow.

I smiled. 'Me? No. Never met anyone — you know what it's like. Big city. Working too hard.'

She nodded at that. 'I dated a few people — you know. But I never met anyone like Lee. He's very — special. But of course, you know that.'

I looked at her because it was such an odd choice of words to use. She glanced at the patio doors, as though she'd heard something in the flat, and a dawning horror came to me then.

He was there. He was inside the flat. He had been in there the whole time.

'What are you going to do?' she asked, her voice quieter. An edge to it. She hadn't taken her eyes off the patio doors, the darkness of the living room beyond it.

'Nothing,' I said, quietly. 'I'm not going to do anything.'

'That's alright, then,' she said brightly, turning to me with a smile, a warm and happy smile.

We'd finished our tea, and I had no reason to stay. I wanted to run as far away from here as possible, and never come back, but before I could do that I would have to go through the flat.

I forced my legs to move, and once I was inside again it was a bit better. The flat was

457

silent, apart from the sounds of Sylvia rinsing the mugs in the sink, chatting away about how we should meet up for coffee, go out one night, how she was planning to go out for her birthday and could I make it?

From the narrow hallway I could see into her bedroom, the door open wide, the bed unmade, the wardrobe door open and the sides of it bursting at the seams with a multitude of bright fabrics bulging off hangers — the bathroom to the other side, the bath across the far wall. I must have imagined it — there was simply nowhere to hide. He wasn't here at all.

At the doorway she gave me a warm smile. I had come here to warn her, and now I couldn't do it. I had wanted to say to her, tell him if he comes near me I'll kill him. I will actually kill him. But I said nothing.

Instead I smiled at her, promised to be in touch, and strolled off down towards the main road and the bus stop, feeling her eyes watching me from the black front door.

I felt more free than I'd felt for years. The further I walked, the lighter my steps, until I reached the main road and I was practically dancing. I didn't have a plan of action — not yet — but now at least I could start to think about making one.

★   ★   ★

From Herne Hill I went back towards Camberwell. The number 68 bus took me to the Maudsley and I hopped out. Stuart was finishing

458

work in half an hour. Of course, it could end up being hours after that, if there was some kind of emergency, but I could hope. I was also relying on him coming out of the main entrance rather than some side entrance, but I wasn't going to worry about that either.

I sat in the sunshine on a wall, swinging my legs. The road was busier up here, but still quieter than on a weekday. I watched buses coming and going, people walking past.

I almost missed him. I just glanced towards the bus stop and there he was. He'd come out early.

'Hey,' I said.

Stuart turned and saw me and his face lit up. He ran back to me, kissing me hard on the lips. Then he sat down next to me on the wall.

'Hey yourself. What are you doing here?'

'Waiting for my ship to come in,' I said.

'Ah. Any luck so far?'

'It's looking good, actually.'

'We could always go and find a nice pub and wait there instead? What do you think?'

We went to the Bull, which wasn't by anyone's standards a nice pub, but it was handy. The beer garden was full of people who clearly had been sitting there drinking for most of the day, so we sat inside. We got a bottle of wine to share and sat in the cool, listening to the random conversations wafting in through the open door.

'I've been thinking about that holiday,' he said.

'What holiday?'

'The one we were going to book when the

weather was freezing. We never got around to booking it.'

'That's because of you and your Protestant work ethic.'

'Even so. We should book something.'

I looked out of the window and sipped my wine. I could manage more than a couple of glasses without being wasted these days.

He said something else, but I wasn't really listening. Then I half-realised that what he'd said was important. 'What did you just say?'

'I said we should book somewhere nice, maybe for the autumn.'

'That wasn't what you said.'

He was blushing. He looked at me, his head tilted on one side.

'Alright. I said maybe we could book a honeymoon. Don't laugh.'

'I'm not laughing. Isn't there something you have to do first, if you're going on a honeymoon?'

'I guess maybe I asked in the wrong order.'

I couldn't quite believe what I was hearing. He had my full and undivided attention now. From outside came sounds of roaring laughter, as though the best joke in the world had just been shared to great acclaim.

'So ask in the right order.'

He took a big swig of his wine. 'Alright, I will. Cathy, will you marry me and then can we go on a nice holiday somewhere hot?'

I didn't answer straight away, and I think he thought he'd somehow messed up because he said then, 'I'm no good at all this. I have no idea what to say, or how to say it. I just know that I love you, and that sooner or later we're going to get married and be happy forever, and that at some point I should just check you want to go along with that. And I got you this.'

He fished around in his bag and pulled out a small box.

I looked at the box, closed on the table between us, for a long time. I wasn't deliberately trying to torture him. It wasn't even that I was confused about how I felt. I knew that getting married to Stuart and being with him for the rest of our lives was absolutely what I wanted more than anything.

But just not yet.

Stuart was looking completely impassive, apart from his eyes. His eyes were breaking my heart. 'It's a no, isn't it?'

I took a deep breath. 'It's a 'not yet'.'

'Is that good?'

I couldn't bear the look in his eyes any longer. I got up and sat in his lap and kissed him, long and deep, feeling him respond even though he was hurting. Even though I'd hurt him by not saying yes. One of the idiots came in from the beer garden to replenish supplies and whistled at us, made some comment about a free show, but I didn't stop. I don't think Stuart even heard.

In the end we went home to Talbot Street, straight up to the top floor, running up the stairs without me even checking the front door. Not even once. We ran into the flat and just about managed to slam the door behind us, shedding clothes all the way, not even making it to the

461

bedroom but instead naked on the living room floor, and after that naked in the kitchen and for good measure naked in the bathroom too.

Hours later, when it was dark and the breeze coming in through the window had turned cold, he whispered, 'Keep it. Keep the ring, won't you? Keep it until the *not yet* turns into a yes.'

Tuesday 22 April 2008

I woke up suddenly, asleep to wide awake in seconds. Heart pounding.

What was it?

Stuart stirred beside me, one hand lifted, on my arm, pulling me gently back down. 'Hey,' he murmured. 'Go back to sleep.'

'I heard something,' I said.

'You were dreaming.'

He fitted an arm around my middle. I lay back down, still, my heart still hammering. It had been a noise again, like before. A bang.

Silence, just my heart, just Stuart's breathing. Nothing else.

It was no good. There was no way I was going to go back to sleep.

I got out of bed, trying not to wake him up again, pulling on a T-shirt and a pair of shorts. Barefoot, I tiptoed out of the bedroom.

The flat was in darkness. I looked down towards the front door. It looked back at me, solid, silent, reassuring. The front room was bright, orange lights from the streetlights below illuminating the ceiling. I crouched down and sat on one of the low windowsills, looking down into the street.

It was utterly quiet, no movement, no cars. Not even a cat. The only sound was the distant drone of a plane, lights like stars flashing in the dark orange sky.

I was just thinking about going back to bed when I heard it again. A bang. A thump, dull, like something soft falling a long way.

It was in the house somewhere, downstairs. Somewhere below.

I thought about waking Stuart. My anxiety levels were high, somewhere around a seventy or eighty. My fingers were shaking and my knees were unsteady as I stood up. I waited for more. Nothing.

Fuck it, I couldn't be doing this for the rest of my life. I was going to check.

I padded in my bare feet to the door and, after a moment's hesitation, opened it. The stairway was dark, chilly, with a draught coming up from the floors below. I waited for my heart to stop thudding quite so hard. There's nothing to worry about, I told myself. It's just our house. It's just Stuart and me, there's nobody there. Go and have a look.

I went downstairs, leaving Stuart's door open. There was light from the front door, below, and dull light from the window on the landing. Otherwise it was dark.

When I was outside the door to my flat I stopped and waited, listened. Nothing at all.

This was ridiculous.

I went downstairs, one step at a time, keeping

to the edge so it didn't creak. The draught was worse now, almost a breeze. It lifted the hair on the back of my neck. Dank air, stale air — the scent of cold soil. The smell of graveyard earth.

I could see the front door now, firmly shut. No sign that it had been opened.

Then, suddenly — BANG — close by.

Not loud, but certainly loud enough to make me jump. I crouched down so I could see through the banister to the door to Mrs Mackenzie's flat.

The door was open again. Wide open.

Frozen to the spot, I looked into the inky blanket of blackness inside the flat. The noise I'd heard was like a cupboard door shutting. Echoing in the empty flat. Someone was inside.

Breathing as deeply and slowly as I could, I tried to concentrate, to think. This was crazy. There couldn't be anyone in there. If they were, they were fumbling around in the dark. Why didn't they just put a light on? I hugged my knees and waited for the panic to ease off. Of course it would have been easier and quicker to go back upstairs, to shout for Stuart, to go and start checking my own flat to make sure it was safe. But I'd come all the way down the stairs on my own and I wasn't going to give up now.

'Cathy?'

The voice behind me, right behind me, made me scream and jump. I screamed louder and harder than I'd thought possible.

'Hey, it's me, it's okay — what on earth — ? Cathy, sorry, I didn't mean to creep up on you.'

I was shaking from head to foot, pressing

464

myself against the far wall. I pointed at the open door, the yawning, gaping blackness. 'I heard — I heard . . . '

'It's okay. Come on, take some breaths.'

In addition to the panic I was furious.

'What the fuck . . . ?' I said, when I could speak. 'Why the hell didn't you just say something? You just about gave me a fucking heart attack.'

He shrugged. 'I thought you might be sleepwalking.'

'I've never fucking sleepwalked in my entire life.'

'Well, what are you doing, then?'

I looked at the doorway. If there was someone inside, we'd probably given whoever it was a fright. My scream alone must have woken up half the street.

'I heard noises. I came to have a look. And — see — the door's open. I bloody locked it. I locked it and I checked it. And now it's open.'

He made a tutting noise, an 'oh, no, here we go again' noise, and moved me out of the way. He went to the ground floor and turned the light on. We both blinked and shielded our eyes from the sudden brightness. The doorway still stood, black and empty. I could see a few feet of crazily patterned carpet.

Stuart looked at me with a world-weary expression and stood in the doorway.

'Hello?' he shouted. 'Anyone there?'

Nothing, not a sound. He went inside.

'Be careful,' I said.

The lights went on in the flat a few moments

later. I crept down the stairs. Everything was suddenly less threatening with the lights on. Stuart was in Mrs Mackenzie's living room, standing there next to the sofa in his boxers and bare feet. 'There's nobody here,' he said. 'See?'

I could still feel a draught. 'Look,' I said.

The bottom pane of glass in the kitchen door was broken, a wedge-shaped piece of glass about a foot wide smashed on the floor. Through it the smell of the garden, a night breeze, was breathing a chill onto the skin on my legs.

'Don't go closer,' he said, 'you might cut your feet.' And then, ignoring his own advice, he went closer.

'There's fur on the glass at the top. Looks like that fox has been getting in.'

'That bloody fox again,' I said. 'And do you think it used a hammer to smash the window?'

He stood up and crossed the kitchen floor to me, avoiding the broken glass. 'There's nobody here,' he said. 'Let's go back upstairs.'

We shut the door, slammed it. Stuart wouldn't let me check it. The latch had shot home, we'd both heard it. We went back upstairs and Stuart went back to bed. I sat in the kitchen with the lights on, drinking a cup of tea. My hands were still shaking, but even so I felt quite calm. I couldn't believe I'd actually done it, gone down the stairs in the middle of the night, left the safe place, left Stuart's bed, and gone out through the door and down the stairs.

Despite the broken pane of glass, despite the fact that Mrs Mackenzie's flat had clearly been broken into — and not just by a fox or any other animal for that matter, it had to have been a person — I felt calm and free and composed.

And still angry. Not just that he'd sneaked up behind me, not just that he'd made me scream and so alerted whoever it was who'd been in the flat, but that he thought I'd done it. He thought that I'd opened the door to the flat. He wouldn't say it, but I saw it in his eyes.

He was starting to doubt me, the same way Claire did, and Sylvia, and then the police, the judge, the doctors, everyone.

★ ★ ★

I didn't go back to bed. I put the television on and stayed up until it got light, half-watching, half-practising thinking about Lee. I was already wired; it didn't seem hard to take a step further and test my anxiety levels to the extreme.

I thought about him breaking into Mrs Mackenzie's flat. I thought about him living down there, in the darkness, listening to Stuart and me in the flat upstairs, listening to us talking, listening to us making love. I thought about him and what he might be planning to do.

When it got light, finally, I had tears on my face. I wasn't panicking; my breathing was steady. Controlling it, the panic, was definitely getting easier.

When I heard Stuart stirring I went to put the kettle on.

I took him in a cup of tea.

'You alright?' he said, his voice sleep-slurred.

'I'm fine.'

'I'm sorry,' he said. 'I'm sorry I scared you last night.'

'It's okay.'

'I'll ring the management company later, get them to send someone over and fix that broken glass. And put another lock on the door. Okay?'

'Sure. I'm going to go down and get ready for work.'

He touched my arm. 'Already? Come back to bed.'

'It's nearly seven. I'll see you tonight, okay?'

I kissed him. He rolled over in bed for another five minutes' sleep and I left him to it, heading down the stairs to my own flat. The urge to start checking everything was still there, but now I always restricted it. Instead of checking the windows and doors, checking the curtains were exactly as I'd left them, I checked other things.

If Stuart, or Alistair, or anyone else for that matter, had asked why I did it, why I checked, I would not have been able to explain. Nobody else would notice the things that I noticed, the little signs that Lee had been in here. The door was always locked, just as I'd left it, but that meant nothing. I couldn't explain how I knew he'd been in here while I'd been away.

I just knew.

Wednesday 23 April 2008

Stuart knocked on my door when he came up the stairs from work. I considered ignoring it, the way I'd ignored it the first time he knocked on my flat door, months and months ago.

'Hi,' I said.

He looked tired. 'You coming upstairs?'

'No, I've got some work to do. I'm going to do that, then have an early night. Do you mind? I didn't get much sleep last night. And you look just about done in.'

'I am quite tired. Just come up for dinner. Just for an hour. Please?'

I contemplated this for a moment.

'I've got lamb fillet. I was going to do some kebabs with lemon and cumin, and rice.'

I relented. He let me have five minutes to lock up. When I went up to the top flat he was already skewering bits of lamb.

'I rang the management company,' he said.

'Oh, yes?' I got some wine out of the fridge and the bottle opener from the cutlery drawer.

'They were going to send someone round to fix the glass in the flat downstairs, and sort out the lock.'

'I think they must have been. There's a load of sawdust on the floor by the door to the flat. Maybe they've put on a mortise or something.'

He turned on the grill. Already it was smelling good, garlic and spices and lemon. 'They asked me how Mrs Mackenzie is.'

'Haven't they been to check on her?'

He shrugged. 'Didn't sound like it. I rang up the ward after I'd spoken to them. No change. I don't think they've got high hopes for her. And they've still not managed to track down a next of kin.'

'Poor Mrs Mackenzie. I'll go and see her next week.'

We sat down to eat.

'We should go somewhere again, now the weather's warmer,' he said, chewing.

'Go somewhere?'

'For a weekend or something. Just to get away from it all.'

'This is yummy,' I said.

'We could go to Aberdeen. Or Brighton — we could go and have a weekend in Brighton, what do you think?'

I didn't answer.

He stopped chewing and watched me, drinking from his wineglass. He was looking at me in that psychologist's way he had: reserved, concerned, curious.

'I don't know,' I said, 'I've got such a lot on at the moment with work. I need to go through all those employment contracts with Caroline, and then there's the therapy with Alistair, and I wanted to think about decorating the flat — '

'Hey,' he said quietly, interrupting. 'Stop it.'

'Stop what?'

'Stop pushing me away.'

'I'm not. I'm not pushing you away, I'm just really busy, and — '

'Stop pushing me away.'

I'd made the mistake of catching his eye, and I was lost. I stared at him, cross at first, just for a moment, and then melting. I didn't want to do this on my own. I didn't want to do it all without him.

'The door, Mrs Mackenzie's door . . . '

470

'What about it?' he asked, reaching for my hand.

'I thought last night — you thought I did it. You thought I left it open on purpose. Didn't you?'

He shook his head. 'No.'

'It felt like you didn't believe me.'

'I do believe you, Cathy.'

'Someone tried to break in. Downstairs. That's why the glass was broken.'

'Yes,' he said.

'Why did you say it was the fox?'

'I didn't say the fox broke the window.'

He was right — he hadn't actually said anything of the kind.

'Why aren't you worried? Someone might have been inside the flat.'

He shrugged. 'Cathy, we live in London. Break-ins happen all the time. I got burgled when I was in Hampstead. My car got nicked two years ago, I never got it back. Ralph got mugged in Hyde Park once. This sort of thing happens all the time. It doesn't have anything to do with Lee.'

'But — '

'And whoever it was who broke the window, there was no sign of them getting in. The back door was still shut and locked.'

'The flat door was open!'

'You and I both know that latch wasn't exactly reliable. The draught from the broken pane probably blew it open.'

I bit my lip. This wasn't going anywhere.

'It's not Lee, Cathy,' he said, gently. 'He's not

here. It's just you and me. Alright?'

I cleared the plates away. While I was rinsing them and putting them in the dishwasher, I felt misery and general exhaustion. He stopped me, took the plate carefully from my soapy hand, made me turn to him. He tilted my chin up so I was looking at him, at his eyes.

'I love you,' he said. 'And I'm so proud of you. You're brave and strong and bold. You're braver than you think you are.'

The tears chased each other down my hot cheeks. He kissed them away. He held me and rocked me gently, and after a while I forgot all about going downstairs to do the work that I'd pretended I had to finish. I forgot all about the broken glass, and the sawdust on the floor, and the draught of cold that blew around my ankles. I forgot about everything except him, Stuart, and the warmth of his hands on my skin.

Wednesday 7 May 2008

For another two weeks, everything was fine. The new warehouse had its official opening ceremony and all the supervisors and warehouse staff we'd recruited were busy finding their feet and doing really well. The CEO sent a letter thanking us for all our hard work.

I had weekly therapy with Alistair and worked on getting the checking down to nothing. I'd managed it a few times. When I did check, it was for the things that might have been moved in the flat. But after that night we'd found Mrs

Mackenzie's door open, there had been nothing. No noises in the night, no evidence that he or anyone else had been in the flat. Nothing at all.

Stuart had been busy completing his research project and had been working late on it before getting home. I'd been sleeping in my flat so that he could sleep undisturbed when he got in. As a result, I'd hardly seen him all week.

Caroline and I were enjoying a cup of tea and a chat, something we'd not had much time to do in the last few weeks. She was asking me about Stuart when I got a text:

C — Forgotten what home looks like. Trying to get weekend off. Love you. S x

A few minutes after that, my work phone rang. I half-expected it to be Stuart, but it wasn't. To my surprise, it was Sylvia.

'Hi,' she said. 'Sorry to ring you at work, but I don't know your home number.' Her voice sounded strange, an echo to it, and I could hear traffic in the background.

'That's okay. How are you?'

'I'm fine,' she said, 'I've only got a minute. Would you meet me for lunch? Today?'

'I'm a bit busy, Sylvia.'

'Please. I wouldn't ask if it wasn't important.'

I glanced at my desk calendar — a meeting at 2pm, but I should be back well before then. 'Alright, then. Where do you want to meet?'

'John Lewis, Oxford Street — the coffee shop on the fourth floor. Know it?'

It wasn't the typical place you'd expect to see

Sylvia, but her tone was so familiar — she expected everyone to move at her pace, meet her in her world, as if the planet revolved too slowly around her. 'I'll find it.'

'Twelve?'

'I'll do my best.'

'See you then. And Catherine — thank you.'

Breathless at the end, still sounding as if she was in a cavern somewhere, she rang off.

I thought about it all morning. It felt like a trap, but a clever one. I shouldn't be afraid of meeting someone in a place like that — very public, busy, lots of entrances and exits, no way Lee could take me, difficult for him to follow me in and out. Unless she helped him. If she'd invited me round to her flat again, I would have refused.

I thought back to the sunny Sunday morning all those weeks ago, when I'd caught her by surprise, and probably him, too. I didn't see where he could have been hiding, in that flat, but there was something about the way she'd looked into the dark cool interior that had made me certain that he was listening, that he was there.

In any case, whether it was a trap or not, I was going to go.

Out of the air-conditioned office, it was surprisingly warm. The sun was shining and the streets were full of office workers heading to the parks and green spaces to get some sun. I walked three streets, crossing the road a couple of times, and then on a whim grabbed a solitary taxi. I don't know why; if Sylvia wanted to meet me, then it was clear he would know where I was going, if he was watching me. In all probability he was already at John Lewis, waiting for me. Maybe this meeting was going to be her way of getting us together for some sort of civilised chat on neutral territory. I wasn't afraid, but I did feel more than a little bit queasy — unsettled, as though I was heading for something terrible and unpredictable.

I sat enjoying the breeze through the open window as the taxi stopped and started its way through the streets. Ten minutes later, I was in a side street, outside one of the back entrances to the department store. It was cool and shaded, the breeze blowing around my bare legs.

The fourth floor coffee shop was crowded, and, having had a quick look around, I thought I'd got there before her. But then as I turned to go I saw her, rising from her seat, her hand lifted in a wave. She was sitting right at the back, near the toilets, but that wasn't why I hadn't noticed her. She was wearing a black skirt and a white short-sleeved blouse, black pumps. I'd been looking for her usual peacock-brilliant colours, and here she was dressed almost like an office junior.

'Hello,' she said, to my surprise offering me her open arms and her cheek to kiss.

'I nearly didn't recognise you,' I said.

'Oh, you mean this?' She gave her tinkly laugh. 'I just bought it. I'm off to interview the head of legal services in a minute; sometimes it pays to dress down a bit. If you get my meaning.'

She'd already bought me a tea, and two cinnamon buns sat on the table waiting for us. 'Just like old times,' she said, as I sat down. 'It reminds me of the Paradise Café.'

I glanced around at our surroundings; I couldn't imagine a coffee shop less like the Paradise Café, but didn't say it.

'So,' she said brightly, chewing, 'how's things?'

'Good, thank you,' I said. Waiting.

'He didn't get the job, then. Mike, I mean.'

Mike. 'No. Not enough experience, in the end. I mean, running a bar in Spain for eighteen months — hardly useful work experience for warehousing, is it?'

She shot me a look.

'It wasn't my decision, I'm afraid. Everything gets scored, and, well, he didn't score as well as the others. That was all. Nothing I could do.'

Sylvia shrugged as if to say it was no skin off her nose, and watched me as I drank my tea. It was barely lukewarm. I wondered how long she'd been sitting here. I fought the urge to look behind me, around the room, through the entrance to the shop floor. He was here somewhere, I was pretty sure of it.

'It was me,' she said, 'in case you were wondering.'

'What was?'

'It was me who told him how to find you. I saw that job advertised in the *Evening Standard*, and your name and contact details. 'For further information and an application form, please contact Cathy Bailey . . . ' I just thought it was likely to be the same Catherine.'

I considered this for a moment. 'Well, you were right. It was.'

'I'm sorry,' she said.

'It doesn't matter now,' I said, still not sure which bit of the immense betrayal she was referring to. 'How are you, anyway?'

She never got the chance to tell me, because just then her phone, which was sitting on the table between us, rang. She almost jumped out of her skin and snatched it up, answering it with a nervous, 'Hello?'

I pretended not to listen.

'Yes. No, I'm just having coffee with a friend.' She looked at me then, and tried to smile. 'No, nobody you know. Why, do you want to join us? . . . Okay, then. No, I left it at work. Why? . . . Alright. I'll see you in a bit.' She hung up and looked almost relieved.

'Sorry about that,' she said. She was pale, I noticed, the make up she usually wore not as bright. She looked as if she'd been washed too many times on a hot cycle. She looked faded. I wanted to ask if it was him, but there was no point, I already knew. It was a set-up, I decided. He wanted me, for some bizarre reason, to trust Sylvia, to confide in her. The phone, sitting on the table, was bugged, recording our conversation.

'Boyfriends,' she said. 'You know what they're like — always checking up on you.'

I shrugged, and smiled. 'Are they?'

'Anyway,' she said, trying to sound bright, 'I can't stop long. I just wanted to say hello, see how you are.' She downed the last of her coffee, leaving the rest of her bun untouched. When she stood, I saw she'd lost weight, even just in the weeks since I'd last seen her.

'You're going?' I asked.

'Yes, sorry. I've got that interview to do. I'll be in touch, okay? Keep yourself safe, Catherine.'

Her voice was strange, quiet, as though she was holding back something vast and uncontrollable. For a moment I caught her eye and saw something in there I'd not expected to see.

She hugged me, held me tight for a moment longer than I'd expected her to, then picked up a large Planet bag which had been tucked under the table, and which seemed to contain a jumble of jewel-bright fabrics, and some red patent high-heeled shoes with a gingham flower on each toe.

I watched her go, skipping between the tables and disappearing into the crowd of shoppers queuing at the till with trays and bags of designer clothes and Egyptian cotton bed linen.

Sunday 11 May 2008

I didn't find the note until just now, a whole four days since I met Sylvia in the coffee shop. Stuart was at work and I got around to sorting my washing.

It was tucked into the pocket of my loose skirt, so small that I might never have found it had it not been for the force of habit making me check every pocket for tissues before shoving my clothes into the bag for the launderette.

I stared at it for a moment, knowing what it meant, before opening it slowly. Just four words, printed — they could have been written by anyone, and yet they could only have been written by her.

I BELIEVE YOU NOW

Four words, scrawled across the back of a John Lewis coffee shop receipt, folded and folded again.

It all dawned on me in a couple of seconds, the horror of it, and already I wondered if it might be too late. I thought about going round there, getting her out, running away. Where would we go? I thought about going to find him, taking a knife, taking him by surprise, finishing it the way I wish I'd finished it four years ago. I thought about phoning Stuart at work, asking him what I should do.

In the end I did the only thing that, realistically, I could do.

I went upstairs with my mobile and let myself into Stuart's flat. It was silent and empty without him. The sun was setting over the rooftops and his kitchen was bathed in golden light. I sat at the kitchen table and dialled the number.

'Can I speak to DS Hollands, please?' I asked, when the call was answered.

I had to wait a few minutes before she came on the line. In the meantime I listened to the background noise of the Camden Domestic Abuse office, someone talking on the phone, trying to calm someone down.

'*. . . Try to take some deep breaths. No, don't worry, take your time. I know . . . It's very difficult. Not at all — that's what we're here for.*'

'Hello? Cathy?'

Her voice sounded brisk, businesslike. I suddenly wondered if I was doing the right thing.

'I'm sorry to bother you. I'm worried about someone. A friend of mine. I think she might be in trouble.'

★ ★ ★

The Rest Assured was quiet this early on a Sunday evening, a few regulars at the bar, nursing pints of real ale and talking about the housing market. I was early, got myself a glass of white wine and sat on the same sofa where Stuart had held my hand and told me how Hannah had betrayed him. We'd both come a long way since then.

She was only ten minutes later than she'd said she would be. I don't know what I was expecting, but I knew who she was as soon as she came in through the door propped open to let the evening breeze in. Jeans, black T-shirt, short natural blonde hair cut in a style that might once have looked like an early Lady Di, but which was too thick and heavy to maintain the necessary sweep to the side. Shorter than I'd expected, but with the build of someone you'd like to have on your side in an argument.

She breezed straight to the bar and got herself

a half-pint of something, then came over. 'Cathy?'

I shook hands with her. 'How did you know it was me?'

She grinned. 'You're on your own.'

Sam took a glance around the bar and suggested we try the beer garden instead. I hadn't realised there was one, but through an open door to the back of the bar, there it was. Just two tables, but enough of a breeze to make the temperature bearable.

'Thanks for meeting me,' I said. I'd been surprised by it, to be honest, the readiness with which she'd agreed to give up her evening to hear the whole sorry Sylvia story.

'S'okay,' she said cheerfully, 'it's too nice an evening to be stuck indoors.'

She took a swig of her beer and licked her lips, then looked at me expectantly.

I told her the whole thing. My friendship with Sylvia, how it had gone cold when she'd left for London and I'd been trying to get out of the relationship with Lee. How I'd seen her on the bus and how Lee was using her address as a base to try to get a job at the place where I worked. Then I told her about the visit a few weeks ago, and how I'd met up with her, and finally — the note.

I took it out of my pocket, unfolded it and passed it to her. She studied it for a moment and then handed it back to me.

'What do you think it means?' she asked.

I felt my patience fray a little. 'Well, that she believes that Lee was violent towards me because he's now doing the same to her.'

'Has she told you she's in a relationship with Lee?'

'Not exactly.'

'Did she tell you she was afraid of him? Or give you that indication?'

'She didn't tell me, but lots of things made sense. When she phoned me to set up the meeting on Wednesday, she called me from a phone box, not from her mobile. Lee used to bug my phones and read my emails, that's how he knew I was planning to escape, so he's probably doing the same to her. The place she chose for us to meet was somewhere public, with lots of different entrances and exits, suggesting she thought either one of us might have been followed there. And when I met her she was dressed in the most peculiar clothes.'

Sam looked at me quizzically. She had deep blue eyes, big baby-blue eyes, yet set in a face that didn't look innocent or beguiling.

'Sylvia always wears really bright colours — she's like some sort of bird of paradise, always in yellows, pinks, purples, turquoise — that sort of thing. Silks, cashmere, leather. Nothing plain, ever. On Wednesday she was wearing a black skirt and a white blouse. She told me she'd just bought them, that she was going to go and do a serious interview and wanted to tone down a bit. Her normal clothes were stuffed into the carrier bag she had with her. But I'd never known her to do that before. She thought her dress style made her stand out from the crowd — that's why she did it.'

'So you think she was trying to blend in with the crowd?'

'Exactly. He must have been following her, the way he used to do with me. And she didn't have her handbag with her. Just the carrier bag.'

'No handbag?'

'I didn't think about it at the time. But it's likely he's put a bug in there somewhere, or a tracker. I know this all sounds crazy. It does until you've lived with someone like that.'

She gave a little shrug and nodded. 'But she didn't say anything about him, about being unhappy? Even though she didn't have her bag?'

'No. I guess she was working up to it, when she got a call on her mobile. I assumed it was him. And then she left almost immediately after that. We'd only been there a few minutes.'

'And you think she slipped the note into your pocket.'

'It was the receipt for the drinks and food she'd bought. Look — the date and time shows that it was when we met. She must have written the note before I arrived.'

Sam picked up the note again and regarded it, not the printed receipt but the words scrawled hastily on the back. I wondered whether she was considering that I could have written it myself.

'Look, why would she suddenly believe me? She testified in court that Lee hadn't hurt me, that I was a complete psycho, that my injuries were all self-inflicted — and she was my best friend! What could have happened to make her believe me, all of a sudden?'

Sam Hollands took a deep breath in and let it

out in a long sigh, casting a glance across the rest of the small garden before leaning a little closer to me.

'I called at the address you gave me, before I came here. There was no reply. I'm hoping that we don't have anything to worry about, with this, but I'll admit that it concerns me that Mr Brightman does seem to be trying to make contact with you.'

'It's not me you should be worried about,' I said boldly. 'I know exactly what he's like, what he's capable of.'

She gave me a smile, reassuring. 'I'll do what I can, all right? I'll make some enquiries, check on her, make sure she's okay. In the meantime, I'm afraid there's still nothing he's done that we can prove as harassment, and until he does we can't start considering an injunction against him to keep him out of your way.'

I shrugged. 'The person he was pretending to be — Mike Newell. I was wondering if the police checked up on his CV whether his friend in Spain would still be prepared to pretend he's been working there for the past year. Although that still doesn't prove that Mike Newell and Lee Brightman are the same person.'

'Leave it with me,' she said, finishing the last of her pint. 'I'll keep in touch. And in the meantime, I'll check up on your friend, too.'

She stood up and stretched.

'Christ, it's been a long day.'

'Are you off duty now?'

Sam nodded and smiled. 'Yes. I'm going to

have a curry and a long soak in the bath, I think.'

I walked with her as far as the junction with Talbot Street, then shook her hand as she turned towards the Underground.

'Don't forget,' she said. 'If you need help. Easter.'

'I won't,' I said, and left her with a smile.

It was nearly dark by the time I got home. I was still smiling as I put the key in the lock on the front door, and it opened without me even turning it. Someone had left it on the latch.

★ ★ ★

The flat door was locked, as I'd left it, and there was nothing out of place inside. Nothing out of place, and yet still I was uneasy.

I stood in the middle of the living room, looking out towards the balcony doors and the garden beyond, the trees still, the air in here stale and stifling. I checked the balcony doors again — still locked and secure — and then opened them wide. The breeze that had chilled my skin in the garden of the Rest Assured had dropped, and despite the sun going down it felt warmer still.

The gate at the bottom of the garden was open, half-hanging on its hinges. It had been like that since a gale last February. I'd asked the management company to fix it, and they'd sent someone round, once, who propped it up again. It was a half-hearted effort. Nobody used the garden anyway, in fact I'd never seen anyone else using the path that ran along behind the gardens, so the fact that it was half-open wasn't what was bothering me.

There was no sound at all, not a breath, not a bird song, not a whisper. But it felt strange nonetheless. The air was close and heavy, the clouds gathering overhead.

I wondered what he was doing, where he was, whether Sylvia was locked in her bathroom, bleeding, waiting for someone to come and save her, the way Wendy had saved me.

Wendy had told me afterwards that she'd been unpacking her shopping from the boot of her car when he came out of the front door. He looked dazed, she said, as if he was a bit drunk, as he got into the car and drove away. But that wasn't what had disturbed her. When he'd turned to get into the driver's seat she'd seen the blood on his hands and down the front of his shirt.

And, luckily for me, he'd not shut the door properly. When she was certain that he'd gone, she pushed it open, she told me, calling out 'Hello?' up the stairs, finding me lying on the carpet in my spare room. She thought I was already dead. The recording of her 999 call was played out in court. Wendy, so together, so calm, so gentle, screaming for help and sobbing with the shock of finding someone naked, bleeding from a hundred different places and scarcely breathing. I found it hard to listen to. I think that might have been the last day I made it into court — I don't remember much else from the trial, anyway.

Suddenly my mobile phone rang from my

handbag on the sofa, and it made me jump.

'Hello, you,' Stuart said, his voice unbearably tired. 'I missed you today.'

'You, too. Are you nearly done?'

'Yup. I'm just writing up some notes, then I'll be on my way. Shall I get us something to eat on the way home?'

'That sounds good,' I said. 'Listen — I'm just going to pop out for a bit. I want to check something at work.'

I heard his voice change. 'You're going back to work?'

'Yes, don't worry, it won't take long. I'll probably be back before you get home.'

There was a pause on the other end of the phone. 'Cathy. You are okay? Aren't you?'

'Yes,' I said, putting a smile into my voice, 'of course I am. I just want to get this out of the way so that I won't be worrying about it all night.'

'All right,' he said. 'Take your phone with you.'

'I will. I'll see you later.'

'I love you.'

'You too,' I said.

When I rang off I stood for a moment, thinking about what I'd said and what it might have sounded like to anyone who might have been listening. I'd avoided speaking to Stuart in my flat before, just in case Lee had bugged the place, and was listening in. I wondered how long I could keep it up.

I found a bus that was going in roughly the right direction, South of the river. Traffic was starting to get lighter, and it was completely dark by the time I got to Sylvia's road. I walked from the station where the bus had dropped me off, trying to remember which of the almost identical roads was the right one. It was nearly an hour since Stuart had rung me in the flat.

The painted black door was shut fast this time. I rang the buzzer for Flat 2. I could hear it ringing all the way from the back of the house, but there was no answer. I waited a moment, then rang again. I checked my watch. Ten past nine. Surely she should be at home? Most people were on a Sunday night, even in London. I rang again, and this time the intercom crackled into life. Not Sylvia, though — someone else.

'Look, she's clearly not at home. Why don't you piss off?'

'I'm sorry,' I said. 'I'm supposed to be meeting her, would you mind letting me in?'

No reply — the intercom was silent.

Well, I couldn't just sit here all night. I walked to the end of the street, turning left, following the gable end of the terrace to the inevitable alleyway running along the back of the houses. It was pitch-dark down there, no doubt full of dog shit, overturned rubbish bins and all sorts of horrors — but at least, somewhere down there, was the back of Sylvia's flat and the garden where we'd sat and drunk mugs of tea in the sunshine.

Two hundred and ten steps across rough ground, exactly the same number as it had taken me from the front of her house to the end of the street, and I was faced with a gate, overgrown with weeds at the bottom, and a dilapidated wall. I felt the rough bricks, ran my fingers along the top, shoulder-height, and pulled myself up, scraping my knee, trying to get a toe-hold with my sneakers.

Once I'd got my elbows up on the wall I could see into the garden, and the downstairs windows — all in darkness. Upstairs on the first and second floor all the windows were brightly lit, and wide open to the warm night. I'd have to be quiet.

I pulled myself up onto the wall, balancing my behind precariously on the top, and debated what to do. It was more than likely that she just wasn't home. She'd gone away for the weekend, gone to visit friends somewhere, or even her parents back up in Lancaster. She'd escaped from him, maybe for good, the way I never managed to.

Or else she was inside. With all the lights off.

Well, I'd come this far — I couldn't just go home without checking. I scissored my legs over to the garden side of the wall and lowered myself down, scraping the backs of my legs down the brickwork and cursing myself for not wearing something more sensible than a sundress.

I could hear voices, laughter, from the flat upstairs. Some sort of classical music — a piano, soothing, melodic. Perhaps they were having a dinner party.

I trotted down the garden, lit up bright as day by the lights from upstairs, hoping to God that they wouldn't choose that moment to cast a glance outside. Only just remembering in time the low wall which dropped down onto the patio, shrouded in shadow.

Once my eyes had adjusted to the darkness I peered in through the glass to the living room beyond. It was much as I remembered — the prints, the misshapen sofa covered in satiny throws, books, magazines piled haphazardly. Through the doorway and into the gloom I could just about make out the doors in the hallway, bathroom on the left, bedroom on the right as far as I remembered.

Both of the doors were ajar.

That was it, then. Wherever she was, she wasn't being held prisoner in her flat.

I took a step back and my foot gave a little beneath me. It was the grille above the windows to the basement flat. I looked down into the dark pit beneath, the lights from above just showing the outline of the windows, also in complete darkness, and it made me shudder.

Feeling rather foolish now, I chanced a quick run to the bottom of the garden, expecting a shout at any moment as someone upstairs noticed me with my bare arms and legs scooting across the grass.

But before I took another breath, I was at the wall. It looked much higher from this side, and the brickwork was smoother. I was going to really struggle to get over. The gate leading on to the alleyway had a huge shiny padlock on it, so that wasn't going to make it easy for me either. An old dustbin with a metal lid stood a few feet back from the wall. It was empty, as far as I could tell, although it didn't smell too pleasant. I dragged it the remaining few feet across the tussocky grass and leaned it close against the wall, every scrape and clang sounding deafening above the pleasant sounds of Shostakovich's second piano concerto from the rooms above.

I tested my weight on the lid of the bin and it held. I only needed a leg up, really, and that was all I got, for as soon as my arms had enough grip on the top of the wall, the bin lid slid away from under my foot and clattered and clanged onto the grass. As I scrambled over the wall, the music suddenly fell silent and the voices — worried, 'What was that?' . . . 'Oh, probably just a fox . . . don't worry, darling, honestly.'

I was on the other side of the wall, then, breathless, feeling stupid, wondering what the fuck I was doing clambering over walls when I could be at home with Stuart, who by now would be there wondering when I was going to be getting back.

Time to go. Wherever Sylvia was, at least I'd checked.

★ ★ ★

I jumped back on the only bus heading in the right direction. It left me on the other side of the park, less than a mile away, and I half-walked, half-ran through the darkness to get back to Talbot Street. The heat was getting worse, the odd rumble of thunder from a long way away punctuating my walk and threatening rain.

I walked the length of the street, looked up at Stuart's windows on the top floor as I passed and noted that the lights were on. He'd beaten me home. I fought the urge to go straight in and instead carried on walking, to the end of the street, turn left, round the back to the alleyway.

I wanted to think.

I'd not seen a soul on my walk from the bus stop; a few solitary cars and one cyclist had passed me, but no one on foot. Nobody walked in London these days, not in the suburbs at any rate. And not after dark.

Just me.

Something bad had happened to Sylvia. I knew it as surely as I knew my own name. She'd seemed so different. Not abrasive any longer, she was quieter, her eyes — haunted. I'd thought he was just using her to get to me, but what if he wasn't interested in me any longer? What if he'd found someone else to control?

That was my thought, right up until the moment when I peered through the gap between the gate and the hinge at the back of the house, and saw my dining room curtains wide open, and a light coming from within.

I stood for a moment, frozen to the spot. He had been inside. He was probably still in there.

I thought for a second, wondered about phoning Sam Hollands, and then considered that it might actually be Stuart — I'd given him a key — wondering whether I was downstairs and deciding to go and have a look to see if I was all right.

Just then a figure appeared at the window and I shrank back, only to let out a long breath a moment later. It was Stuart, standing by the window with his mobile phone in his hand, pressing keys. At that moment the phone in my pocket vibrated.

C — Where are you? Are you all right? S x

At that moment I wanted to see him more than anything else in the whole world. I ran to the end of the alleyway, stumbling over rough ground and laughing, almost, because he was there and everything was all right after all.

All the way round to the front door. I put my key into the lock but somehow I already knew I wouldn't need it. I pushed it with the key in the lock and it swung open. I flipped the latch and pushed it shut, checking once through force of habit, feeling stupid and happy and wanting to be upstairs now, wanting to be with Stuart, wanting to hold him and forget all about the past and just think about the future.

At my flat door, I stopped for a moment and listened. Not a sound. Not a breath, a whisper.

I turned the key in the lock, opened it and let it swing open. In front of me, I could see through to the living room and the dining room, both dark. The only light came from my bedroom.

Something was dreadfully wrong. Why had Stuart turned the lights off?

But then, standing in the doorway, I could smell it, smell *him*. Only faintly, but I recognised it and it made my heart pound, my stomach turn.

Lee.

He must be in there, in the living room.

I tried to picture where he might be hiding,

waiting for me to get home.

I took a step into the hallway, another step until I was level with the open door, the light from my bedside lamp casting a soft glow across the floor, long, deep shadows.

Stuart was lying on my bed, looking for all the world as though he'd fallen fast asleep. For a moment I breathed out and felt myself relax a little, but there was something unnatural about his position — and his shoes were still on. Then I saw something red on the pillow, spreading out onto the white cotton from the side of his head.

I moved before I thought. 'Stuart! Oh, no!' and I was beside him, lifting his head in my hand, gazing in utter horror at the red on my fingers. He was breathing, regular shallow breaths.

I heard a noise behind me and I froze.

I stood up slowly, turned.

He was in the doorway of my bedroom, blocking my exit.

It was the strangest thing. Even though my heart was thumping, even though I felt nauseous and light-headed, I had a strange sense of calm. I recognised it: it was that dreadful inevitability I'd felt just before he was going to kill me last time. Of course he hadn't managed to finish me off then, either. If he hadn't managed it then, he wouldn't manage it now. I almost laughed as I automatically calculated my anxiety level — probably about a sixty.

'Mr Newell,' I said, 'how nice of you to stop by.'

He laughed. At the same moment I sensed

uncertainty from him. He wasn't as big as he used to be, or maybe I'd just created this huge monster of a man in my mind? In any case, I don't think he recognised me, either. I was a very different Catherine from the one he'd left behind.

'Don't think much to your new bloke,' he said. 'Bit of a pushover.'

'What do you want?'

'Just to talk.'

'Come on, then.'

To my surprise he let me pass. I cast a glance at the front door, wondering whether to chance it, and at the same time knowing that I wouldn't leave Stuart behind.

I put the light on next to the sofa and sat down. In the pocket of my skirt, my mobile phone. As he moved to sit opposite me, I pressed the button on the phone keypad that I hoped would redial the last number called. I gave it a few seconds and terminated the call. Hoping it had had time to ring the other end.

'You look good,' he said. And then, to my horror, 'I missed you.'

'Really?'

'Of course I did. I thought about you every day, every single day. It should never have ended the way it did. It was all wrong.'

'What do you mean?' I felt anger rising. It made me more defiant. I tried to consider my options. Be nice? Or be mean? Which was likely to buy me the most time?

'You should have told me.'

'Told you what?'

'That you were pregnant. You should have told me, Catherine.' His voice was quiet, almost tender.

I couldn't believe what I was hearing. 'What are you talking about?'

'You lost the baby, our baby. Didn't you? If you'd told me . . . it would have been so different. We'd still be together.'

'You mean you wouldn't have tried to kill me if you'd known I was pregnant?'

'I would have stopped you . . . being so tough on yourself. I would have taken better care of you, got you some help, before it came to all that . . . '

I shook my head slowly. 'You actually think it was my fault? You believe your own lies?'

'Catherine, come on. You know what you were like. Of course it was your fault. That's why I had to find you, to see you again. To stop you hurting yourself. To stop you doing it again. We could do it properly — try for a baby. We could be a family.'

I stared at him for a moment, almost wanting to laugh. Of all the things I'd been anticipating for the last four years, this certainly wasn't it. 'I need a drink,' I said at last. 'Do you want one?'

He looked at me for a long moment, those blue eyes contemplating. 'Sure.'

I went to the kitchen and got a bottle of wine out of the fridge. I was thinking about using it as a weapon. I think he realised that too, because he was on his feet and heading towards me when my mobile phone rang in my pocket.

We faced each other. I pulled the phone out

and looked at the display.

'Don't answer,' he said, in exactly the same moment as I hit the 'accept' button.

'Hi! Sam! How are you?'

Sam Hollands' voice on the other end, my salvation. Sounding tired. 'I had a missed call. Everything okay?'

'How was your Easter?' I said. 'I was thinking of you . . .'

Lee grabbed the phone from my hand and threw it against the kitchen wall. It smashed into several pieces, scattering across the tiled floor. 'I said don't answer. Were you not listening? As usual?' his voice rising, using his bulk to try to intimidate me.

'That was a bit stupid,' I said. 'What if she comes to check on me?'

I'd crossed the line. He hit me across the face with the back of his hand and I backed into the kitchen counter. My cheek stung, blood on the inside of my mouth. I should have been scared. I should have been terrified. Instead, I had simply had enough of this man controlling my life for so many years.

'Who was it?'

'Sam,' I said. 'Thought you'd have heard me say that. Of course, since you've broken my phone, you won't be able to check if I'm telling the truth, will you?'

He smirked at me. 'Sam's in Lancaster, so she's not likely to call round, is she?'

'Different Sam.'

I took the moment of relaxation to grasp the wine bottle around its neck and swing it as hard as I could, a scream of rage from within me that probably half-deafened him. I was aiming for his head but I caught his shoulder, not hard enough to cause damage but hard enough to knock him off balance. The bottle slipped out of my fingers and crashed to the floor.

I seized the chance and ran for the bathroom, slamming the door behind me and locking it.

'Go away!' I screamed. 'Go away, leave me alone!'

As if he would. It was only a second later that the hammering started, followed by the pause, then the thump as he shouldered the door. It jumped on its hinges but held. It wouldn't hold much more.

When the door slammed back against the edge of the bath with a noise like the world coming to an end, I was ready for him. The only weapon I had was a can of deodorant, which I sprayed in his face whilst his arms flailed at me, punches flying, but none of them connected. He backed out of the room, his hands over his face, coughing, yelling, 'You bitch! You crazy fucking bitch, Catherine!'

And I was screaming too. 'What have you done to Stuart? What have you done, you bastard! You shit!'

I pushed past him, running for the kitchen, for a knife. Anything. My fingers felt like jelly as I pulled out drawers, whimpering, searching for anything, and all I could find was a potato peeler. I gripped it as hard as I possibly could and turned to face him.

He wasn't there. No sound except the crazy thumping of my heart, and the first heavy drops of rain landing on the balcony outside, splashing off the glass. Minutes passed.

'Come out!' I yelled. 'Where are you? You bastard! Where the fuck are you! I am not fucking afraid of you any more. Come on then, you fucking chickenshit coward!'

My hands were shaking but my grip on the peeler was tight, held aloft as though it had a six-inch blade of steel instead of two blunt inches and a plastic handle.

If he'd been standing in front of me I would have rammed it into his body, as far as it would go, into his neck, into his face. But he just wasn't there.

In the half-light from the bedroom I looked around, frantically. He could have gone out of the front door. I chanced a glance around the kitchen and saw something else — the lighter for the gas stove. I shoved the peeler into my pocket and picked up the lighter instead.

'Show yourself!' I screamed. 'What are you waiting for?!'

From here I could see to the front door, slightly ajar, the light from the hallway filtering in. 'No,' I muttered to myself, and ran towards the door after him.

He was behind the sofa and stood suddenly, tripping me up, the can of deodorant and the lighter skittering out of my hands and across the floor as I landed face-down on the carpet with an almighty thump.

He laughed, his face manic in the half-light,

his face wet with tears, residue from the spray smeared around his eyes. 'You're not afraid? Huh? Is that what you said?' He was sitting astride my chest, my fists pounding him as hard as I could everywhere and anywhere I could reach, but clearly not bothering him in the slightest.

'Get off me, you shit,' I hissed. 'Get the fuck off me!'

He caught one of my hands and was trying to get the other one whilst I slapped him and punched him and tried to get to his eyes, scratching anywhere I could get to. If he got my other hand, if he tied me up, it was all over.

'Where's Sylvia?' I shouted at him, snarled. 'What have you done with her?'

He laughed, again, as though what I'd said was funny. 'Sylvia — Christ. Let's just say she won't be putting in a complaint.'

A car's headlights outside brightened the room for a second and I saw his eyes, the expression in them — and the fear almost took over me. Until then I hadn't been afraid. But now I saw he was going to kill me. And this time he was going to be quick.

Instead of going for his face, my left hand grasped into my pocket and found the potato peeler. With as much force as I could muster, I rammed it into his side and almost immediately he fell off me, yelling and clutching his side.

The handle of the peeler stuck out from his side. He twisted round to look at it and touched it gingerly.

I crawled away into the shadows, feeling

around the carpet for the can and the smooth metal of the lighter, and my fingers made contact with them just as he grabbed at my ankle. I kicked backwards as hard as I could and my trainer made contact with something that made him yell.

In the meantime I turned, sprayed and clicked.

The jet of flame shot halfway across my living room, over the figure that was sprawled on his back. I saw his eyes and the shock and the fear in them for a moment before I adjusted my aim full into his face. And then he was just a figure, engulfed in flame, falling backwards with his hands over his face, arms flapping. I thought he would be quiet but he was screaming, his mouth full of flames and the sound coming out of it the most terrible noise I'd ever heard.

My hands were burning too and I managed to drop the can. I stood for a moment wondering if I should do something, as he dropped to the carpet and rolled left and right, writhing like a man possessed. The flames were gone and he lay still, his face blackened, his shirt tattered.

I let out a breath, a sob, just as I heard feet on the stairs, louder than the rain hammering on the window outside, louder than the bleeping smoke alarm above my head, and the door flew open. I looked behind me at the shapes coming through the doorway, only two of them, only two of them in uniform — what did they think? But I was never more grateful to see two people in my whole life.

I fell to my knees onto the carpet, and wept.

From where I sat on a low wall outside the main building, I saw him running across the car park, watching for a gap in the traffic then risking it and weaving between the cars, slowing down as the lights changed.

He was out of breath when he finally got to me.

'Hi,' he said. 'Am I late?'

I shook my head. 'There's some sort of a hold-up — they're not starting until half-past. They're all still waiting in the corridor outside.'

'Is she in there?'

'Yes.'

He kissed me, a quick kiss on the cheek and then another one, lingering. His fingers on my cheek were cool.

'Stuart. You're nervous.'

'A bit. Aren't you?'

'A bit.'

'Let's go inside. Get it over with.'

Sam Hollands was waiting for us inside.

'How are you feeling, Cathy?' she asked. She looked smart today, in a trouser suit and with a fresh haircut. She'd given her evidence this morning.

'I'm okay. Thanks.'

'They've delayed the start,' Sam said to Stuart. 'It seems Mr Brightman isn't feeling well again.'

'What a surprise,' Stuart said.

I was half-listening to them, scanning the waiting area, watching the people coming and going, looking for her. Where was she? She was supposed to be here.

'Sam, where . . . ?'

'She went to the loo.'

Stuart still had tight hold of my hand. He kissed it. 'Go and look for her,' he said. 'I'll see you in there. Don't look at him. Just look at me, if you need to.'

'Just go in,' I said. 'I'll be fine. Really.'

He went through the door, looking for a seat in the public gallery. The courtroom was filling up.

'I'd better go in, too,' Sam said. 'Unless you want me to wait?'

'No, you go in. I'll go and find her.'

She hesitated for a moment. The usher was hovering by the door, looking fidgety.

'We're going to nail him,' she said.

I smiled, and she went inside.

Inside the ladies' toilets, Sylvia stood by the sink, staring at her reflection in the mirror. 'Hey,' I said.

She'd made an effort to put on some make-up, brighten her face up a bit, but she still looked terribly pale.

'I'm afraid, Catherine,' she said.

'I know.'

'You were so brave, yesterday. They listened to you.'

'They'll listen to you, too.'

I watched her face start to crumple and stepped forward to hold her. She was shaking, her thin shoulders rigid with fear.

'It's alright,' I said. 'It's alright to be scared. But you know what? He's more scared than you

503

are. You're the one with all the power now. You know that? He can't hurt us again. We've just got to get through this, and it will be alright.'

She pulled back, fiercely dabbing at her eyes with a tissue. 'I know, I know. You're right. But — '

'Did you hear his voice on the first day? Remember when they asked him his name and he entered the plea? It was just a squeak. That's all he has left. He is nothing.'

She nodded, and smiled, a slight smile. A deep breath.

'Don't look at him, if you don't want to. Look at me, or Stuart, or Sam. We're all there for you. We're all in this together. Right?'

'Yes.'

'Then let's go,' I said.

'One more thing.' She fiddled around in her handbag, and found some lipstick. Bright red. When she applied it, her hand was steady.

It was time.

Inner London Crown Court

R-v-BRIGHTMAN

Wednesday 4 March 2009
Morning Session
Before:
THE HONOURABLE MR JUSTICE McCANN

MRS SCOTT	Would you please state your full name?
MISS BARTLETT	Sylvia Jane Lesley Bartlett.
MRS SCOTT	Thank you. Now, Miss Bartlett, how long have you known Mr Brightman?
MISS BARTLETT	About five and a half years.
MRS SCOTT	And you formed a relationship with him?
MISS BARTLETT	Yes.
MR JUSTICE McCANN	Would you speak up, Miss Bartlett?
MISS BARTLETT	I'm sorry. Yes.
MRS SCOTT	You maintained a relationship with the defendant whilst he spent some time in prison, did you not?
MISS BARTLETT	Yes, I did.
MRS SCOTT	And when he was released from custody in December

	2007, you were able to spend time with him again?
MISS BARTLETT	I was living in London at that time, and Lee was supposed to stay in Lancaster. He was supposed to sign on at the police station every week, and see probation, things like that. So I didn't see him that often.
MRS SCOTT	Did Mr Brightman visit you in London?
MISS BARTLETT	Yes, whenever he could.
MRS SCOTT	And how would you describe your relationship at this point. Were you both happy together?
MRS SCOTT	Take your time.
MR JUSTICE McCANN	Would you like to sit down, Miss Bartlett?
MISS BARTLETT	Thank you. I'm sorry. Lee was very different when he came out of prison. He was difficult to be around sometimes.
MRS SCOTT	What do you mean by that?
MISS BARTLETT	He could be — er — argumentative. He was prone to mood swings.
MRS SCOTT	Was he physically violent towards you?
MR JUSTICE McCANN	Miss Bartlett, do you need a glass of water?
MISS BARTLETT	No, no. I'm sorry. He could be nasty in the things he

	said, and I was scared of him. But he was only ever violent to me that last time.
MRS SCOTT	Thank you, I understand this is very upsetting for you. When he was released from prison, did Mr Brightman mention Catherine Bailey to you?
MISS BARTLETT	No. I saw Catherine in January last year. I was on the bus and she was outside, waiting at the bus stop. When I saw Lee I told him that I'd seen her.
MRS SCOTT	And how did he react?
MISS BARTLETT	He made no comment on it at the time. But he must have been looking for her. I saw a job advert in the paper and noticed Catherine's name as the person to contact. Catherine worked in personnel, I assumed it was her. When I showed it to Lee, he said he was going to apply for the job, just for a laugh. He wanted to use my address on the application form.
MRS SCOTT	And how did you feel about that?
MISS BARTLETT	I wasn't happy that he wanted to contact her again.

507

	We had an argument about it.
MRS SCOTT	Now, a few moments ago you said that Mr Brightman was only violent that last time. Could you tell the court the circumstances that led up to that event?
MISS BARTLETT	(*inaudible*)
MR JUSTICE McCANN	Miss Bartlett, could you speak up for the court, please?
MRS SCOTT	Are you alright to continue?
MISS BARTLETT	Yes. Thank you.
MRS SCOTT	My question was in relation to the last time that you saw Mr Brightman prior to his arrest.
MISS BARTLETT	I looked in his bag. He brought a bag with him when he came. Usually he took it with him when he went out, but on that occasion he left it behind, and I looked inside it.
MRS SCOTT	And what did you find?
MISS BARTLETT	It was mainly clothes, a pair of shoes, just things you would take for a weekend away. But at the bottom of the bag I found — other things. There was a photo of Catherine. A pornographic photograph. And some equipment,

508

	electronic devices, I don't know what they were. And a knife.
MRS SCOTT	I see. And just to be clear, what date did this happen? Do you recall?
MISS BARTLETT	It was Tuesday the sixth of May last year.
MRS SCOTT	And when you next saw Mr Brightman, did you tell him what you'd found?
MISS BARTLETT	Yes. It was the next morning. I don't know where he'd been that night, but he didn't come back to the flat.
MRS SCOTT	And how did he respond?
MISS BARTLETT	He was very angry. He hit me across the back of my head. I lost consciousness for a few moments and when I came round, he was . . . he was . . .
MRS SCOTT	Take your time.
MISS BARTLETT	I'm sorry. He was on top of me. He was raping me.
MRS SCOTT	He raped you?
MISS BARTLETT	Yes.
MRS SCOTT	What happened next?
MISS BARTLETT	He left. He just took his bag and walked out.
MRS SCOTT	Did you call the police?
MISS BARTLETT	No. I was too afraid. I didn't know where he'd gone. I thought he might come back at any moment.

MRS SCOTT	What did you do?
MISS BARTLETT	I had a bath. Got dressed in clean clothes. I went to a public telephone box and phoned Catherine at work, and asked her to meet me.
MRS SCOTT	You met up with Catherine in Oxford Street, is that correct?
MISS BARTLETT	Yes. I wanted to meet somewhere public, in case he was following me.
MRS SCOTT	And was it your intention to tell Catherine what had happened to you?
MISS BARTLETT	Yes. I wanted to warn her.
MRS SCOTT	To warn her?
MISS BARTLETT	I thought he was going to go after her. I thought he was planning to attack her again.
MRS SCOTT	When you met with Catherine, did you explain this to her?
MISS BARTLETT	*(inaudible)*
MRS SCOTT	Sylvia, for the benefit of the court, would you please answer?
MISS BARTLETT	No. I didn't. I didn't get a chance to tell her. Lee phoned me just as Catherine arrived. He was normal on the phone, but I knew he was watching us. He asked why I was wearing those clothes.

510

MRS SCOTT	Could you explain what you thought he meant by that?
MISS BARTLETT	I normally wear quite bright clothing. I'd chosen to wear a plain black skirt and a white blouse. I thought it would make it harder for him to spot me, if he was following me.
MRS SCOTT	And he commented on your clothing?
MISS BARTLETT	Yes. And he asked who I was meeting. I told him no one he knew. He said I was lying, it was someone we both knew very well. I knew he was watching us.
MRS SCOTT	What did you do?
MISS BARTLETT	I left. I thought if I could leave Catherine behind, she would be safe. I thought he would follow me rather than her.
MRS SCOTT	And is that, in fact, what happened?
MISS BARTLETT	Yes.
MRS SCOTT	Where did you go?
MISS BARTLETT	I walked around for a while. I tried to lose him. I went to a gallery, I went to the shops. When I finally went home it was nearly dark. He was waiting for me on the steps. I was terrified to see

	him. He was . . . very calm about it, almost reassuring. Then he said he wanted to show me something and he took me down the steps to the basement flat.
MRS SCOTT	Could you explain what you mean to the court? This is not your flat, is that correct?
MISS BARTLETT	No. The basement flat in our building was empty. It was being done up, I think. There was no furniture in it. I don't think the electricity was switched on.
MRS SCOTT	What happened when he took you into the flat?
MISS BARTLETT	I'm sorry, I just . . .
MR JUSTICE MCCANN	Miss Bartlett, do you need to take a break?
MRS SCOTT	In fact there are just a few more questions, if the witness is able to continue.
MISS BARTLETT	I'm alright. I'm sorry.
MRS SCOTT	Are you able to tell us what happened when you went into the flat?
MISS BARTLETT	He punched me and kicked me. He shouted at me, told me I was stupid over and over again. He told me I didn't deserve to live.
MRS SCOTT	How long did this attack last?

MISS BARTLETT	I'm not sure. It felt like a long time. He dragged me into the bathroom. There was a toilet and basin there, and fittings for a shower, but otherwise it was bare. No windows; it was a small room. Then he locked the door behind me.
MRS SCOTT	And was that the last time you saw him?
MISS BARTLETT	No. He came back some time later. He was wearing gloves. I thought he was going to kill me.
MRS SCOTT	Did he attack you again?
MISS BARTLETT	No. He told me he was going to find Catherine, said he wanted to sort things out.
MRS SCOTT	And what did you think he meant by that?
MR NICHOLSON	Your Honour, the witness is being asked for her opinion.
MRS SCOTT	Your Honour, I feel that the witness was in a situation where she could have interpreted what was meant by the words spoken by the defendant.
MR JUSTICE McCANN	I understand what you are saying, but I would prefer it if Miss Bartlett were directed to stick to the events in question. Please continue.

MRS SCOTT	Mr Brightman came into the room and told you he was going to find Catherine. What happened after that?
MISS BARTLETT	He went. He locked the door behind him and he went. He left me there. I tried to get out, I tried banging on the door but nobody could hear me. I couldn't get out.
MRS SCOTT	I believe you were there for four days, is that correct?
MISS BARTLETT	Yes.
MRS SCOTT	So you had access to water but he left you no food?
MISS BARTLETT	No.
MRS SCOTT	Thank you. Your Honour, I have no further questions.
MR JUSTICE MCCANN	Thank you, Mrs Scott. Ladies and gentlemen, we will take a break at this point. We will reconvene at three o'clock.

— CROSS-EXAMINATION —

MR NICHOLSON	Miss Bartlett, how did you and Mr Brightman first meet?
MISS BARTLETT	Catherine introduced us.
MR NICHOLSON	When you commenced your relationship with Mr Brightman, was he still romantically involved with Miss Bailey?

514

MISS BARTLETT	Yes, but he told me —
MR NICHOLSON	Thank you. And you were aware that he was continuing his relationship with Miss Bailey whilst he was also seeing you?
MISS BARTLETT	Yes, but —
MR NICHOLSON	Would you describe yourself as a truthful person, Miss Bartlett?
MISS BARTLETT	Yes, of course.
MR NICHOLSON	In 2005, did you give a statement to police concerning your friendship with Miss Bailey?
MISS BARTLETT	Yes.
MR NICHOLSON	Do you recall stating that in your previous years of friendship with Miss Bailey, you were aware that she had harmed herself by cutting her skin with a knife?
MISS BARTLETT	Yes.
MR NICHOLSON	Was your statement truthful, Miss Bartlett?
MISS BARTLETT	No.
MR NICHOLSON	You admit that you lied in a police statement?
MRS SCOTT	The witness has already answered that question.
MR JUSTICE MCCANN	Mr Nicholson, I must say I'm very concerned about this line of questioning.

MR NICHOLSON	Your Honour, I would suggest that there is a point of law that needs to be raised and I would ask for a private hearing.
MR JUSTICE McCANN	Very well. Ladies and gentlemen, at this point we are going to discuss a matter further, and I would ask that you all go to the jury room. I will ask that you are called back in as soon as we are able to continue. Thank you.

— *The jury departs* —

— PRIVATE HEARING —

MR JUSTICE McCANN	Mrs Scott?
MRS SCOTT	I would like to point out that Mr Nicholson is fully aware that there is a second statement made by Miss Bartlett in which she states clearly that she was directed to lie by the defendant. Miss Bartlett has been interviewed under caution about this very matter.
MR NICHOLSON	Your Honour, it is clear that Miss Bartlett cannot be relied upon to provide a consistent testimony. That is

516

	merely the point I am keen to bring to the attention of the jury.
MRS SCOTT	She was terrified of Mr Brightman, Your Honour, I would suggest that she would have made a statement denying her own existence if he had told her to do so.
MR JUSTICE McCANN	Mr Nicholson, my feelings on the matter are that if Miss Bartlett gave a second statement which provided an explanation of why she was untruthful in the first, then that too should be put before the jury.
MR NICHOLSON	Very well.
MR JUSTICE McCANN	Thank you, would you please call the jury back? We will continue where we left off.

Sam Hollands was waiting for me outside.

'Morning,' she said, as I slid into the passenger seat. 'Nice day for a mystery tour. Where did you say we're going?'

'St Albans.'

We drove off towards the main road.

'I'm really grateful for this. I know you've probably got better things to do on your day off, Sam.'

'Tell me again. You got a letter?'

It had been waiting for me when I got home from the shops yesterday. Nothing at all to indicate the nasty surprise that it contained — an ordinary envelope, my name and address typed on the outside, a first-class stamp, a smudged postmark. I read it out to Sam.

Dear Catherine

I've been thinking about you a lot. I wanted to tell you that I'm sorry about everything that happened. I'm sorry for lots of things and I have a gift for you which I hope might make things better.

You need to go to the Farley Road industrial estate to the north of St Albans. Unit 23 is right at the northern end of it. If you park in front of the unit you should be

able to walk around the side of the building.
At the back is an open space with trees.
Follow the line of trees to the end and you'll
find what I've left for you.

I hope you will do this last thing for me and
take it as my way of saying sorry.

'Is that it?'

'What?'

'It just seems like an abrupt way of ending a letter. You know, people who start a letter with 'Dear Whoever' usually end it with 'love from Whoever', don't they?'

We were on the M1, heading towards the M25. The traffic on the other side of the motorway flashed past us. I bit my lip.

'Cathy . . . ?'

'There are a few more sentences on another page. It's personal stuff.'

'What sort of personal stuff?'

'It's nothing that will make any difference. Really.'

'Cathy. This isn't just a letter, it's evidence. You know that, don't you?'

'Let's wait and see what this is all about, shall we? It might be something really silly.'

'What does Stuart make of it all?'

'He's away for a couple of days. Gone to a big new hospital in Belgium for a conference.'

She kept her eyes straight ahead and expressed her disapproval through the firm line of her mouth. I would end up showing her the letter anyway; I'd have to. But just for now I wanted to keep it between me and him.

519

'What do you think it is?' Sam asked.

'I don't know. I don't think it's anything good, put it like that.'

'Me neither. I'm glad you rang me.'

'I wondered if it was a trap.'

'Well, he's still safely inside, so you don't need to worry about him being there to meet us. I rang the prison this morning.'

'It's not a prison letter,' I said.

'I noticed. He must have got someone to smuggle it out for him. Whatever happens, I'll be putting in an intelligence report about that.'

We turned off the motorway and listened to Sam's satellite navigation telling us in a calm voice to take the next turning left, right, continue straight for two point four miles.

'So how's Stuart?'

'He's fine. We're fine.'

'What's it like being married?'

I laughed. 'Not much different from how it was before. Anyway, it's only been five months, give us a chance.'

'No babies yet?'

'Not yet. Don't tell me you're feeling broody?'

'I'm not, but Jo is. We're going to get married next year, I think.'

'Sam, you never said.'

'Well, we've been together ten years. It's about time.'

'Have you asked her?'

'Not yet.'

'You should get on and do it. It's worth it. Can we come to the wedding?'

'Of course you can. I was going to ask Sylvia, too.'

'She'd love it.'

'Anyway, we're here.'

The Farley Industrial Estate was deserted, long wide streets empty of traffic, litter blowing across the pot-holed roads. We passed a kebab van, shutters down. Half the units were unoccupied, the whole area had a sense of desolation, and Unit 23 was no exception. It was as far as you could go, round a final corner. It was like the end of the world.

Sam parked the car in front of it.

'Round there, look.'

Amidst the weeds growing around the building, a narrow dusty path twisted off between the chainlink fence and the wall of the unit. Stinging nettles grew to chest height, swaying towards us in the breeze.

Sam went first, weaving her way along the path, one hand on the wall of the unit. A rabbit scuttled across the path in front of us and made me jump.

Behind the unit the narrow space suddenly widened into a patch of wasteland. We walked across a large expanse of concrete, weeds growing up through the cracks. The sun shone over our heads and a bird sang from somewhere high up. It was completely deserted, not a person anywhere in sight.

'Now where?'

I shaded my eyes from the sun and looked around, towards the trees he'd described, and saw it, a flash of colour in a landscape of grey

521

and brown and green.

'There. See it?'

It was a patch of red, scarlet, like a flag, and as we got closer it fluttered at us as though it were alive. I already knew what it was but it was still a shock to see it. I felt the tears start in my eyes and they were falling before I could stop them. It was like seeing an old friend, and a nightmare.

'What is it?' Sam said.

'It's my dress.'

The edges of it were ragged, and it was dusty and filthy, but I still recognised it. All of the buttons had gone from it, and sections of it had been cut out, leaving the bare edges to fray and catch the wind. It must have been here for some time.

'That's it? Just an old dress?'

It was anchored to the rocky soil by an old spade, rusted, which had been placed across it, and a heap of stones which had been laid over the top, like a cairn, like a grave.

'No,' I said. 'It's a marker.'

She saw it just a few moments after I did. At the bottom of the ditch, the movement caught my eye as the wind blew against a hank of dark hair. At first it looked artificial, like frayed hessian, and the skin like old canvas. And then the sudden whiteness of the broken bone, and there was no confusion any more.

'Oh, shit, shit.' Sam grabbed her mobile and started phoning, calling for back-up, and I sank to my knees amidst the dry soil and the stones, and stroked my fingers against the softness of the fabric for comfort.

'I think she's called Naomi,' I said.

From the back pocket of my jeans I pulled out the second page of the letter.

'Sam. You'd better look at this.'

I'm sorry for what I did to Sylvia, and to the old woman who lived in the flat downstairs. They meant nothing to me other than as a means to find you. You should realise that nobody and nothing can ever stop me from finding you, Catherine. I've left you this gift as a sign that I am prepared to take the blame for everything. But it won't stop me. However long it takes, I will wait for you. One day I will be free, and I will find you and we can be together.

Wait for me, Catherine.

I love you.

Lee

Acknowledgements

The book you're holding now would never have come into being if it were not for the help and support of many people. Most of all I'd like to thank Vicky Blunden, Candida Lacey, Corinne Pearlman, Linda McQueen, Dawn Sackett and everyone at Myriad Editions, for taking my original ramble and turning it into something immensely proud of, and for taking a chance on a complete novice.

Into The Darkest Corner was originally written in 2008 as part of the annual National Novel Writing Month challenge, run by Chris Baty and a brilliant team of people, and if it had not been for the encouragement of the Nanowrimo website (www.nanwrimo.org) I doubt I would have made it past the first chapter. Thank you, guys! I hope you like it.

I would like to thank my friends Ellen Doughty and Linda Weeks, who read the first draft and thenceforth encouraged me every step of the way. It was my cousin Michael George's idea to actually send it off (even though he hasn't read it yet), so I have him to thank for that.

Greg Mosse, for his insightful and thought-provoking Crime Writing course at West Dean College, and in particular for his encouragement with regard to this book. Thank you Greg!

Thank you too, to Lillian Fox, a gifted and inspirational writer, who steered me in the right direction many times and kept me going when I most needed a push. Vanessa Very read the manuscript when it was nearing completion and came up with some brilliant suggestions which changed everything. This book would be nothing without Lillian and Vanessa, so thank you both.

Thank you to my lovely friend Alexia Fernholz, consultant clinical psychologist, who generously shared her expertise, and to Stephen Starbuck for assistance and advice with matters of procedure.

Thank you Mary, Vicky, Hannah, Sonja, Ella, Hanna, Fiona, Shelagh, Nadia, Mia, Sophy, Jenna, Steven, Janet, Alison, Sarah, Tricia, Michael, John and David, Nickie and all my online friends who were all so supportive of me throughout this enterprise.

To the wonderful and talented Medway Mermaids, thank you so much for your insightful comments, and for cheering me on.

Specail thanks are due to the fantastic Moscicki family (Jackie, Julie, James, Phoebe and Anna), and to Jane Mellinger, Nicola Samson, Maxine Painter, Lou Bundock, Naomi and Will Lay, Chris Gambrell, Clare Howse, Russ Shopland, Alexandra Amos, Lucy Smith, Emily Mepstead,

Paticia Cox, Katie and Wayne Totterdell, Matt Liston, Tara Melton, Clive Peacock, Claire Eastham, Phil Crane, Bob Sidoli, Gordon Lindsay, Emma Dehaney, Lindsay Brown, Angela Wiley, Karen Aslett, Jenny Harknett, Pam Wiley, Judy Swan, Robert Nicks, Trish Cross and all my other dear friends who kindly put up with me talking about my book and encouraged me far beyond the call of duty — thank you.

Last, but not least, thank you to my Mum, and to David and Alex, who put up with most of all, and still love me nonetheless.

We do hope that you have enjoyed reading this large print book.

Did you know that all of our titles are available for purchase?

We publish a wide range of high quality large print books including:
Romances, Mysteries, Classics
General Fiction
Non Fiction and Westerns

Special interest titles available in large print are:
The Little Oxford Dictionary
Music Book
Song Book
Hymn Book
Service Book

Also available from us courtesy of Oxford University Press:
Young Readers' Dictionary
(large print edition)
Young Readers' Thesaurus
(large print edition)

For further information or a free brochure, please contact us at:
Ulverscroft Large Print Books Ltd.,
The Green, Bradgate Road, Anstey,
Leicester, LE7 7FU, England.
Tel: (00 44) 0116 236 4325
Fax: (00 44) 0116 234 0205

Other titles published by
The House of Ulverscroft:

THE PLAYDATE

Louise Millar

Sound designer Callie Roberts, a single
mother, has come to rely on Suzy, her best
friend and neighbour. Suzy has been good to
Callie and Rae, her daughter; welcoming
them into her large, apparently happy family.
But Callie knows that Suzy's life is not as
perfect as it seems. It's time she pulled away
— and she needs to get back to work. So why
does she keep putting off telling Suzy? And
who will care for Rae? The houses in the
anonymous city street hide families, each
with their own secrets. Callie's increased
sense of alienation leads her to try and
befriend a new resident, Debs. But she's odd
— you wouldn't trust her with your child —
especially if you knew anything about her
past . . .